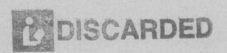

COSMOPOLITAN'S

Winds of Love

ROMANTIC & EROTIC TALES

COSMOPOLITAN BOOKS/NEW YORK

Acknowledgments

Many writers contributed to Cosmopolitan's Winds of Love, and we are grateful to all of them. Specifically we wish to thank the authors of the following stories originally published in Cosmopolitan magazine for permission to reprint their works here: "Zalman's Galatea" © 1966 by Lynne Reid Banks; "Marching Through Delaware" © 1969 by Bruce Jay Friedman, by permission of Robert Lantz–Candida Donadio Literary Agency, Inc.; "Green Love Later" © 1968 by Herbert Gold; "Rain Queen" from Livingstone's Companions by Nadine Gordimer, copyright © 1969 by Nadine Gordimer, all rights reserved, reprinted by permission of The Viking Press, Inc.; "A Break in the Weather" from The Egg of the Glak and Other Stories by Harvey Jacobs, copyright © 1968 by Harvey Jacobs, reprinted by permission of Harper & Row, Publishers, Inc.; "Girl Overboard" by Garson Kanin, © 1968 by TFT Corporation; "An American Marriage" copyright © 1969 by Norma Klein; "It Will Pass" © 1971 by Ella Leffland; "A Girl Worth Two Million" © 1969 by Joyce Carol Oates; "Space Ant" © 1970 by Gilbert Rogin, by permission of Robert Lantz–Candida Donadio Literary Agency Inc.

In addition, the following © 1965, 1966, 1968, 1969, 1970, 1971 That Cosmopolitan Girl Library, Inc.: "The Smile" by A. Alvarez, by permission of Robert Lantz–Candida Donadio Literary Agency, Inc.; "The Wife-Eater" by Myrna Blyth; "Lemmings Are Lonely" by Babs H. Deal; "Subject to Change" by Sonya Dorman; "East of the Sun" by Chloe Gartner, reprinted by permission of Paul R. Reynolds, Inc., 599 Fifth Avenue, New York, N.Y. 10017; "St. George" by Gail Godwin, reprinted by permission of Paul R. Reynolds, Inc., 599 Fifth Avenue, New York, N.Y. 10017; "The Winds of Love" by Rosemary Hamilton; "The Chameleons" by William Harrison; "Iatro's Djinn" by B. L. Keller; "Names and Faces" by Eleanor Leslie; "Jimmy from Another World" by Vin Packer; "Voyage of the Earth Maiden" by Judith Rossner.

To say that you can love one person all your life is just like saying that one candle will continue burning as long as you live.

Count Leo Tolstoy, THE KREUTZER SONATA, Chapter 2, *1890*

Love keeps the cold out better than a cloak.

Henry Wadsworth Longfellow, THE SPANISH STUDENT, act 1, scene 5, *1840*

Contents

Foreword

*L*ove is the most beautiful emotion we have! And there has *never* been more of it around than there is *right now!* All right, perhaps it's been *ages* since you've seen a young man pinning a corsage on his date's formal gown, or a woman blushing delicately at a man's compliments (perhaps you've *never* seen those things!), but that doesn't mean (as some gloomy souls believe) *true* love is dead. It isn't! Love takes many different forms, but I believe people give and get more affection than ever . . . do you agree? We all feel freer to express love— to kiss hello, touch, hug, even go to *bed* with each other—so much more directly and honestly than we used to. I think this new freedom and openness is *wonderful*. Because today *every* woman has so many chances to experience what love is *really* about—sex, tenderness, sharing—instead of being forced to sit around looking docile and pretty, hoping Prince Charming will step out of his Jaguar XKE and awaken her with a kiss.

In choosing the twenty-two stories in this book, our fiction editors read many, many thousands (yes thousands!) of manuscripts, looking for writers who express *contemporary* ways of loving and being loved. (That doesn't mean some selections aren't romantic—and I don't think there's a single one that isn't *real*.) Several stories are by world-famous authors. Others were written by talented newcomers—*Cosmo* "discoveries." What all the writers share, I think, is an understanding of a very forthright language of the heart. I'm sure you'll find many of these stories seem to be speaking directly to *you*, about love feelings and experiences you *know* are true. And that's why I believe you'll want to read and reread *Cosmopolitan's Winds of Love* for years to come.

Helen Gurley Brown
Editor-in-Chief, Cosmopolitan

Introduction

These are *real* love stories, not the kind of Cinderella romance or earnest, life-can-be-beautiful-even-in-the-suburbs tale that some ladies' magazines still prefer. (Honestly, after reading such *Cosmopolitan* articles as "I Didn't Have the Baby, I Had the Abortion" or "How Sexually Generous Should a Girl Be?" could *you* believe a short story in which all the heroine's problems are solved because the sun comes out from behind a cloud or she observes a small child at prayer?) Our fiction department never even looks for the old-formula love story with its happily-ever-after ending. Those stories ended at the bedroom door. Many of ours *begin* there. (Isn't that where love starts to get *really* fascinating?)

Fortunately, there are many fine writers who write about present-day love with depth, humor, and feeling. Because their stories are about real characters in real situations, you'll find that each story takes you on an emotional "trip" which may leave you soothed, or possibly exhausted, but always *satisfied*.

There are many kinds of love today and many ways of loving, and the writers represented in *Cosmopolitan's Winds of Love* seem to have touched on nearly *all* of them. If you are looking for romantic and more-or-less tender stories of young love, then turn first to "Voyage of the Earth Maiden," by Judith Rossner; "Rain Queen," by Nadine Gordimer; "The Winds of Love," by Rosemary Hamilton; or "Lemmings Are Lonely," by Babs H. Deal. If you love the especially frank, daring, or far-out story that many people associate with *Cosmopolitan*, try "East of the Sun," by Chloe Gartner; or "Names and Faces," by Eleanor Leslie. Perhaps you like to be made slightly sad (even to shed a tear or two)—turn to "Jimmy from Another World," by Vin Packer, or "The Wife-Eater," by Myrna Blyth. If strange, violent, or savage emotions fascinate you, sink into "Green Love Later," by Herbert Gold, or "A Girl Worth Twenty Million," by Joyce Carol Oates.

Best of all, just start reading and let these stories speak for themselves. Someone once said that a short story, to be any good at all, must be a minor masterpiece. We think *all* these stories are minor masterpieces—and we hope you agree!

Jeanette Sarkisian Wagner
Editor, Cosmopolitan Books

Voyage of the Earth Maiden

by Judith Rossner

In June of 1960 I came to New York from Nebraska armed with a B.A. in history from the University of Iowa and my mother's assurance that even if I wasn't related by blood to Willa Cather, I had relatives who practically had been. My aunt, who made yearly trips to Chicago and thus knew how cities worked, had given me extensive instructions. Upon leaving the Greyhound and setting foot on New York soil I was to: look in the nearest available phone directory for a Young Women's Christian Association residence; write down the address; secure a taxicab, without speaking to any strangers; give the driver the residence address; write down the driver's number; and, upon disembarking, pay the driver the amount indicated on his meter, plus, if he had been polite and the trip smooth, ten percent of that amount.

The crowds, which I'd been instructed to hate and fear, were actually no more dense than those at a school football game, and I did manage to find a row of phone booths, without even leaving the terminal. But I was stopped cold by the size and variety of the directories on the rack; each displayed some unfamiliar name in addition to the words: New York City. I put down my suitcase and studied the titles. A small man was leaning against the candy counter nearby, smoking a cigar, half reading his newspaper and half watching me; probably the exact sort of stranger my aunt had had in mind for me not to approach. As I hesitated, he lowered the paper and took the cigar out of his mouth.

"Whaddya wanna know, dolly?" he asked. "Which way is up?"

"Not exactly," I said. "I——I didn't know New York had so many parts to it."

1

He came over and stood next to me at the rack, the top of his head just level with my shoulders. "Anything you gotta know is in here," he said, pointing to the Manhattan book. "These two"—his finger skimmed the row of other books—"is empty lots, this one's sand and swamps, and this one"—he shook his head sadly—"ain't even on the right side of the river."

"Manhattan," I said gratefully. "Thank you very much."

"Forget it." He waved away my thanks and walked back to the candy counter. I opened the Manhattan book.

"Say, dolly," he called as I incredulously made my way through hundreds of pages of names. I looked up. "How the hell big are you, anyways?"

"Six feet," I said. "Six feet and a quarter of an inch, actually."

He stared at me thoughtfully. His lips worked back and forth, and squat smoke puffs danced up from his cigar.

" 'Sokay," he said finally. "You're all peaches and cream, dolly."

I thanked him again and he told me to forget it again and then he disappeared around the other side of the candy counter. I found the Y.W.C.A. listings but, here again, was confounded by the fact that there were several residences to choose from. I took a pad and pencil from my shoulder bag and dutifully copied their addresses, but I felt no farther along than before. Most of the street numbers were preceded by an E, which I understood to mean East, but how could I know without looking around whether I wanted to be on an E street or a W street? Obviously, I couldn't. I picked up my suitcase and walked out of the terminal.

It was around noon on a Saturday. There were a lot of people, but certainly the stories had been exaggerated; there was room to walk on the sidewalk. I reached a corner and got weak-kneed with excitement because stretched out down the street I could see as many movie houses as I had seen in my life. I put down my suitcase and looked up at the street signs: 8th Ave. and—someone banged into me. I looked down.

"Jeez," the woman said. "Why 'oncha watch where you're standing?"

"I'm sorry," I said. "I didn't mean to be in the way."

She glanced at my suitcase. "Whaddya, lost, honey?"

"Not really." But she looked offended, so I added, "Can you tell me, though, if I'm in the east part of town or the west part?"

"Not lost, she tells me," the woman said, looking straight at me. "Where you from, honey?"

"Nebraska."

"Oh, my God, Nebraska!" she exclaimed pityingly.

I smiled to reassure her. "I think New York is wonderful. I haven't seen so many movie houses in my whole life."

"Stay away from them," she said sharply. "They're full of bums out of work. You wanna see a picture, go to your neighborhood movie. You godda be wired for electricity before you go into one of them places."

"All right," I said uneasily; but then, when she didn't go away, I glanced at my list and saw a Y listed on Fifty-first Street and Eighth Avenue, and asked her for directions.

"Look," she said, after telling me, "you go ahead. I'll watch you cross in the right direction. Not now, you don't have the light. You know about lights?"

"Oh, yes. We have them in Nebraska." I thanked her again and walked to the curb.

"Hey, honey?"

I turned around.

"How tall are you, anyhow?"

"Six feet," I said. "Six feet and a quarter of an inch, actually."

"You're a nice girl. Good luck to you; you're missing your light!"

I hurried across Forty-second Street, but I really wanted to look around a little more before registering at the Y. Besides, I was getting hungry. I crossed Eighth Avenue and went back to Forty-second Street, where I ate lunch in an Italian restaurant that advertised thirty-five-cent spaghetti dinners in the window.

"Thanks for the tip, girlie!" the counter man called as I was leaving.

"I'm sorry," I said. "I didn't know. At home we don't tip at counters."

"Well, you know what they say, peaches; when in Carthage do as the Carthaginians do."

"My goodness," I said, handing him a quarter from my change purse. "Do you mind my asking what an educated man like you is doing at a job like this?"

"That supposed to be funny?" he asked, looking from me to the quarter as though he was trying to make up his mind about something.

"Good heavens, no. It's just that at home, anyone who knows where Carthage was is teaching school or gone."

"That's me." He grinned and put the quarter in his pocket. "I'm gone."

"Oh," I said uncertainly.

"Actually"—he put one foot up on a ledge behind the counter and leaned toward me in a confidential manner—"I'm doing a watchamacallit, a survey. On people who eat spaghetti. May I ask you a few questions? How long are you going to be in our city? What are you doing tonight? May I pick you up in front of the Y.W.C.A. of your choice?"

I felt myself blushing. "Does everything about me show or is it just that New Yorkers are all smart?"

"Where you from?"

"Nebraska."

"New Yorkers are smart."

"If you don't mind awfully terribly much," a girl sitting at the counter said, "I'd like a cup of cawfee, please."

"So long, stretch," he said to me, turning to the coffee urn. "I get out of here at eight. Meet me in front."

"All right," I said. "If I'm not too tired."

But by three o'clock I was terribly tired. I'd gotten to the Y and then it had somehow seemed a shame to go right in when there were so many things to see. I was at Fifty-third Street and Fifth Avenue, having walked up and down so many streets that numbers and sights were jumbled in my head. My suitcase seemed to weigh a hundred pounds and my tongue was thick with thirst. Down the street I saw an ice-cream and soda-pop cart; I practically ran to reach it. I bought two containers of orange pop, then set my suitcase down in front of a strange-looking building that turned out to be the Museum of Modern Art. I sat on the suitcase and leaned back against the building wall, drinking the pop.

When I'd finished it, though, I was still too tired to walk, so I went into the museum. I left my suitcase at the checking counter and paid my admission, automatically nodding my head when the cashier asked if I wanted a movie ticket. The lounge downstairs was crowded but I found a seat and closed my eyes. Then someone was shaking my arm.

"Hey, blondie," he was saying. "Wake up. Alice? Betty? Shirley? Little Red Ridinghood?"

With some difficulty I opened my eyes. I'd never seen anyone who looked quite like this young man—even in Iowa. His brown hair was thick and wildly tangled; his eyes were deep and dark; his nose was impressively long and so bony that it looked more like some other part of the body, perhaps a bent elbow. His face, in general, as a matter of fact, seemed to have more pits and bends and bones and directions than any whole body I'd ever seen. He smiled at me in a friendly way.

"You have beautiful teeth," I said sleepily.

"Would that my father, the dentist, could hear those words," he said.

I looked around. The lounge was almost empty.

"Look, Alice," he said, "the movie's going on in a couple of minutes. Wouldn't you rather sleep in there?"

"I never sleep at the movies," I said.

"Fine. Go splash some cold water on your face. I'll get a couple of seats."

"Thank you."

He got up and walked toward the auditorium entrance. He was very tall, but so narrow, except at the shoulders, that his clothes could have been hanging on a coat hook. I found the ladies' room and splashed cold water on my face, then I combed my hair and went back to the lounge. The auditorium doors were closed, but a neat young man took my ticket and let me in. *I Walked with a Zombie* was just beginning.

"Hey, Alice! Over here!" he shouted from the other side of the auditorium as I waited for my eyes to get accustomed to the dark. I walked across the back aisle and up the balcony steps, then slipped in next to him. He put his arm on the back of my seat and once or twice, during very frightening parts of the movie, I grabbed his hand without thinking. But because of his fragile appearance I was reluctant to squeeze it hard, and I ended up biting off most of my nails,

4

instead. He stood up the second the lights went on and stretched his arms, yawning loudly. I stood up next to him.

"Jesus," he said, his eyes traveling slowly from my face down to my feet, "how many pounds of meat do they give you every day?"

"Who?"

"Forget it, Alice. Come on, I'll buy you a few cups of coffee."

"All right," I said as we shuffled out of the auditorium with the rest of the crowd. "But I'll have to pick up my suitcase."

"Suitcase? Where?"

"In the checkroom."

"Were you figuring on pitching a tent here?" We reached the steps and started up.

"No-o-o. I just got to New York today and I haven't registered at the Y, yet."

"You haven't registered at the Y, yet," he repeated in a thoughtful way, as though I'd said something very deep. "Tell me, Alice—your name is Alice, isn't it?"

"Janice."

"Same thing. Tell me, Alice, why were you going to register at the Y?"

I took my aunt's instructions from my shoulder bag and handed them to him. We'd reached the checking counter and I got my suitcase while he stood over at the side and read.

"Who gave you these, Alice?" he asked when I got back to him.

"My aunt."

" 'Number fourteen,' " he began reading aloud as he went through the revolving doors and I followed. " 'Do not order any food whose contents you may not be acquainted with, such as egg salad, chicken salad, tuna-fish salad, meat loaf; also meat balls and other food of that type.' " He looked up. "What does she mean by 'that type'?"

"Italian food. My aunt thinks Italians are dirty," I explained.

"Maybe they are," he said, "compared to your aunt."

"Oh, yes," I agreed. "Everyone is dirty, compared to my aunt." Then I laughed, although I wasn't sure I should.

"Now," he said abruptly, "suppose you tell me what you *did* do upon your arrival."

He listened solemnly as I told him; then he asked me to explain my disobedience.

"Well," I said slowly, "sometimes things are different when you get there from what you thought they would be before you got to them."

" 'Sometimes things are different when you get there,' " he repeated thoughtfully, " 'from what you thought they would be before you got to them.' " Suddenly, he became cheerful. "O.K., Alice, you're on. Let's find an Automat."

My right arm was tired again, so I shifted the suitcase to my left hand.

"My God," he said disgustedly. "Are you still dragging around that idiot thing?"

"I'm sorry. I didn't know where to leave it."

"Well, you can't lug it all over town with you. Come on. We'll get a cab and drop it at my place."

"That's very nice of you." I had to half-run to keep up with him and the suitcase kept banging against my leg. "My aunt said that cabs were too expensive for general use."

"And dirty, too," he said. "But we'll have to put up with one for now."

I giggled.

"What's so funny?" he asked.

"I was just thinking that I don't know your name."

"Jonathan," he said, "Jonathan Meltzer. You can call me Nathan."

A little while later, we were climbing up a dark, rickety flight of stairs to his apartment. He unlocked the apartment door and I followed him in. It was nothing like any apartment I'd ever seen, but, of course, I'd never been in an artist's apartment before. As a matter of fact, I'd never been in *any* apartment until Iowa City. It was one great big room, mostly dark, except for the front end, where there were two windows. In the back, there were a bed and two armchairs and, in one corner, a sink. In the middle of the room, backing up one end of the bed, was a big wooden wardrobe, and next to that, a chest of drawers. In the front there were a table and some chairs and an easel. The table was completely covered with newspapers, tubes of paints, jars, paint-smeared rags, and so on. Every inch of wall was covered with paintings, some of them abstract but most of very pretty, naked girls.

I put down my suitcase.

"O.K.," Nathan said. "Let's get some coffee."

"Could I rest for just a minute?"

"Sure, sure. Have a seat, stretch out on the bed, crawl under it; no, you better not, the phone's there. Anything. Make yourself at home."

I took off my shoes and stretched out on the bed with a grateful sigh, flexing my toes to uncramp them. I had to make an effort to keep my eyes open. Nathan came over and stood looking down at me, smiling in a sort of dreamy way.

"Do you have a mummy and daddy, sweetheart?" he asked. "Or did you just tumble through some oversized looking glass?"

"Of course I do," I said.

"But there aren't any more at home like you."

"One."

"You're kidding me."

"Mmm-mm. My sister Pamela." My eyes were closing in spite of me.

"Pamela."

"She's seventeen," I said, trying not to mumble. "She's going to the

University of Iowa in the fall. . . . She's four years younger so . . ." But I couldn't remember the rest of the sentence.

"I don't know if this is going to be worth my while," he said when he awakened me. The room was dark except for a faint glow from the street lights. He was sitting on the edge of the bed; his hand was on my shoulder. "I met you seven hours ago and twice I've had to shake you out of a deep sleep."

"I'm sorry. I didn't get much rest on the bus."

"Well, all right. But if you want to stay in New York, you'll have to get along on less sleep."

"Oh, I want to stay," I assured him.

He patted my cheek, then smoothed the hair back from my temples and forehead.

"When did you have your last haircut?" he asked.

"Real haircut, you mean? I guess I was around twelve. My mother trims the ends every few months."

"Take out whatever's holding it back."

I took out the clip and he lifted my head and brought the hair around to the front, so that it practically covered my chest. Then he asked if I was hungry and I admitted that I was starved.

"We'll go get a pizza," he said. "No, I have a better idea. *I'll* get a pizza. You stay here and figure out how you're going to pay your share of the rent."

"Rent?"

"Did you think apartments were free in New York? Like traffic?"

"Of course not. I just hadn't thought about *living* here."

"That's what you're *doing*, isn't it?"

"Well," I said slowly, "I guess I am. Right now, anyway."

"Say, what's going on here?" He stood up and walked away from the bed, then turned to me. He seemed very angry. *"Right now, anyway.* Are you trying to take advantage of my good nature?"

"Oh, no!" I sat up on the bed. "Please—"

"Do you think I let every hicklet who breezes into town flop in my place for a few hours and pass on? I'd lose a lot of good silverware that way."

"Oh, Nathan—"

"Are you"—he stalked back to the bed and stood glowering down at me—"are you leading me up the primrose path?"

"Oh, Nathan." I sighed. "I can't tell when you're teasing me and when you're serious."

"All right," he said after a moment. "Now listen carefully. Are you paying attention?"

I nodded.

"When you get to the point where I say things and you can always tell absolutely positively whether I'm teasing you or not . . . *that's* when you can pass on." He turned, walked out of the apartment, slamming the door behind him.

I stood up and stretched. I was smiling to myself. I felt as though I were in grade school again and we'd just turned on the radio and heard it was a snow holiday. I went over to one of the front windows and looked out just in time to see him come out of the house and start down the street. *"I found me a million-dollar baybee . . ."* he was singing, *"in the five-and-ten-cent store."* His hands were in his pockets. He had a wonderful jaunty side-to-side walk. I left the window when I couldn't see him any more.

I felt rumpled and dirty and eager to be out of the dress I'd been wearing since Omaha. I took it off and washed, using the dress to dry myself because there was just one towel hanging near the sink. I started to get another dress out of my suitcase but it seemed silly to be putting on a dress at that hour, so I slipped into my yellow kimono, instead. I was putting my dirty clothes into one of the paper bags my mother had given me for the trip when the phone rang. I reached under the bed to get the receiver.

"Hello?"

"You can't fool me," a man's voice said. "You're not Nathan."

"No," I said. "I'm Janice."

"I must have the wrong number."

"No, this is Nathan's telephone," I said. "I'm just li—"

He hung up. Nathan came back a few minutes later with a big white pizza box and some other packages.

"Good morning, sunshine," he said, looking at my kimono. "I see you've been sewing in my absence."

I laughed. "No-o-o. I made this at home. I don't have a machine here."

"Too bad." He took a bottle of Chianti wine from one of the bags. "I need some sewing done."

"I can do it by hand."

"Mmm. Why didn't I think of that?" He opened the bottle and filled two glasses giving me one and then handing me a slice of pizza.

"I suppose you can cook."

"Sure. I'm really not an orphan, Nathan. I have a regular family at home."

"Can you bake a cherry pie quick as a cat can wink its eye?"

"I can bake a cherry pie, anyway."

"That settles it. Let's get married."

"My goodness," I said, "don't you think we could just go along like this for a while?" Not because I didn't want to marry him but, because he was so changeable, I wasn't sure he'd feel the same by Monday.

"Damn it," he said, standing up so quickly that half his wine splashed out of his glass. "I'm out of the house for ten minutes and when I come back I'm playing straight man."

I went over to him but he moved to the windows. As I was standing there, holding the wine in one hand and the pizza in the other, straight out so that the drippings wouldn't run down my kimono sleeve, there were two knocks on the door and a young man came in. He stopped short when he saw me and opened his mouth as though he'd just eaten something very hot and had no water to drink. He looked a bit like Nathan, except that somehow there was less of everything; he was a little shorter, a little narrower in the shoulders, and a little less narrow everyplace else. I supposed the girls at home would have said he was handsome, but there was nothing in his face you'd particularly want to look at forever.

"Oh, my God!" he said, "it's the original Earth Mother!" He dropped to his knees and bowed over, his hands touched the floor. "Oh, Earth Mother, please accept the homage of your supplicant, Markham Sobel, known to mortals as Max."

I looked at Nathan.

"Get rid of him," Nathan said.

Max stood up and closed the door behind him.

"Don't bother," Nathan said. "You're leaving."

"I hate to prostrate myself and run," Max said.

"Are you two boys related?" I asked.

"Only by idolatry," Nathan said, opening the door.

"You should say by a previous idolatry," Max told him.

"Out."

"I trailed him worshipfully through Scarsdale High School and Yale," Max told me, "assuming the man must be as great as the talent. Then we came to New York and I discovered that my idol had feet of clay."

"And ever since," Nathan said, dragging him to the open door and pushing him out to the hallway, "he's been trying to grow a pair." He slammed the door shut and locked it. Max began banging on the door.

"Earth Mother, Earth Mother," he called, "are there any more at home like you?"

Nathan was eating his pizza and staring up at the ceiling.

"My sister Pamela," I called.

"Phone her and get her over here, for God's sake."

"I'm sorry, she's going to the University of Iowa in the fall. You'll have to wait four years." I sat down on the edge of the bed. Nathan continued to ignore me.

"Four years," Max groaned. "What am I going to do with myself for the next four years?"

"You could try some other girls in the meantime." I started eating my pizza and decided not to answer Max any more because of the way Nathan was looking at me.

"Can't hear you," Max called.

I took another bite of pizza and drank some wine.

"Earth Mother, say it again! I couldn't hear you!"

"Go to the Art Students' League!" Nathan shouted. "You, too, can burn with a hard gemlike flame!"

It was quiet outside. Then there were slow, heavy footsteps on the stairs. I smiled at Nathan. He took another slice of pizza. I poured more wine for both of us and we finished the pizza without talking. I put the pizza box on the floor and poured the last of the wine.

"This is so pretty," I said, looking at the straw bottle-basket. "It would be a shame to throw it away."

"Oh, Jesus," Nathan said, "don't go artsy-craftsy on me."

"I just thought I could use the basket for something."

"What have you been reading? *Drivel for Young Homemakers? Womb and Tomb?* You'll have to cancel your subscriptions. I won't have that pornography coming into the house."

I giggled.

"Or maybe you want to write for them," he said. "*Make Your Dead Canary a Chianti Casket for Christmas.*" He was a little less angry now, though. "*Make Your Widow Friend a Stuffed Husband for Christmas.*"

I giggled again.

He sighed. "You giggling, Alice, is like . . ."

"Like what?"

"I dunno. Like some huge, beautiful piece of fruit quivering in its own juice. That's not exactly what I mean, though . . . or maybe it is." He put his hand on my thigh. "Still hungry?"

He got the other paper bags from the chair and began emptying peaches and cherries and coconut macaroons onto the bed. "Here, have some. Keep up your strength." He popped a macaroon into his mouth. I had a peach, then a couple of macaroons and some cherries.

"Jesus," he said, "I'd be crazy to marry you."

There, he's changed his mind already, I thought. I got a heavy sick feeling all through me.

"For the same upkeep I could have a Buick."

I looked away from him.

"Is that why you don't want to marry me?" he asked. "Because I'm crazy?"

"Oh, Nathan," I said quickly. "I didn't say I didn't want to marry you, I just thought you might change your mind in a few days."

"Oh, for crying out loud," he said. "You have enough to do taking care of your own mind. Don't worry about mine."

"All right," I agreed happily.

"Then, it's settled," he said. "We'll go up to Scarsdale tomorrow. I'll get my suit and you can meet my parents. Hah!" He bounced off the bed, knocking all the food down to the floor. "You don't know how happy you'll make them. They live in constant terror that I'll marry some dull plump rabbi's daughter and throw a good suburban-agnostic boyhood down the drain." He picked up one of the paper bags, blew it up, and popped it. "Now, what about you, Alice, love? Do you have something virginal to wear? You *are* a virgin, aren't you?"

I nodded.

"Why?"

I thought about it.

"I can take the truth, Alice. You musn't pander to my puritanism. I mean, I've heard about the University of Iowa."

"Really? What have you heard?"

"Never mind. Just tell me how you spent four years there without getting laid."

"Well," I said, "I guess it's that I went out mostly with ball players."

"Sick ball players?"

"Oh, no, they weren't sick. They were just tired Saturday nights."

He stared at me seriously for a while; then, suddenly, he shouted, "Whoopee!" and leaped onto the bed so hard that I nearly bounced off it.

"I found me a giant gentile virgin," he began singing, "in the Muzeem of Modern Arty-arty-art in the Muzeem of Modern Art." He finished and flopped down near me.

"What does gentile mean?" I asked.

He propped himself up on his elbow and looked at me. "Not Jewish."

"Oh. Are you Jewish?"

"Yes, Virginia," he said, "there is a Jewish lad beside you in the sack."

"My goodness," I said, "you don't look Jewish."

"You're doing it again," he groaned. And without explaining what I was doing, he said, "Tell me what Jews look like."

"Well, the Jewish boy at school was very short. And he had curly black hair."

"Maybe it was my grandmother. She disappeared a few years ago."

"You're teasing me again."

"I'm clowning to cover my sadness."

"Nathan! Why are you sad?" I wanted to touch his nose to see what it felt like but I was afraid of annoying him.

"I'm tortured by the notion that you want me to be short and have curly black hair."

"Oh, no," I said quickly, putting my hand on his arm. "I'm crazy about the way you look."

He smiled. "Well, I'm crazy about the way *you* look, Alice, but that's easier to understand." He put his free arm around me to bring me down against him, then he kissed me for a long time, his hand sliding under my kimono sash and all around me. His body felt much stronger than it had looked under his clothes.

"I also like the way you feel."

I touched his nose. It wasn't like an elbow but it didn't feel like any nose

I'd ever known, either.

"You like that nose, huh? Twenty-seven pounds and not an ounce of fat on it." He pushed me back gently so I was lying on my back, and leaned over me. "I haven't even begun to tell you about my—"

The phone rang.

"Son-of-a-bitch," Nathan said. "Ignore it."

It rang again.

"Son-of-a-bitch, I can't stand it," he moaned. "Get it, Alice."

I leaned over the edge of the bed and groped past the fruit and the pizza box to the receiver.

"Hello?"

"What the hell does a girl that looks like you want with a college education?" Max's voice asked. "She *does* look like you, doesn't she? Same size and everything? I'm not in the market for a midget, you know, midgets are a dime a dozen."

"She's just under five eleven," I said.

Nathan grabbed the receiver and roared, "Is that you, you stupid bastard? All right, now listen to me." He caught his breath. "If you don't get off this phone and stay off it and refrain from any attempt at communication with the tenants of this apartment for the next twelve-hundred hours, I will cut you up into small pieces and donate you to the children's art class at the museum for experimentation in collage." He handed me the receiver. I put it on the floor, rather than in its cradle.

"He shouldn't worry so much," I said. "I'm sure he'll like Pam."

"I haven't even showed you the hole in my chest."

"Pamela's more—"

"Give me your hand."

I gave it to him. He made it into a fist, opened his shirt, and put my hand right into the hole in his chest. It was so deep that most of my fist fitted into it.

"My goodness," I said. "How did you get such a large hole in your chest? It doesn't hurt, does it?"

"Nope. I've always had it."

"Does anyone else in your family have it?"

"My father doesn't. I'm not sure about my mother."

"Mother says Pam's more ingoing and I'm more outgoing."

"If you're so damn outgoing, what are you doing on the edge of the bed?"

"Max talks the way you do," I said, moving back to him, "but he's really a more serious sort of person, isn't he? Not so happy-go-lucky?"

"Oh, God," Nathan said, playing with the belt of my kimono, "is this what the next hundred years are going to be like? Me failing to shock you, and you confounding me with no effort at all?"

"It's not that Pam doesn't like to have fun," I explained, running my fingers through his wonderful, thick, tangled hair. "It's just that she's more intelligent than I am."

"Good for him," Nathan said, carefully draping my kimono sash over one of my ears. "The stupid bastard."

Then he kissed me again.

~~~~~~

Judith Rossner, born and raised in New York City, now lives in a tiny New Hampshire town ". . . where fifty percent of the population bakes whole wheat bread, drinks too much, and is regarded with deep suspicion by the other fifty percent." Ms. Rossner is the author of three novels: To the Precipice, Nine Months in the Life of an Old Maid, *and* Any Minute I Can Split. *She is married to writer Robert Rossner, and they have two children.*

13

A Break in the Weather

by Harvey Jacobs

Amos had a cold and made sounds like *aieeehoom* every third or fourth breath. It was unnerving. Lisa gave him Hycomine, Triaminic, and aspirins on top of the penicillin.

"Look at the little drug addict," she said. "He's so congested. He must be having terrible dreams." Amos twisted in sleep, looking for a comfortable position. My heart went out to him. I am terrified when Amos gets sick. He is our only child. I love him in a way that is painful. He is the best thing I have going for me. But there is only one of him. And I am a hypochondriac. I worry about diseases they might bring back from outer space. "We got to have more kids," I said. "Jesus, how brutal," Lisa said. She knew what I meant. She knew that in my deepest insides I was thinking about spreading the base of my emotional investments. Since I began reading the *Wall Street Journal,* I tend to think like that, despite my poetic nature. I have developed a conglomerate personality, aggressive and fearful. Lisa read that thought, too.

"Diversify. Right?"

"All our eggs, you should pardon the expression, are in one dear basket," I said. "It wouldn't hurt to have more kids around. It would be good for Amos, too. Of course, if you're not up to all that fornication . . ."

"Don't punish me," Lisa said. "It's your office dinner party. If you don't want to go, I'll cancel the baby-sitter."

"I have got to go."

"Go yourself."

" 'Go yourself.' You're saying that because it's my thing. You know I can't go myself. It would be bad for my image. You are absolutely essential at this dinner party. The whole party is so we can look at each other's wives and have a deeper human sense of one another."

"Very funny," Lisa said. "First you make me feel guilty about leaving Amos, then you make me feel guilty about wanting to stay home. That's some technique. It stinks."

"At least the sitter is a nurse. Almost a nurse. And the party is only fifteen minutes away. God forbid if anything did happen she could call us."

"What can happen? Every kid in the city has a cold."

The student nurse rang the bell at seven-thirty. I answered the door.

"Hello," the little nurse or nursling said. "I'm Amy Pokko. You must be Mr. Craft."

The embryo nurses who sit for us come from St. Vincent's Hospital. They have names like Amy Pokko, where the first name is beautiful and the second kicks you in the stomach. Beside the fact that their names do not hang together, they are mostly pert and pretty. And they carry books depending on their term and current course. Amy Pokko did not have pediatrics books. She had kidney books.

"We haven't met before," I said. "We usually use Leslie, Marie, Angela, or Sue. Horslip, Didliglia, Xekopolis, or Beerbider. They're all on retreat this weekend."

"I know. I room with Angela Didliglia."

"Ah."

"Is that Amy Pokko?" Lisa said. "Would you ask her to come in, Harry."

"Of course," I said. "Come in, Miss Pokko."

Amy Pokko came, examined the living room, and apparently approved of the furniture because she smiled.

"Take her coat, Harry."

I took her coat. Amy Pokko had a marvelous body like all of them. The St. Vincent's nurses have a very sensual quality, slightly starched. They look so crisp and cute in their white uniforms and blue capes. But in civilian clothes they are loose and languid. Walking those children back to the hospital at curfew time you pass a corridor of parked cars in which freshmen, juniors, and seniors are kissing good night until the last and final moment of freedom is done. You turn your sitter over to a nun and you get a blank, beatific look, not even a receipt. It is sweetly unnerving.

"Aren't you a pretty girl," Lisa said.

"Thank you," said Amy Pokko.

"When they come out of the ether they must think they're in heaven," I said. "Ha hee."

"Don't mind my husband," Lisa said. "He has an odd sense of humor."

"Angela told me."

I went into our room to finish dressing. I could hear Amos breathing in his room and, in the living room, Lisa telling Amy where the TV was, how to find food, filling her in on Amos' condition, showing her various medications, and listing telephone numbers ranging from our number at the party to our doctor's number to numbers for police emergency, the neighbors, and the doorman.

"Double-lock when we go and don't open for anybody," Lisa said.

"I know that," Amy Pokko said.

"You won't have trouble with Amos."

"I hear he's a darling."

"Amy and Amos," Lisa said.

"His respiration is funny," Amy Pokko said.

"What do you mean his respiration is funny?" I yelled from our bathroom. Coming from a student nurse that comment was pregnant.

"Your husband must be some character," Amy Pokko said. "Angela said he's a laugh a minute."

"Sometimes two laughs a minute," Lisa said.

In the bathroom I buttoned and put on shaving lotion. There were two bottles of lotion, Royall Lyme and Monsieur Balmain. A year ago if anybody had said I would be using perfume I would have gone into homosexual panic. Now I used lotion. Lisa gave me the bottle for Christmas and I was trapped by the gift. The worst part was, I liked it.

"Smell me," I said when Lisa came in to finish her hair.

"Leave me alone," she said. "You have already ruined the party. And who the hell wants to go to the damn thing, anyhow? I'd rather go see *Bonnie and Clyde*. The whole apartment is a mess. I should do laundry. Damn."

"You look disgusting when you're mad," I said. "Look at your face in the mirror. Hide that charming expression under tons of makeup."

"Get out of here," Lisa said.

"I was just making my toilet," I said.

"There's a hydrant down the street," Lisa said. "Use that."

Before we left, Lisa looked in on Amos. I refreshed Amy Pokko on the telephone numbers, medicines, and security preparations.

Aieeehom

"He seems to be breathing better," Lisa said.

"Really?" I said.

"Now look," Lisa said. "If you . . ."

"Come on. We're already a half-hour late."

When we left, Amy Pokko locked all three locks on the apartment door. Lisa, bundled in a great fur, waited for the elevator in deep silence. I listened to hear if we could hear Amos breathing better from around the curved hall and behind the bolted doors.

In the car Lisa asked me if I realized that she had not been out of the house since Amos started running a fever a week ago. I realized. And I reminded her that I wasn't exactly playing backgammon at Monte Carlo. I was working and on hardly any sleep. Suffering is mutual in a marriage, especially when there

16

is an only child and he has a cold. I reminded Lisa that she should have expected that.

"Naturally, though, being brought up as a little art genius in Connecticut there may have been things Mummy and Dada didn't tell you. All this responsibility may come as a surprise to you."

"Let me out of the car. I'm going to the movies."

"You are going to the dinner party. If you give me any trouble whatsoever I am going to make lewd and suggestive advances to your mother the next time she comes merrily to visit. I am going to place a frozen pea under her pillow on the sofa and expose her as a royalist sympathizer. I am going to paint myself with gentian violet and do a violent naked foxtrot around the cup where she keeps her uppers. There is no telling what I will do. But she will not be the same woman, Lisa, I promise you that."

"Harry, if you don't like the way things are, why the hell don't you . . ."

"Because I am sick," I said. "Sick."

We drove as recklessly as possible in New York traffic. Lisa sat in the death seat and knew it. She was too proud to fasten her seat belt. I used that against her.

No words were spoken. Our wheezing baby, a few miles back, was in the car, somehow, pointing accusing fingers.

We entered the party, in the penthouse of a new apartment building called The Dylan Towers, all warmth and smiles. I browsed the wives of my fellow workers. Most of them were bland as yogurt. Mine was the best. That was pleasing and also depressing.

The party, predictable, went well enough. At one o'clock we said our goodbyes. Two calls to Amy Pokko established the fact that while Amos was restless, he was still alive. But Amy Pokko had a one-thirty curfew.

"If those seedling nurses are late, they get beaten by the Pope," I said.

"Well, that's that," Lisa said in the car. "Another glorious Saturday."

"The telephone woke him," said Amy Pokko, holding a warm but not burning Amos.

"He's a sleepy-poo," Lisa said, taking him. Amos snuggled into her soft coat.

"Who called at this hour?" I said. I say lines now that I never believed I would ever say like *who called at this hour* . . .

"A long distance from Rome. Rome, Italy, Madam Vinip."

"Did she say Mona called from Rome?" Lisa said from Amos' room.

"Yes, Mona called. Isn't that wonderful? She called to wake Amos. It's the hot line from some spaghetti orgy."

"You have to call overseas operator twenty-five," Amy Pokko said.

"I wonder what's happening," Lisa yelled from Amos' room in a voice loud enough to joggle a growing subconscious.

I paid Amy Pokko and walked her home.

"I never took a call from Rome before," she said. "It's exciting."

"Yes and no," I said. "Mrs. Craft had this friend from her schooldays who inherited a bundle. She's a sculptress."

"They have to know anatomy."

"She knows a lot of anatomy. See, Amy, she had this marriage going for ten years, a decade, has a couple of kids and so forth, but she broke up the marriage about a year ago to go into Stud, so to speak. Anyhow, she took up with this Fawn, John."

"Fawn?"

I put my fingers up over my forehead like horns, feeling a little guilty about inflicting the story on Amy Pokko. I have a tendency to experiment on living subjects that is certainly evil.

"A human Fawn. A beautiful boy. You know there are men who live off rich ladies, Amy. Sexual and social acrobats."

"My goodness."

"Mona says the Fawn used to sleep with this movie star and is quite a catch."

"Good night, Mr. Craft."

"Are we at the hospital already? I got carried away. The thing is, Lisa— Mrs. Craft—thinks this Mona is herself with wings. If anybody else called at dawn and woke the kid, Lisa would absolutely flip. But Mona is another story."

"Well, good night. It was a pleasure sitting for Amos."

"And every time Mona writes or calls there's an open invitation to go over to the good old Eternal City. Not to knock Rome."

"Mr. Craft . . ."

"Oh. Good night, Amy."

In she went past the check-in nun. I lit a cigarette and watched baby nurses pour out of Chevys, Fords, and Volkswagens, and run for the door. They were revolved inside where Sister Checkin greeted them with a nod and a smile. There is a tremendously stimulating scene there at the hospital every Saturday night.

I walked home in a slouch, heading for certain punishment. It was like going to a dentist without a mouthful of pain. With pain at least relief is in prospect. Lisa was in a lousy enough mood, what with looking after Amos. Now she would be turned on by Mona's call. All kinds of restless winds would blow inside. Who could blame her? Mona the brave, Mona the free, was a powerful symbol. She had probably called to ask Lisa to send her a dress she saw in *Vogue* or a record by The Fugs or some such. Lisa, mired in domesticity, would trudge slowly up to Bergdorf's or The Record Hunter, in between taking temperature.

"He's snoring," she said when I got back. "What took you so long?"

"I slept with Pokko," I said. "Is he hot?"

"Medium rare," she said.

"Did you find time to call operator twenty-five?"

"Not yet. I'm a little nervous about it. It's not like Mona to phone at this hour."

"She called at this hour in 1965 to ask you if you remembered the name of your freshman art teacher. She called in 1966 to ask you to ship her a subscription to the *Village Voice*. She called twice in 1967 for Day-Glo paints and hippie buttons. Always at this hour."

"Just forget it," Lisa said. "Forget the whole thing."

"You might as well call instead of sitting around speculating and savoring."

"Just go away."

I sat on the sofa with an old newspaper while Lisa made the call. While she waited for a connection, she bit her nails. Nail biting was the start. The storm would last at least three days. At least. Operator twenty-five said she would call back. Lisa began cleaning. She began scrubbing the kitchen floor. She was feeling as much of her drudgery as possible to increase the pleasure of contact with the golden expatriate bird.

I took my pulse. It was fast, fast.

It was nearly three when the telephone rang. Lisa was washing a baseboard. Her knee cracked when she stood up.

"Are you all right?" I said and she never answered.

"Mona? Mona? I can't believe it. I can never get used to the idea of talking to you . . ."

While I read I listened for Lisa's side of the international conversation.

"Oh no . . . oh, Mona. . . . It sounds terrible. . . . the doctor!"

Maybe the call was not about a printed pantie advertised in *Bazaar*.

"Never said a word . . . is he in pain? . . . No cure? What are you going to do? Oh, Mona . . ."

When the call ended, Lisa stood staring at the telephone. I continued to read. She would have to say something soon. A million years of biology guaranteed that. And finally she did after a commendable struggle.

"It's too late to call Dr. Armon."

"Dr Armon? Why do you want to call Dr. Armon?"

"I've got to get some information for Mona."

"Is she sick?"

"No. John."

"Is it serious?"

"I think so. Mona is very upset."

"Do you want to share the details?"

"We're getting a cable. A long cable. That's what Mona called to tell us. She didn't want us to be shocked by getting a cable in the middle of the night."

"When are we getting the cable?"

"Soon. All I know is, John is sick. He's got something."

Lisa bit a nail again. The worried look replaced the harried look. It was a softer look. I welcomed it. At least she was more *reachable*.

"Do you want a cup of tea while you cable-watch?"

"Yes," Lisa said. "Do you feel like making it?"

"Sure, dear."

So I made two cups of Earl Grey and we drank them slowly.

The doorbell rang. It has a loud, ripping sound. Amos whimpered but he didn't wake up, thank God. I buzzed for the doorman. He told me there was a delivery coming up.

"Here we go," I said.

"Do you have any change?"

I took the cable but Lisa grabbed it from me, then handed it back because she was too nervous to open it herself.

We read:

DEAR HARRY ETLISA STOP EXTRAORDINARY TURN EVENTS STOP FAWN LETHARGIC LAST TWOMONTHS STOP NO GOING OUT ETREADS BOOKS STOP UNLIKE FAWN ETATTRIBUTED TO INEVITABLE SETTLING STOP AFFAIR RESEMBLES MARRIAGE AFTER WHILE STOP WRONG JUDGEMENT INPART ANYHOW STOP NO OTHER BROADS STOP FAWN SUSPECTED SOCIAL DISEASE CAUSED ANTISOCIAL BEHAVIOR STOP TERRIFIED SEEK MEDICAL HELP BUT FINALLY WENT DOCTOR DUE CONCERN MEMBER OF WEDDING SOTOSPEAK WOULD FALL OFF STOP DIAGNOSIS HORRIBLE EYE DONT UNDERSTAND ENTIRELY STOP SOMETHING LIKE HARPIES HERPIES HIPPIES SKINRASH STOP PRESCRIPTION UNCERTAIN ETSUGGESTION TOTAL ABSTINENCE STOP REPEAT TOTAL TOTAL TOTAL STOP NO GUARANTEES STOP EYE FRANTIC STOP QUERY PLEASE CHECK LOCAL DOCTOR ON HARPIES HERPES HIPPIES ETAL POSSIBLE MEDICAL BREAKTHROUGH IN USA STOP EYE FEELING COMPRISED DEPRESSED UNNERVED NOT SLEEPING STOP HE VICIOUS NASTY INSECURE STOP REMEMBER HARRY SAID ONE SHOULD ALWAYS DEMAND AFFECTION FROM PETS STOP REASONABLE STOP DONT WANT BE KIND WOMAN KICKS MAN WITH HARPIES HERPES HIPPIES WHEN DOWN BUT LOSING GRIP STOP WELCOME ADVICE MEDICAL SOCIALHUMAN ETAL STOP REGARDS AMOS ETAL KNOWN IMPOSING YOU BUT UNDERSTAND HANGUP STOP WIRE COLLECT INFO HARPIES HERPES HIPPIES URGENT STOP PLEASE HURRY STOP MUST REACH DECISION BASED ALLFACTS BEFORE SPRING THAW STOP PROBLEMS PROBLEMS PROBLEMS STOP LOVE MONA

"That must have cost a bloody fortune," I said.

"What does it mean? Does it mean what I think it means?"

"It means the Fawn is both domesticated and for all practical purposes out of action."

"They can't make love?"

"Nope."

"And what does he have?"

"The word is herpes. That I remember from pre-med."

"Get the dictionary."

We read:

her-pes n. L. fr. Gk. *herpes*. fr. *herpein* to creep—more at SERPENT: any of several virus diseases characterized by the formation of blisters on the skin or mucous membranes—**her-pet-ic,** *adj.*

"He has *herpes*. He is *herpetic*. Or, here, *herpes simplex*, same difference. It's interesting that it goes back to the Greek."

"Dear god, what in the world waits in the wings to snag at us," Lisa said.

"Plenty."

"He has blisters?"

"On the skin or mucous membranes."

"Stop, Harry. Don't run it into the ground. You sound so clinical. It's a person we know. You sound gleeful."

"I don't sound gleeful, Lisa. And we don't know the person; at least, you don't."

"Are they catching?"

"How the hell should I know? Mona didn't say she was herpetic."

"Boy, you squeeze the juice out of a word, don't you."

"It's not my word. I didn't make it up. I didn't give the Roman candle his herpes. I am sitting here, dead tired, coping with this which is all I can do. And, frankly, I don't understand why. What has it got to do with us?"

"Not us. Me. Mona asked me to ask our doctor, not us. And don't think I'm not going to do it. I'm doing it first thing in the morning."

"Good. Do it. But don't you think if it's been around since the Greeks that Italian doctors are on to the latest herpes poop? Mona is an expatriate, but when the chips are down it's the old Stars and Stripes. Very typical. Your faith is where your money comes from."

"You reduce everything to money."

"That's not what I said. Look, cool it. Mona's Fawn-of-the-Moment has a few shoddy mucous membranes, right? He'll probably get over that. He's strong willed, I mean he never worked a day in his life and survived. So he has the odds going for him. The thing that's bothering Mona is the part about his being domestic all of a sudden. Settled. Sitting around. She bought a fawn and she got a hippopotamus and that's what's bothering her. And there's no cure for that. It's really pretty funny when you think about it objectively, which you can't do because you think that Mona is you with wings."

I had used that line on Amy Pokko and it was too good to waste.

"Me with wings? That's insane."

"It bothers you more that Mona's seminal fairy tale is tainted than it does that you have no nails left. You couldn't scratch a back if your life depended on it."

"I'm sick, right?" Lisa said. "Psychotic, right?"

"I never said that."

"Well, I can't help feeling deeply for Mona and for John. How would you feel if the tables were turned?"

"I wouldn't expect you to cable the story of my herpes across the Atlantic Ocean."

"You'd love it if you had those things. And I know exactly who'd be to blame."

"Now you've got yourself suffering from my herpes. You've got some mind on you, Lisa. Your head would make a hell of a transplant."

"You don't have to pick up on everything I say. Can't you have the sensitivity to see I'm all keyed up over this? Mona broke up a marriage to have John come live with her. She had a terrible childhood. She needed some fire in her life. And look what happens. The girl must be so lonely. So lonely."

"If she's lonely, she'll find another Fawn. And if she's tired of Fawns she'll relate to John as a mortal with herpes."

But the idea of lonely Mona, overwhelmed in Rome by as insurmountable a problem as the Emperors faced at the first rumbling of Christianity, pleased Lisa more than any glib solution.

She mellowed again, as she had before the tea.

"Darling, you must be dead tired, what with Amos and the party and Mona and all. The best thing for you would be some sleep."

"I am exhausted. Throbbing," she said.

"I notice that Amy Pokko ate three bananas."

"I'll go down in the morning."

"No problem. We can have eggs."

"All right. I didn't get any fresh bread, either."

"Just go to sleep. Go on."

Lisa sighed and went into the bedroom. I sat on the sofa, reading Mona's cable. I confess the idea of the temporarily indisposed Fawn gave a certain lift. And Mona's conundrum, in a time when the world is falling into a jigsaw, did not bother me too much. And the whole event had given Lisa something to think about beyond Amos' last sneeze and the budget.

"Harry, are you coming to bed?" She said it in a soft voice.

The Lord works in mysterious ways. Especially in a marriage. There was a definite break in the weather.

I am awed and amazed at those satellite pictures Tex Antoine shows on television—those that spread-eagle the continent and detail storms, clearings, clouds, and soft sunlight.

"Harry, look in on Amos." She said it in a soft voice.

"I will."

"See that he's covered."

"I will."

You can see all America from miles in the thin air and know that it will rain in California, snow in Nebraska, be gray in St. Louis, and fair and warmer in New York. The changes can be predicted, too. To date, nobody has come up with little satellites to spin over individual heads. We must take things as they come and accept the surprises.

"Harry, I'm freezing in here," Lisa said. "Don't mess up the blankets."

"I won't," I said.

And I was careful not to. Not in that climate. It was a climate that had been missing from the apartment for days. I slid into the envelope of sheets, displacing as little of it as possible.

"Thank you, Fawn," I whispered. "And good luck."

"What, Harry?"

"Nothing, honey," I said. "I was talking to myself."

Harvey Jacobs's short stories have been published in many countries. Presently a public relations consultant for the American Broadcasting Company, he has worked for The Village Voice, *taught a writer's workshop at Syracuse University, and helped the international division of ABC with satellite telecasting. At the age of twenty, he published his first story in* Tomorrow *magazine—as the winner of a search-for-talent contest, judged by Patrick Dennis, author of* MAME. *Years later when he met Dennis, Jacobs says, "Patrick told me about the time he had to judge a contest for* Tomorrow. *It seems he forgot about the manuscripts until it was too late to read them, so he just put them all into a barrel, closed his eyes, and drew the winner." Mr. Jacobs has published one book,* THE EGG OF THE GLAK. *He lives in Greenwich Village with his wife and son.*

Green Love Later

by Herbert Gold

𝒜 quarrel is only a quarrel, Sam thought, but we suffer it poorly. Who said it clears the air? It lays the heart and belly open. We poison the air afterward, yes; we breathe an air which sweetly buzzes, welcoming the poison.

Before the party, Helen and Sam Donner had quarreled because she refused to go. She didn't like their hostess; he did. Sam said, "She's funny, even though I admit what you say. She's tricky. She likes to make trouble. But she's pretty and smart, and sure I get a kick out of her."

"Your trouble is she's got eyes for you, Sam."

When Helen talked tough—bad news. He shrugged. "Maybe that's my only trouble."

"Listen, Melinda is a bitch," Helen said. "She knows I think so—and you like her. It just gives her the chance to make that little mouth at me."

"Nothing *happens*, Helen. She plays that game all by her lonesome—"

"Nothing happens! Just the way she says, *Feeling any better lately, Sam?* is enough. You looked tired last time, she says. She's—"

And always one thing leads to another. How Helen didn't let him kid the boys. How Sam was so quick to criticize but never saw when *he* did anything wrong, like that time at the resort. How and how and how. And the sense of it was that they loved each other but despaired of loving after the first ten years of their too-early marriage and something still missing between them. Not children; they had two. Not place; they were young, healthy, handsome, and installed in Sam's career. Not the obvious delight of marriage! They were grateful for each other's pleasure.

Some expectation had not been fulfilled, some desire for a perfection found nowhere on this earth, some nagging wish for felicities other than their own. They were intelligent and sensible and could talk to each other. It was not enough. They were twisted with discontent. Her perfume had a faint animal strength of anger, but still sweet to him off her arms and throat. Not enough.

They went to the party, anyway. Sam held Melinda's hand just a second too long at the door, while she told him what she had heard of his tennis-playing from a mutual friend—another young blond person who admired Sam Donner— and the look that Sam received from Helen was a crash of diamonds. There was nothing harder in the world. Would he have to explain to her all night that it was Melinda who held his hand? Trouble, trouble.

Truce in the automobile, yes.

A shake-hands with Melinda at the door and it fell into grit.

Can Helen ever have loved me to do this? If she is dead to me now, could she have been alive that night on the train from Chicago and that day in the park when we bought the Popsicles? Oh, I remember the ledge of rock, the lonely beach we found on our bicycle, her hair all flowing careless in the sand, how she touched me—was it ever true?

Melinda, seeing all evil, hearing it, sucking it into a small bud of pout, was after Helen to introduce her to a new friend. "Helen darling, I want you to meet Harold Dowling. Isn't that funny? You have the same initials. Harold Dowling—Helen Donner."

"I'm pleased to meet you, Mr. Dowling."

"I'm very happy, Mrs. Donner."

Fuming, distraught, feeling the hard draw on her scalp where her hair was pulled and tied, she let him guide her to a sofa where they sat. It was a large party. Helen had one drink, had two. This Mr. Dowling was a very amusing, a very bright, a very nice young man. He had traveled and such, and he wasn't a slug like most engineers. He kept his eyes open. He had his eyes wide open on her. They were talking and he was leaning and searching for something in her eyes and she was laughing at his stories and taking a third quick drink and he was still looking at her eyes. Yes, at her eyes, but all busied with the proud, used-to-love, demanding-it perch of her body from the waist up—it was the way to look at her. It made her feel awake and challenged. Then a strange thing happened. He leaned away and said, "You know, I only said hello to your husband."

He left her brusquely, he deserted her on the couch while he went to stand near Sam. Sam had hardly noticed her. Sam left his wife alone in these moods. Annoyed, piqued, still amused, Helen finished her third drink (one over her limit) because Harold Dowling had deserted her just when she was feeling better.

But she still felt better. He said nothing more to her for the remainder of the evening, although he occasionally smiled at her across the room. She remembered that he had told her his troubles, making inconsequential fun of them, so that she had to think about it afterward to realize that he was unhappy, really he was, to be divorced and lonely and yet so sweet about everything. It made her less lonely to think about his troubled sweetness.

He and Sam had a long talk during which they each appreciated the other's ideas about Cleveland politics and the problems of urban development—Harold as an engineer, Sam as a city planner. It was a business they loved. They found the same politicians ridiculous. Sam liked Harold so much that he suggested they get together for lunch next Monday. Afterward, alert with the afterglow of companionship, he remarked to Helen: "This Dowling is a good fellow. You don't meet his kind so often in Cleveland. We'll have to get to know him better."

Helen said nothing.

"Look, honey, let's forget about it. I didn't pay any attention to her that you could object to."

"That's right." *Melinda.*

"Then stop fretting. Did you like Dowling?"

"Who?" Why should she say that? What a silly little deceit.

"Harold Dowling, that engineer up from Venezuela. He's lonely. I think we ought to invite him to the house sometime."

She felt very far from Sam at this moment after a noisy, smoky, rattle-headed party at Melinda's. Deceit was no good, but it came easily. "That new fellow with the bad teeth? I don't mind," she said. "I hardly spoke with him."

Sam needed his friendship with Harold Dowling after the heavy, flesh-loosening, steam-heated winter. It flowered in the spring. Sam drove him out to Shaker Heights for dinner cooked by Helen, then back downtown to his apartment hotel; it was no trouble late at night on the lightened highway. "How long do you suppose before they start air conditioning the streets? It should be easy, just build a machine big enough. Warm air rises—the cold air lies down flat for us to walk through."

"They're working on it. It's no secret, Sam. Even in politics the hot air rises."

Nice to smile with a friend!

His life in business had always seemed too purposeful to Sam. The touch of lazy wit and fanciful thought that had always kept him apart from his earnest-after-money, earnest-after-improvement associates now served to draw him to Harold Dowling. They talked of Venezuela and skyscrapers, slum clearance and decentralization, the local art museum (a Greek gas station! bank Doric! a prison for painting!). Harold Dowling, waspish and more self-sufficient—a man who worked barbells but lonely, anyway—warmed to the friendship of this crew-cut young man who sold large civic ideas and collected Mozart records to which he sometimes listened. When Sam said, "It's O.K., this lunch is on me," Harold smiled through his jagged teeth and said:

"It's O.K. then, but are you busy tomorrow? How about an Italian lunch?"—which would, of course, be on him.

A sudden friendship is a surprise gift from the world. Sam felt good about it. The pressure between Helen and him had gone down, too. Spring was really here, whether or not the streets were air conditioned.

At the third week of lunching together he proposed that Harold celebrate April Fool's Day by again having dinner with them at home. "The first of April is a kind of anniversary—the first day I got up the courage to talk to Helen. We were still in high school. She was the prettiest girl in cashmere."

"It would be disrespectful of true love to refuse," Harold gravely stated.

The dinner was very pleasant, very relaxed, with Helen doing special casserole things and a holiday mood in waiting until the kids were asleep and sitting down to table late. But an odd little occurrence surprised Sam and annoyed him. They were, of course, on familiar terms. Harold said "Helen" very often, bending to her, saying "Helen," leaning and finishing a statement with her name, saying "Helen," inquiring of Helen this and wondering if Helen agreed about that. Perfectly all right. A lonely, terribly alone grasping for intimacy. Harold and Sam had already talked together so much that they felt like old friends. However, this evening, in Helen's presence, Harold suddenly referred to him as "Sammy." It shouldn't have annoyed him. It didn't mean anything. Years ago a few people had called him "Sammy," but it didn't go with him any more. It made no difference.

But it did.

"Helen," Harold was saying, "you ought to take better care of Sammy's socks. A man in his position doesn't need holes for his feet to cool off."

She laughed. "He insists on wearing the ones with holes around the house. Husbands are known for their little quirks."

"Don't you have any, Helen?"

"Not many," she said softly, slyly, laughing for no reason, "not as many as Sammy does."

It was the first time she had ever said his name like that. A silly complicity with Dowling. He thought of calling Harold "Harry," but that sounded all right, and why show his trivial exasperation?

Afterward they spent a lazy late evening, playing a side of a new Italian recording of *Don Giovanni*, listening, smoking, talking quietly. Helen seemed relaxed and happy. It was probably good to have two men occupied with her. Any woman, even one as pretty, yes, as beautiful as Helen, with her long light hair and body of an athletic girl and soft watchful eyes and mouth, yes, even a woman as worthy of admiration as Helen could be improved by the fact of admiration. She was at her best.

Harold knew when to leave. He made them promise to go to the theater with him that Saturday. "Good night, Helen," he said with a surprising formality and seriousness at the door. "It's a real pleasure to know people like you. I was afraid of the Middle West."

"We're not just *natives*, you know. You New Englanders are barbarians. Go to Caracas and you expect the life of art. But come to Cleveland and it's a desert you look for."

He took her hand again and smiled, and then shook Sam's hand firmly. "Good night, Sammy," he said, showing all at once the frayed, tobacco-dirtied edges of his teeth in a grin.

Cleveland is a large city, but like all cities, not so large as it seems. An entirely unexceptional thing happened the next day in this town—this *urban area*—of over a million people. Helen Donner went downtown to buy a record at a shop she knew in the Colonial Arcade. She might have tried the neighborhood music store, but she was looking for a European recording of some cuckoo-clock music by the young Mozart and she was certain that they would have to order it. She might have saved herself the trip by telephoning, but this didn't even occur to her. Anyway, it would be good to get dressed up and tuck her hair under a smart black hat and leave the children with a neighbor and escape the house and suburb on an afternoon when Sam had to work late. They didn't have the record at the Colonial, either. She should have telephoned.

The coincidence was that she should run into Harold Dowling just looking in the window of the shop. A coincidence and yet not; his office was in the Colonial Arcade. It was nothing to be startled over. They both wanted coffee, took it in the little coffee shop in the arcade (they sat in a booth because Harold looked tired and she thought it would be more restful than the counter), and then spent longer than it seemed and separated with the warmth of new friends who know that they matter to each other. What Harold had said about himself worried Helen and made her feel close to him. Confiding makes confidence. He asked no confiding in return, or if he did, he asked it without questions.

That evening she forgot to mention that she had met Harold Dowling downtown.

The next night, after supper, when they had divided the evening paper and put some music on the player, Helen sat without reading for a time. Then she said, "Sam?"

"What?"

"Melinda called. She wants us for Saturday night."

"O.K., are we busy?"

"I don't want to go, Sam. It's silly to accept her invitations and not return them—"

"Return one, then."

"I can't bear that woman, Sam."

His short harsh laugh was worse than patronizing. "O.K., then we won't go," he said. This wasn't what she had asked of him. Helen wanted her husband to share her feeling, not just submit to a demand. He agreed that Melinda was a bitch, but it didn't seem to disturb him. She amused him; she still pleased him. They talked of this and that, and when it was clear that Sam didn't care whether or not they saw Melinda on Saturday night and whether or not she was a bitch, but only wanted to finish the paper, they both returned to their reading.

For five minutes.

Then: "Oh!" said Helen. She had been so busy. Now she remembered what had been on her mind. Yesterday she had met Harold Dowling—a really nice fellow. So intelligent, sympathetic, kind, witty, and such an unhappy life.

Sam Donner's newspaper crackled to the floor beside his chair. "Who is this character from a movie?" he asked. "You talking about our little friend, that Harold?"

Helen remarked that it was silly to call Harold little when he was exactly Sam's height. She had always felt that it was a nice size for a man. Yes, Harold had really talked freely, like an old friend. His wife had not been right for him, but he had tried for several years to make it work—really tried—but now he was sad because he knew he had failed and they were getting divorced. An unlucky break. It could happen to any very young man. Harold's wife had been pretty, charming, captivating, in fact. Too bad, too bad.

Sam was listening with very close and serious attention to all this news.

"We had coffee together at the Colonial," Helen said. "He insisted. He needed someone to talk to."

Sam seemed to be thinking hard, but he said only, casually, after a few moments and a rattling straight of his newspaper: "You didn't mention it yesterday. . . . You know how much I like Harold, but that kind of thing causes talk." He flushed. He wished it were someone else using such words.

Helen pouted and laughed, a merry, excited, entirely pleased laughter that made Sam feel still more suburban, foolish, and distant from himself. "Really, Sam!"—really-Samming him was unusual in their marriage. "Really, Sam, I never said there was anything wrong when you met Melinda by accident and had martinis with her. *Martinis,* I think you said they were, and you don't even like Melinda. You really agree with me about her. But Harold is a good friend to both of us. Who's going to talk that doesn't talk about Melinda's curious attitude toward you?"

"You don't have to flatter me about Melinda. I don't need her."

"Maybe not. I don't know. I'm not flattering you, Sam. She'll do what she does to any husband. And any wife. But Harold, he's—"

Sam tried to be calm but succeeded only in looking awkward and confused. "I know, he's a good friend. In fact, we're having lunch tomorrow. Never mind, forget it, Helen. I must be tired." He pleaded fatigue in order to avoid pleading worse. In some way this conversation about a meeting which had taken place yesterday but had not been mentioned until today changed Sam's feeling toward Harold Dowling. No, it hadn't exactly changed his feeling; it had only brought back the itch of heat in his cheeks when Harold called him "Sammy" before Helen. Harold—what kind of a name was that? Just as funny. Just a name for a sissy kid.

Foolishness.

Sam tried, the next day, to recall his first fellow feeling for this engineer whose deep tan had turned yellow in Cleveland after the trip from Caracas.

Dowling never told Sam about his troubles in marriage. He never hinted that Helen and he had talked; he seemed to like secrets. When he lunched with Sam he seemed to be all ease and no trouble at all It was a lot of confidence for a man who then turned around and excited the sympathy of another man's wife. It was as if he knew that her sympathy was overready, overhidden, a swollen and tired-of-waiting thing.

Still, you couldn't properly make a fuss over a manner. Just because Dowling was lonely and needed a woman to whom he could tell his troubles was no reason for Sam Donner to look for unpleasant tics. That sly sideways grin with the yellow tips of teeth showing? Well, it was only a smile and lots of people have smoke stains on their teeth. That way of saying *Sammy*? It was his name, look! The sour scent of male shaving lotion? Maybe he had sensitive cheeks.

Don't be foolish, Sam Donner told himself. Don't be a dope.

But he knew that, if this is what it is to be a jealous dope, then he was a dope and jealous.

When Helen met Dowling again by accident at the library—but he knew her day for the library—Sam made no effort to hide his irritation. It only made him feel more angry, more silly, that she told him about it as soon as he came home, that she felt no embarrassment, that she treated the whole thing as unexceptional and made appointments for the three of them without allowing him his discontent or giving him the chance to be foolish in a less foolish way.

Then, when they were together, Sam had to admit that Harold was a likable guy and what was the matter with him? Harold didn't do anything to them but exist.

One day it happened for the first time. Bill Stowe said, "Say, Sam, does your wife have a cousin or something in town?"

Sam knew that this was it, the kind of talk after a season of refusal that would make his trouble real to himself. "No, why?"

"Oh, nothing,"—malice is so nice! "This fellow sort of looks like her. I thought maybe they were relatives or something and he was staying at the Park Villa—"

Hiding his rage made it worse. He went home choking with it, sweating and sticky with it, sick and heavy and swollen with it on the seat cover of the Studebaker. He felt the question come slow and wheezing.

"Why, no!" Helen cried, her laughter trilling out.

He believed her. He knew at once. He *knew*.

"Why no," Helen said, "I told you about the time we met at the library— we just stepped into the Park Villa to get cigarettes. The way people like to talk!" But even in her amusement her eyes darkened and he looked away under the emotions that ran in flood over her face: triumph because he doubted her, a heat of power and a cold of contempt.

The fact that it was the truth and she was hiding no lunches with Harold

Dowling made it harder for him at this moment. It would almost be better if it were true and he could rage at her. This fantasy which was obsessing him—these images of Dowling leaning over the table to her, touching her elbow over wet spots in the little park behind the library, looking at her and playing her and making his ironic sad little jokes—led straight to still more grotesque imaginings. Sam Donner shivered. The thought that Dowling's initials were the same as his wife's enraged him. His thoughts were splitting to nonsense.

He tried to be reasonable. He asked her to stop seeing him, to be busy if they met by accident, to avoid listening to his troubles, and to let him know that she didn't keep secrets from her husband. "Of course we'll go on seeing him together. I know he's a nice guy"—liar! liar! hypocrite before Helen! But his brand of loneliness can be dangerous for us. I don't blame him for falling in love with you."

"No, Sam, no!" Such merry, merry laughter!

He insisted on laying down the conditions under which they could meet.

Laughter again, and that name: "What about Melinda? Does this mean I have the right to order you to refuse to buy her a drink when she just happens by the parking lot at five?"

"Melinda has nothing to do with anything. You know what I think of her. We've known her for years."

"You know what I think of Harold, darling. I've told you." She bent her head and gave him the line of scalp dividing her strong light hair.

The quarrel was a serious one. While they put the children to bed it simmered and steamed. It began again downstairs in whispers, conspiratorial, while the kids were falling asleep. It was more destructive because they were hissing and spitting at each other so that the children would not be infected, and more destructive because it had no reason, she had done nothing—only because Sam felt that Dowling had his ideas and that his wife's refusal to recognize what Dowling meant implied a complicity with him. "But I don't see it, Sam! There's not a sign!"

"There's a reason you don't see the signs, Helen."

"I can't stand you when you stand there looking so hurt and smart!"

She was frantic; she didn't want this, either.

At last they were in bed, exhausted, nothing settled, but she turned and touched his back and he too turned and held her.

"I love you, Sam," she said. "I wouldn't do anything to hurt you. I just don't see—"

"Let's not start again," he said warningly.

They got warm in silence for a long time, eyes closed but not sleepy. Helen touched him and whispered, "Look, it's important, I know it, Sam. Don't get upset again, but I want to tell you."

"What?"

"If everything were right with us, this couldn't happen and we wouldn't be this way."

"Everything is all right in no marriage I ever heard of. I can't imagine it."
Eyes open all at once.

"Then it isn't *his* fault if you feel upset by him."

Sam, without moving, said stubbornly, "Then it's exactly his fault if he
knows how to profit from something he has no right to."

"My fault, Sam. Your fault."

His head turned on the pillow. "O.K., O.K., but that's our affair. No right
of his. He has no rights here."

She seemed to know that his eyes had opened, because she brushed her
hand over to close them again. He touched her. They hushed each other. Nothing
was settled, but they slept.

Twice during the night he was awakened by her hand on his face, green
in the dark, green touching his eyes to make sure they were shut, greenly brushing the lids down as if this art were a ritual mercy and his face a dead one to be
set in the green regard of rest and peace. The spatter of her hand's pressure on
his eyes sent sea flashes deep into his sleep.

Sam had his Architects' Association evening meeting and said good night
to the kids and goodbye to Helen. At the door he met Dowling just coming up
the walk in the late-spring drizzle. Sam turned back into the house and sat deep
in his coat while Helen greeted the visitor.

"I just thought I'd drop by for a minute. I didn't know you were going
out"—Dowling.

"The first Monday of the month. Reports"—Sam Donner.

"But stay, Harold! Sam will be back early." Helen was busy and young
and full of pleasure as she settled him with cigarette, ashtray, and the prospect of
a drink.

Dowling let her touch his shoulder to oblige him into the chair. "Don't
bother," he said. "If you have a beer, though—but I think I ought to be going."

Helen: "No! no! no!"—and that sweet animal scent of anger.

Sam sat and waited with his coat on while Helen hurried about in a fever
to keep Dowling from looking at him and, incredibly, succeeded. Dowling seemed
easy at his place on a cushion. He said not a word about Sam's sitting there in
silence, his trench coat buckled, his face glistening. Helen glanced at him once
ferociously, triumphantly, and chattered at Dowling. He was staying.

"Helen," Sam started to say.

"What, Sammy?"

Her pleasure in his jealousy made him more hurt, more hopeless, more
jealous. The easy delight on Dowling's face was unmistakable, too. The flattering
lean toward Helen was also directed toward her husband.

Little Julie, upstairs, must have heard his voice. "Daddy," she called, "is
Uncle Harold here? I want to see him."

Jealousy is located in an exact spot at the lowest part of the belly.

"I came to see you, honey." Dowling called back. "Come down and give Uncle Harold a kiss."

Helen said nothing, although usually bed was bed and no visitor could disturb this rule. They were not the sort of parents who switched on the light for relatives to admire sleeping eyes and fists. Now she said nothing, waiting.

"We don't get the kids out of bed for company," Sam said hoarsely.

Helen was silent. No solidarity with him at all. But the child did not come down, it was not her habit; perhaps she had not heard. She was silent, probably dropped off to sleep—but no solidarity with Sam from Helen. He knew what jealousy tasted like, and the weight of it, and where it was located.

Once when they had talked about why Helen liked Dowling, he himself had suggested that there was nothing wrong in her being flattered by the man's attention. No love can satisfy every desire for love, and therefore no love has the right to be exclusive. Even the child who is most attached to a parent will sometimes run for other needs to a grandmother, an uncle, or a friend. A life fits to ours always less perfectly than a shoe. He himself had said it. Melinda flattered him although he knew she was vain and self-centered; this flattery and his warming to it took nothing from Helen.

Then, why his fury about Dowling? What was Helen withdrawing that was his right?

He felt it in his belly at that sick place.

The courageous thing was to admit this most shameful of feelings—this sick, green, belly-pulling fear. He took a breath and said in a harsh voice that surprised him (he caught a glimpse of his swollen face in the mirror): "Harold, I have to leave now. I'm sorry, but I suggest that we leave together."

Dowling's amusement was something luxurious, a woman's pleasure even in his way of saying it. "Oh, why of course! I should have known you were waiting for me, Sammy."

Helen's eyes were wide to cracking with anger. Her lips were moving, mumbling, and he thought for an instant murmuring the reminder *Melinda*.

"No!" she gasped.

Dowling was still laughing without a smile. He went for his coat himself and left his beer untouched and his cigarette burning in the ashtray. "Sammy?" he said softly.

A jerk of the head that Sam Donner could not control.

"Sammy, I don't blame you for watching out for your wife."

"What-what-what-do-your-mean-by-that?"

"Oh nothing, Sammy, nothing but the best and purest. Just that she's charming. A delightful person. Lovely"—caressing her with his voice, exciting her with words, covering her with discretions of kisses. "Worth taking care of, Sammy."

He went.

Sam missed his meeting.

Helen locked the door to her room and it was only at dawn that she would open it to say that she didn't care about Harold Dowling or anyone, but that she would take her revenge for what her husband had done to her. (Shame! Both ashamed!) He tried to say that he was sorry, but he could not speak for fatigue. He could not speak for wondering why, if Harold Dowling meant nothing to her but an unhappy young man, her face had to be stained with crying all night and her door locked to him because he had taken away that which Harold Dowling was giving her. And distant and mysterious she seemed because she did not regret what she had made of him.

"It's your problem, not mine." Sam was never convinced, as the weeks went by, that Dowling had really said this to him, but it was certainly the sense of his smile and the reason of his jaunty tipping walk out that evening. If you're intelligent, a problem is something that you solve.

Therefore, long drives in the country for dinner, a cautious flattery (nothing too *willed*), flowers, a searching attention. An effort of devotion was the intelligence of this problem—that Helen no longer lived in solidarity with him.

But something was coming to birth again between them through the dusty summer. He was bringing her to him. Her head came down on his shoulder. In this effort of wooing, he was touched by her as he had once been. The children, too—those shrewd creatures whose first social life is to comment on their parents' ways of walking, eating, and loving—passed through a time of querulousness. They knew what was happening without knowing. Sending them to a summer camp made the house seem like a honeymooner's cabin, the Pullman burrowing into the night, or the friend's room on the other side of Ithaca. They returned to the abrupt fullness of first desire, when each nip and circle of flesh was a new miracle of becoming that other to whom they each had said: *Dear; Dearest.* Sometimes Sam wondered if the demands he made upon love, to which Helen also vibrated, were not an intolerable burden upon children. Romance means a solitary devotion, and families are busy kitchen events. But this was the only marriage they knew. Someday it, too, might have its kitchen and its picnic side, with apples roasting and a steady ease with kids. Someday, later.

During this season a steady, hot dry wind blew up from Columbus, and when it shifted, there was only the wet, heavy stir from Lake Erie over Cleveland. The secretaries in Sam's office were mussed and mouth-parted when they came in from the street, suffering as if from an effort at love, but just hot, only hot, fearfully hot. The children were at camp for a few days more. One July afternoon Sam decided to come home soon after lunch and surprise Helen for a drive out to swim at Huntington Park.

Surprise. She was not at home. The house was dark and shaded, but hot with an air through which nothing had moved. The doors were locked. The house looked put away.

The pain in the lower part of his belly came pinching sharp and quick.

Stupidly, his head pressed between enormous thumbs, he spread his handkerchief over the telephone and called Harold Dowling's office. Mr. Dowling was out for the day. It meant nothing. That Mr. Dowling was out for the day did not mean that he was in his automobile some place with Helen, did it?

No, it did not.

But Mr. Dowling was out, sir, for the day. The sickness made it hard for Mr. Donner to walk straight.

Mr. Donner was wandering through his empty house, which looked strange to him, his children absent (he longed for them now), his wife gone, the objects that were his property bathed in a thieving glitter of sun through blinds—stolen from him because he had to look at them in a new way. Mr. Donner walked upstairs and downstairs. Mr. Donner washed his hands and left the faucet dripping. There was glass on the kitchen floor. He had broken something, but it was something empty and dry. Mr. Donner ran to the window because he heard a footstep up the walk, taking a pipe so that he could say, "Just smoking and waiting for you to come home, dearest. Where were you, anyway? How about a drive out for a drink to cool off?"

It was the boy leaving a circular from the Big Bear Market.

Sam Donner was in a chair with sickness everywhere within him and tears, harsh and hopeless, hurting his eyes because they were turning in so many bad ways and breaking so many new paths.

It stopped. Time stopped. He sat and the sun crossed his face and he did not move. The thousand legs of a bug crossed his foot. He was watching, counting, not seeing.

Oh!

Her little gracenote because the door was unlocked. "Oh, you're home early," she said. "It was just so hot I took a bus and went to the beach alone." She threw down a little bag with her swimsuit, towel, and book. "Now, I'm hot again. How are you, Sam? Been here long?"

"No, just a few minutes—just got in." He came up with an effort from a deep place.

"How about a kiss?"

Yes, yes, *that*. She put up her face, flushed and tanned and tired, and said, "A big one, ohh," through his fierce, teeth-clashing embrace. He trusted himself to say nothing now, only to explore her mouth while he felt the poison of that place in his belly turn and search and pull at him. He knew he was bruising the soft lip-flesh. She caught her breath but said nothing, clinging to him, her fists on his back. He would take her now. He would take her for nothing but dread. She would not dare to know why. He would demand her now, here, in this heat, his hand toppling her, there, fast, terrified, rolling wetly on the polished floor from which the rug had been lifted.

She was crying softly.

She had lovely hair. She went to the beach alone. She knew that she had lovely hair. If she went to the beach alone, then why did she have sand in her hair? If she were at the beach alone, what vanity held her from wearing a bathing cap? Why didn't she protect her hair from the sand if there was no one to tell her it was lovely? Her hair smelled of sand and sun, and in their dark house in the suburb he tasted its grit in his mouth and he kissed her there and again and everywhere.

She was gasping with dry tears as they crashed together and then there was silence. Why didn't she ask why? Why the grit in his mouth and the deep belly pain? Her breast lay hot and thick and swollen by his lips. It made no difference that the thickness and the throb were his doing now. In the empty house they lay together on the floor and she stroked his eyes shut, making green flashes in the dark of his sight.

She asked nothing. Did she think him asleep? He knew nothing at all about her.

Loneliness is only loneliness, and there are worse ways to be alone.

One of America's most widely known writers and critics, Herbert Gold has won more literary prizes than can be listed in this space. Born in Cleveland, Ohio, he graduated from Columbia College, and studied at the Sorbonne in Paris. Mr. Gold taught at Cornell, the University of California at Berkeley, Harvard, and Stanford University. Among his best-known works are THE PROSPECT BEFORE US, THE MAN WHO WAS NOT WITH IT, THEREFORE BE BOLD, LOVE AND LIKE, FATHERS, *and* THE AGE OF HAPPY PROBLEMS. *He lives in San Francisco with his wife and daughter.*

Rain Queen

by Nadine Gordimer

⚬⚬⚬⚬⚬⚬⚬

$\mathcal{W}$e were living in the Congo at the time; I was nineteen. It must have been my twentieth birthday we had at the Au Relais, with the Gattis, M. Niewenhuys, and my father's site manager. My father was building a road from E'ville to Tshombe's residence, a road for processions and motorcades. It's Lubumbashi now, and Tshombe doesn't live there any more. But at that time there was plenty of money around and my father was brought from South Africa with a free hand to recruit engineers from anywhere he liked. The Gattis were Italian, and then there was a young Swede. I didn't want to leave Johannesburg because of my boy friend, Alan, but my mother didn't like the idea of leaving me behind, because of him. She said to me, "Quite honestly, I think it's putting too much temptation in a young girl's way. I'd have no one to blame but myself." I was very young for my age, then, and I gave in. There wasn't much for me to do in E'ville. I was taken up by some young Belgian married women who were only a few years older than I was. I had coffee with them in town in the mornings, and played with their babies. My mother begged them to speak French to me; she didn't want the six months there to be a complete waste. One of them taught me how to make a chocolate mousse, and I made myself a dress under the supervision of another; we giggled together as I had done a few years before with the girls at school.

Everyone turned up at the Au Relais in the evenings, and in the afternoons when it had cooled off a bit we played squash—the younger ones in our crowd, I mean. I used to play every day with the Swede, and Marco Gatti. They came straight from the site. Eleanora Gatti was one of those Mediterranean women who not only belong to a different sex but seem to be a species entirely different from the male. You could never imagine her running or even bending

37

to pick something up; her white bosom in square-necked dresses, her soft hands with rings and jewel-lidded watch, her pile of dark hair tinted a strange tarnished-marmalade color that showed up the pallor of her skin—all was arranged like a still life. The Swede wasn't married.

After the game, Marco Gatti used to put a towel round his neck, tennis-star fashion, and his dark face was gilded with sweat. The Swede went red and blotchy. When Marco panted it was a grin, showing white teeth and one that was repaired with gold. It seemed to me that all adults were flawed in some way; it set them apart. Marco used to give me a lift home and often came in to have a drink with my father and discuss problems about the road. When he was outlining a difficulty he had a habit of smiling and putting a hand inside his shirt to scratch his breast. In the open neck of his shirt some sort of amulet on a chain rested on the dark hair between his strong pectoral muscles. My father said proudly, "He may look like a tenor at the opera, but he knows how to get things done."

I had never been to the opera; it wasn't my generation. But when Marco began to kiss me every afternoon on the way home, and then to come in to talk to my father over beer as usual, I put it down to the foreignness in him. I said, "It seems so funny to walk into the room where Daddy is." Marco said, "My poor little girl, you can't help it if you are pretty, can you?"

It rains every afternoon there, at that time of year. A sudden wind would buffet the heat aside, flattening paper against fences in the dust. Fifteen minutes later—you could have timed it by the clock—the rain came down so hard and noisy we could scarcely see out of the wind screen and had to talk as loudly as if we were in an echoing hall. The rain usually lasted only about an hour. One afternoon we went to the site instead of to my parents' house—to the caravan that was meant to be occupied by one of the engineers but never had been, because everyone lived in town. Marco shouted against the downpour, "You know what the Congolese say? 'When the rain comes, quickly find a girl to take home with you until it's over.'" The caravan was just like a little apartment, with everything you needed. Marco showed me—there was even a bath. Marco wasn't tall (at home the girls all agreed we couldn't look at any boy under six feet) but he had the fine, strong legs of a sportsman, covered with straight black hairs, and he stroked my leg with his hard yet furry one. That was a caress we wouldn't have thought of, either. I had an inkling we really didn't know anything.

The next afternoon Marco seemed to be taking the way directly home, and I said in agony, "Aren't we going to the caravan, then?" It was out, before I could think. "Oh, my poor darling, were you disappointed?" He laughed and stopped the car there and then and kissed me deep in both ears as well as the mouth. "All right, the caravan." We went there every weekday afternoon— he didn't work on Saturdays, and the wives came along to the squash club. Soon the old Congolese watchman used to trot over from the laborers' camp to greet us when he saw the car draw up at the caravan; he knew I was my father's daughter. Marco chatted with him for a few minutes, and every few days gave him a tip. At the beginning, I used to stand by as if waiting to be told what to do next, but Marco had what I came to realize must be adult confidence. "Don't look so worried. He's a nice old man. He's my friend."

Marco taught me how to make love, in the caravan, and everything that I had thought of as "life" was put away, as I had at other times folded the doll's clothes, packed the Monopoly set and the sample collection and given them to the servant. I stopped writing to my girl friends; it took me weeks to get down to replying to Alan's regular letters, and yet when I did so it was with a kind of professional pride that I turned out a letter of the most skillful ambiguity—should it be taken as a love letter, or should it not? I felt it would be beyond his powers—powers of experience—to decide. I alternately pitied him and underwent an intense tingling of betrayal—actually cringing away from myself in the flesh. Before my parents and in the company of friends, Marco's absolutely unchanged behavior mesmerized me: I acted as if nothing had happened. He was not pretending to be natural with my father and mother—he *was* natural. And the same applied to our behavior in the presence of his wife.

After the first time he made love to me I had looked forward with terror and panic to the moment when I should have to see Eleanora again; when she might squeeze my hand or even kiss me on the cheek as she sometimes did in her affectionate, feminine way. But when I walked into our house that Sunday and met her perfume and then all at once saw her beside my mother talking about her family in Genoa, and Marco, my father, and another couple, sitting there—I moved through the whirling impression without falter. Someone said, "Ah, here she is at last, our Jillie!" And my mother was saying (I had been riding with the Swede), "I don't know how she keeps up with Per, they were out dancing until three o'clock this morning—" and Marco, who was twenty-nine, December 1st, Sagittarius, domicile of Jupiter, was saying, "What it is to be young, eh?" and my father said, "What time did you finally go to bed, after last night, anyway, Marco?" and Eleanora, sitting back with her plump smooth knees crossed, tugged my hand gently so that we should exchange a woman's kiss on the cheek.

I took in the smell of Eleanora's skin, felt the brush of her hair on my nose; it was done, forever. We sat talking about some shoes her sister-in-law had sent from Milan. It was something I could never have imagined: Marco and I, as we really were, didn't exist here; there was no embarrassment. The Gattis, as always on Sunday mornings, were straight from eleven-o'clock Mass at the Catholic cathedral, and smartly dressed.

There was a shortage of white women in Katanga and my mother felt much happier to see me spending my time with the young married people than she would have been to see me taken up by the mercenaries who came in and out of E'ville that summer. "They're experienced men," she said—as opposed to boys

39

and married men, "and of course they're out for what they can get. They've got nothing to lose; next week they're in another province, or they've left the country. I don't blame them. I believe a girl has to know what the world's like, and if she is fool enough to get involved with that crowd, she must take the consequences."

She seemed to have forgotten that she had not wanted to leave me in Johannesburg in the company of Alan. "She's got a nice boy at home, a decent boy who respects her. I'd far rather see her just enjoying herself generally, with you young couples, while we're here." And there was always Per, the Swede, to even out the numbers; she knew he wasn't "exactly Jillie's dream of love." I suppose that made him safe, too.

If I was no one's partner in our circle, I was a love object, handed round them all, to whom it was taken for granted that the homage of a flirtatious attitude was paid. Perhaps this was supposed to represent my compensation: If not the desired of any individual, then recognized as desirable by them all. "Oh, of course, you prefer to dance with Jeelie," Mireille would say to her husband, pretending offence. He and I were quite an act, at the Au Relais, with our cha-cha. Then he would whisper to her in their own language, and she would giggle and punch his arm.

Marco and I were as famous a combination on the squash court as Mireille's husband and I were on the dance floor. This was the only place, if anyone had had the eyes for it, where our lovemaking showed. As the weeks went by and the lovemaking got better and better, our game got better and better. The response Marco taught me to the sound of spilling grain the rain made on the caravan roof held good between him and me on the squash court. Sometimes the wives and spectators broke into spontaneous applause; I was following Marco's sweat-oiled excited face, anticipating his muscular reactions in play as in bed. And when he had beaten me (narrowly) or we had beaten the other pair, he would hunch my shoulders together within his arm, laughing, praising me in Italian to the others, staggering about with me, and he would say to me in English, "Aren't you a clever girl, eh?"; only he and I knew that that was what he said to me at other times. I loved that glinting flaw in his smile, now. It was Marco, like all the other things I knew about him: the girl cousin he had been in love with when he used to spend holidays with her family in the Abruzzi mountains; the way he would have planned Tshombe's road if he'd been in charge ("But I like your father, you understand?—it's good to work with your father, you know?"); the baby cream from Italy he used for the prickly heat round his waist.

The innocence of the grownups fascinated me. They engaged in play-play, while I had given it up; I began to feel arrogant among them. It was pleasant. I felt arrogant, or rather tolerantly patronizing, toward the faraway Alan, too. I said to Marco, "I wonder what he'd do if he knew"—about me; the caravan with the dotted curtains, the happy watchman, the tips, the breath of the earth rising from the wetted dust. Marco said wisely that Alan would be terribly upset.

"And if Eleanora knew?"

Marco gave me his open, knowing, assured smile, at the same time putting the palm of his hand to my cheek in tender parenthesis. "She wouldn't be pleased. But in the case of a man—" For a moment he was Eleanora, quite unconsciously, he mimicked the sighing resignation of Eleanora, receiving the news (seated, as usual), aware all the time that men were like that. Other people who were rumored or known to have had lovers occupied my mind with a special interest. I chattered on the subject, ". . . when this girl's husband found out, he just walked out of the house without any money or anything and no one could find him for weeks," and Marco took it up as one does what goes without saying: ". . . well, of course. If I think of Eleanora with someone—I mean—I would become mad." I went on with my secondhand story, enjoying the telling of all its twists and complications, and he laughed, following it with the affectionate attention with which he lit everything I said and did, and getting up to find the bottle of Chianti, wipe out a glass, and fill it for himself. He always had wine in the caravan. I didn't drink any but I used to have the metallic taste of it in my mouth from his; he said it was terrible Chianti that you got in E'ville—often he would wash his mouth out with it, as if the wine were a gargle.

In the car that afternoon he had said maybe there'd be a nice surprise for me, and I remembered this and we lay and wrangled teasingly about it. The usual sort of thing: "You're learning to be a real little nag, my darling, a little nag, eh?" "I'm not going to let go until you tell me." "I think I'll have to give you a little smack on the bottom, eh, just-like-this, eh?" The surprise was a plan. He and my father might be going to the Kasai to advise on some difficulties that had cropped up for a construction firm there. It should be quite easy for me to persuade my father that I'd like to accompany him, and then if Marco could manage to leave Eleanora behind, it would be almost as good as if he and I were to take a trip alone together. "You will have your own room?" Marco asked. I laughed. "D'you think I'd be put in with Daddy?" Perhaps in Italy a girl wouldn't be allowed to have her own hotel room. Now Marco was turning his attention to the next point: "Eleanora gets sick from the car, anyway—she won't want to come on bad roads, and you can get stuck, God knows what. No, it's quite all right, I will tell her, it's no pleasure for her." At the prospect of being in each other's company for whole days and perhaps nights we couldn't stop smiling, chattering, and kissing, not with passion but delight. My tongue was loosened as if I *had* been drinking wine.

Marco spoke good English.

The foreign turns of phrase he did have were familiar to me. He did not use the word "mad" in the sense of angry. "I would become mad"; he meant exactly that, although the phrase was not one that we English-speaking people would use. I thought about it that night, alone, at home; and other nights. Out of his mind, he meant. If Eleanora slept with another man, Marco would be insane with jealousy. He said so to me because he was a really honest person, not like the other grownups—just as he said, "I like your father, eh? I don't like some of the things he does with the road, but he is a good man, you know?" Marco was in love with me; I was his treasure, his joy, some beautiful words in Italian. It was true; he was very, very happy with me. I could see that. I did not know that people could be so happy; Alan did not know. I was sure that if I hadn't met Marco I should never have known. When we were in the caravan together I would watch him all the time; even when we were dozing I watched out of slit eyes the movement of his slim nostril with its tuft of black hair, as he breathed, and the curve of his sunburned ear through which capillary-marbled light showed. Oh, Marco, Eleanora's husband, was beautiful as he slept. But he wasn't asleep. I liked to press my feet on his as if his were pedals and when I did this the corner of his mouth smiled and he said something with the flex of a muscle somewhere in his body. He even spoke aloud at times—my name. But I didn't know if he knew he had spoken it. Then he would lie with his eyes open a long time, but not looking at me, because he didn't need to: I was there. Then he would get up, light a cigarette, and say to me, "I was in a dream . . . oh, I don't know . . . it's another world."

It was a moment of awkwardness for me because I was entering the world from my childhood and could not conceive that, as adults did—as he did—I should ever need to find surcease and joy elsewhere, in another world. He escaped, with me. I entered, with him. The understanding of this I knew would come about for me as the transfiguration of the gold tooth from a flaw into a characteristic had come. I still did not know everything.

I saw Eleanora nearly every day. She was very fond of me; she was the sort of woman who, at home, would have kept attendant younger sisters round her to compensate for the children she did not have. I never felt guilty toward her. Yet, before, I should have thought how awful one would feel, taking the closeness and caresses that belonged by law, to another woman. I was irritated by the stupidity of what Eleanora said; the stupidity of her not knowing. How idiotic that she should tell me that Marco had worked late on the site again last night, he was so conscientious, etc.—wasn't I with him, while she made her famous veal scallopini and they got overcooked?

And she was a nuisance to us. "I'll have to go—I must take poor Eleanora to a film tonight. She hasn't been anywhere for weeks." "It's the last day for parcels to Italy, tomorrow—she likes me to pack them with her, the Christmas parcels, you know how Eleanora is about these things." Then her aunt came out from Italy and there were lunches and dinners to which only Italian-speaking people were invited because the signora couldn't speak English. I remember going there one Sunday—sent by my mother with a contribution of her special ice cream. They were all sitting round in the heat on the verandah, the women in one group with the children crawling over them, and Marco with the men in another, his tie loose at the neck of his shirt (Eleanora had made him put on a suit), gesturing with a toothpick, talking and throwing cigar butts into Eleanora's flower trough of snake cactus.

And, yet, that evening in the caravan he said again, "Oh, good God, I don't want to wake up . . . I was in a dream." He had appeared out of the dark at our meeting place, barefoot in espadrilles and tight thin jeans, like a fisherman.

I had never been to Europe. Marco said, "I want to drive with you through Piemonte, and take you to the village where my father came from. We'll climb up to the walls from the church and when you get to the top—only then—I'll turn you round and you'll see Monte Bianco far away. You've heard nightingales, eh—never heard them? We'll listen to them in the pear orchard, it's my uncle's place, there."

I was getting older every day. I said, "What about Eleanora?" It was the nearest I could get to what I always wanted to ask him: "Would you still become mad?"

Would you still become mad?

And now?

And now—two months, a week, six weeks later?

Now, *would you still become mad?*

"Eleanora will spend some time in Pisa after we go back, with her mother and the aunts," he was saying.

Yes, I knew why, too; knew from my mother that Eleanora was going to Pisa because there was an old family doctor there who was sure, despite everything the doctors in Milan and Rome had said, that poor Eleanora might still one day have a child.

I said, "How would you feel if Alan came here?"

But Marco looked at me with such sensual confidence of understanding that we laughed.

I began to plan a love affair for Eleanora. I chose Per as victim not only because he was the only presentable unattached man in our circle but because I had the feeling that it might just be possible to attract her to a man younger than herself, whom she could mother. And Per, with no woman at all (except the pretty Congolese prostitutes, I suppose) could consider himself lucky if he succeeded with Eleanora. I studied her afresh. Soft white gooseflesh above her stocking tops, breasts that rose when she sighed—that sort of woman. But Eleanora did not even seem to understand that Per was being put in her way (at our house, at the Au Relais) and Per seemed equally unaware of or uninterested in his opportunities.

And so there was never any way to ask my question. Marco and I continued to lie making love in the caravan while the roof made buckling noises as it contracted after the heat of the day, and the rain. Tshombe fled and returned; there were soldiers in the square before the post office, and all sorts of difficulties arose over the building of the road. Marco was determined, excitable, harassed, and energetic—he sprawled on the bed in the caravan at the end of the day like a runner who has just breasted the tape. My father was nervous and didn't know whether to finish the road. Eleanora was nervous and wanted to go back to Italy. We made love and when Marco opened his eyes to consciousness of the road, my father, Eleanora, he said, "Oh, for God's sake, *why* . . . it's like a dream. . . ."

I became nervous too. I goaded my mother: "The Gattis are a bore. That female Buddha." I developed a dread that Eleanora would come to me with her sighs and her soft-squeezing hand and say, "It always happens with Marco, little Jillie, you mustn't worry. I know all about it."

And Marco and I continued to lie together in that state of pleasure in which nothing exists but the two who make it. Neither roads, nor mercenary wars, nor marriage, nor the claims and suffering of other people entered that tender, sensual dream from which Marco, although so regretfully, always returned.

What I dreaded Eleanora might say to me was never said, either. Instead, my mother told me one day in the tone of portentous emotion with which older women relive such things, that Eleanora, darling Eleanora, was expecting a child. After six years. Without having to go to Pisa to see the family doctor there. Yes, Eleanora had conceived during the rainy season in E'ville, while Marco and I made love every afternoon in the caravan, and the Congolese found themselves a girl for the duration of a shower.

It's years ago, now.

Poor Marco, sitting in Milan or Genoa at Sunday lunch, toothpick in his fingers, Eleanora's children crawling about, Eleanora's brothers and sisters and uncles and aunts around him. But I have never woken from that dream. In the seven years I've been married I've had—how many lovers? Only I know. A lot—if you count the very brief holiday episodes as well. Five, really.

They are another world, these dreams, where no wind blows colder than the warm breath of two who are mouth to mouth.

~~~~~~

Born in a small town in the gold-mining area of South Africa, Nadine Gordimer has been called "South Africa's unchallenged First Lady of Letters." She is the author of four collections of short stories and five novels, one of which, The Late Bourgeois World *(1966), was banned in her native land. An outspoken defender of civil liberties, legal reforms, women's rights, and equal educational opportunities, Ms. Gordimer says, "Somehow, the decision for any white South African is on the wrongness of apartheid. . . . If you oppose apartheid from within and are not a revolutionary, you have a duty to speak out." Having recently completed a teaching and lecture tour of the United States, she lives in Johannesburg with her husband.*

Jimmy from Another World

by Vin Packer

A year out of Wellesley, twelve months as a copywriter for Flood & Gilholder, when you think you know pretty much all there is to know about New York City, because you're a very hip girl and you've been to pot parties and seen underground movies and stood in line at Friday's on a Saturday night with other girls, left with a man you met there; when you've dug the Village scene and the East Village scene, gone to the Egyptian Gardens and sipped retsina until the wee hours watching the belly dancers, and been chic at Ondine's, blown your mind at Trudy Heller's, dined on paella at Spanish Pavilion, played pool on Third at Twenty-third, brunched at Martell's, and turned on to live jazz at Slug's, some night, very late, when the bartender cries, "Last call," someone may say, "Let's try an afterhours club."

Which was exactly what happened to Iris King on a Saturday night in August, one of the few times she had triple-dated with her roommates. Kevin Austin, Franny's boy friend, an art director for a small ad agency, knew the address of a place over on Manhattan's West Side, where they served drinks until nine or ten in the morning. He had never been there, but he had heard that it was a swinging club on the top floor of an old building near the river. Want to try it?

They all did. They all piled into a cab: Iris was with Alan Clark, a junior stockbroker she dated at least one weekend night; Ellie was with her fiancé— Kevin led on.

When they got out of the cab he said, "Let me do the talking," and they agreed and followed him in. The elevator creaked slowly to the twenty-second floor and they emerged in a hallway confronted by five hefty men of the cigar-smoking, zircon-on-the-little-finger school, and a closed door with a cloakroom to the right.

Kevin told the men someone named Phil sent them and they doubted this for a while, looking the six of them over with distasteful expressions while Kevin continued to argue that all they wanted was a few drinks, they'd come all the way from the East Eighties, how about it, *please*, and finally one of the men signaled the elevator operator not to wait and mumbled that all coats had to be checked.

Then they were let into a large dark room teeming with people, filled with smoke, noisy with Johnny Mathis singing "Chances Are," and waiters pushing their way through the crowds, carrying trays loaded with glasses.

They found a table in the rear. Alan, who had the drink order memorized, pinned down a waiter and gave it to him. They looked around at the woman with the mink sweater and dark glasses, and the fellow with rouge on his cheeks and dyed red hair, and the girl in leotards with the boy in the striped polo shirt and bell-bottom trousers, barefoot; the ones with evening gowns and dinner jackets, the man in bermuda shorts, the woman in the electric dress, the couple in riding clothes—and they all grinned at one another: it was a groovy place to be at four-thirty on a Sunday morning. Kevin kept saying, "What do you think?" trying to suppress a self-congratulatory smile.

Iris saw him first. He probably never would have noticed her but for the fact she began to stare at him. When he became aware of this, he occasionally glanced in her direction, uncertainly, as though she might know him or know someone standing near him. He looked around to check on this; he had a puzzled expression. Then, gradually, he sensed that she was simply looking at him, that's right, with a very open and unamused curiosity. What? Attracted to him? He seemed to disbelieve it, but with each glance back at her he became a little more sure.

Iris King was not the type for this—perhaps that was the reason he hesitated. Everything about her said she wasn't, from her date in a Hickey-Freeman suit to their whole crowd of upper-class-youth-explosion glancing around with expressions of wow-look-at-this-place, to her fresh-from-the-campus quality of cool-but-square innocence, in-but-out way of sitting there with a cigarette as though she came to these spots frequently, so what.

No, not the type at all. An English major who had done her master's thesis on the ambiguities of Herman Melville's *Pierre; or, The Ambiguities*, straight A's, only one physically serious romance with a hopelessly academic Princeton graduate student of anthropology, public schools in Oak Park, Illinois, the type of girl who received something like a Hunt & Winterbottom sweater from a beau at Christmas, and shared an apartment with girls who split the cost of a bottle of good brandy for afterdinner when they had their dates over; a watcher of Tony Bennett specials on the boob tube, and Huntley-Brinkley, Dean Martin; a turkey eater at Thanksgiving and an eggnog drinker on New Year's . . . traditional, predictable, blond, attractive, wasp.

You didn't figure that Iris King would look twice at him.

Name of: Jimmy Marshall. Clubs like these, which opened and closed with the whim of a floating crap game, were filled with his kind. Black silk suit, white-on-white shirt, fifteen-dollar light-blue silk tie, large gold cuff links some woman had given him; no, he was not a pimp, not kept; no, you would never find out what he did for a living—Mafia, maybe; gambler? Who did he come in with or leave with? Friends, was all you ever learned from him. Black & White and soda, not a big drinker but a good drinker, standing and not smiling, often there, not often noticed.

Alan said, "Stop staring at him. He'll come over."

"What if he does?"

"Listen, Iris, this isn't an ordinary place. We're not at Maxwell Plum's or Daly's. Don't try and make friends here."

Franny said, "He looks like something out of an old gangster picture."

"This whole place gives me the creeps," said Ellie.

"You want to go?" her fiancé asked.

Ellie said, "Are you kidding? I love it!"

"How can these places stay open?" Franny said.

Her fiancé said "they" pay off the police.

Kevin ordered another round.

She saw him this way: handsome, one of the most handsome men she had ever seen. If nobody else could see it that way, it didn't keep her from feeling the most electric kind of sensation when she studied his face, and she admitted that Franny was right—he was out of those old gangster movies but she had sat through the awkward part of her early teens watching things on TV like Bacall telling Bogart that if he wanted anything he should just whistle, and Garfield telling Priscilla Lane not to get mixed up with a guy like him, and part of her was a loser-lover who had understood every single one of James Dean's pained gestures of helplessness against a world of rigid convention, who had felt prickles on her skin when Brando went after Blanche in *Streetcar*, or Paul Newman zapped into that dusty Southern town and shook up those proper belles. Was that part of what she saw?

"I don't know why I was staring at you."

"You were, though."

"I know I was."

"I mean, why?"

"Does it bother you?"

"Yeah, I mean—"

This desultory conversation in a corner of the crowded room on her way to the Ladies.

When she came out of the Ladies he was waiting nearby.

How many drinks had she had? It must have been plenty for she told him her name and gave him her phone number. He said he was Jimmy; he'd call.

Alan said, "What took you so long?"

"It was crowded."

"We're going after this round."

She shrugged but she was disappointed. She wished she had the nerve to say, "I'm not." She wished Jimmy would come over and ask her to go with him; she would have. She watched him across the room and he gave her an "I'll call you" look a few times, once patting his breast pocket where he had the slip of paper with her name on it.

When they got up to leave she didn't see him. Reluctantly, she let Alan hold her coat in the hallway; Kevin was yawning; Franny was asking them all back for scrambled eggs; Ellie was saying no, she was too tired. Ellie won. Thank God.

It was daylight out. Some people were hurrying to early Mass. The boys dropped them in a taxi. Alan said maybe tomorrow they'd go to a movie, meaning today. Before they all went to sleep, Franny said Kevin scared her because he was so turned on to things like the afterhours club—for instance, what would he want from a girl in bed; and Ellie said go to bed with him and find out, while Iris thought to herself: that is absolutely the only time I've actually felt sexually drawn to a stranger.

Monday night the phone was for her at eight thirty.

"Who?"

"Jimmy from Another World."

"Why do you say you're from another world?"

He laughed as though she were a Lucille Ball-caliber comedian.

"That's the name of the place where we met," he said.

"Oh."

"Yeah." Another long laugh.

Then, "Yeah," again.

But she wasn't disappointed by the conversation. She hadn't expected it would be any different. She wasn't going to be disillusioned about much of anything he'd do or say; she had an idea, and she didn't care.

Yes, Franny and Ellie were hysterical. She might as well have told them she was meeting Richard Speck for dinner the next night. She screamed back at them and her face got as red as theirs, and no one was talking after an hour; oh, Ellie and Franny were, in whispers, while she went into the bedroom to calm down, and when she looked at her reflection in the mirror she thought: how long are we going to be friends, you and I, because I intend to see him, Goody Two-shoes, so let's have a real wide-eyed expression of horror from you . . . and received an ironical grin instead. Your picnic, ducky. I've taken you this far—but he's something else.

She did the girls a favor and met him out. He named a restaurant on Broadway and he was sitting at the bar waiting for her when she arrived at seven. It was the kind of restaurant with the prices of brand whiskey soaped on the mirror and all men at the bar. There was a jukebox which he fed quarters before leading her back to the table carrying his drink, and she said, "How do you know what'll play? You didn't even look."

"I punched numbers from the old-favorites' section. That way I don't get The Beatles and that stuff."

"I like The Beatles."

"Not me. I like Sinatra and Andy Williams and Perry Como. You know?" They were sitting facing one another.

"Yes, I know."

"You know? I saw your face in London town and 'Night and Day.' "

"Yes."

"What're you drinking?"

"Scotch and water."

"Black & White and water," he said to the waiter, "and gimme another."

She volunteered a lot about herself because he had so little to say about himself. He lived in a hotel, unspecified. He wasn't married. He went to Another World two, three times a week. Why? Something to do. She asked him if he worked nights and went there after and he said he didn't work nights. She said, "What do you do?"

"I've got this job," he said. "I'm going to be changing it before long."

"What do you do exactly?"

"Looking around for something else. . . . You really write those commercials I see?"

"Not the ones on TV . . . not yet."

"Yeah? Like what do you write?"

And they were off on her again.

But she liked talking to him. There was a strange part about it, too, which she understood but wanted to deny to herself, because it seemed snobbish or upper-handed, not right—yet, wasn't it? She enjoyed letting him know that she was a very decent type, a bright woman who had a good job, probably not the kind of woman he had ever known well, as though she were presenting him with a gift, or was it a way of telling him she was better than he was and didn't care? If it were happening to Ellie or Franny, she could have analyzed what it was in seconds; she was a very sharp parlor analyst, but she couldn't figure out her own motivation in this instance: just that she didn't pretend to be anything but what she was with him, and she felt proud of what she was—you decide—and when he said, "I don't know why you want to bother with me," she was very Priscilla Lane with a slightly jaded Bacall edge and answered, "Don't put yourself down, Jimmy."

Was that all there was to it, role-playing?

No. If he had asked her to go back to his hotel room with him that night, she would have. There was that to it, too. But he didn't ask her. They had tough steaks in the restaurant and she had two stingers; after a while he had more Scotch, and she even had some money ready in case she had to pay her own way or the whole bill, but that didn't come up, either.

He put her in a taxi without offering to take her back to the Eighties. He said he'd call. On the way to the taxi he said, "What if I fell for you? Where would it get me?" She wanted to say, "Everywhere," but there was still a lot unreal about their being together and she was shy and not a little confused.

O.K., it was wrong to tell Alan, and that was how she lost Alan. She had nothing but respect for him when he said the hell with it, he wasn't going to run any races with a pool-hustler silkie. He didn't think it was funny or cute or adventurous or anything but stupid of her, and she said good night to him, goodbye to him, wondering if she'd live to regret it until she was ninety. For she had been very attracted to Alan, and found it easy to be with him; there weren't half a dozen Alans loose in New York City, either, and how many Jimmys were there, probably? Stand on Forty-second and Seventh someday and count them; when you get tired you'll have been there five minutes.

". . . never coming here, never setting foot inside our apartment!" Ellie said after Iris' second date with Jimmy, "and don't forget it! And don't mention Franny's name or my name to him, and don't tell him anything about us!"

"Don't worry!"

But he was curious about them now; he wondered at the end of their second date why she didn't ask him back for a drink. She said her roommates were washing their hair, wouldn't like a surprise.

"My room's crummy," he said. They were dawdling on the corner of Forty-seventh and Sixth; it was still early.

"I don't care," she managed.

"Naw. Not picked up or anything."

She said, "I'll pick it up."

"I couldn't take *you* there," he said.

Instead, he bought her a few drinks at a bar and put fifty cents in her hand to pick out songs she liked on the jukebox, and they had many meaningful looks back and forth while they listened to what she selected, and once again she tried to know more about him.

"What do you do with your days, Jimmy?"

"I get up, shave, fool around, do things, business, come home, think about you."

"Aren't you ever going to tell me what you do for a living?"

"Does it make any difference?"

"No."

They held hands and then he walked her up to Central Park. They sat on a bench and kissed, and after a while they lay down on the grass, something she'd seen others do and wondered why they had to make such a public display —and disapproved. Everything she felt for him was confirmed: the Princeton anthropologist had never even come close, Alan had never made a dent; this was what it was all about and now she knew, and there was nowhere to go.

"...a hotel," she mumbled into his coat, "I wish."

He put his fingers to her lips.

She said, "Why not?"

"I'm not going to treat you that way."

"No. Don't do me any favors."

"I've got a friend's got a big place on Long Island; some weekends he goes away. It's a real mansion. I'll give him a call."

At midnight a policeman said it was time to leave and Jimmy took her to the Eighties in a cab this time and said he didn't last time because he figured she was in a hurry to ditch him.

"I wasn't at all."

"I know that now. Then I thought you were bored, I don't now."

"Jimmy, I wish I knew you better."

"Then you would be bored." And he gave that long laugh he had the first night he had called and said he was Jimmy from Another World; they held hands very hard, and then forgot the cab driver, and he had to tell them when they were there.

When he said good night he said he was going to call his friend on Long Island.

Kevin was there when she got in, and it was obvious Franny had asked him to speak with Iris. Kevin tried. He wanted to know more about Jimmy, he said, before he passed judgment, and Iris made up a lie and said he sold shoes, why she had to say that was beyond her, and no he wasn't college, he wasn't the catch of the season, he wore a shirt jac that night and pointed shoes, and there were whole areas lacking they never talked about like theater and the galleries they all liked to go to on Saturday afternoons, and he picked up his fork before she did when they dined, and—oh, yes—he said "consensus of opinion" and approved of the war, wished we'd drop an H-bomb on Vietnam—so their dialogue was broken down in many places, but...

"If you ever need me," Kevin began. He put his arm around her shoulder and she broke down. This in the kitchen while Ellie and Franny waited in the living room. Then he went in and they talked in hushed voices and after he left Ellie said why didn't they all have coffee, and they all did and pretended Jimmy didn't exist as they talked and laughed like old times.

Jimmy and she never went to the movies, never went anywhere but to those restaurant-bars he favored in the West Forties and then up to the park. If he knew anything about Italian food or French food, she didn't know about it, though one night they had Chinese, but mostly steaks or roast beef or corned beef, and always the jukebox and now he was telling her about things he read or saw: he liked Edison Marshall novels and best sellers and he devoured the *Daily News* word for word, and he had a winning way of telling stories about this fellow in a bar, for instance, who always said things nobody could figure out like one day he asked Jimmy what happened to an old friend of theirs and when Jimmy said he had "appendicities," this fellow said: "Well, that doesn't surprise me," and then Jimmy would laugh very hard and say, "What kind of an answer is *that?*", and she would laugh with him; it would seem terribly funny. He could also explain in detail how some bars sold drinks in false bottoms or made steaks look bigger by putting them on smaller plates, and which one on the street was a pusher, and which one was a cannon, which Iris learned was a pickpocket, and always there was talk of the place on Long Island and soon, soon, soon.

Once she bought him a tie but he wouldn't accept it. He left it beside him on the table and she kept asking him to please put it on, but he shook his head and said he didn't want her giving him things. He protested so much she finally put it back in her purse. She gave it to Kevin one night when he called for Franny. While Franny was dressing Iris told him, with a little pride for some unknown reason, that Jimmy wouldn't accept it, and Kevin said it was a sure sign he was probably on the take, otherwise he wouldn't be so self-conscious.

"He's never taken anything from me, not a nickel."

Kevin shrugged. "Well, maybe he's been that way with everyone but you and you're different, and that's why, but most men will accept a gift."

"Would he be married and not telling me?"

Kevin threw up his hands in a gesture of helplessness.

She realized it wouldn't matter if he were married.

One night he told her his friend with the place on Long Island would let them have it Sunday night through Tuesday. Could she get off work?

She arranged it.

They would leave Sunday afternoon.

From Ellie's and Franny's point of view she was already pregnant and doomed to marry a markdown and live her life in grubby hotel rooms never knowing where he was, what he did; she was ruined. Kevin said no fooling, had she really thought this out, and she hid the nightgown she had bought at Bonwit's and spoke for the first time of moving out.

Then she announced that Jimmy was being asked in for a drink before they left just as any of their dates would be, and they could be there or not— it didn't matter to her, but he was going to sit in their living room and drink from one of their glasses, and be treated the way Kevin was and Alan had been and Ellie's fiancé was; that was that.

Sundays they always made dinner for their dates and that Sunday was no exception. Ellie's fiancé was there, poker-faced, superior-sounding as he helped Ellie work the *Times* crossword, and Kevin was being patronizing and saying why shouldn't Jimmy come up, and Ellie and Franny were being brave about it.

When the downstairs buzzer rang Iris said, "And if he wants another drink, he'll get another drink! And if he wants a third—"

"He'll get a third," said Kevin. "Don't worry."

But as she glanced at Ellie and Franny she doubted that it would be anything but a catastrophe.

In came Jimmy.

Yes, handsome . . . couldn't they *see* that? But there were things wrong, too. The first thing Iris noticed was the white tie . . . then, he was wearing both a boutonniere and a breast-pocket handkerchief. Overdone. All right. And he was awkward.

Kevin said, "We've heard a lot about you," as though he were Iris' father.

Jimmy said, "Same here."

But she loved that wistful expression in his dark eyes, the way he gave Kevin that sort of sideways do-you-mean-it look as though he wasn't quite sure that Kevin was sincere. Ellie's fiancé made an effort, too, talking about sports suddenly which he knew nothing about but sensed Jimmy did—and was right. There the men were relaxing and talking in the living room with Ellie and Franny and Iris fixing them drinks and dips with crackers in the kitchen.

"Can't you see he's nice?" Iris pleaded with Franny, the more humane of the pair.

"Did I say anything?"—which meant no, I cannot, but they were going to be decent, all of them, Iris could tell.

And Jimmy tried, he really did. He didn't just clam up, even when Ellie's fiancé started talking about the bonus plan his company had and Kevin countered with the benefits his agency offered. Jimmy balanced a drink on his knee and said "sounds good" and smiled pleasantly, and he wasn't too aggressive: he discussed gin brands quietly with Kevin, he complimented the girls on their taste, albeit gauchely ("some of the things are very tasteful here"), and while she never relaxed, Iris felt the first glimmerings of hope; dammit, they'd just have to get used to Jimmy, and one day his coming here would be as natural as anyone else's. There was even a possibility they'd all laugh about it one day. She watched him, fell in love all over with his face, didn't care all over what he did for a living; if there was mystery behind the mystery or banality, she would trust him until he trusted her enough to tell her, and love him regardless, such were her thoughts as she sat there across from him.

Then Kevin took it on himself to say suddenly, "Hey, why don't you two have dinner here before you go? There's enough, isn't there, Franny?"

And Franny said, "Why—yes," surprised, but not unwilling.

Ellie said, "There's plenty."

Ellie's fiancé was talking about a forthcoming college reunion; he interrupted himself long enough to ditto their mild enthusiasm, then went back to a description of the SAE house at the University of Missouri.

Jimmy was perspiring; he mopped his forehead, smiling so regularly now that he looked as though his mouth were paralyzed in that position.

"We can't stay," Iris said.

Jimmy said, "Sure we can. Why not?"

She looked at him to fathom if he really meant it. He nodded. "Why not?" he said.

"You *want* to?"

"Why not?"

Kevin said, "Put two more plates on, Franny."

Iris wouldn't have blamed Franny if she had answered, "Let her put the two plates on," but Franny got up and Iris did, too, and they set the table together.

Iris whispered, "I'm surprised he wants to."

"Maybe he's hungry," Franny said, and her tone was loaded with double entendre, but that was more like Franny than for her to have let it go by, and Iris began to feel happier: she wasn't going to worry about it any more. She wasn't going to sit wondering what Jimmy would say next or they'd say next; it was just going to happen, however it did, and they could all fend for themselves.

There were no miracles; it was what you could expect. Jimmy was miserably outclassed. Franny and Ellie could at no point change their minds about him. The subject of his work came up and was disposed of with his usual noncommittal grunts. He said "yellow jaundice" and "irregardless" and called the Vietnamese "gooks" and spoke of "me and Iris." He rattled his ice in his glass when it was empty to signal he wanted a refill, and as he grew more euphoric with his drinks, he beat out a rhythm to an Eydie Gorme record, atop the coffee table, and jiggled his legs and exposed the fact he was wearing ankle-length socks. No one had any illusions left about Jimmy, and Iris, defensive, was glad, cheered him on, invited him to be himself, invited them to think what they wanted to.

Ellie's fiancé stopped talking down to him; Kevin disagreed with him about nearly everything; Franny asked him to watch his ash; Ellie announced that the coffee table wasn't all that sturdy.

I don't care, they don't care, Jimmy doesn't care, Iris thought as she slugged herself with a fourth drink, but she made Jimmy's weaker because he had to drive that night. He had rented a car for the trip; they were going to get there safely come hell or high water.

Don't say men you pick up in afterhours clubs who wear black silk suits and white-on-white shirts and know as much about grammar as they do about early Greek tragedy don't have manners. Jimmy was beautiful. Just as Kevin announced he was going out to buy dessert, Jimmy sprang up and said let him contribute that, and he said, "Who likes what?", and he wouldn't hear of Kevin going. He repeated "some kind of goopy pie," when Ellie said it, and "maybe a chocolate cake," when Franny said it.

He said, "I like anything with coconut in it."

A surprise to Iris, but it was an afternoon of surprises. Surprise surprise: turn the animals loose and they won't necessarily eat one another, even if they won't become friends; surprise surprise: the human being was resilient, accommodating, and tractable, and never again would she dread Jimmy's buzz from downstairs . . . surprise: he had read a little Emily Post . . . surprise: he pushed Kevin's hand away with the five clutched in his fingers and told Kevin, "Don't be silly; my treat."

When he left, reciting "chocolate cake and goopy pie," the door was shut behind him, and Ellie said, "Groan!"

Franny said, "Double groan!"

Ellie's fiancé said, "Yiiik—is love blind!"

Kevin said, "It's going over O.K., though."

"Get it all out of your systems now," said Iris, "because we're going right on with things when he gets back."

But he never came back.

Days later when Iris King went to the afterhours place to find him, there was a whole roomful of people playing cards under a sign which said: ALLNITE BRIDGE CLUB. No one had ever heard of Jimmy or "Another World."

A year out of Wellesley, twelve months as a copywriter for Flood & Gilholder, four weeks after an eight-thirty phone call on a Monday night in August, Iris King appreciated you never learn all there is to learn about New York City: but you discover—when you are looking for a man about whom you know little more than that he likes anything with coconut in it but doesn't like The Beatles—how large the city is, and how unlikely it is that you'll ever run into him again.

Vin Packer is a pseudonym of the prolific (thirty novels and countless short stories) and highly successful author Marijane Meaker, who also publishes under her own name. "Vin Packer used to be much better known than I am," says Marijane, "but I've been gaining on her lately." Ms. Meaker is a University of Missouri graduate and lives in Brooklyn Heights, New York. Vin Packer's latest novel is DON'T RELY ON GEMINI. *Marijane Meaker's latest is* SHOCKPROOF SYDNEY SKATE.

St. George

by Gail Godwin

~~~~~~~~~~~~~~~~

*U*ntil tonight, Silas had been working out perfectly. Lusty, uncomplex, the archetypal man of few words, he had hooked onto Gwen's well-ordered life like a charm. He had served as her antidote against Love, the disease that had felled all her friends in the midst of whatever they were pursuing and left them handicapped forever after, trapped in mortgaged homes with rather ordinary men, all their grand possibilities extinguished.

But tonight, as Silas stood over her bed, buttoning up his shirt, his usual blond, untroubled countenance clouded over and he said, "This isn't much of a relationship, is it?"

"Of course it's not!" exclaimed Gwen. Imagine Silas using a word like "relationship." "It's not supposed to be one. Relationships take too much libido and right now mine's all booked up." She was getting her master's degree in English next June. Then she could go out and make her demands on the world. Then she could begin to look for someone, her equal or better, with whom to fall in love. Silas was her Now man. She had picked him up in an all-night coffee shop. Having cleared her life of bearded graduate students who wanted to latch onto her psyche like leeches or lie in bed afterward discussing D. H. Lawrence, she had been on the prowl for a simple man, a truck driver perhaps, a non-soul-sharer she couldn't get serious about, but who would stand between her and loneliness in this impersonal city. Lonely people, she knew, were the most susceptible to the Disease of Love. "I thought we understood each other, Silas," she added, a little sadly, from her pillows.

"I understand," he said in his unruffled monotone. "I'm just feeling a little cold. Never mind." He gave her rump a friendly little pat. "If you're lucky, maybe I'll see you later in the week."

He always said this. She, in return, said, "That would be nice!" It was part of their unspoken ritual, never to plan ahead or "promise" anything, though in fact he came almost regularly every Tuesday, Thursday, and Saturday, subwaying to her place at ten, ravishing her by eleven, and departing at twelve for his all-night job in some plant. She could not get much information out of him, so most of the time she talked about herself. He had heard her opinions on everything, most of all concerning the Disease. He would scratch his blond curly hair and lie beside her, a remote smile on his big bland face, and listen to her go on and on about why she loved medieval literature the best ("It's full of saints having visions and great perfect love affairs and knights slaying monsters to win the love of their ladies"), and how utterly, hopelessly dull her married friends had become ("They got the fever and attached it to the first thing in pants that came along and now look at them"), and once in a while he would nod, or murmur "Mmm," or ask a question. She was never sure what he was thinking or how much he understood, but he was so warm and comfortable and always left at twelve. It was working out so well!

"You're not mad at me, Silas," she said, flirting a little to make up for her "libido" speech.

"Nope," he replied pleasantly. He let himself out of her apartment with a neat click of the lock and there he went, light-footing it down the stairs, headlong into a December's starry cold.

She got up at once, put on a Bach cantata, ran herself a hot bath, and while it was running flicked open the little white compact and punched out Tuesday's pill, being careful to lick up all the crumbly parts round the edge. Then she climbed into her bath, letting solitude fold warmly around her with the water. "Oh, Silas, don't you dare spoil things," she said aloud. After which she gave herself up to the pure, ethereal Bach, uncluttered by human emotions, and soaked for a while in daydreams of possible futures.

Silas did not come on Thursday. Gwen frowned but was not unduly worried. She listened to some Brandenburgs, made herself a radish-and-bacon sandwich, and translated thirty lines of *Beowulf*.

He didn't come on Saturday, either. Her weekend stretched endlessly ahead. Classes had let out for the long Christmas break. "That's all right, I have plenty to do," she said to herself. She made out a rigorous schedule: nine books to read for course work, two papers to write, and a volume of *lais* to translate from Old French. For several days she did not leave her comfortable little apartment on the top floor of a made-over warehouse near the river. How lovely to be answerable to nobody but yourself, to sleep in the afternoons if you wished, and stay up all night reading Boethius, underlining passages of strength and beauty. Tuesday evening, she went to an early movie, hurrying home past the lighted windows of others to be there when Silas came.

But ten o'clock passed, and then eleven, and no Silas. "Perhaps he's sick, maybe I should call him." But she didn't have his number. She didn't even know where he lived. She didn't even know his last name! Just for the hell of it, she put in a long-distance call to her parents, whom she'd outgrown years ago, but their phone rang and rang. "They must have gone to the movies." Then she just sat for a while, listening to the boats on the river, the night sounds. A strange thought crossed her mind: "If nobody in the world knows I am sitting here in this chair at this moment, how can I be sure I exist?" Enough of that. She translated some more of an Old French *lai*, about a knight who goes to a strange land locked in the thrall of a monster-king. About midnight she got hungry and wished for an omelet, whole-wheat toast with soft butter, strawberry preserves, and black coffee, and being free and alone to follow such whims whenever they arose went at once to her kitchen to satisfy these.

She got everything out, broke the first egg in the bowl, broke the second, and something dark came out with a *plop*. It moved beneath the sticky yolk in which it was entrapped. God, could an embryo chicken get through all that modern dairy apparatus alive? It was too horrible. She lost all appetite, made ready to dump the whole mess down the sink, turn on the hot water, and hope it died. But she hesitated. What would it look like? With a kind of morbid curiosity, she ran some tepid water into the bowl, loosening the yolk's stickiness and freeing the thing. It was a reddish color and began paddling slowly round the bowl. It had little legs and a tail which flicked drops of egg water in her face. "Ugg!" she cried, turning away, then had to look back at it. It was some sort of tiny lizard trying to blink open its eyes, which were stuck together with egg.

She ran to get her magnifying glass.

For some moments, she peered through it at the creature in the bowl and tried to get her bearings. In her mixing bowl swam a tiny but perfectly formed dragon. And she knew one when she saw one. She was, after all, a medieval-lit. scholar, and the thing that came out of her egg was an exact miniature of the dragon on the cover of her *Beowulf* book. Although it was scarcely an inch long from snout to tail, it was equipped with all its legendary parts. No bigger than inverted commas, its tiny nostrils flared. It had stand-up ears so straight they might have passed for horns. The birdlike talons had minuscule toenails, and a mane of fiery points ran like rickrack from the crest of his flat reptilian skull down to the tip of his very active barbed tail. Now he had got his eyes unstuck. They were comically large in proportion to the rest of him and regarded her sharply, with just a hint of coyness.

"God," she said aloud. "I am not insane, I'm not. He is down there in that bowl." How did she know he was a he? Gently she eased him onto a spoon, took a matchstick and probed at the soft red underbelly, trying to discern a hint of gender. The hackles sprang up all along its back, its tail stopped dead still and it plunged like a dart from the spoon into the bowl. She could see its shadow underwater, swimming round and round in a huff.

"Oh, dear, I've offended you. I'm sorry, I'm very sorry, really I am. We'll assume you're a man. O.K.?"

The shadow slowed down, as though considering. The whole thing was too much. She was overcome by a violent moment of disbelief. Taking down a clean Pyrex bowl from the shelf, she heard her own voice bribing him with some clean water. "And I'll even make you a small island," she coaxed, inverting a dessert dish into the bigger clean bowl which she filled almost to the top with water. "You're going to love this!" she said. The shadow paddled on, submerged in the eggy water, but some of the fury had gone out of him now. With just a hint of a shudder, she spooned him into his new kingdom. He seemed to enjoy the greater freedom but would neither look at her nor come up on his island.

Next morning when she went rather queasily into the kitchen, he was languishing on his dessert-bowl island. He wagged his tail several times, very listlessly, and appealed to her with the oversized eyes. He was undoubtedly hungry, but what did he eat? She offered him graham-cracker crumbs, bacon shreds, and slivers of lettuce. From all of these, he turned away sadly. Groaning, she knelt beneath the sink where a family of ants insisted on living and murdered one quickly between paper-toweled fingers. She thought she was going to vomit. The dragon refused the dead ant and wedged his head between his two front feet. The eyes rolled up at her imploringly.

"What can I *do!*" Gwen cried. "I don't know what you eat. Oh, why couldn't you have stayed in your egg!"

He was too weak to dive like a dart into the water. He stood up wearily and did a half-turn round the dessert bowl and lay down again with his back to her.

Gwen went out reluctantly into the city. Her palms were sweating and her heart beat loudly. The people she passed seemed to be wearing masks. The watery winter sun shimmered like lemon water on the streets. Everything seemed unreal. She went into a pet shop and asked the man what lizards ate. He sold her a box of turtle food. In a sort of automatic trance, she took the crosstown bus to the main library and went to the encyclopedias to look up "dragon." The *Americana* had but one paragraph on the creature and was careful to put the word in quotes. *Collier's* left it out altogether. *Britannica* gave the etymology of the word (Gk. for "sharpsighted") and went on to show its Oxbridge education by name-dropping Sigmund, Beowulf, Arthur, and Tristan, all of whom had bouts with the creatures. *New Catholic Encyclopedia* was *slightly* more helpful. Dragons could be found on land or in air, it said, but their most natural habitat was water. Gwen was proud of her dessert-bowl-in-Pyrex-bowl innovation. After paying tribute to St. George and a St. Margaret of Antioch, who had confronted dragons unflinchingly, this liberal source quoted Posidonius' story of a dragon covering an acre of land who swallowed a full-grown knight as though he were a mere pill. St. George's dragon ate two sheep a day until sheep ran short and then he decided he would eat the king's daughter.

Not a word about what very small dragons ate.

She checked out all the books on dragons and took the bus back across the unreal city where she didn't know a soul—except Silas, who seemed to have vanished. She was rather interested to see whether the little dragon would take the turtle food.

Dumping the books on the nearest chair, she hurried to the kitchen, calling "Don't give up! Help is coming!" But he was not in his bowl. She got down on her hands and knees and searched the floor. Could he have tumbled down the drain? She shone a flashlight down it and saw nothing but a nasty coating of grease. Sadly, she ran a fast slosh of cool water from the tap to speed him on his way in case he was stuck halfway down. The unopened box of turtle food lay abandoned on the sink counter.

Feeling very empty, Gwen sat down in a chair and surveyed her four walls, which were white. Deliberately, she had hung no pictures. She loathed the graduate-student style of sticking posters and unframed prints up everywhere, just to cover the emptiness. Until she could afford good originals, she would have nothing. But in her present isolation, the bare white walls appeared sinister—like an asylum or an anteroom between this world and the next.

The thought of the papers she could be writing for her courses nagged but did not spur her. She wished there was a pill she could take that would put her to sleep until Christmas vacation was over and classes started. She played a little Bach and went to sleep on the couch and when she woke up it was dark. Fumbling into her bedroom, she undressed, dropping her clothes on the floor.

"There's nothing wrong with me, Silas," she said reproachfully. The tall wraithlike girl leered at her from the mirror with rather hysterical eyes, and for a minute Gwen thought it was someone else. Shaken, she paused in front of her dresser and deposited her watch into her open jewelry box.

The little dragon leaped up with a start and she screamed.

He had been sleeping in the golden embrace of a pearl-studded bracelet which had belonged to her grandmother. His nostrils expanded and contracted exactly above the space where two pearls had formerly lodged. He seemed bigger. He wagged his tail ecstatically and costume jewelry clanked beneath his red belly. He was all attention, waiting to see what she'd do. After a long pause, she said aloud, "Well, *somebody's* glad to see me."

He leaped out of the jewelry box and scuttled across the dresser to hide behind a Shalimar bottle.

"Oh, you want to play, do you?" The tail thumped wildly to one side of the bottle. She tried to corral him with the pearl-studded bracelet, wondering where she'd lost those two pearls, when he caught hold of it like a baby will grab a finger, aimed a tiny flame from his mouth round the prongs of another pearl, and gulped it down with a wide grin.

"No, you idiot, that's an heirloom!" she cried, unclenching him from the bracelet. In doing so, she touched him for the first time. He was warm and dry; he throbbed slightly. She thought she was going to faint. When she didn't, she was so grateful she stroked him again and said, "I'll name you St. George."

Later that night, after St. George was asleep on his island, worn out from chasing round the dresser (he had knocked over the Shalimar, finally, and was the sweetest-smelling dragon ever), Gwen lay in bed, books lining the crack of her bedroom door, and read the dragon books. According to Grafton Elliot Smith (*The Evolution of the Dragon*, Manchester, 1919), "the dragon dines on precious gems and is partial to pearls. . . ."

She went into the kitchen and woke him up. He slept rather quaintly, with his tail curled round over his eyes, to keep out light.

"Look here, St. George," said Gwen, "I hope you're no gourmand. Because tomorrow and tomorrow and all the days after, you're getting the Woolworth's special." He wagged his tail happily and regarded her with the big sleepy eyes. There was no doubt about it, St. George *was* getting bigger. He covered almost the entire surface of the inverted dessert bowl.

Next morning she forced herself to make the trip downtown. The people on the streets seemed another species from herself, their faces grimly set toward a destination she could not see. "And not one of them will speak to me," she said aloud. An old woman, who looked like she'd been run through a strainer, turned to glare at her. Gwen looked at her reflection in a store window and saw she'd come out without combing her hair. Raking it down with her fingers, she went to Woolworth's jewelry counter. They sold a fairly long strand of imitation pearls for $1.99. She picked up one and, under the curious stare of the salesgirl, counted the pearls: forty-two. That should be enough. No, better get a couple of them.

"I'll take these," she told the girl. How croaky her own voice sounded. When was the last time she had talked to anybody? Was it yesterday she had spoken to Sarah? Time seemed to be stretched out of shape. Usually her life was neatly marked off by class schedules and Silas' three-times-a-week nocturnal visits.

By the end of the week, St. George was the size of a Chihuahua. He had eaten seventy-nine of the pearls by Saturday night, and the stores were shut on Sunday.

"You'll have to take potluck from my jewelry box when you run through your other five," Gwen told him. They were curled up on the sofa, the little dragon in her lap, watching the Saturday-night movie, which was a bore. But St. George loved it as he loved all TV programs. His tail lashed delightfully from side to side, snagging her best wool skirt and tearing the stuffing from the upholstery. A great silent chuckle seemed to be in progress inside him as he watched human beings going about their business on the screen. "But please remember, the diamonds and the turquoises are no-no's." St. George had cunningly pried open the box and eaten a diamond earring and several turquoises out of a favorite ring. He was ingenious and energetic as a naughty child, or a kitten. Gwen had never owned a pet. She was amazed at the destruction one could wreak in a simple act of play. Already, with one swipe of his barbed tail he had irrevocably scarred her Queen Anne writing desk, the most superior piece of furniture she had. He could not control his fiery tongue: Every time he got excited, out it came, and when the smoke had cleared there was another scorched tablecloth, towel, or book. Gallumphing tirelessly across her rooms, his razor-sharp toenails cut into the finish of her hardwood floors. As he no longer fit into his bowl, she'd given him the plugged-up kitchen sink, but he crawled out at night to roam wet-footed about the dark apartment. She would wake to hear him scratching at her bedroom door, which she kept locked, or playing by himself in the living room. On one of these late-night romps, her Dresden Satan came crashing to the floor, losing a foot, an arm, and a horn.

"Where does it all go?" asked Gwen, referring to the pearls and other jewels he'd gobbled down in the course of the week. But it was merely a rhetorical question. She spent half her time now creeping round with paper towel in hand, searching out his indiscriminately placed droppings. What St. George ate went *in* diamonds and pearls, but there the uniqueness stopped.

At that moment, an Alka-Seltzer ad came on and St. George snorted with excitement. Gwen's skirt caught on fire and she rushed to pour water on herself. On her way back to the sofa, she saw that the electric clock read close to ten. She wondered what she would do with St. George if Silas called.

But they watched News and Weather and Johnny Carson and the late movie, and Silas did not call, and she wondered what she would do without St. George. He was, after all, company. Absorbing herself in his erratic behavior— he was enormous fun to watch—she had less chance to sit listening to the hollow river sounds and the buzz of the electric clock and wonder whether or not she *did* exist.

On Monday morning, she went back to Woolworth's. "Forty-two, eighty-four, a hundred and twenty-six, that ought to hold him," she muttered, counting pearls. The salesgirl looked at her as though she were mad. Hurrying along the decorated streets to the tune of Salvation Army Santa Clauses ringing their bells, Gwen caught the Christmas spirit. She had someone to buy presents for! She bought a small tree, some shiny ornaments, a bunch of silly toys, and psychedelic wrapping paper.

That night, after they played an exhausting game of hide-and-seek followed by a game of ball made from a yard or so of scrunched-up aluminum foil, Gwen crept to the kitchen to make sure St. George was asleep. Sometimes, he slept curled on a dish towel folded on the sink counter; other times, when he was feeling secure, beneath the water. Tonight he was submerged. A straight line of peaceful bubbles ascended from his nostrils to the surface of the water. Gwen hurried back to her room, locked the door, and wrapped all his presents in the psychedelic paper. She hung the little tree with colored balls and tinsel. The latter she put in the living room. She left his presents in her suitcase, fearing they'd never make it till Christmas otherwise.

By Christmas morning St. George was the size of a beagle puppy. He went berserk over all his wonderful presents and accidentally set the tree on fire. He frolicked in the bucketfuls of water as Gwen doused the flames. For his dinner, she placed the final turquoises from her ring, the ones he hadn't got, atop his Yuletide dish of imitation pearls. She was a little dismayed at how quickly it all disappeared. If he kept growing, with an appetite to match, she would soon be bankrupt.

About seven o'clock in the evening, the telephone rang. St. George scuttled in terror beneath the Queen Anne writing desk. He had never heard the sound before. Silas!

It was only Gwen's mother and father, calling to wish her a Merry Christmas. Gwen said yes, her work was going very well and, yes, she had made some friends. "I'm going out to a party later this evening," she lied. The dragon's yellow eyes danced at her from the gloom beneath the desk. Her mother sounded relieved. "There's no need to be so *ruthless* about things," she said. "Enjoy life. You're young."

"Yes, Mother."

After Gwen hung up, she played her one Beatles record for St. George—he loathed Bach—and gave him a bubble bath. He loved to duck beneath the suds and come up spouting bubbles which he would blow carefully into the air with his hot breath before shooting them down in flames. She dried him in a thick Turkish towel, for the sake of her floors, and carried him to the kitchen.

"You're getting too big for the sink, aren't you?" she said, worried. "Well, give it another night's try and we'll put you in the tub tomorrow." He wagged his tail delightedly and knocked over a canister of flour. Before Gwen could fetch the sponge mop, he had found a new pastime, rolling in the flour.

"Damn you, I'm tired!" she cried. "I've just bathed you and I haven't the energy to bathe you again." A powdered dragon rolled comic-tragic eyes at her. He wagged his tail, stirring up more flour, and made her sneeze. Sighing, Gwen picked up the white, wriggly bundle. Back to the bathtub they went. "No bubbles this time, my friend." He shimmied delightedly at her feet. She felt exhausted as she gave him a second bath. Afterward, she deposited him on her bed and went to mop the kitchen. When she returned, he was curled up at the foot of her bed, snoring gently.

"Oh, what the hell," she said, climbing beneath the sheet. "If you set us on fire, we'll ascend together in glorious smoke. Nobody will miss us." The dragon moaned in his sleep. The red rickrack along his back rose and fell. She closed her eyes and saw unwelcome visions of her next bank statement. St. George's food bill was growing along with him, by leaps and bounds. Her scholarship did not make allowances for keeping dragons in pearls—even Woolworth ones.

By New Year's Eve he was the size of a St. Bernard. The floors shook when he rollicked and romped. Gwen had sold three of her favorite art books to a secondhand bookstore and pawned her watch to feed him. Over the past week, a dark and desperate plan had gradually worked its way into her conscious mind. She was going to have to kill St. George. Aside from the fact she could not afford even one more round of imitation pearls, he was too risky to leave alone in the apartment while she attended classes. He seldom got through the day without setting a fire and as he grew bigger, so did the fires. She doubted if a zoo would take him. There was probably a state law against the harboring of mythical animals. Since Christmas, she had taken to leafing stealthily through the dragon books, collecting bits of information on their disposal, while St. George lay beside her, singeing the sofa with every other breath as he ogled the TV commercials. "In China," she read, "the emperor ordered his men to beat the drums in order to attract the Dragon King. When he came out of his cave, the men riddled him with arrows until the ocean became red with dragon blood. Some weeks later, however, the emperor died in a dream." In ancient Guatemala, two crafty brothers, Hunahpu and Xbalanque, visited a dragon's house and pretended to be dentists because the dragon had a terrible toothache. When he let them in, they pulled out all his teeth, put out his eyes, and slew him. Upon reading this, Gwen winced so violently she frightened St. George off the sofa. Madly, he raced about the room. With a flick of his tail, which was now several yards long, he scattered a stack of thesis note-cards like a flurry of snow. God, how cruel. She could never do it the Guatemalan way.

Once again, Mr. Grafton Elliot Smith (op. cit., p. 135) came to her rescue. The most humane way of killing the creature, he explained, was to get him drunk on beer (the beer of Osiris, if possible) and clout him on the head with something made of iron. An alchemical connection was made between beer and iron and the dragon was snuffed out painlessly.

At sunset, on New Year's Eve, Gwen opened the first of four six-packs. She turned on the stereo and unsheathed a brand-new Beatles album, a sort of going-away present for St. George, though he would never know. "Come here, Georgie!" she called, trying to keep the sadness from her voice. He lumbered into the kitchen, thrusting his funny face expectantly up to hers. He came to her waist now. She hoped four six-packs would be enough, and she would have to have a little for herself, to get up courage.

"Try a little of this." She gave him half a canful in a plastic dish. Oh, God, what if he didn't like beer?

But he lapped it up and rolled his eyes for more.

She poured him a bowlful and a glass for herself. She had no such ugly courage of a Margaret of Antioch. They drank to side one of the Beatles' new record, then side two; then side one again, and after that it didn't matter what was playing. St. George grew gayer. He wanted to play hide-and-seek. But he was too big for most of his favorite hiding places. Gwen lurched about the apartment, pretending not to see three-fourths of his tail hanging from the linen closet.

"I wonder where St. George is!" she cried drunkenly. The tail wagged violently. There were tears in her eyes. He thudded gaily to the floor, bringing half the linen closet with him. "There you are! How 'bout another drink?"

St. George eagerly lapped up another bowlful while Gwen got down the steam iron and set it in an easy-to-reach spot on the kitchen table. She remembered how St. George, when he was smaller, had learned the knack of perching beside her book, on the table, and turning the pages for her with his tail, so that she could read and eat. She burst into a flood of maudlin tears. St. George looked up at her, his head cocked to one side. His eyes had gone rather crossed. Then he wobbled drunkenly into the living room, tried to go beneath her desk, bumped his head on the too-low underpass, and dropped to the floor with a snuffly snore.

Still weeping, Gwen went to get the steam iron, decided to go to the bathroom first, and passed out on the return trip.

She woke, chilled and weak, to hear a terrible retching coming from the bathroom. She hurried in and found St. George being violently ill. He hardly recognized her, he was choking and spluttering so. His talons scraped wildly at the tile floor. His scarlet rickrack trembled like tissue paper in a storm. He looked up at her, helplessly, very apologetic, and vomited again and again. Then he collapsed at the foot of the toilet, wrapped his barbed tail listlessly round its base, and passed out from sheer exhaustion.

She was sponging up the beery vomit, weeping incoherently—he had looked up at her so *trustingly* just before he'd passed out!—when the phone rang. She stumbled through the dark apartment and groped for the phone.

"Hello?"

"Silas here," came the laconic voice. "How've you been?"

"Silas! Where in God's name are you?"

"Home. You O.K.? You sound a little hysterical. Did you miss me?"

"Miss you! I almost went out of my mind! I thought I was never going to see you again! I was all alone, except for—oh, God, I'm too drunk to make sense."

"You alone now? I thought we might get in a little New Year's celebration."

"Oh, please, Silas, come over quick. Yes, I'm alone except for—look, there's someone desperately sick here, not someone, I mean, something—a poor helpless animal—you wouldn't believe me if I told you what—"

"I'll be there as soon as I can," Silas said.

Gwen went back to the bathroom and lay beside St. George, who was still out cold. "Help is coming," she crooned. "Silas is a big, capable guy. You'll feel better the minute he comes." She sponged his nostrils, his slack jaws, his mane, which had gone soft as overcooked spaghetti. She covered him with a blanket and dozed with her arms around him.

The doorbell rang. At last! Gwen ran to open it and threw herself at six-foot-three of reassuring bulk. Silas was sun-tanned and smiling puzzledly. After she had mauled him for a few moments, he said: "Where's the sick animal? Did you get yourself a cat?"

"Listen, Silas, let me explain before we go in. . . ." She listened to her own voice, pouring out details of St. George. Silas listened with no more expression in his face than usual. They were still standing just inside the doorway. Once he scratched his mop of dry blond hair." . . . but now I realize I can't possibly kill him," she concluded. "I've gotten attached to him. I think I'd stand by him if he grew big enough to swallow the world. Silas, you have to help me save poor George." She grabbed his fingers and tugged him to her bathroom. "There. Look at him. Who could murder a helpless dragon. You should have seen him when he was littler. He was so cute. He was vomiting his heart out, just before you called. We drank almost four six-packs between us."

Silas stood in the doorway of the bathroom. He reached a hand inside his jacket and into the top of his shirt and gave his chest a thoughtful scratch.

"Poor little guy," he said. "What he needs is some fresh air. That's obvious."

"Oh, he's never been out. And he's much too big to carry."

"I can manage," said Silas. He stooped down and gently collected the creature in his arms.

"Watch out for his tail, it's hooked around the toilet bowl," Gwen warned.

"Oh, yes." Silas stood up, carrying St. George easily.

"Thank God you're a big man," Gwen breathed. "Where will you take him?"

"Down by the river. There's a good wind blowing. He'll be all right. You look pretty bad, though. Go to bed."

"Will you come back?"

"Of course I'll come back. As soon as this dragon gets his air."

Some time later, Gwen woke. The bedroom was dark. From the living room came the sound of TV, turned down low: noises of the nation celebrating the New Year. She heard someone opening a beer can, then the soft gurgle into the glass, then a pause and a deep male sigh. "Silas?" she called. A strange lassitude had attached itself to her; she couldn't move. She felt like an invalid who had been very, very ill.

"You slept," he said, sitting down beside her in the dark.

"What happened? What did you do with St. George?"

"Ah," he began, stroking the back of her neck with his big fingers. "You aren't going to like this. I took him down to the river and sat beside it—so he could get the breeze—and all of a sudden he woke up and jumped right into the river and went swimming away. I never saw anything swim so fast. Not even the river police could have caught him. Don't cry. Look: On the way back, I was thinking how I could tell you. And I decided that now he's much better off. He has the whole river to himself. If he keeps growing at the rate you said, he'll need the ocean, and that's available, too. What could you offer him here?"

"A bathtub," she sobbed. "And you're right. He was getting too big for that. But I'll miss him. He's all I had for two weeks. At least, this way, he can stay alive. Where did you go? You've been on a holiday in the sun and didn't even send me a card."

"No, I was working. I had to cover an international scientists' meeting in Miami. The married reporters don't like going away over Christmas. So I volunteered."

Gwen sat up in bed. "But you said you worked in a plant!"

"A newspaper plant."

"But you're not a factory worker, then."

"I never said I was," came the bland reply in the dark.

"But you let me *think* you were. You had hundreds of opportunities to correct me. You knew I thought—"

"I would much rather have gone on listening to you," he said, rubbing her neck some more.

"That feels good. Oh, yes, I'll bet you were enjoying my grand speeches, weren't you? Did you even miss me, in Miami?"

"Yes." The hand went on rubbing.

"Then why didn't you call me, or write, or something?"

"I wanted to worry you," came the noncommittal voice. How she wished she could see his face. From the TV came sounds of tipsy America howling "Auld Lang Syne" to the tune of paper horns. Somewhere a gong began ringing in the New Year.

Gail Godwin was born in Alabama and brought up in Asheville, North Carolina. With a B.A. in journalism from the University of North Carolina, she worked for a time on the Miami Herald, then lived for several years in various Spanish cities, the Canary Islands, and Denmark. Ms. Godwin has worked as a travel consultant with the U.S. Tourist Office and as a researcher for The Saturday Evening Post. *While at the Post she won a scholarship to the Iowa Writer's Workshop of the University of Iowa, where she earned an M.A. Her recently published first novel,* THE PERFECTIONISTS, *was highly praised by the critics. Ms. Godwin lives in Iowa City and teaches writing at the University of Iowa.*

A Girl Worth Twenty Million

by Joyce Carol Oates

~~~~~~

Dr. Blouin was on duty in the emergency ward when the girl was brought in. She was dead but that was no more than a technicality. They brought her back to life with an artificial heart and an artificial lung and other kinds of pumps and machines that were delicate, powerful extensions of the body—expensive organs set out onto the floor and made solid and immortal. It was a grinding, sweating wonder, how they brought her back to life; Dr. Blouin felt in his exhaustion and his excitement that he was being drawn closer to death himself. He was very tired.

The girl's doctor was Max Stern, whom Dr. Blouin knew slightly. He was a busy, tongue-clicking, perspiring man with thinning hair and a monkeyish face. It was rumored that he had become wealthy through his investments. Out in the lounge the girl's people waited—a mother, a mother-in-law, other related weeping women, a few men. They smoked and wept at the same time. Dr. Blouin did not want to talk to them but he had no choice; he stood with Dr. Stern and spoke gravely to their immensely weary, lined faces, faces that were somehow still handsome—the women's hair, even at this time of the night, was neat and professional-looking as if just combed out by their hairdressers. Dr. Blouin was fascinated by their hair, which had been sprayed to rigidity. What they said was less fascinating because it was exactly what he knew they would say . . . "But Irene would *never*" . . . "Irene has been going through *too much*" . . . and so he did not really listen to them. He gathered that the girl was being divorced and that her husband was out of town. "We were just there at the wedding, all of us here, all together at the wedding like this," one of the women cried. Her voice was elegant and not suited for grief.

When Dr. Blouin left he kept thinking of the girl, who was more vivid now than she had been when he was working on her body. She was a beautiful girl, but it was a peculiar kind of beauty. Blond hair, light freckles, perfect white teeth that looked formidable, a little prominent. Denuded of makeup and shiny with sweat her face had still been beautiful—her beauty lay in the structure of her bones, which was angular and lean. Working with death so much, working against death, Dr. Blouin did not think of the precariousness of life any longer. He thought instead of the struggle that life made, of the toughness of the body and its silent secret organs; the girl's body had been very strong. Her heart had been very strong. She must have taken twenty to thirty pills, barbiturates, but still her body had not been overcome.

He washed and changed his clothes and kept thinking of her. He had saved the lives of other people before, but he had never quite brought anyone back from death. Of course, it was a technicality: In a sense she had not been dead. But in another sense she had been dead and he had brought her back. Bringing her back like that was like giving birth to her, or to the idea of her. Dr. Stern came into the lounge and sat down heavily. He was a middle-aged man of dark, nervous, intense mannerisms; Dr. Blouin resented him. He had wanted to think about the idea of the dead girl but now Dr. Stern talked about her. "Irene Jacobsen, you know her probably as Irene Schlechtman—no?—never heard of her? What do you think? That's something, isn't it? I shouldn't talk about her, her father is a good friend of mine, a very good friend, but frankly I could see this coming—isn't it something? Isn't it?"

Dr. Stern was a familiar type, a very expensive doctor and a kind of philosopher, very bitter and fast-talking, bitterly comic, nervous, quite hard. He was an excellent mechanic and silent in his work, and he charged extraordinary fees for what miracles he performed, but his darting, puzzled mind could not quite accept his career. He said bitterly, "What do you think, eh? A girl worth twenty million? They come in and we bring them back and we give them the prescriptions—they can't sleep at night, of course—and they take the pills and we bring them back, that's how it goes. I'm a doctor so I make money. Why are you a doctor?"

Dr. Blouin, who was twenty years younger than Dr. Stern, indicated that he did not know and that he was very tired. Dr. Stern said, "Tell me why Morris Davie, that's the neurosurgeon at Ford, tell me why he killed himself. Huh? Tell me why, take a guess."

"When was this?"

"Midnight tonight. You tell me the answers, you're the younger generation. Supposed to know everything, aren't you?"

"Not my generation," Dr. Blouin said. He was thirty-one, himself. He had once been a tall man, in his early youth. Now boys of fifteen and sixteen were taller than he and he was a man of perhaps moderate height. There was something slow and gentle about him, even about his hands; he had dark, thinning hair and a shy mouth. He was the kind of doctor to whom doctors like

Stern lectured without bothering to notice if they were being listened to. Stern said, "She watched a Marilyn Monroe movie on the television, don't ask me which one, and then she took the pills. My prescription. The divorce hearing comes up next week. So, what do you think? You think she's the first of my patients? And what do you think about that face? Huh?"

Dr. Blouin fled and as he drove home he kept thinking about the girl, not about the circumstances of her life and death, and not about the people so attendant upon her in the waiting room, but simply about the fact of her body—her life and her death, which were uniquely hers and yet out of her power. He remembered her lying sunk deep into her body on the table—it had been a rather long body, stretched out like that and so exposed. She was about twenty-six years old. In dying she would have been no age at all, but in living she would have to continue at a certain age. Dr. Blouin felt feverish with exhaustion and could not control his thoughts; it seemed strange that she would have to continue at twenty-six years of age.

Dr. Blouin and his wife were no longer poor, though they had once been quite poor and the memory seemed to still be with them. They had one child, a girl. Returning to them he felt as if he were entering another world, a slow-paced dreamy world in which nothing significant could happen; the other world, rapid and dangerous, continued back at the hospital or in the lives of his private patients, and in a way his mind was always with that world in spite of his efforts to enjoy his own life, his own world. He had been very poor as a medical student and his wife had supported him. There was something about money, something about the idea of women with money, that unsettled him. Part of Irene Jacobsen's beauty was the fact of her immense wealth, which was unconscious in her as her facial bones were unconscious in her, beneath her skin and invisible. Talking to his wife, Dr. Blouin sometimes found himself thinking about Irene Jacobsen. Even the terrible foul odor of her insides had been somehow magical. . . .

"You seem tired," his wife said, accusingly, in her way. "Why are you always tired? Shouldn't you take better care of yourself?"

One day in his own office he dialed Irene Jacobsen's number, on an impulse. He was terribly agitated and seemed not to know what he was doing. Someone answered the telephone, a maid probably, and he hadn't the courage to speak—he hung up. The experience shamed him and made him doubt himself; as an undergraduate and as a medical student he had worked himself to the brink of a nervous breakdown more than once, and he was terrified of losing control of himself again. In his dreams the figure of that girl pursued him with the schoolgirlish postures of ballet; he despised himself. The fact of his good, solid marriage had nothing to do with his wishes, which lay elsewhere. He believed that he had fallen in love with a girl whom he had never really met—he had met only her body.

The other emergency patients who were brought in to him made him understand that his fascination with the girl was based upon something accidental in her. Her beauty, her suicide, her money. These were not matters that should have been significant to an intelligent man. These other people, victims of automobile accidents or smaller, foolish accidents, or the sudden failures of their own bodies, were not handsome like that girl—and in a way they were not people. They became people slowly, in agony. Of course, some of them did not become people again; they died, or they remained at a strange unconscious level, not quite asleep and not awake, as if lying motionless just beneath the surface of water. He worked upon them but he did not remember them for more than a few days. In the lounge the doctors talked about their golf scores and their squash scores, and their talk helped Dr. Blouin to see how very real the personal, private world of an individual was, after all. He should have been able to talk with enthusiasm about his own life. He had a good, intelligent marriage and he was proud of his six-year-old daughter. Yet he could not quite believe in them.

Months passed, and one day he saw Irene Jacobsen in a hotel lobby downtown. He himself had come down to have lunch with someone and after lunch he had gone to the lobby to buy a paper, and there he saw the girl. It was his day off. He stared at her and felt resentment at her light, yellow suit and her face. She looked healthy; she must have gone south after her recovery—she was still rather tan. She was coming toward him and his heart began to pound frantically, like an artificial heart gone out of control.

"Mrs. Jacobsen," he said.

She stared at him, half-smiling, polite, and yet very careful. Dr. Blouin felt a wave of dizziness rise and subside in him, confronted so suddenly with this apparition, but he heard himself talking to her in the ordinary daylight language of the sane world. He introduced himself and mentioned Dr. Stern's name, which was a magic name. The girl seemed to move backward without actually moving, as if sinking backward into her heels; then she understood. She knew. With an immediate gratitude, an enthusiasm that was like a child's, she reached out to touch his arm with her gloved hand and said, "Oh, thank you, Doctor, for saving my life!"

She smiled and her smile was dazzling. Her teeth looked powerful, enormous. Dr. Blouin stared at the eerie whiteness of her teeth. She began to chatter, passing quickly over her "accident" and going on to talk about Dr. Stern, who was marvelous and deserved his reputation, and about a certain hotel in Jamaica where she'd gone, with her parents, and how wonderful a rest had been for her. . . . She seemed so happy about the idea of a rest that she might have discovered it herself, and wanted Dr. Blouin to share it. He smiled, he agreed with her. He asked her something. She seemed to notice none of his anxiety, his desire to keep her here, keep her talking; she obviously liked to talk. She was only a few inches shorter than he, in her high-heeled shoes. Her hair was longer than he had remembered. So wet and seemingly thin that night, plastered back against her head and neck; now her hair was puffed out about her face, its tawny blond ends turned up. Her hair did not look like real hair. Her eyes, which might have been amber, or light green—were skillfully outlined with black so that they looked enormous, like the eyes of someone under a spell, and her smile was so persistent and so perfect that certainly she must be under a spell. She wore yellow, a very light wool, a yellow suit that made Dr. Blouin love her, he couldn't help himself . . . it was absurd that he should stand here so helplessly, listening to her, and unable to think. . . .

"You mean in the evening?" she said, startled.

"No, at noon. Lunch sometime. Sometime during the week. . . ."

"That would be very nice," she said. She smiled and thought. "Well, tomorrow is impossible, and Friday I have my hair done, I have a fixed appointment. So it can't be this week, I'm sorry."

"Then, next week? Any time next week?"

"Next week isn't impossible," she said vaguely.

He was forty-five minutes early for lunch with her. He had wanted to come early and to sit waiting for her, in the lobby of the same hotel, luxurious in the peculiar knowledge that he was waiting for her and that she—wherever she was—was coming toward him, irreparably toward him. He did not even buy a newspaper. The girl was as late as he was early, and he kept staring at the revolving doors that led to the street, waiting for that single, special woman who was coming to him, out of the dozens of other women who came into the lobby and who did not matter. Finally, she did appear, surprising him, coming up the marble stairs quickly and with good, firm, almost athletic steps, like a vision, something crazily exciting. He stood. He believed that he had never seen anyone so beautiful before. But she came to him, in a flurry of embarrassment that might have been real, and took both his hands in hers, and said, "I'm late, I don't know what happened. I'm terribly sorry."

She wore a light-blue coat. Her hair had a brittle, gleaming look to it; it was faintly perfumed. Her eyelids had been dampened with a thin metallic paint, light blue, and her eyelashes were absurdly thick and seemed to weigh her eyelids down, as if with shame. Her lips were pale, but pale with art and not nature, skillfully outlined. Dr. Blouin felt that he was being confronted with a preposterous creature, something decked out with ornaments from another civilization—a sunken city beneath the sea—both outlandishly expensive and tawdry, quite useless. The uselessness of her beauty, particularly the beauty of her face, overwhelmed him.

"You look a little tired. Have you been waiting long?" she said. Her concern rose as easily as her eyebrows; she looked at him as if he were an old, intimate friend. There was something both maternal and boyish about her femininity. When she did not express joy and wonder her voice lowered a few notes and was rather husky; that was the familiar sound of women of wealth, the way she would sound when she was middle-aged.

Don't become middle-aged, don't change, he wanted to tell her anxiously. But, instead, he answered some conventional answer and they walked somewhere. "There's a lovely restaurant right through there," she said, knowing what she wanted and where they would go, and he was grateful for her firmness. She talked, chattered. In the restaurant she drew off her gloves as if presenting him with a gift, her graceful, narrow hands and her pink-lacquered fingernails. She noticed nothing of his silence, his uneasiness. She talked about the Franklyn Shop, where she'd been trying on suits all morning. "I was really looking forward to lunch with you, Doctor. There's nothing so boring as that—when you can't find what you want, just can't find it. I have to go back after lunch."

They ordered drinks. She was still talking; she leaned forward and rested her chin on the palm of her hand, her elbow neat on the edge of the table. Dr. Blouin kept thinking of her dead. She was far more beautiful now, alive, but truly it was the same girl; something about her being the *same girl* obsessed him. He began to sweat. There was something strange about her, something sinister, which she herself knew nothing of. She said with a smile, "I just had my twenty-seventh birthday, isn't that awful? I feel so old. You know, I majored in art illustration in college, mainly clothes and things, you know, and I never did anything with it—I should have a career, everybody says so—it's just awful how I never get anything done. . . . Dr. Stern always says I should get a job. He takes such an interest. Isn't that nice of him, such a busy man?"

Dr. Blouin thought that perhaps she meant that he, Dr. Blouin, was not busy; that there was something suspicious and inferior about him. But she seemed to have meant nothing. Her lunch arrived—an expensive salad—and she began to eat hungrily. Her appetite was all that his wasn't. He watched her pick around in the salad with a kind of pride in her health and appetite—good, eat, keep on eating. . . .

"Why are you staring at me?" she said.

"I'm sorry, I didn't mean to stare."

She wiped her mouth with her napkin and laid it down, lightly smeared with pink lipstick. If she felt discomfort at his obvious interest in her, she did not show it. She said, "What are you thinking about, Doctor, you look so serious. . . ?"

"About you."

"About me, why? Why about me?"

"I've been thinking about you for some time. Since December."

"Really?" She made a face and smiled, almost grinned, as if he had said something that should be challenged. Now she became boyish and insolent. "Just because you did me that favor, you did so much for me—you believe that we have something in common? That I owe you thanks?"

"No, I don't think that."

"Yes, you do. You think that."

"I would like to think that—"

"You big dumb nut, you're really a nut," she said. Her smile slid across her face and she had a fox's quick, meaningless look; her cheeks had colored lightly. He wondered if she spoke in this way to hide her embarrassment, or whether she could not have felt embarrassment. "You know, Doctor, you act just like all the doctors I've known, except my brother who's different because he's my brother. And my cousin Tyrone. Yes, all the doctors I know are like fathers—they sit there listening and they take everything in, they're so wise, they make me feel like a dope, really. I feel so inferior. But still—there's something very dumb about them, I can't explain it. You're like that."

She spoke as if they were at a party, surrounded by other clever people, and he tried to smile and reply in the same way. "A doctor is led into his career by an interest, sometimes an obsessive interest, in the way the body works and the way pathological conditions work upon it," he said, tapping his fingertips together lightly. "He thinks then that he does know these mysteries. But the fact is that he doesn't know, he never finds out, and that might account for this air of incompleteness you find in so many doctors of your acquaintance. . . ."

"You talk so well, like a lawyer," she said, surprised and pleased. "Oh, I like to hear you talk! You're very nice. I wish I could stay but I have to leave, you know; I have to go back and check out those suits."

"Already?"

"Then, at four-thirty, I have to be somewhere. I'm sorry, it's a party for an artist who just came to town, a sculptress you've maybe heard of? She does all those things out of lead and burlap, that look like sand dunes. So I have to hurry, I'm sorry."

"I can walk you over to the store."

"No, no, it's all right."

"Wait until I pay the check."

He was really afraid she would not wait. He went to the cashier and paid the bill and when he returned Irene was putting on her coat. He helped her unnecessarily with it; he felt a stifled pleasure in touching her.

"Oh, it was a lovely lunch, it was such an interesting conversation," she said. They left the restaurant and were in the lobby again. While she chattered he watched her, warmly and uncomfortably, and interrupted her to say, "You couldn't—stay with me a while longer? I mean—just a little while more? I've been thinking about you so much, and I—"

She looked at him seriously, her lips parted. "What do you mean?"

"I've been thinking a great deal about you, and so—If we could go somewhere together it would mean so much—Upstairs here, or somewhere else—"

"Why, what?" she said. She touched his arm again and her voice rose to a thin, alarmed shriek, almost a delighted shriek as if he'd said something very funny. "Why, what do you mean? Do you mean here, in a hotel room here? Are you serious? What are you saying?"

"I'm sorry—I don't—"

"But here, here? People know me here, what are you thinking of? This is crazy," she said, laughing and suddenly stopping, suddenly very serious. "Doctor, you should know that I'm probably going to get engaged again. I'm thinking seriously of it. Why are you always staring at me like that?"

"You really have to leave now?"

"I told you about those suits."

"But—is it that important?"

"Goodbye."

"Can I see you again?"

She was half-backing away, waving vaguely at him, smiling in that rushed, intimate way as if they were old friends, meaningless friends, and she said again, "Goodbye, Doctor," in a voice that could have been a mechanical voice.

So he called her again and they met again. He resented her power over him but did not quite blame her for it; it was the strange power of her body and her life, the secret of her existence that fascinated him. In his ordinary everyday life, with his wife and daughter, he was exactly the same as he had always been; left to himself he began to think at once of the girl. What a strange mystery it was, to know nothing of the secret of one's own body, to walk around without the knowledge of one's death—which others have witnessed. He craved to get somewhere with her fast, to spirit her away, bundle her off, hide her, elope with her, overpower her, and cut off all the telephone lines that bound her to a busy, noisy world and distracted her from him. At their second meeting she was a little more self-conscious, as if she had actually thought about their last conversation in the intervening week.

She said, "Doctor, are you married?"

"Yes."

She nodded as if expecting this, but unmoved. She said, "Doctor, what do you think about self-hypnosis? There's such an interesting article in *Harper's* this month."

"I don't think anything about it at all."

"You don't? But—how strange! You really don't think anything?"

As they talked he felt stirred by her, summoned to her perpetually, not by her words which were just chatter but by certain gestures of hers which she seemed not to know about—the rapid closing and opening of her fists, resulting in the outward flick of her pretty nails, and a bemused sly smile that was like a second thought, added onto her broad, social smile. She complained to him about her mother and about her ex-mother-in-law, about a shower she had to go to for a girl she hated—he realized after a slow second that she didn't mean *rain* but a shower, a party—about her ex-husband, and about this man who took her out often now. "You'd know his name if I told it to you," and he listened with the helpless sweat of someone doomed and inert in his doom. He was almost immune from ordinary human considerations, standards of conduct or sense, when he said to her, begging, "Can't we go somewhere today? Just this afternoon?"

She brought her gaze around to his—she'd been looking at someone at another table—and with a faint coloring of her cheeks she said, "Well, Doctor, I'm very puzzled by you. I don't know what to say."

"I'd just like us to be alone once. It means a great deal to me."

"Well, as a favor . . . I suppose as a favor. . . ."

She rose, polite and resigned in her pink suit, clutching a bone-colored purse. Her gaze was easily distracted as they left the restaurant and entered the lobby—it was very important to him that they always meet here, always in the same place. But out in the lobby she touched his arm and said, "Doctor, you don't mean in *here*. . . ? Not here, please. You can't mean in here."

"We could go out somewhere else, then . . . another place. . . ."

"Yes, all right, another place," she said, frowning slightly as if caught with a bore, someone who was disappointing her. She instructed him to get a cab and, once in the cab, she told the driver where to go. He wheeled around in the street and took them back to an obscure hotel Dr. Blouin had never seen before; he was very nervous. She was already checking her wristwatch as they entered that hotel, and entered its elevator a few minutes later. He felt a dizzy impulse to snatch it off her wrist. She stood in the elevator with him as if ascending dutifully to an appointment, a doctor's dreaded but necessary examination. Now that they were alone she had the look, still, of being in public. In the privacy of the hotel room it was as difficult to talk to her as it would have been to approach her at a party—she was dressed, and she behaved, as if she were somehow at a party. Dr. Blouin, sweating, realized with dismay that it was almost impossible to be with her, to exist with this girl in the same close space: the very fact of her breathing, the fact of her thinking was somehow uncanny. It was as if a store-window dummy were to exhibit a faint sign of life.

"My hair, please don't hurt my hair," she said seriously.

He seemed to fall upon her as if from a great height, anguished and desperate, burdened with a love that was mysterious in its violence—it was more like an acting-out of fantasies he had imagined as an adolescent. He seemed to have skipped back past the normal period of his marriage altogether. The girl had kind arms and a manner vaguely maternal, the antithesis of the thin, stark, staring, frigid girls of Dr. Blouin's infrequent acquaintance before his marriage but, in her generosity, just as unfeeling. There was a sense in which she was unconscious. She was less feeling than those girls for they at least felt disorder and shame and injury; she looked slowly around the room and was obviously thinking of something else.

"Please, I don't want to sweat. Don't make me sweat," she said. She was petulant; thrusting her lower lip out, she blew her bangs up off her forehead. It was an uncanny, absurd gesture, like a boy's. Dr. Blouin felt a maniac's love for her.

He lay beside her and stared at her. She did not seem to mind, as if she were accustomed to this sort of thing. Her eyes had a flat, golden, flecked look, a friendly look. He said, to get her attention, "Tell me why you did it."

"Why what? Because I like you."

"No. I mean the pills. Why did you take those pills?"

Her smile disappeared. She looked at him. "I don't think it's necessary for us to talk about that."

"But I want to know. It's important to me."

"Why?"

"Because I want to know. You're very important to me."

She looked away. Her face was blank with disapproval. Finally she said, "You're too morbid."

"But I thought we could talk together—about ourselves—"

"Why? Talk why? Why are you so morbid?"

"I don't think I'm being morbid. I'm in love with you."

"Love, hell."

"You don't think I'm in love with you?"

"Whether you are or not, my business is my own business, Doctor," she said rudely. It was the first time she had been less than charming to him; the effort of it left tiny lines on either side of her mouth. Touched, he brought his thumb up against one of the lines and tried to wipe it away.

"I don't want you to die," he said. "I want you to live."

She moved her head so that his hand fell away. Quiet, impatient, breathing in long heavy drafts of disapproval, she was casting her mind about for some way to get out of here. He tried to think of something to say. To keep here here he would have to hold her down, to seize her in his arms and keep her still, shut her mouth with his own mouth, own her. He wanted to own her. She said apologetically, "There is this person I have to meet in an hour. . . ."

The next time they met, at the same hotel, she wore white and a white felt hat. "I had to wear a hat, my hair looks like hell," she said breathlessly. In the elevator this time, she looked down at her smart shoes with their white buckles, and her slim, pale-stockinged legs, and the skirt of this impeccable white suit. Her delight in herself was a child's delight, without vanity. "I'm so glad you came, I was worried you wouldn't come," he said to her, forcing an idea upon her she maybe hadn't thought of yet herself, regretting it, despising himself, incredibly clumsy and she stepped out of one embrace in the elevator, disengaging herself from him politely, and in the hotel room stepped into another with the same politeness. She even put her arms around his neck and kissed him as a greeting, in response to his obvious need, and once more her mind drifted off while her body remained with him.

If you don't love me, why do you come here? he wanted to ask in anger. But he said nothing like that, he muttered to her only the anguished and unlistened-to declarations he had vowed he would never make to her. After a while she turned over so that the long, curving expanse of her back made him blind with alarm, and said, "Do you see that thing by my shoulder? That mole or whatever it is? Do you think it's dangerous, should I have it removed?"

He touched the small mole with his forefinger. It was soft. He felt like crying, he hardly knew why, and instead of answering her question he pressed his hot face against her back and closed his eyes. He remained for some time like that, silent. Irene finally said, "Is something wrong? Is it malignant or something?"

"No, no, it's nothing. It's beautiful, it's nothing," he said weakly.

That day she had to leave early for a two-o'clock appointment at her hairdresser's. He watched her prepare for leaving, for the public street, and he understood that she left nothing of herself behind, that she would not think of this room once she had left it . . . and how mysterious that was, he thought with an aching, sick brain, how mysterious to go from place to place and retain nothing, recall nothing. . . .

Before she left he said suddenly, "Tell me why you tried to kill yourself."

She was adjusting her hat. Her hands froze.

"Why don't you want to talk about it?" he said.

"Why are you so morbid?"

"Is it morbid, to be frank about these things?"

"But you have nothing to do with me. You should talk about something else, other things, Doctor. You have nothing to do with me."

"Why do you come up here, then?"

She looked at him through the mirror, thoughtfully. "I don't know," she said, "I think it's because of a favor, to make you happy. Because you saved my life and all that before Dr. Stern came."

"But Dr. Stern is still your doctor?"

"Of course he's my doctor," she said, a little surprised. "I've been going to him all my life. Of *course* he's my doctor."

"You don't like me?"

His question was too pitiful for her to answer. She turned away, looking for something. He stared at her and was already sickened by the loss of her, for he knew that he would have nothing to remember of her—nothing—once she left. The absence of so empty a woman would be no different from her presence. And the bitterness in his mouth was formed by the knowledge that, with such a love, nothing added up to anything, there was nothing to love. There was nothing in her for him to love, and yet he loved her.

"Say, don't you have any work to do?" she said. "Shouldn't you be busy like other doctors? You know, my father takes work very seriously. He can take two months off from work if he wants to, each year, but in the last five years he only took a month. And do you know why? He took that month off because of me, no other reason. He loves to work."

"Yes, I feel the same way," he said slowly, not knowing what he said.

"Will we be seeing each other again?"

"But don't you have a wife—where is she?" The girl laughed. "Oh, you're so strange—you're even beginning to look strange. It won't be good for your profession, if you keep losing weight."

"Should we meet again next week?"

"Oh, go to hell," she said, turning, laughing, without resentment. "Men I know are nothing like you. They're normal and real, they're *nothing* like you!"

"Should I call you in a few days?"

"Goodbye."

But she did agree to meet him again, in two weeks. For Dr. Blouin these meetings were precisely timed and enormously important; for Irene they appeared accidental. She seemed to be remembering him slowly as she talked, becoming accustomed to him again as her eyes became accustomed to the chic semidarkness of the restaurant. She talked, she chattered. Did he know her father was called Mr. Moderno, as a joke, that he owned the Moderno Stereo Company, which was putting stereos in cars? He was so lucky with his investments! And her Uncle Soskin, her uncle's hobby was making money—just pure money, on the stock exchange. Dr. Blouin thought suddenly about strangling her when they were alone. She said, lowering her voice, "I have some news, Doctor. The engagement will be announced at a party before we leave. We're going to Greece with some friends of his."

"What engagement?"

"Haven't you been listening? My engagement. I'm getting married."

"Married?"

"I told you. You're so strange, why are you surprised?"

"So you're getting married again,—second husband?"

"Actually, this is my third time," she said, lowering her gaze for a moment. Then she raised it. "Here's my ring, do you like it? I just love it, myself."

He ignored the ring. "You're really getting married, then?"

"Of course."

"Are you in love?"

"Yes, of course."

There was a slight emphasis on *course,* as if she were a child defending some outlandish desire. He watched her resume eating. Her long fingers with their two good, expensive rings seemed made for the heavy impersonal silverware of dark, pretentious restaurants attached to hotels. He had never seen this girl in a home, in a normal domestic setting. She was the kind of person who seemed dressed and arrayed only for public places; even the emergency ward had been a kind of theatre for her.

"And so, you're . . . getting married?"

"I thought I told you about it."

"And what about me?"

She chewed slowly, thinking. It was clear that she had not thought about him at all. "Well, I'll be gone to Europe for a while. . ."

"I could take you to Europe myself. The two of us could go."

She pretended to be considering this, politely. He could see the visions rising in her brain of the hotels they would stay in and the dinners they would eat. But the chartered boat promised by her fiancé's friends and her father's business connections in Rome—he could provide nothing like that, he was only a doctor. She shook off her contemplation and said, "But I'm going to get married. Aren't you married yourself?"

"Do you still have faith in marriage?"

"Look," she said chattily, preparing to count something off on her fingers, "my Aunt Brenda says this: The first marriage is almost always a mistake, you're too young. The second marriage comes right after the first, when you're broken down and don't know where to turn, so it's almost always a failure. *But*, by the third marriage, you know what's what, you're older and you don't jump into a mistake. Of course I have faith in marriage."

"But when are you leaving?"

"Oh, a week or so."

"Will I see you when you come back?"

"You mean like this? Like we've been?"

She wiped her mouth with the heavy linen napkin. "Well, I don't see the necessity of it," she said.

His hands twitched with the desire to get hold of her. And now had he become what he had always despised?—a man enamored of his work, his doing? He felt dizzy. He was a doctor. A doctor is a man, yes, but a doctor is also more than a man. So many bodies yielded to his dissecting instruments, and so many textbooks turned themselves inside out for him! A body was a diagram to him, or an X-ray. How was it possible that death—which he had always half-thought a kind of sick air breathed in by the dying—could expel itself in a simple "Thank you, Doctor," like a mechanical doll's squeaking? Even this girl's frigidity was a way out of dying, a way out of feeling. She was so empty that one could fall forever in her, reaching out for something, daring, grasping, struggling—and what besides her hollow, weightless bones would he reach? Always Dr. Blouin had feared he might lose his mind. Like all orderly, clean, sane people he had feared chaos and filth and madness, and now he saw himself trembling on the verge of some small, quick act—could he strike her head against the bathtub? Seize her beautiful head between his hands and strike it until it shattered softly, until it was his again?

"Will you come somewhere with me today? For the last time?"

She was too simple or too distracted to hear the strange urgency in his voice. She was looking at herself in a compact mirror. "But I have an appointment somewhere," she said.

"Just this last time?"

"I'm sorry, I have too many things to do."

"Then I won't see you again?"

She patted his hand maternally. "Of course, sometime."

"In the emergency ward again?"

She flashed him a fast, hateful grin. She stood.

"But you won't come back with me, really?" he said. He had begun to tremble and her summery flowered dress blotched before his eyes. "You don't understand. You owe me something. You wouldn't be alive except for me—and getting married again. All this you owe to me—"

"Please, don't be upset," she said, as if moved by his stammering. She patted his shoulder and was about to leave. "There's nothing to be upset about."

"Wait," he said, stumbling to his feet. She indicated with a shrug of her shoulders that she would wait or not wait, he wasn't sure. He paid their bill blindly, his eye on the door that led to the hotel lobby. The girl was waiting outside. She looked idle and impatient at once, walking in a small restrained circle. Her dress was bold green and red, of a silky material, with a puffed-out skirt. A middle-aged man passing her turned to stare; Dr. Blouin was seized with a terrible fear. If someone should approach her? Someone else? If someone should interfere with him, with his need for her? What if another man got to her before he did? There was something so hateful in her beauty that any man, certainly, would want to destroy it: he wondered why he had never guessed that secret about beauty before. It was true of all beautiful women, the unconscious secret they held sure and damning as the very structure of their faces' bones. . . .

He hurried toward the door, brushing against someone on his way back to her. He had to get to her. But then he saw that the middle-aged man, who was a well-dressed, handsome gentleman had decided to approach the girl; he approached her hesitantly, asking her something, and then as if by magic both burst into smiles. They embraced. Obviously, he was someone Irene knew, an acquaintance of her father's, or an ex-father-in-law, or someone with the key to her pleased, astonished, rapturous face, which was now more beautiful than Dr. Blouin had remembered. He stood watching them and did not know what to do. They talked with great gestures, friendly and excited, and he knew that she'd forgotten him and would turn with a vague surprise should he approach her, trembling with lust to drag her off somewhere and force his love upon her and the whole terrible weight of his desire, which would crush her body beyond all remaking. . . .

And so, with a shudder, Dr. Blouin took the other door out of the restaurant, the door leading to the sidewalk. The street. Freedom.

He read of her engagement on the society page of the newspaper, and he read of her trip to Greece. She seemed in a way more real to him, in a blurred and very flattering photograph, flanked by women beautiful as she and men firmly jowled and handsome as the man who had saved her life in the hotel lobby that day; he could believe in her at that distance. When, some time later, he was to read of her second suicide attempt, which was also a failure, he was able to read the news item without too much emotion. He had accustomed himself by then not to feel much emotion, certainly not excitement, at his work or at home. He felt that he had saved his own life, had somehow desperately remade himself that day—taking the door out to the street and so saving himself. He had saved himself. He was not a murderer and it was not possible that he could have been a murderer, but still he felt that he had saved himself.

And he forbade himself to think about it any further.

Joyce Carol Oates is one of America's most highly regarded younger writers. Her work has brought her many honors, including several O. Henry prizes (for short stories), the Rosenthal Award from the National Academy of Arts and Sciences, and the National Book Award (for the novel THEM*). Ms. Oates is a literary phenomenon: A writer of rare sensitivity and depth, she is also enormously productive. At the age of thirty-three, she has appeared in almost every American magazine or literary periodical of importance, has published five novels, two collections of short stories, and a volume of poems. Her latest novel is* WONDERLAND. *Ms. Oates lives in Windsor, Ontario, where she and her husband are both professors of English at the University of Windsor.*

The Winds of Love

by Rosemary Hamilton

She was walking an old, beaten path under greening trees. Around her were the springtime seekers, the bearded ones and their tattered girls and the crisply shorn ones and their scrubbed, tailored women, and she smiled at them tolerantly. She and Josh were so different. She stroked the thought. Everyone else on campus fell into neat categories; they lined up solidly to the left or the right, and they were marked by their clothes and their hair. By a glance, you could tell their inclinations, and within the groups there was a stultifying sameness. But she and Josh went their own way, like no others, absorbed in nothing but each other. She paused a moment to savor the thought of him. Sometimes, she teased herself so, hesitating briefly in her rush toward him so that she might contemplate the happiness that awaited her. Around her there were small rustlings and coaxing calls from the piercingly bright birds to their bark-colored mates, and she felt as if she should respond. She wanted to trill an answer. She wanted to hurl herself upon the young grass and breathe deep of its musty odor. She wanted to make love to the pushing newness of the season. Weary with awareness, she leaned against a tree. Her hand touched the tiny ridges of the old tree-flesh, and she mourned for the long life it had known, standing there, frozen still for year upon year. The tree was an ancient mother, patiently putting forth its leaf-children, forced to live on when the children died, a scattered, heedless death in the fall winds. The sticky green birth taking place on those twisted limbs was useless, she thought sadly, strangely like the having of human children who would grow to want nothing but to be off and away. It was odd, she reflected, that she could not bear the thought of having children, not even Josh's child. Perhaps it was her guilty knowledge of her own restless escape that filled her with caution. Already she had left her parents. Soon now they would sense that she was truly gone, and there would be sorrow in her house. She shook her head. She had no time for regrets, she told herself. There was too much *now* to cope with; there could be no time wasted on once-was and yet-to-be. She began to run.

He was sitting in a crowded place. At a table uncleared of used coffee cups and fragments of bread, he slumped in a chair, his long legs stretching thoughtlessly in the path of others. He frowned at the chatter about him. He shoved disgustedly at the clutter on the table. He was waiting for her to put things to rights. She hurried through the fat snake line at the food counter where she filled a tray with plump, raisin-dotted rolls and cups of steaming coffee. Swiftly, she brought her burden to the table, and with brisk, neat movements she removed the soiled dishes and flicked away the crumbs. Before him, she ranged the food, and he began to smile. Something inside her burst into pain as she watched him eat. He needed her so. For little things like rolls and coffee. For big things like life and love.

After he had drained his cup, he massaged his stomach. "That's better!" he declared. She smiled. He was so natural. Unlike herself, he never wasted time with dreamy thoughts and unnecessary comparisons. He simply existed, large and marvelously male. "How's my Carole?" he asked, and she rejoiced. He had called her *mine*, and that was all she wanted to be.

"I'm fine," she smiled. "I love you, and that makes everything fine."

"Love you, too," he announced offhandedly. "Hell of a nice day today. Too nice for anything but fun. Want to come along?"

"Yes! Let's take the whole day for ourselves," she agreed delightedly. "What shall we do?"

"Oh, I'll think of something!" He grinned. He reached out and rubbed her arm, pushing his fingers up under the short sleeve of her linen dress. "I'll think of something we can do!" He threw back his head and laughed. His vigor seemed to lunge at her. He was dressed carelessly in an old dark-blue sweatshirt from which he had chopped the sleeves and which he wore inside out, its shaggy interior exposed. She mused that he looked like a healthy young Basque sheepherder clad in a dyed skin. She wanted to tell him her thought, but she knew it would bother him. He would puzzle over what a Basque was, so she hugged the thought secretly to herself. There were many little secrets she kept from him, but not her adoration. Never that. "Might as well enjoy myself," he said, suddenly frowning. "Haven't got too many days left."

She couldn't have heard right. He had misphrased his meaning, often he did. "What do you mean?"

"Time's up. I'm off to the rice paddies! This weekend I'll have to take my stuff home, and next week I'll be a soldier boy." He stopped and snapped his fingers. "Hey! I never did tell you about enlisting, did I? Did it right before I met you. The old grades were at the danger level, and I decided to beat the draft board to the draw. Traveled down to my friendly, neighborhood recruiter and signed my life away." He scowled. "Got to call my folks tonight and tell them. Figured I wouldn't tell them until the last minute. Otherwise, they'd have hauled me home to do my waiting stretch there. No thanks! It's more fun here. Pretty girls. Beer and buddies. They are going to be one shocked set of parents! Man!"

She sat very still and straight. Oddly, all the faces around him were coming into bright focus, and his was receding. His face was becoming undistinguished, like that of any stranger. She waited for him to say something that would erase the dreadful obscuring he was undergoing.

He looked at her uncertainly. "You look funny. Mad? That's it! You're mad! You can't do that. Nobody gets mad at soldier boys. They have to have love and consideration. I'm going to be swatting my way through a lousy jungle while you get a new boy friend, you know. I may be dying while you get engaged. Think of my side of it."

"Yes," she said through dry lips. "I'll think of your side of it. My side is unbearable. I can't stand to think of how you tricked me. If I think of that, I may kill you, myself, before you ever get to that miserable, uncomprehensible little war."

"Harsh words, baby. Very harsh. I never tricked you. I just helped you get rid of your frustrations. Did a damned good job of it, too. You were a stick when I met you. Little, old, frozen Carole, the Popsicle girl. I made you into a female instead of a walking dictionary. The way you talk! No wonder you'd never had a man before. Scared them off with words. Only I was smart enough to figure out a way to shut you up."

Her chin ducked back as if he'd struck her. He was right. He had shut her up. They had never talked at all. Her book lore had bored him, and so it wearied her, too. Between them, there had been nothing but touch. Their fleshly boundaries they had learned well, but they had never exchanged an idea. And during each of their nearly mute meetings, she had persuaded herself that they were in love. When they were apart, she dwelled on the forever of which he never spoke. When she was alone, she spoke for him the promises he never made. She had dialogued their love. She had given him eloquence. Now this stranger, whom she knew so well yet not at all, was at last revealing himself in common words and tawdry intentions. He was not even allowing her the dignity of desertion. He assumed, with easy camaraderie, that her feelings had been as temporary as his. He was monstrous. "I have to go!" she said wildly. "I have to get out of here!"

He soothed her with agreement. His car, he suggested pointedly, was outside. It would take them away to privacy where they could indulge themselves for one of the last times. She pushed away from the table and hurried to the door. He followed her amiably as if nothing were wrong. His hands were on her shoulders. His breath was on her neck.

Outside, she turned on him. "I could be pregnant," she snarled. "I could be pregnant and alone. What am I supposed to do about that?"

"You're not pregnant," he said easily. "Do you think I'm crazy? I never took any chances with you. Hell! What kind of a marriage do you think we'd have? You with your nose in a book all the time, and me with itchy feet. I'm not as stupid as you think. I never wanted to get into anything like that!"

He had ripped through her last pretense. He had been smarter than she! She who had been condescending about his need for her had been gulled by his superior common sense. He had never been lost in a grand passion, he had merely been wenching, and she, poor dreamer, had given herself to an imaginary lover whose lofty phrases and extravagant praise she had supplied herself. She was filled with the fruitless anger of the tricked.

She noticed with surprise that she was moving. He had his hand on her elbow, and he was steering her toward the car. "*No!*" she said with horror. "Find yourself someone who doesn't have to have love mixed in with it. Someone who can't be hurt." She jerked away and began to run. It seemed as if she could not force herself to go fast enough, yet she knew he was not pursuing her.

She ran back over the same path she had traveled such a short time before, but now the blurry anonymity of the walkers no longer existed for her, and she was frightened of them. Each sound of laughter seemed directed at her. Each snatch of conversation was a whispered comment about her. Stripped of her folly, she was no longer chosen or special. She crouched as she ran as if someone might strike at her. When she emerged from the woods, the broad stretches of green lawn and the twisting sidewalks appalled her. Now, she must cross in the open. From the windows of the buildings, eyes would be watching her. She sheltered her head with an arm and darted toward the wide steps of her home building.

There was a cool breeze moving down the dormitory hall, and the doors to all the rooms were open to catch it. She made her way past unmade beds and book-cluttered rooms. She was whimpering. A head appeared from a doorway, and a girl looked at her curiously. As she moved past, the girl caught her arm and pulled her into the room. "You sound like a dog hit by a car!" she said, pushing Carole toward a rumpled bed. "Lie down!" she commanded. Obediently, Carole curled into a knot on the bed, her hands clenched against her mouth. The girl caught up a towel from the back of a chair and ran water in a basin in the next room. Soon Carole felt a cool wetness on her forehead. Her arms were being rubbed, and there were gentle, encouraging murmurings being said over her. Her knees unfolded and slid flat. Her fists unclenched, and the whimpering became replaced with hiccups. A part of her, she decided, must be feeling better. A part of her was going to live. She searched for the girl's name, the girl who was being so incomprehensibly kind to her. It had been so long since she had paid attention to anyone but Josh. Other people and their names had ceased to exist. "Sheila?" she ventured.

"I'm here," the girl said comfortingly. "Feel like talking about it? I suppose the boy friend dumped you?"

"How did you know?" She was alarmed. She was marked. To look at her was to know what she was.

"Maybe because I know the feeling so well," Sheila said philosophically. "That old rejection! The first time it happened to me, I was sixteen. I thought I was going to die. I ran away from home, a perfectly good home, but I couldn't stay in it after I became a locker-room joke. It was because of my mother. I was sixteen, but she always looked at me as if I were six and on my way to Sunday school. It was sweet of her, you understand, but not very practical. I couldn't bring myself to tell her I'd stopped being a little girl in the back seat of a Corvair. I moped around, and she kept asking me things like did I want hot cereal or cold for breakfast. Breakfast! Hell! I couldn't even get my toothbrush in my mouth without gagging. I couldn't eat a thing, so she got me vitamins. I couldn't sleep, and she bought me a new mattress. I thought maybe I was pregnant, and she talked about dragging me to the doctor to see if I had anemia! God! I felt a hundred years old, and she was worrying about whether I was wearing the retainer for my braces. It was horrible. So I ran. Not too far, nor for too long, but when I got back, she didn't look at me in the same way. Not ever again. Now, it's always with a question. A question she won't ask, and I wouldn't answer even if she did. I stay here at school nearly all year round, and she seems to like it that way."

"Love!" Carole said hoarsely. "How could you think you were in love at sixteen? He couldn't have been more than a boy."

"I know that now. But then, I thought he was man incarnate. A sixteen-year-old quarterback with shoulders like a packing crate. I thought he was something! It was love, all right, as far as I was concerned. For him, it was something else again." She shook her head. "Oh, well, if it hadn't been him, it would have been someone else. I've found that out about myself. He opened little secret doors for me, but once I learned the secrets, I've been opening doors ever since. Poor old Brian," she said reflectively. "I don't suppose I'd even shake hands with him today. He was too simple. Now, I have to have the flourishes." Absently, Sheila reached out for a huge stuffed rabbit and hugged it to her. She was a large girl, with softly sloping shoulders and rounded, full breasts. Everything about her was flowing, her long hair, the folds of her batik gown. "Sometimes, I wonder about myself. I wonder if I am always getting even with Brian, or if I'm just unusually hungry. But I'm the only one who wonders about it. My folks have settled for me staying out of town, and no one I go out with cares what I feel. One of these days maybe I'll find someone who cares, even just a little bit, and then I'll get married. But I'll tell you one thing, that marriage had better work out exactly right or I'll move on like I've always done. I've lost that certain something that it takes to stick with a man, no matter what. New faces," she said thoughtfully. "They're really habit forming."

She was far too nice, Carole thought sadly, to go on endlessly doling herself out. "You can't do that!" she said with concern. "It won't work. Sooner or later, you'll run out of luck. Or you'll lose some of your looks. Or you won't be able to find any desirable men."

The rabbit held closely in her arms, Sheila turned a suddenly childlike face toward Carole. "But that's off into the future. I never think about that. I can picture a year, maybe two years, but not my whole lifetime. Maybe I won't have a lifetime. Nobody says anything encouraging about lifetimes anymore. Nobody promises that the world will last a long, long time. So what's there to live for but right now?"

"You're wrong!" Carole protested. "There has to be a future. It has to be worth waiting for and planning for or there wouldn't be any sense in anything."

Later, she remembered how Sheila had looked at her fearfully and admitted she dreaded the possibility that there might be a long, humdrum life spinning out before her. She wanted her youth and then nothingness. To become involved in years of sameness was not for her. Alone in her room, Carole understood. She lay on her narrow bed and was panicked by her understanding. From all along the hall, there came a sound of incessant giggling as the girls rushed back and forth preparing for the evening. Their silliness was maddening as they prattled and tittered their way through showers and hair washings and impetuous lunges at ringing telephones. They were preparing for their men. A flowery scent from their perfumes sifted into the room, and Carole felt a wave of nausea. Yet, she longed to be adorning herself. She moved restlessly against her flat pillow. She could have been readying herself for Josh. There could have been today and tomorrow. She could have clung to him until the very last second. He had expected her to be honest, to admit her enjoyment and share it with him until necessity parted them. Weakly, she blamed herself for the bitterness that had caused her to turn from him. She put her feet to the floor and shakily made her way to the phone. From memory, she dialed his number. She lost count of the rings, and it was minutes before she could bring herself to return the receiver to the hook. He was gone. Her hate flooded back. She was glad he would never know that she had called. It would only have added to the smirking pride he would display when he strutted and boasted of his conquest. And he would boast. She knew he would. She bent double with an insane desire to hurt him. But a short time later, she was dialing his number again.

The evening was at its mid-hour when she walked into the street. A small girl, groomed with deliberate care, she walked with purpose. She was searching. He would be where there were people. He would be in the midst of a crowd. She cut across the mall, her sun-browned legs moving swiftly. There would be music tonight, outside in the soft warm air, and he would be listening to it. Soon, she was on the hillside, and below her was the group of entertainers in a bright arc of light. They wore rag-tag, gypsy clothes, varicolored vests, trailing scarves, and flopping trousers. They looked unreal, like fairy-tale minstrels come to lure all the young people away into a land where there was no aging or hurting. A land of panting, pumping, never-ending motion. The musicians were frantic with their desire to seduce, maddened by their double wish to both play and dance to their own tunes. Far away as she was, she could see the pain on their faces as they grunted out the sounds which were not music at all but a kind of cabalistic entreaty. All around her, the healthy, young people were sitting on the grass. Bolt upright, they bobbed back and forth as children do when they are coaxing for an outing. Take me along, the bodies said, take me along into your mystery, take me into your mindless cacophony. The hillside swayed with their movements as if a coating of locusts were upon it. She peered into the darkness. All the young males looked alike in the gloom. Hundreds of Joshes. Multiplied, he was all about her. Suddenly, a pair of warm hands were on her shoulders, and she clasped them with her own. The hands manipulated her so that she began to jerk with the music. At her back, he duplicated her motions; standing slightly apart, they began to beat out the grinding rhythm with snaps of their hips and thrusts of their chests. She smiled secretly. They were dancing once more in the furious, heated way he loved. She gave herself into the undercurrent of the drum. At last, the players dropped their instruments and leaped from the stage as lightly as if their own sounds still propelled them with endless energy. In the sudden stillness, he twisted her around and pushed his mouth onto hers. His body still twitched with the remembrance of the songs, and his kiss was greedy. She moved toward him in the old, familiar way and made small, spurring motions with her fingers on his shoulders. His kiss deepened. He moaned as he always had with his painful wanting of her. She grew suddenly gentle in her sweeping forgiveness. He had come to find her. He had hungered for her. Soon, he would discover that the hunger would never leave him.

He pulled her after him as he began to plunge away from the crowd. Down the hill, toward the mall, she followed hastily, stumbling and righting herself before he could assist her. Now, they left the hillside behind and sped onto the clipped grass that surrounded the lighted fountain. From the shadows, she could hear the music throbbing once more. She pulled her hand from his and he turned impatiently. She looked up wonderingly into the face of a stranger. He moved toward her, and, incredibly, he kissed her once more with Josh's lips.

When she broke away and ran from him, she heard his angry protests until she was far along the way that led to her room.

Her fingers fumbled ineffectually at the telephone, but at last she heard her mother's voice, sleepy, startled. "I want to come home," Carole said simply. "I need to come home."

"Are you all right? It's so late!" her mother said confusedly. "We've been in bed for hours. What are you doing up so late?"

"I want to come home," she said stubbornly. She wanted no inquisitive probing, no wintry advice. It should be enough that she expressed her need. It was her home; she had a right to its comfort. Why, she thought wearily, can't things be simple? "I can't stand this place another day," she insisted.

She was in a mood, her mother said soothingly. In the morning, things would seem different. Mornings always made things seem better. But Carole interrupted. "You wouldn't have to come and get me. I could take the train. Or maybe get a ride with someone. Anything! I can leave tomorrow."

"Now, Dad and I will drive down to see you this weekend." Her mother ignored her urgency. "We'll have a nice visit and take you out to dinner. Won't that help?"

"I'm not talking about coming home for a visit. I want to come back for good. I don't want to stay here. It isn't working out."

"Now, Carole, listen to me!" her mother instructed firmly. "I want you to go to bed immediately. Obviously, you are not getting enough sleep. At this hour of the night, we cannot make any important decisions. Get some sleep and call me tomorrow, do you understand?"

"Yes, Mother," she said hopelessly.

"That's better! I love you, honey, and so does Dad. You'll never know how much we love you and how proud we are of you."

"I love you, too." And she dropped the phone into place as if the weight of it had become unbearable.

In Sheila's room, Carole leaned against the rabbit and waited. It was very late when she came. Her mouth was full and swollen from kisses, and she looked tired.

"I kissed a complete stranger tonight," Carole said bluntly, "and it was every bit as good as with Josh."

Sheila sank onto the bed. "It's surprising, isn't it, when you find that one person doesn't have a monopoly on your responses?"

"I wish I hadn't found it out. Now what am I supposed to think of myself? That I can't allow myself to be touched lest I melt?" Nervously, Carole braided and unbraided a strand of her hair. "What if I leave a kind of spoor behind me that attracts all the wrong kind of men? I did that tonight. What if it happens again and again?"

Sheila dropped back flat on the bed and stared up at an orange felt pennant on the ceiling. "Well, then I guess you'll be like me."

"Are you happy?"

"No! Excited, maybe. A panicky, scary kind of feeling like playing tag in the dark when you know you could get caught any minute."

Carole shook her head. "That's not what I want."

"I know." Sheila sighed. "In the beginning, it wasn't what I wanted either. All I wanted was love. But it never seems to happen."

"I'm sorry!" Carole thought of all the sleeping girls in their lonely beds along the hall. "How many of us will ever find love? You aren't the only one who is searching."

"No. But it always seems to me that everyone else has found it. Couples. Each couple I see looks all wrapped up in love like in a nice, warm, woolly blanket, and I'm still shivering in the cold."

Carole touched her shoulder. "Someday. It will happen someday."

"Sure. Sure it will." And Sheila closed her eyes.

In her own room, Carole lighted the lamp and settled her books upon her desk. She opened one and began to read. She knew that if anyone were to see her, they would be impressed with her studiousness. Nice Carole! Studying into the night. At her books on a night filled with warmth and springtime invitations! But soon, her mind caught at the neatness of the phrases on the pages. Soon, she told herself that she was enjoying the steady memorizing of the old, proven facts. This was the way she had been before she met Josh, and this was the way she would be again. She would lock the wanton part of herself far inside the conscientious student. Hidden away like that, it would never be found by the love winds that blow so easily, so caressingly, one would never suspect the hurricane betrayal they can bring to the unwary.

Toward morning, she slept, her head dropped forward onto her cradling arm, and a mischievous breeze fluttered her papers about the room and tossed shut the cover of her book, but she slumbered as a child, confidently and innocently.

Rosemary Hamilton is the author of many short stories, as well as a housewife with four children. Although family and writing leave her little time for hobbies, she manages to paint (usually in tempera), sculpt, and sew. A self-taught writer, Ms. Hamilton is, in her words," . . . one of those persons who, willy-nilly, are going to write despite lack of education, opportunity, encouragement, or understanding." She lives with her family in West Lafayette, Indiana.

An American Marriage

by Norma Klein

*B*efore calling it quits definitely, Carol and Mike Bonner agreed to both try being analyzed.

Carol's analyst was a tall, thin Viennese man who looked like an Austrian version of T. S. Eliot. He was famous as a theoretician; since Carol's parents were paying, she could afford someone well known. His office was dark and messy, with books and papers stacked all over the place and a green velvet couch in one corner. It looked like the pictures of Freud's office that Carol had seen in photographs. There was even a cocker spaniel who came to the door when she entered, though he did not, like Freud's spaniel, remain in the office during the session.

Carol could not help feeling the bridge in age, experience, and background between herself and this man. She would not have wanted a woman, God forbid, but sometimes she wondered, wouldn't an American have been better? Of course, her parents had wanted her to have the best, just as when she was growing up, they had wanted her to have the best education, the best clothes, the best summer vacations. The best, in this case, meant a man old enough to have studied with Freud: From his person wisdom would trickle down, as it had from the disciples. But Dr. Furstenberg terrified her with his German accent and his dry, ironical laugh. He was as remote from any influence of feminine charm as a man could be, and Carol, who was used to using such influence when it might be of use, disliked him for it. The prig!

She felt terribly small and petty as she sank, mink-clad, sunglasses pushed visor-like against her streaked blond hair, into the green wool basket chair and told all about herself. She could not help feeling that he despised her, though he would not admit it, for the disorder of her life. But, of course, he was too wonderfully discreet to say anything of the kind. She hated the doorman, too, and the way, recognizing her, he smiled obsequiously each time she entered the building. She hated the little crouched waiting room with its copies of *Medical Newsletter* and *M.D.*, which were never up to date. Especially she hated the other patients who all looked so god-awful: the fat lady in suede boots, the gawky lawyer who asked her for a date, the little girl (or midget) dressed always in plaid who carried a bright red patent leather purse. She even resented the money, though she knew her father, an ear, nose, and throat man with a lavish office on Park Avenue, could easily afford it. Usually Carol would have derived some pleasure out of knowing she was spending his money. It made her feel loved and wanted to run up huge bills at Bergdorf's and overtip cabdrivers and waiters. But now, seeing some Pucci lounging pajamas on sale for a hundred dollars, she would think, For two lousy hours, I could get a whole outfit! Why, if you took all those hours and added them up, she'd be the best-dressed manic depressive in New York! For revenge—though at whom the revenge was aimed was a mystery—she tried cutting sessions or arriving late, but, of course, the next time she had to talk about "why she had felt the urge to 'act out.' " You just couldn't win with these characters: They had all the answers.

It was worst during the time when Ben, her first husband, came to New York for a month and she began seeing him again and sleeping with him. She knew it was bad, bad for herself—she had been down this one-way road to nowhere too many times—and bad for the kids, who could not help getting all mixed up, what with Ben leaving at 10 A.M. Saturday morning and Mike arriving half an hour later to pick them up for their weekly "day with father" outing. But, hell, why must she account for everything? She was an adult, wasn't she? For what that was worth.

Mike was going to an American analyst who, though he belonged to the New York Psychoanalytic Institute, had an office in the Village. It was a trek for Mike, who worked as assistant editor for a literary quarterly in midtown Manhattan. But he had no choice. He was going to the Treatment Center in order to pay less; he was still supporting Carol and the girls.

His analyst was the swinging type, a short, stout man with longish black hair and a wrinkled, but friendly, basset hound face. He wore dark sports shirts and flowing navy blue ties with giant red polka dots. His waiting room had a dozen doors, each leading off to some unknown, mysterious realm. One door was painted bright orange, another a scarcely less subdued shade of violet. The plastic coffee table was littered with copies of *Ramparts* and *Mad*, and large white bowls of leafy plants were suspended from the ceiling by chains. Over the couch an Andy Warhol cluster of vibrant flowers made a blotch of color against the white wall.

As an analyst, Dr. Nachmanson was scarcely the conventional type either. Mike had expected a silent presence, stern, patriarchal, sparing in remarks of any kind, but Nachmanson reacted to everything. Guffaws, chuckles, snorts, hoots—all these sounds came trumpeting forth with unrepressed vigor from behind Mike's head, interspersed with terse but vivid comments: "She really bitched you up that time, huh?" or "Let *them* eat shit for a change, Bonner. How about that?"

In general, Mike found he had a harder time with his analysis than he had expected. He had, of course, read a lot of Freud and consequently it had seemed to him that his case would be a pushover. Certainly there were no suggestions about his character or subconscious that he would have any qualms about entertaining, nothing that would take him aback. Had he wanted to sleep with his mother? Sure, why not? He'd go along with that (though the memory of her squeezing into her size 18 girdle was hardly calculated to evoke the most erotic memories). "Just tell me," he said at one of the first sessions, "tell me honestly what you think my problem is and I'll go home and think about it. I won't say I'll change right away, but I'll take it into consideration."

But Nachmanson didn't see it that way. "You have *enough* ideas rattling around in your head," he said, puffing on his cigar (he always smoked Schimmelpennincks during the hour, giving the air in the room a strangely acrid smell). "That's one of your hangups, pal. . . . Did you ever stop and think how many times you say, 'On the one hand . . . on the other hand'?"

Though taken aback by this appraisal, Mike could acknowledge it to be valid. But in his work it was precisely this quality for which he was valued, his tendency to look at things calmly, from all angles. Did he really want to change all that?

One Friday evening in December Mike came over to Carol's apartment to spend a half hour with the girls. He was leaving that night for a weekend in Boston to give a lecture and visit some friends, the Helmstedders. Hence he would be unable to make his usual Saturday morning visit. On the way in, following Carol, he glanced at himself in the hall mirror. Tall, heavy set, beginning to gray, he still had a deceptively boyish, genial appearance, as though he had been cast for the wrong part in a play. Under his arm he had his leather briefcase, an old battered one, dating from graduate school days. It contained, along with the notes for his lecture, a pair of wrinkled blue pajamas. He thought of how his never having his pajamas ironed used to drive Carol crazy. But they got wrinkled in bed anyway, didn't they?

He had just had a crummy session with his analyst. He always hated going late in the day. By six o'clock he was pretty exhausted and the long drive downtown, plus the search for a parking space, was a final irritant. This session he began quite unexpectedly to talk about Carol and the affairs she had had, both when they were together and now that they were apart. Some had been with people he knew. Others he had only suspected or heard about. It seemed to him he had resolved all this; he could talk about it with detachment. He could see it her way. She had a right to have affairs, in a certain sense. Maybe he had been too uncommunicative, too. . . .

"Is that what you really think about it?" Nachmanson said. He kept battering Mike with questions, one after the other, until finally, at the end of the hour, Mike yelled, "Okay, I hate her for it! I hate her! I hate *them!* Does that satisfy you?" Naturally Nachmanson said nothing to indicate either satisfaction or dissatisfaction. The smiling Freudian bastard! What did it matter to him if she'd gone down for the whole Bulgarian merchant marine corps! Mike hurried out, only nodding to him briefly. When he got out in the cold December evening, wrapping his maroon scarf around his neck, he felt more than a little shaken at this burst of dark feeling that seemed to have come from nowhere and momentarily overwhelmed him.

Carol was going out on a date with a girl friend, the wife of the professor of Slavic languages at whose house she and Mike had met eight years earlier. The professor had a gourmet society meeting—he was taking lessons in Chinese cooking—and the two girls (they called each other girls, though Carol was thirty-three and the professor's wife forty-one) were going to see a double feature: a sexy Swedish picture and a Japanese horror movie that someone had said had remarkably good photography. Carol always went to the movies when she was depressed: good movies, bad movies, any movies. She sat, benumbed, munching Snickers bars, as entranced as a ten-year-old at Radio City. Mike had never liked movies, but then he was never depressed: He always sublimated. But for his sake, although she told herself the time for these childish games was past, she would have liked it to be a man with whom she was spending the evening. Two women of a certain age, husbandless. Maybe if we're lucky, we'll be picked up by two fairies in the lounge and get a free *caffè espresso* at Rienzi's afterward—great! She had arranged to meet Virginia at the theatre.

She, too, had just come out of an analytic session. Hers was at five thirty, leaving her just time to bolt home and give the girls their usual Friday-night supper: chicken chow mein, matzos, raspberry-ripple ice cream. She was fuming when she came out. It was the first time she had said nothing, not one solitary word, the whole hour. Oh, she had been silent before, deliberately or not, for five minutes, ten, but never once had she thought a whole hour would go by without a single exchange, even of hostilities. But once it had started, the silence, as though by inertia, had gone on and on until finally she felt that, even if she had wanted to, she could not have broken it. Sitting there in the chair, Carol had glanced up once and seen Dr. Furstenberg's intent, colorless eyes fixed on her, just the trace, she thought, of a smile on his lipless lips. Oh, how she hated him! He reminded her, sitting there, of her father, who would always come home after work and plotz into a chair in front of the seven o'clock news, not wanting or caring to talk to her or her sister, even if something special had happened at school. He reminded her of Mike who, at dinner, would listen to her when she was telling about the Women's Strike for Peace, outwardly sympathetic, inwardly detached, eyes glazed ("Can you repeat what I just said?" "Yes, I can.

You just said . . ." Even there he never missed a trick!). A kind of rage, a cold fury built up in her until she felt she wanted to get up and smash every damn Chinese vase in the office (Dr. Furstenberg collected Chinese vases set into small lighted alcoves, like prayer stands. Ought one to put pennies there? God, make me a more interesting neurotic!). At the end of the hour he got up, smiled, openly this time, and said, "So . . . we'll continue next time." Continue *what*? It was like Alice and having more tea when you hadn't had any to begin with.

For the first half hour Mike played with the girls. Carol stayed in the bathroom, ostensibly getting ready for her big night on the town, in fact, sitting morosely on the toilet seat reading the second half of *The New York Times*. When it was time for the girls to go to bed, Carol emerged, perfumed, gleaming, in a new striped dress. Mike looked at her with that blank, I refuse to comment expression she had seen on his face when he was lusting after some forbidden creature at a party. This gave her a small token of satisfaction.

They returned to the living room and sat warily facing each other.

"How're tricks?" she said.

"Okay." He still had that expression: I will say nothing that can be used against me. Did he think the place was bugged?

"You're going to—"

"Boston." He watched her cross her legs and begin unclipping her watchband, a habit she had when she was ill at ease. Why the perfume? She never wore it. He didn't like perfume. To show that someone does. Please, that's been proved, he felt like saying. Proved, proven.

She sat back and regarded him.

"I hear Ben was in town," he said.

"Oh, who was your source?"

"Muriel said she saw you at the Pinter."

"Yes, it wasn't very good."

"How *is* he?"

"Well enough . . . his wife may be divorcing him."

"That's a pity."

"Why?"

"Well, a two-time loser."

She sat forward, suddenly hostile. "Is *that* losing? What's winning, then?"

"Okay."

She continued examining him. "What's with the tie? Is this your mod phase?"

"Isn't it conservative enough? I thought you liked outlandish people."

"You're not the type."

"Maybe I'll *become* the type."

Carol smiled. "We could do this all night, couldn't we?"

"Sure."

"Why don't we not?"

"What, then?"

"Leave, if you like. . . . Don't you have a train to catch?"

"Ultimately."

She poured herself some sherry and sat coiled with the glass in her hand. "So, let's screw."

She said it just to test him, for no more or less devious motive.

"No thanks," he said.

"No time between trains?"

"There's time."

"Just not interested?"

In fact, he had had this fantasy a hundred times—coming back, screwing her, and leaving, and if it could have been just like that, as coldly and nastily satisfying as it was in his fantasy, he wouldn't have hesitated one second. Just do it and leave, leaving her to howl and scream and pull whatever tantrums she had up her sleeve at the moment, leave her to complain about too many orgasms or not enough—whatever! But it wouldn't work that way and he didn't feel like chancing anything else.

"Not interested," he said.

She said nothing. So, he was going to Boston. She knew whom he'd stay with, too—the Langens, probably, that bastard Hank Langen who, while she had been married to Mike, always used to take her aside, hold her hand, tell her how much he commiserated with her, and now, under the influence of his wife, that prissy slob, had dropped her completely, wouldn't even say hello when they met once in F. A. O. Schwarz's in front of the Teddy bears. Murder, she thought. One day I will commit murder. Not suicide: That would make him too happy. She said, "I took Janie around to Dalton today."

"Oh?" Mike lit a cigarette and didn't look at her. Having rebuffed her sexually, he felt, at the same time, an enormous sense of pride and an equally great sense of uneasiness. He would not be allowed to escape free for that.

"They have this special program for two-and-a-half-year-olds. I want to get her in it if I can."

"I thought there were all these local nursery schools," Mike said. "I thought you were going to try one of those."

"You can't *do* that," Carol said.

"Why not?"

"Because they're lousy, that's why."

"I thought Margie Klinger said—"

"Who cares what Margie Klinger said? . . . Look at her kid! She's a fat Mongoloid."

"But Dalton is pretty expensive, isn't it?" He tried to sit back and regard her calmly. He shouldn't have come, should have skipped a week and come next Saturday.

"Nine hundred," Carol said flatly, looking up at him deliberately, challenge in her eyes.

Mike tried to smile. "For nursery school? That's crazy!"

She stiffened. "In what *sense* is it crazy?"

"No, I take it back, not crazy—it's just, well, it's a hell of a lot of money, isn't it? I mean—"

"As a matter of fact, it isn't! No! Not at all. Nursery school is the most important experience a child can have. Are you going to ship them off to some pound, some—"

"Anyway, two and a half!" He crushed the cigarette out, not having taken two puffs. Wasn't he giving up smoking? "Can't she wait a year?"

"No, she cannot wait a year." She sat on the edge of the couch, legs crossed, looking tense and ready to leap at his throat.

Mike stood up. "Carol, listen, let's not get embroiled in some unnecessary thing. . . . I'd love to send her. I don't have the money. That's it. That's all there is to it."

"You do have it."

"I don't."

For a moment she wouldn't even answer him. Then she blurted out, "You don't have it for us, but you have it for the things you want, for your damn records, for your causes. You can donate to them, you can do plenty, if you want. Don't give me that."

"I don't have the money," Mike said, trying to hold back.

Suddenly Carol leaped up. She rose so quickly that her stocking caught; there was a tearing sound as the run slithered down her leg. "You do have it. Why do you lie?" she cried. Rushing into the bedroom where the girls were asleep, she stood, pointing, shouting, "Here! Tell them you don't have anything! Tell them you won't give us a cent! Here they are—tell them!"

"Damn it, why do you drag them into it?" Mike, furious, grabbed his coat and briefcase and headed for the door. "What kind of hell do you want to make for them?" In a minute, he thought, he would have hit her, something he had never done; he wasn't sure he was sorry to have been spared that satisfaction.

That Spring Carol went with her father and stepmother to Miami Beach for a three-week vacation. They thought she was looking run down and needed a rest. Her father rented a suite in a big luxury hotel overlooking the sea. Every day they all went down to swim. The girls loved it. They discovered a drink called Piña Colada, half pineapple juice, half coconut milk, which they consumed three or four times a day. The rest of the time they spent on the beach, running into the waves, playing in the sand, collecting sea shells. Carol's stepmother was a heavy woman with coarse, dyed red hair and a tendency to overdress. She wore cashmere sweaters with sequins all over them and plastic sandals through which you could see her purple-pink painted toenails. Each afternoon she and

Carol went up to the solarium and lay nude in the sun. Like a town through which a flood has passed, leaving its mauled and mutilated victims, the terrace was littered with the bodies of middle-aged women in varying stages of disintegration. Once, between marriages, Carol's stepmother had been a masseuse, going to the homes of rich women and massaging their opulent backs and bellies with firm, unsparing hands. She offered to massage Carol: It would "relax" her, she said. Carol refused and then, one day, accepted. With the sun beating down on all parts of her body, Carol lay on a red-and-white-striped mat while her stepmother, like a butcher tenderizing a piece of beef, pounded her all over with quick authoritarian gestures. It was not relaxing, it was a punishment, and Carol accepted it as such. With each blow Carol's stepmother kept on talking, derided men, accused them of infidelity, lust, cruelty, stupidity, and incompetence. These remarks, too, Carol accepted as a punishment, seeing in her stepmother the woman she would some day become. But she said nothing, simply lay, as still as a corpse, her eyes masked with blobs of cotton soaked in witch hazel, offering her beautiful, tanned face to the hot rays of the sun. At dinner she flirted, but ungraciously, with the hotel manager, a fattish man in a straw hat, and after that they all went down to watch little dogs racing around on a sandy track. Carol's father won a lot of money.

Mike was invited, in the month of July, to be a judge for a literary contest on an island off Italy. He was glad to go, not giving beans for the contest, for the sake of the free vacation and the chance of escape from Carol's lawyers, who were pursuing him with impossible demands for money. The island was nice; it was sunny. Mike was given a room in a villa with a British homosexual of fifty, a withered man with a face like a lump of Roquefort cheese who, over Italian vermouth, related long, droning stories about his hopeless love for an American boy who took his money and blackmailed him among his friends. Mike felt sorry for the man and was repulsed by him. He was glad when he met a girl, someone connected with the business end of the contest, who attached herself to him and with whom he began having an affair. She was an Italian girl, homely, with a long face and somber, suffering eyes. She knew English quite well, bit her nails and always insisted on paying her own way at cafés and in the theatre, calling this independence. She had read his essays in Italian and admired them. He liked her because she was quiet and didn't wear a girdle and cooked incredibly good meals for him which they ate in a courtyard in back of her house. He stayed with her in the evenings, usually leaving the next morning for one of the meetings connected with the contest.

One morning he woke up late—it was after eleven—and decided the hell with the contest. Filemina rushed out to her job. Alone in the airy, sunlit apartment, Mike made himself a large pot of coffee. Each morning Filemina made coffee for him and each morning he left hurriedly and had time only for a few sips. This morning, however, relishing his leisure, he sipped the coffee slowly, adding an extra pour of milk to mask its bitter taste. It was in this carefree, curiously detached mood (a foreign country, a foreign girl, a foreign cup of coffee) that he ambled to the door at noon to receive and sign for a telegram.

THOUGHT YOU'D BE GLAD TO KNOW IT'S OFFICIAL (OUR DIVORCE, REMEMBER?). P.S. GOT MARRIED YESTERDAY TO WIL TRAMPLER. LOVE, KISSES, CAROL.

Wil Trampler? Who the hell? The gastroenterologist who had told her she had beautiful jowls? The man who'd made a pass at her in her analyst's waiting room? It was only later in the day, sipping Chianti with Filemina on a moonlit terrace overlooking the Piazza Navone, that it came to him. Wil Trampler was the children's dentist, a genial, freckled man who was always wiping his hands on paper towels and giving out free lollipops. Mike saw him as in a vision, like those stuffed animals in the showcases at the Museum of Natural History—permanently surrounded by plaster casts of open, grinning mouths, joyfully tilting people back in his Formica chair, the better to torment them to health and future happiness. He raised his glass of wine. "To their health!" he said. "To the teeth of future generations!"

"Who?" Filemina, smiling charmingly, was afraid she had missed some reference in English. But Mike leaned forward and kissed her nose and she forgot all of that.

Norma Klein began publishing short stories while a student at Barnard College. Her work has appeared regularly in magazines such as Sewanee Review, New Campus Writing, *and* Mademoiselle; *and in 1963, 1968, and 1969 her stories were selected for the O. Henry Awards. Born and raised in New York City, she is a perceptive observer of human relationships set against a modern, urban environment. Several years ago Ms. Klein received a master's degree in Slavic languages from Columbia University, but she has since devoted herself exclusively to writing. She lives in Manhattan with her biochemist husband and two young daughters.*

The Smile

by A. Alvarez

*I*t had been years, and in that time her image had come and gone like a face in water. Now you see it, now you don't. At every moment of inattention it had been ready waiting to solidify, like a family ghost. It had no meaning in his everyday life, yet he couldn't lose it.

He had spotted her in the audience in that drab little college hall and thereafter had given his performance at her and for her. It was a charity function, raising money for one of the usual liberal causes—to stop some war or other; God knew which. He was a veteran of these occasions and was following standard procedure: Find a pretty face and then act to it; it improved his performance and gave him something to think about. At one point she smiled up at him, a slow, beautiful smile, like an exquisite change in the weather. That was a bonus he hadn't expected.

Afterwards, she stood by the wall near him while the old birds from the audience clucked admiringly around. Finally she managed to get in a question, and they began to talk. But almost immediately he was whisked away by the organizers. Just his luck.

He was, however, reckoning without her. He was to perform again that night at a club banquet twenty miles away: an all-male affair, black ties and pomposity. As he drove off the campus she was standing by the roadside with a girl friend, waiting for him. She was wearing a green silk blouse and a long velvet evening skirt that bagged slightly, as though she had made it herself. It seemed oddly inappropriate against the pine trees, and somehow pathetic. He stopped the car and the two girls climbed in. Where were they going? To hear him again. But it would be the same old performance. That was all right. And it was an all-male affair. They would worry about that. He should have been glad. Instead, he was appalled.

He had left them in town, thinking that would be that; male isolationism would triumph. He drove to his motel, took a long, slow bath, and slept uneasily until a car arrived to collect him. But when he got to the hotel ballroom where he was to perform, they were already installed, a clutch of young men fluttering hungrily around them. The chairman, in his introduction, had made some lumberingly graceful remarks about breaking the club rules for these two beautiful young ladies, twinkling at them over his spectacles.

So he had gone through his routine again, and couldn't take his eyes off her. When it was all over, the chairman drove him back to his motel and she, without saying a word, came with them. He sat in front of the little car, leaning slightly back; she was behind, leaning forwards. He could smell her hair, faint and clean. The chairman rambled on and on about the war and neither of them answered him, sunk in their own mute communications. When they reached his motel she simply got out with him, smiled charmingly at the chairman, thanked him, and said good night. The poor man sat on in his Volkswagen, not knowing what to do in his embarrassment. They walked into the motel room together, letting the sceen door bang to noisily, and didn't bother to turn on the light. The car engine churned away outside as though it were trying to apologize. She turned into his arms, her mouth soft and open, and they were far into their first parched kiss when the startled chairman finally drove away.

"What the hell," he said, "it's a charity performance."

For such a young girl, her body was full and easy and very experienced. Her expertise surprised him.

"Daddy is a doctor," she explained. "He put me on the Pill when I was fifteen."

"How old are you now?"

"Twenty," she lied.

At five o'clock the next morning he drove her back to the village among the pine trees. In the faint green dawn he kissed her quietly for the last time.

"I don't even know your last name," he said.

"Pike," she answered. "Nancy Pike. Like the fish."

He put her down at the edge of the village where he had found her—or she him—and drove on a little way to turn the car. When he came back, accelerating with relief away from the whole improbable scene, she was still standing forlornly where he had left her. They waved at each other and he watched her dwindle in his rear mirror. When he finally lost sight of her, she still hadn't moved.

Three months and several girls later he was back in New York. He lived by casual affairs, which tickled his actor's vanity, and this tour had provided a rich harvest. Yet he kept seeing her face: her long, blue eyes and soft, slightly pushed forward mouth. Her teeth were strong, even, and very white, as though they had been expensively looked after. Suddenly it became important that he should see her again. It took him an hour of telephoning to trace her to her doctor father's house. It was a smart address, just outside New York. Mercifully. She sounded surprised to hear him, and curiously shy. Sure, she would come on in. But it would take a little time. She would be there by five.

It was only noon. He wandered nervously around the apartment, unable to settle or read. Finally, he lay on the bed, his body hard and tense, as if wires had been drawn through it, and stared at the ceiling, his mind blank. Somewhere he felt irritated; this wasn't the usual procedure at all.

At five sharp the doorbell rang. She seemed smaller and younger than he had remembered. Her hair, when he kissed her, smelled of shampoo. So that was why she had been so long. But it was a good sign: Years of experience had taught him that a girl won't sleep with a man if she thinks her hair is dirty. A shampoo is a way of saying yes.

Not yet, however. She went and perched on a narrow chair, very proper and separate, and when she spoke her voice was guarded. But there was no hurry; he was pleased merely to be in her company again. So they sipped their drinks and chatted inconsequentially. Finally, he asked her about her father. Her face softened.

"Oh, he's fine. Just fine. But since Mummy left, he can't find anyone right for him."

"Maybe *you* should marry him."

"Maybe I should." And she smiled her beautiful smile like a child.

He set down his drink and went across to her, put his hands under her shoulders and drew her up. She came to him willingly and with relief. As they kissed he unbuttoned her blouse and skirt, unfastened her bra, and slipped them off. Then he gathered her up and carried her into the bedroom.

Afterwards, they lay together in silence while the room filled slowly with darkness.

"I'm hungry," she said at last.

"Me too. Where shall we eat?"

"What about Japanese?"

"Very soothing, all those shuffling girls. Which one?"

"I don't know. Tell you what. I'll phone the Japanese Embassy."

And she did. Face down, naked on the bed, she sweet-talked a startled official in a husky lover's voice, while he stroked her soft back: "But where would *you* go? I mean, if you wanted somewhere *really* special?"

"Christ," he said when she'd finished. "Why didn't you simply ask him to join us in bed?"

"You're jealous." She jumped off the bed, picked up a pillow and threw it at him. "Jealous." He threw it back, ducked as she came at him again with pillow upraised, and grabbed her round the waist, pulling her down onto him, his head in her heavy breasts. "She's still a child," he thought. And then she was kissing him seriously, deeply, not at all childishly.

Finally, they had their Japanese meal and went down to the Village to

103

listen to jazz. She held his hand all through the music, and whenever he looked at her she was watching him with wide, solemn eyes. It made him feel uneasy.

Driving back uptown, he asked her, "Are you sure you don't want to go home?" His voice was harsher than he intended.

"I will if you want me to."

"I mean, what about your father?"

"He won't care. He's used to it. But I'll go if you want me to."

"Of course not."

They drove in silence back to his borrowed apartment. He felt obscurely aggrieved, as though the girl were somehow imposing responsibilities on him he did not want. They made love in the pitch-dark, blindly. Despite his resentment, her softness was imperturbable.

He was leaving the next day, going back to his career and his girls in England. He was, after all, a famous actor and a famous supporter of liberal causes. He had done his bit in the States, now it was back to real work and real life.

They drove downtown in the shining summer air, the top of his rented convertible down and the radio playing. She sat close to him, her hand on his thigh. When they reached the bus terminal, they sat for a while in silence. He kissed her gently.

"That's it, then," he said.

"Yes. That's it."

She got out of the car quickly and flashed him her smile. Stunning.

"Take care," he said.

"I will." She smiled again and was gone.

As he drove away, he muttered to himself, "That was a close shave." He felt a great sense of relief and well-being.

That was when the haunting began. Her image kept floating up unexpectedly, breaking the surface of his mind like the bright ring of a fish rising. "Pike. Nancy Pike. Like the fish." He seemed to see her smile out of the corner of his eye at parties, and across the glare of the footlights. He smelt her scent suddenly on other girls and his mind seemed to dissolve. He found himself thinking about their lovemaking in the act of making love to someone else.

In London the girls came and went as usual. He had a long West End run and starred in a smart, arty movie. Both were huge successes. But they didn't stop appearing at the best-advertised political rallies. Everybody loved him: the moneymen, the radicals, the great oxlike paying public. He couldn't go wrong. But he also couldn't get her out of his mind.

Finally the call came, as it always does in the end, from Hollywood. So he arranged to stop off in New York on the way out to the Coast—in order to see his agent, he said.

The first thing he did was phone her father's house. A woman answered, young sounding.

"Is that you, Nancy?"

"No. This is Mrs. Pike. Nancy isn't here anymore. She's living in New York. Who is that speaking?"

He gave his agent's name, since his own was too famous. An old friend, he said. Could he have her number?

"Surely. But it's somebody else's apartment." The second Mrs. Pike sounded vaguely disapproving, but she gave him the number anyway.

When Nancy answered her voice was harsher than he remembered it.

"What are *you* doing in town?"

"Just passing through. Can I see you?"

"O.K. Tomorrow night. Come to dinner tomorrow."

"How's life?"

"Extremes. Sometimes terrible, sometimes beautiful. Never in the middle." The gush didn't sound like her either.

The address was off the Bowery, a drab, filthy building with a rusty fire escape down the outside and a luncheonette at the bottom. He took a long time to find the bell, which was hidden high up in the dark entrance.

A window opened on the top floor and a head peered out into the darkness.

"Nancy?" he called.

"Yeah." Something white fluttered down and landed in the gutter: a soiled handkerchief with a key tied to it. He opened the heavy door and started up the stairs. The walls, which had once been painted green, were peeling, and the iron banister looked too dirty to touch. Halfway up, an elderly man passed him, coming down. His gray hair was combed forward in a fringe, and he had a gray, lined, slightly simian face. His clothes were elegant, faintly queer.

He supposed it was Nancy waiting for him on the top landing, but he didn't recognize her. The face before him had only the vaguest, most tenuous connection with the one he had known years before. It was as though the finger of God had descended and scooped the life from it. The skin was tight over the bones, the cheeks waxy and hollow, the long eyes dull. Even her beautiful mouth was stretched tight over her teeth in a death's-head smile. Her body, which had been plump and smooth, was now frail as a skeleton. The bones showed through at her shoulders and hips, at her elbows and knees. Her hair was lank, her clothes filthy. Her life had gone elsewhere and there would be no resurrection.

"I've brought some whiskey," he said, following her into the kitchen.

"You have it. I don't drink anymore. I smoke. Do you?"

"Smoke?"

"Pot, hash, that sort of thing."

"Sometimes. It's not really my scene."

"Want some now? I do."

"I'd prefer a drink."

"The ice is in there. I'll go fix a smoke. I haven't even started dinner yet." She giggled helplessly, fumbling in the icebox, and brought out a package of pinkish-gray frozen chicken.

"There's no hurry," he said.

"That's nice."

He poured himself a large drink and followed her into the studio, a long room cluttered with rubbish. There was a Mexican hammock at one end, a sleeping cat hanging over it like a dead thing. Against one wall was a plaster rockery, studded with colored lights. From the ceiling hung more colored lights, flashing on and off a sign that read "Joe." At the near end of the room was a workbench scattered with sculptor's tools. By it stood a large, unfinished plaster torso of a woman, convulsed, arms outflung, huge buttocks in the air, as though frozen in an epileptic fit. Whoever had done it had no talent; he simply hated women.

"Who's Joe?" he asked, patting the plaster rump.

"The guy I live with. He'll be back later."

"I passed him on the stairs, didn't I?"

"Yeah."

"A bit old for you."

"He's a year older or younger than my father. Poor old Pa. It took him a year to say hullo. But now he's reconciled to it."

"How long have you been together?"

"A couple of years. Since soon after Pa remarried."

There were mattresses on the floor, covered with fur rugs. He settled down with his drink. Nancy rummaged around at the far end of the room and came back with a large cigar box. When she opened it he saw a jumble of cigarette papers, bottles of pills and powders, lumps of this and that wrapped in silver foil, a sealed pastille tin, a woman's vanity mirror, a cardboard tube, and a small pipe with a rubber stem and copper bowl. She unwrapped one of the silver-foil packets and put some dark lumps into the pipe.

"Hash," she said. "Real good stuff." She lit it carefully, inhaled deeply, and handed him the pipe. He sucked on it dutifully.

"Good, eh?" she said.

"It's O.K.," he answered. "What else do you take?"

"Opium sometimes. Pills. You know."

"What about the hard stuff?"

"No, never. I've got troubles without that. And no acid either. I don't like to lose my cool. I just like to relax a little."

"You've changed a lot," he said.

"I've taken off over thirty pounds," she said, misunderstanding him, "but I like it that way. It makes me feel my body is all my own."

"How did it happen?"

"Well, everything happened. I had some kind of a breakdown. The sum-

106

mer after you left, that was. I'd flunked Spanish, so every morning I had Spanish lessons, and every afternoon I went to the shrink. But that all blew up. I went down to Washington with him and . . ."

"You mean you had an affair with your analyst?"

"Kind of." She seemed unperturbed. "Then I was on amphetamines. That takes off your weight. Then last year Joe and I got busted."

"Why?"

"Dope. They raided us. He was holding some stuff for a friend. We had enough to give all Manhattan a high."

"What happened?"

"Nothing. We spent the night in jail. Then we paid off everybody and they gave us the usual deal. You know: 'When analyzed the substance proved to be sugar.' Blah, blah, blah. And that was that."

She gave him the ghost of her beautiful smile and lapsed into silence, puffing away at her ridiculous, rubber-stemmed pipe.

"How about dinner?" she said at last.

"Forget it. I'd rather drink."

"Fine. I'll fix us a sandwich."

He followed her back into the kitchen. Her skinny buttocks and fragile arms made her seem more of a child than ever. He felt he was falling down a great black shaft of depression.

They ate standing up in the kitchen, then went back to their separate rugs in the studio. The cat unslung itself from the hammock and rolled on its back in the crook of Nancy's thin body, waiting for its stomach to be scratched. She poked around in the box of drugs, and finally selected a phial of white powder.

"Isn't that coke?" he asked. "I thought you weren't on the hard stuff."

She only nodded, carefully tapping two streams of powder onto the vanity mirror. She put the white cardboard tube into one nostril and sniffed up a stream of powder, put the tube into the other nostril, sniffed again, and leaned back smiling. She had a delicate, finely shaped nose. She should have been a great beauty.

"That's fine," she said contentedly, "just fine. Want to try some?"

He shook his head and bent toward her.

"I was in love with you, Nancy," he said. "In all this time, I couldn't get you out of my mind."

"I was in love with you, too, for a while. But that's all past."

"Give me twenty-four hours. Come with me for twenty-four hours."

She shook her head. "I can't anymore. I used to do that kind of thing to Joe, but it's not worth it anymore. It hurts him too much."

"Do you care?"

"Kind of. He's what I've got for the time being. There's no point in screwing it up."

"But it won't last."

"No, it won't last. But it's O.K. for the moment."

"You've grown up," he said, "in a way."

She smiled her ghostly smile, got to her feet, and disappeared into an alcove which served as a bedroom. He could hear her opening drawers and shuffling through papers. At last she came back into the studio and handed him a cardboard folder.

"Remember me?" she said.

He opened the folder. She stood there in a soft white dress, smiling radiantly down at whoever it was who kneeled in front of her with his camera.

"That was taken the year we met," said Nancy.

"With a smile like that you could have gone places, darling."

"I have," she replied.

A. Alvarez is a critic, essayist, editor, poet, and short-story writer. Educated at Oxford, he taught there and in the United States for several years, and still makes occasional academic forays to this country—most recently as Visiting Professor of English at the State University of New York. He has been poetry editor and critic of The Observer, *and drama critic for* The Spectator. *In 1961 Mr. Alvarez received the Vachel Lindsay Prize for poetry from* Poetry *magazine. His latest book is* THE SAVAGE GOD, *a study of suicide. He lives in London with his wife, Ann Alvarez, also a writer.*

Zalman's Galatea

by Lynne Reid Banks

~~~~~~~~~~~~~~~~~~~~~~

Zalman noticed her legs first—partly because he was what is vulgarly known as a legs man, and partly because they were the first bit of her that he saw, coming down the stairs into the basement cafeteria where he was having his lunch. They were not far from being the loveliest pair of legs he had ever seen on a woman, and he was a man who knew.

His eyes moved upward as she descended. Her figure was also something quite out of the ordinary, what could be discerned of it through a highly unbecoming flannel dress and oversize trench coat, both in shades of mud. By the time he got around to her face, she had turned away and was choosing her food at the counter; but she had softly curling hair of a really extraordinary shade of reddish brown, screwed up carelessly at the back of her neck.

Zalman felt outraged. What a little sloven! How could a woman like that, with such natural assets, bury herself in such awful clothes and twist up her hair in that dreary way? Her shoes, too, he noticed, bordered on the criminal— brogues almost; the seams of her stockings wove like convolvulus stalks up those superb legs, and disappeared—too soon—beneath the hem of the putty mac. All Zalman's professional feelings, as well as his personal ones, were affronted, for he was a models' agent and accustomed to beautiful girls whose one obsession was to make the absolute best of themselves.

As the girl moved along the self-service counter, Zalman soothed himself by imagining how he would like to see her dressed. His ideas were conventional, but sound—seamless stockings, black shoes with medium heels (she was above average in height), a suitably fitted dress in . . . sharp acid yellow, perhaps, with cinnamon thingamies, accessories. Of course a lot would depend on the color of her skin and eyes. . . . He waited with some impatience for her to pay her bill, pick up her tray and turn around.

When she did so, he got a highly unpleasant shock.

She was ugly. So ugly that he sucked in his breath and turned his eyes instinctively away. To him ugliness, stark ugliness, in a woman was something unforgivable. Women had to be beautiful; what was the point of them, otherwise? To Zalman, women were in a class with flowers, paintings, music—they had no function but to decorate the world, to amuse, intrigue and delight men like himself. He had never demanded more of a woman than this; but nor could he settle for less, and women who were not clearly lovely and delightful seemed to him almost an insult to his whole philosophy of life.

In the ordinary way he would have put this girl out of his mind at once and taken care not to look at her again; but she was so spectacularly awful looking that he found her perversely fascinating. It would have been rather hard not to look at her, anyway, inasmuch as she was sitting right opposite him at the next table. As soon as she had sat down, she took a book out of the scruffy bag swinging from her shoulder, opened it, put on horn-rimmed glasses and began to read and eat at the same time.

Zalman somehow found he could not take his eyes off her now. His sense of outrage was dulled by pity. Poor little thing, he found himself thinking—poor little wretch! What chance has she of anything in this world? And he found himself feeling angry, too, for surely some of what was so offensively wrong could be put right. To begin with, she had at some time broken her nose, which was now a flattened and grotesque small replica of a boxer's; her upper lip was so short that for a moment he thought she had a harelip, and her chin was long, almost comic, like a clown's. Her eyes were hidden, but her eyebrows were too thick, her forehead too high for anyone but a ballet dancer—an uncompromising shiny dome; and instead of giving herself a fringe to help it, she had scraped her front hair straight back as if defiantly saying: "Have a good look! I'm just as ugly as this, and I won't hide any of it!"

He stared and stared, something burning in him. He wanted to go to her and say, "Look here, I don't know you, but you can't go around looking like that. Go to a plastic surgeon and get your nose fixed; pluck your eyebrows; cut your hair thus and so, and learn something about makeup. . . ." Something could be done. The nose was the worst. Remedy that, and the rest would not be so bad. But meanwhile—no wonder she was badly dressed. What woman would bother about her clothes, if she had a face like that?

Eventually she closed her book, and without bothering to take off the heavy glasses stood up and walked swiftly out. She did not linger or glance about her, as most women do. She walked badly, like a soldier—in fact she marched, her flat rubber-soled shoes lightly squeaking on the floor. She walked up the stairs and disappeared.

Zalman got up and followed her.

What are you doing? he asked himself. You're mad! But it was no use. He couldn't let her go—looking like that. The walk had been too much for him—

that chin-up, defiant, mannish stride. He had watched hundreds of women walk, and could interpret every movement, though he had not even known it until this moment. That girl was on the very brink of *really* not giving a damn anymore, as distinct from pretending she didn't. And that was perhaps the saddest and most compelling thing Zalman had ever seen in all his twenty-seven soft and undemanding years.

Outside, sunshine spilled onto the lunchtime crowds. He had long ago decided that the women of his city were growing prettier and prettier. Perhaps it was the extra milk and orange juice they had had as children (he had had it, too, and jokingly attributed his handsome face and sturdy six feet of never-failing health to this); or maybe it was because they were dressing better; or maybe it was simply that he loved women and could see beauty or at least a certain attractiveness in most of them. But now he did not notice them. He pushed his way quickly after his quarry, who was striding along in the direction of a side-turning off the main road. He turned down it, and he had to break into a run for fear of losing her.

When he turned the corner, she had gone, but there was only one place she could have gone to in the time—into the stage door of one of the big city theaters. The irony of it struck him—a girl like that, involved in that most glamorous of worlds.

Without giving himself time to think, he went up to the old stage door keeper. "Excuse me, could you tell me where I can find the girl who just went in?"

The old boy looked up grudgingly from his racing page. "Which girl? I didn't notice no one."

Nobody would ever notice her pass, Zalman thought. "You know, the one with the—" his hand went automatically up toward his nose, but quite sharply he stopped it, and concluded: "with the beautiful figure."

The old man sniffed. "Didn't see no one." He bent again to study the form.

At a loss, Zalman stood waiting for inspiration. After a moment, the door keeper gave a grunt and mumbled, "Oh. Wait a tick. Yers. I think Miss Stephens went past. Yers, I think she did. She'll be in the prop room. Downstairs and to your right, next the stage. You a friend of hers, are you?" But Zalman was halfway down the stone stairs and didn't answer.

He found her in a strange half room, like a three-sided box with no lid, adjoining the echoing roofless cavern of the stage. Everything was dark but the boxlike room, and that was like something out of a child's dream, half practical reality and half deceptive fantasy. The trestle tables were loaded with artificial fruit and flowers, bottles and baskets, plates of unreal food, a pile of bright clothes, a feather duster, some stuffed animals and a lot of other things which would normally have drawn Zalman, fingering and exploring, into every corner, for he was a man who had never outgrown his childhood delight in ingenious

111

imitations or the trappings of illusion. But in the midst of the bright welter was the girl, busy arranging things in order on the trestle and checking a list. From the back, she excited him again; she had taken off the trench coat and the flannel dress gave her body a touching quality of beauty curtained and disguised. But when she turned at the sound of his footsteps, her face almost made him quail. She still had the glasses on and she looked terrible.

"Hello, are you looking for someone?"

He closed his eyes for a moment as she spoke. Her voice was magic. Funny how rare it is for a beautiful model to have a lovely, low, musical voice like that. What a waste, in a way, like the legs, like the figure! But that was unfair. Nature's compensation. Why shouldn't she have a pleasant voice? It was probably nothing out of the ordinary, really; it only seemed so by contrast with the face it emerged from.

"I think I'm looking for you," he said, and now his mind began to race, for he had made no plan. "Miss Stephens, isn't it?"

"Yes, that's me."

In her own domain, she lost the defensive stiffness he had been so shocked to notice before. She was relaxed, standing with her weight on one hip, an expression of mild curiosity on her face and none of that affectation in her manner which a normally endowed girl will always adopt in the presence of a strange man, none of the muted challenge, the earliest feelers going out: Are you interesting? Are you interested? Is this the beginning of something important? Zalman was only now aware of how inevitable that was, and what a strange relief it was for once to find the challenge absent.

He felt himself wanting to relax, to be himself, to get to know her. But he had pursued and picked up too many girls in too many situations which called for quick thinking and ingenuity, and without stopping to think he launched into his line.

"I'm Zalman Thurston of Darren's—you know, the model agency. I noticed you just now in the cafeteria. I do hope you won't run away with the wrong idea, but I'd be awfully grateful if you'd consider doing occasional photographic work for us."

Her whole manner changed. Without actually having moved, her body seemed to have gone taut, and her face closed. Her voice was like the torn edge of a piece of metal now, when she said, "Is this your idea of a joke?"

He felt for a moment so overcome that he wanted to turn and run. He had said what he always said, unthinkingly, but this time it had been something so terribly wrong that he had hurt her to a point where *he* felt he could not bear it. They stared at each other, he in shame, she in ice-cold patience waiting to hear how he would extricate himself. For a moment he saw strange depths in her eyes, depths of pain that frightened his undeveloped, shallow soul.

At last he swallowed and managed to say, with something like dignity,

"Miss Stephens, you have a beautiful figure. A model's figure. Surely you've been told that before now."

"What would you do?" she asked immediately. "Photograph me from the neck down and give me the head of some girl with a beautiful face and a body like a gorilla?"

The crudeness of the comparison spoke her unhappiness, the constant misery of ugliness. He could hardly forgive himself. Presumably she forgot sometimes, when she was alone here and working, and he had come barging in and reminded her. He saw her move a step backward, and was surprised to see that his hand had gone out toward her without his instruction. He hastily withdrew it. He saw that there was nothing more he could do or say for the moment. She was frozen shut against him.

"Please forgive me if I offended you," he said. She gave a funny, stiff little nod, and he went away. Back in his office, shaken but safe, he decided to forget her. What, after all, could he actually do about her? It had been just one of his crazy impulses. He spent the afternoon arranging sittings and appointments for one flawless girl after another, looking at their photos, dialing their numbers, interviewing them, praising them to fashion editors and photographers. He dealt in beauty for three hours, and at the end of it he wondered why he felt so stale, and why he was still thinking about that squashed nose and those thick brows and that long chin. Could it be that one needs relief, even from glamour?

At half-past five, she was still in his mind; she was there an hour later when he was taking his shower and changing for an evening that he was not aware of having planned, and she was no fainter at half-past seven when, with a feeling of utter helplessness, he presented himself once more at the stage door.

This time the old man was more alert. "Here, you can't go in just now! The curtain's gone up. Miss Stephens can't see you now, she's busy."

Zalman checked. A reprieve—a sign from fate! But he heard himself asking anxiously, "When will she finish?"

"Five past ten, curtain down," said the door keeper. "Want to leave a message?"

"No," said Zalman. "No message."

He went away again. He did not know what to do with the evening—a most unusual situation for him. It was ludicrous to hang around for nearly three hours—why? For what? He stood in the alley, cursing himself for this folly. Why didn't he ring up one of his many enchanting girl friends and take her out to dinner? But he didn't want to.

Eventually he went round to the front of the theater, bought a seat and watched the play. Actually he was watching the props. He recognized many of them, and it was pleasing to think of Miss Stephens having set them all out in their appointed places before the rise of the curtain. He felt obscurely satisfied when the right articles came into the right hands at the appropriate moments. He didn't notice the play. He was trying desperately to think. He wanted to heal the hurt he had caused her this afternoon. Beyond that, he could not plan.

After the show, he went round again and waited until all the actors and their friends had emerged, and then slipped in and down the stairs. She was moving briskly about the empty stage, putting things away and tidying up. She wore a shabby denim skirt and a dark red man's shirt with the sleeves rolled up carelessly on her smooth, round arms. Even her elbows were pretty. She was not wearing the glasses, but her face remained ugly.

She stopped dead when she saw him and there was a long and difficult silence. Zalman, who was never silent with women, unless by design, felt like a complete fool standing there with cold shivers of embarrassment running over his shoulders. Madness! Why was he torturing himself?

But there she stood; her hands were small and perfect, holding a vase of wax flowers, and when he looked at the place where her throat disappeared into the neck of the old red shirt he was more moved than he had been by the whole perfect body of the last girl he had looked at.

"Please," he blurted out at last, "will you come out with me when you've finished and have dinner with me?"

He had never said anything so gauche in his life, nor felt so clumsy.

"Why?" she asked.

"Because I want you to. I want you to," he repeated helplessly.

That face, that face! Every time he looked at it, he shivered. But he could not look away. She had to say Yes—he had to hear that thin, embittered mouth saying Yes.

He took her to a new place, very chic, very expensive. He chose it because of the brightness of the lights there; he didn't want her to think he would only take her somewhere dim and quiet. She had had nothing to change into, and ordinarily he would have been cringing before the headwaiter's disapproving glances, but he was so overjoyed that she had come at all that he did not notice.

They talked—stiffly at first, but then gradually, as the marvelous food and wine did its work, more freely, more happily. The specter of the afternoon's fiasco drifted away. She relaxed a little, putting her delicate forearms on the table and playing with the flower arrangement. Her hands fascinated him. The skin on them seemed to shine with smoothness and he longed to touch them, but then her face would get in the way.

He tried to find out about her, but she was very reserved—oddly so. Her name was Ruth; she was twenty-five—nearly as old as he—and had been in the theater since she was eighteen. She was currently studying lighting and hoped to be a director some day. It was clear the theater was very important to her, yet he felt there were whole areas of her life about which she was deliberately saying nothing. She lived alone, and said she liked it. Of course he did not believe her.

Watching her hands, which she had begun to use in lovely, fluent gestures, he asked idly, "Did you never want to be an actress?"

The hands became still and lifeless, and the exquisite voice lost its musical timbre. "You do manage to say the damnedest things," she said with a flat note of irony.

This was the moment, perhaps. He could retreat, or forge on. He decided to forge. "I don't understand," he said blankly.

"Look at me."

"I am."

"Do you see the face of an actress?"

"Actresses," he said, "have all sorts of faces."

"None like mine, I dare swear," she said with a grim quaintness.

The casual approach seemed best, though very risky. "Well, I don't actually remember one with a broken nose, but that could easily be fixed if it mattered to you."

"If it mattered——!" Her voice went almost shrill for a moment and she stopped at once. There was a longish silence while she looked down at the tablecloth. "It does matter," she said quietly at last.

"Well, then——?"

She looked swiftly up at him; her eyes, which were very dark brown, stared at him intensely. "I can't talk about it casually," she said in a low, strained voice. "Do you mind?"

"I didn't mean to sound casual," he said.

"It would be a little nearer the truth to say that I can't easily talk about it at all," she said. "I know I'm u-ugly." It was the first time he had ever heard anyone stammer over a vowel. "Don't say anything please. It doesn't matter."

"It does matter!" he said with sudden urgency.

"To me, yes," she said. "But not to anyone else. Please let's stop. I——I was having such a good time until we began about it."

Zalman felt the strangest sensation in his throat, as if he were going to weep. But he changed the subject, and gradually she relaxed again. Afterward he took her home in a taxi. It was dark, and he felt strongly moved to take her in his arms. It was partly because being in a taxi with a girl after dinner automatically set in motion certain conditioned reflexes, but what was not so automatic was the fact that he did not touch her. This time it was not her face, which he could not see; it was a reluctance to let her think him the type of man who always makes passes at girls in taxis. Particularly since this was more or less the truth.

She lived in a rather shabbier district than he would have imagined. Surely stage managers in big city theaters were rather well-paid? It was not exactly a slum, but the terraced houses were all alike in their drabness and the street was ill lighted and without trees. It did not suit her. He helped her out of the taxi and went with her through the creaking gate and up the narrow tiled path to her front door.

She put out her hand, and when he held it, his own tasted its smoothness for the first time and found it sweet. There was very little light coming through the glass panel in the door, and with her small hand in his it was almost impossible to stop himself from kissing her, but he held back; the odd thing was that it was not wholly the knowledge of what she looked like that restrained him, but something else. Despite the disturbing depths of knowledge in her eyes, he chose to believe that she was unused to such precipitate behavior and would not welcome it.

"May I see you again?"

"Do you really want to?"

"Yes."

There was a pause, and she gave a small sigh. "I wish I understood all this," she said.

So do I, he thought.

"Come swimming with me on Saturday."

"I can't—we've got a matinee."

"Sunday, then. We could go in the morning and have lunch there."

She hesitated. "Where—the sea?"

"I thought, my club. It's just outside town. It's very nice. The water's heated," he added urgently, for he feared she would find some pretext to refuse.

"But I can't swim."

He nearly said, "With your figure, you should live in a bathing suit," but he didn't because every reference to her looks seemed to offend her, and anyway it sounded cheap. You could say such things to a model, but . . . "Maybe I could teach you," he said instead. "It's just a matter of believing you won't sink."

There was another short silence and then she gave a queer little chuckle. "All right," she said. "But if it's a matter of confidence, I don't suppose I shall be able to learn."

Sunday was a day of sunlight and perfection. He called for her at ten o'clock in a car even more glistening clean than usual, and she came out shyly, wearing dark glasses and a head scarf pulled well forward to throw kindly shadows on her face.

She had on a summer dress of plain dark blue and white, her lovely arms bare to the shoulders and her feet in leather sandals, and carried an old wicker basket containing a rolled-up towel, some apples and a bar of chocolate with nuts.

"I didn't know how far it was," she excused these items. "Perhaps we might get hungry on the way."

Zalman wished he'd thought of it. She got in beside him. The roof was down and the wind of their motion soon blew the scarf back off her face. He kept glancing sideways at her. The squashed profile was immobile, rather tense. Each time he looked at her she turned her head slightly away. After a while he suddenly put his hand over hers which lay in her lap and said impulsively, "Don't do that."

She made a startled little movement of her head, but didn't ask what he meant. "I can't help it," she said. "I don't like to be looked at."

"I wouldn't look at you if I didn't want to."

"That doesn't follow," she said seriously. "Lots of people look at me because they can't quite believe it."

Tragic though this was, Zalman found himself wanting to laugh. He did laugh. She turned right around in her seat to stare at him. "What do you find funny?" she asked him in her defensive voice.

"I don't know," he answered quite honestly. "Nothing, really. I was laughing because I feel happy and silly, not because anything's actually funny."

She stared at him a little longer, and then said slowly, "If you can laugh at my face, I suppose that's better than——"

He was still holding her hand and watching the streaming road. They were out in the country now, and the world seemed utterly free and beautiful. He breathed a deep lungful of fresh air and almost sang, "Oh, never mind about your face today! It doesn't matter! Look how marvelous everything is!"

He put his foot down on the accelerator and the additional speed flung them both back against their seats. After a long moment, she slowly faced forward again and he felt her hand relax in his. Later still, the limp fingers curled round his own as she suddenly pointed—"Look, look! A magpie! Two!"

"One for sorrow, two for joy," he said. "Salute them, quick, or it won't work."

"I waved. Will that do?"

"While you could still see them?"

"Yes."

"Then it's all right," he said judiciously. "They accept waves."

The pool was almost indigo, and cool as a sapphire in the green velvet of the lawns. Miraculously, there were not too many people. He changed into his trunks and spread a towel on the velvet to wait for her. The flowerbeds were like heaps of colored stuffs from a glorious Victorian ragbag; the thrushes and blackbirds sang wildly in the cedars. There was a smell of flowers, pine, chlorine and roasting meat. Zalman lay back and stared at the sky, thinking of nothing specific, only feeling happy in all his senses.

She came walking toward him, in a new bathing suit. Her body moved with a mixture of awkwardness and natural grace; she was embarrassed by her unwonted nakedness, but she must have known that every eye was upon her, and she held herself tall and tried to hide her painful self-consciousness. Her arms were held stiffly, but at least she did not stride. He could not take his eyes off her as she approached. She was so beautifully shaped that even he, confident to the point of conceit, had a moment of disbelief that it was to him that she was coming.

She sat down quickly beside him, trying to curl her long legs up under her. "Why are they all staring at me?" she whispered.

"Don't you know?"

"I feel so embarrassed."

"There's no need. They're looking at you the way you looked at the magpies—in pure pleasure and admiration because you're so lovely."

She did not look at him, but at the grass beside her knees, and she began to play with it with one hand. "It's strange," she said. "I've always known my body was all right. But it's no help. It even seems irritating—a waste, like having a box of treasure on a desert island."

At this, Zalman felt an all but overpowering wave of emotion. What it was, exactly, he couldn't be sure—whether it was compassion, pure physical well-being, or attraction, or what; but he had a wild urge to fling himself at her, knock her over onto the soft grass, and roll about with her as if they had been two crazy children—to twist his fingers in that curly hair, to hold her tight and hear her laughing and shrieking while he tickled and bit and kissed her. He thought he would explode if he didn't let himself do all this immediately. So he jumped to his feet with a violent start, and without saying a word or looking back took a wild, running dive down the slope and into the pool.

When he had churned his way up and down it for four lengths without pausing for breath, he felt safer—or rather saner. He swam to the side nearest her, and found her sitting straight up staring at him with big round eyes, like a startled squirrel.

"Come on in!" he called.

She rose like Venus and came toward him.

"What came over you just then?"

"Don't know—just had to take some action," he said. "Come down here, where it's shallow." She sat on the edge with her legs in the water, and he dared to put his hands on her incredibly slender waist to help her to jump in. She was not wearing a cap, and her hair gleamed like oiled teak in the strong sun. She splashed about, then let him tip her forward, lying trustfully on his spread hands and making inefficient stirring motions with her hands.

"Kick—kick!" he urged her. "Push the water with your hands!" He had never met a girl who couldn't swim with consummate ease; her frowning, concentrated efforts to obey touched him, and so did her delight in the unaccustomed feeling of the water flowing past her skin.

"Don't suddenly let go—don't leave me!" she implored him, and he felt happy that she would soon learn that she could trust him.

Afterward they lay side by side in the sun and then dressed and went into the clubhouse for lunch. Everything in the dining room seemed to sparkle—the white linen, the silver, the crystal; there were garden flowers on each table, and wine in beaded buckets of ice. This club was really an unwarranted extravagance for a young man in Zalman's position; he had actually joined for reasons of conquest—business and social—all more or less unworthy; and although it would not be true to say this was the first time he had enjoyed himself here, it was certainly the first time he had really felt sure it was worth the money.

It was Ruth's pleasure in everything which principally delighted him. Over the loganberries and whipped cream, she gave a sudden sigh.

"What is it?" he asked anxiously.

"Contentment," she replied, adding: "Too placid a word, perhaps."

His heart was stung with joy. He felt genuinely alarmed for the first time.

He had thought himself in love every other month since he was sixteen, but some deep honesty had always informed him that he was only playing at it. This reliable inner voice was keeping remarkably quiet now.

After lunch they went for a walk. She walked at a little distance from him, and every time her hand swung past his he wanted to reach for it. A suddenly awakened instinct of self-preservation prevented him. One could not just pretend that the ugliness of that face had vanished—it had not, in fact he could not understand how he had spent the last three hours in its presence without being aware of it.

Was it conceivable that one's affections could completely bypass a face like that? He did not really believe it, not of himself. Higher, nobler men than he might find it possible, but he had only to imagine for a moment introducing that face to any of his smooth young friends as his special person, be it girl friend or wife, to produce in himself an effect of inward quailing. But the soft, free hand kept on swinging past his, and at last his own reached out of its own accord and took it. . . .

The madness went on. He kept seeing her. Even when he was not with her, he kept seeing her, and he stopped seeing other women. The ravishing faces he had before his eyes all day meant no more to his libido now than pictures on postcards. He tried to reason with himself each week as Sunday drew deliciously nearer. What had set him off on all this? He had wanted, simply, to improve her. A kind impulse, nothing more. Well, perhaps it had a bit of the old power complex mixed in with it, but what harm, if it were a power for good? He was trying to get back to this original objectivity one afternoon as they walked high on a crest behind the club—which in the meantime had subtly become "their place" to such a degree that he could no longer bring other people there.

He broke a long patch of peaceful silence to begin: "Ruth——"

"Yes?"

"May I talk to you?"

"About my face." She did not ask, she stated.

"You once said it mattered. I can see how it might, to you." *I sound as if it didn't to me*, he thought. *I'm not being honest.* "I only wondered . . ."

"How it happened to me?"

"No. That, no." And it was true. He had never wondered *how*, only why she endured it. But now he did. "Tell me."

"It's an unpleasant story," she said in a flat voice in which he was surprised to detect a note of warning. He smiled confidently.

"Nonetheless . . . if you want to, of course."

She paused for a moment in her walk, as if debating with herself, and then walked slowly on, looking ahead.

"I was never exactly a raving beauty, but I used to take steps . . . my eyebrows, my hair—I was clever about makeup in those days. I even managed to make this spade-like chin look vaguely aristocratic. So successful were all these aids to nature that I actually contrived to . . ." Once more she stopped, and this time turned to him, a sudden clear look of challenge in her face. "Do you really want to hear all this?"

"Yes."

"I've never told anyone before."

He felt self-assured, strong and male. He touched her wrist. "Tell me."

She stared at him for a moment, gave a little shrug, and went on. "I attracted a young man. As it might have been, yourself." Her manner had changed. There was a hardness now that threatened into cynicism. "He was a marvelous-seeming young man, more, far more than I had ever dared to hope for. I was so bowled over by my good fortune, that I forgot the advice that all wise mothers give to their daughters. Not that I ever had a wise mother; but I heard the advice, of course, so I can't plead ignorance as my excuse."

Zalman felt a numb whiteness in his head as if he'd been suddenly struck. Underneath his would-be worldliness, he was a very, very conventional young man. That is not to say that he himself was highly moral; but he suffered from the double standard.

Ruth continued, "We both behaved atrociously. I don't, of course, mean by going to bed together. He behaved badly because he made love to me for reasons that were connected with my well-made body and not with his own emotions. I behaved badly because, when I came to realize this, I grew dishonest in my desperation to marry him. I was in love with him, but I don't suggest that that excused my quite deliberately getting pregnant."

Zalman was so shocked that he had to stop walking. His mouth was dry and he couldn't look at her.

"Do you want me to stop?"

Her voice was gentle, but there was a thread of very feminine mockery in it too. He sat down on the turf and shook his head.

She leaned against a tree and stared at the view. "When I presented him with my—ultimatum—he reacted in a way which will perhaps seem shocking to you. It did to me, too, at the time. But looking back on it, perhaps it was no more than I deserved. This strikingly handsome, well-set-up, well-bred and soft-spoken young man suddenly went quite black in the face with rage. He must have guessed at once that I'd done it on purpose. He didn't say a word. He stood in front of me, doubled up his fist, drew it back—I remember looking at it, thinking 'It's coming'—and punched me in the face."

Zalman felt sick. "Enough?" she asked, and now her voice was wholly kind.

He shook his head again, staring at the ground. She continued in the same quiet voice, "I never actually saw him again. I had the baby. It wasn't . . . right. Not because he'd hit me; I asked that. I wanted it to be that. But it wasn't. It had just happened—it can happen. Tell me, do you think one should keep such babies, or put them in homes?"

"I don't know," he said thickly.

"I didn't know either," she said. "I still don't know. I had no one to ask—no one of my own, I mean. So I asked the experts—the doctors and so on. They said I must put her away. They said it was the only thing I could do. So I did it."

There was a very long silence. Zalman was pressing his hand hard down on a sharp stone, and that was helping him a very little to retain a sense of reality.

"They are very expensive, those places," she went on at last. "It's right that they should be, of course. It helped me to have to pay a lot. Of course it didn't really help—nothing does. You think all the time that you should have her at home with you—somehow. But you don't. You go on with your life and you take a check with you each month when you go to visit. I won't tell you about the visits. That is something very private and very terrible, not to be wished onto anyone else."

He managed to look up at her. She was standing perfectly still against the tree trunk, her hands folded in front of her and her eyes moving over the blue misty hills across the valley. He reached out his smarting hand and closed it over her instep and the leather straps.

She looked down at him. Tears spilled down her face, quiet tears of acceptance. "She's dead now," she said. "She died this spring, when she was six years old. The relief is something I can't describe. The relief . . . and the shame that follows the relief."

He felt the tremor go through her foot and upward, and when it reached her face she broke. She came down beside him on the ground and he held her, as any man would, but his soul was frozen. He could not feel anything but shock and numbness. His world was not like this. In his world—his gay, young, flashy, smoothly running world, such injections of raw life were beyond his capacity to take. His pampered spirit felt as if it might blow apart with the numbing inner pressure of what it was being asked to absorb.

After a while she released herself, and sat away from him, drying her face and blowing her nose prosaically. He felt limp and beyond his depth. He could not begin to think what to do or say next.

However, she took charge very competently.

"Well," she said, "now you know. It's been quite a problem, deciding to tell you. And quite an ordeal doing it. For both of us, I see. . . ." She touched his hand for a moment, and then quickly stood up, shaking out her skirt. "Let's be getting back, shall we?"

They walked back to the club in silence, got into the car and drove home. And that seemed to be the end of that.

For several weeks, Zalman was in a turmoil. Not only was every preconceived idea about Ruth shattered; so were all his innocent conceits about himself. He had believed himself man enough to cope with any woman's "past"; he had romantically supposed that his love would not alter where it alteration found —and by now he knew that he was, or had been, properly in love.

But Ruth's story had proved that his emotional stomach was not mature enough yet for such strong meat. He writhed at the realization, but he could not evade it. A whole man would have held Ruth and kissed her and comforted her with a promise that a new life was beginning for her. *He* on the other hand had driven her home in silence, shaken her hand with a mumbled good-bye and not made any effort to see her since. He was ashamed, the more so since he knew why she had told him. "I attracted a young man—as it might have been you . . . ."

In the small accounting hours Zalman learned from his own thoughts. He learned that his condescension had been ludicrously misplaced. She was, in wisdom no less than in experience, older than he. Only in looks had he any advantage—and for the first time in his manhood, he now rated his handsome face at nothing, cursed it, in fact, for the folly of imagined superiority it had led him into.

His days went on as before—except that now he endlessly drew her face on his blotter and note pads and in the margins of books. He had always had this small talent, and now he was surprised at the likenesses he achieved—not the likeness of Ruth as she was, but as she must have been before, and as she could be again if the money for an operation could be found.

Well, no—not found. Zalman had the money in his bank. He made enquiries, and learned that what he had saved in a casual way, during seven years of profitable employment, was more than enough for the best in plastic surgery. He delayed a long time because some instinct told him that such failures as his could not be paid for in money, and that if she chose to regard his gift as a payment she would not accept it.

But at last, some action becoming imperative, he went one morning to his bank, cashed his savings, put the whole lot in an envelope (a check would somehow have lacked immediacy—a check could be ignored; hard cash could not) and sent it to her at the theater.

Just to make sure that she could not misunderstand the purpose of the money, he enclosed one of the sketches he had done of her, with her nose straight and perfect above a relaxed and smiling mouth.

No sooner was the envelope in the mail than he was assailed by the most horrible misgivings. What would she think when she got it? Either that he was trying to buy himself off, or (worse? better?) to buy himself on again. The worst of it was, he didn't understand the real truth himself. He both longed for her, and feared the thought of her; she attracted and repelled him at the same time. Was his gesture one of generosity, or guilt? Or—oh, God!—was it merely one of his silly, ungrown-up impulses to make himself feel good, which his thrifty soul would later meanly regret?

He passed four days of the most acute mental discomfort and personal insecurity he had ever experienced. Then, one morning in the middle of work, she telephoned.

He became speechless at the sound of her voice. He had an important client sitting opposite to him, and he stared fixedly into his bilious little eyes to give himself a point of balance.

"Zalman, may I see you, please?"

He cleared his throat and tried to summon words, feeling like the vilest of criminals, caught and trapped.

"Will you come to the theater after the play this evening?"

He managed to croak something affirmative. She thanked him in her beautiful voice, and hung up at once.

Zalman looked at his watch. Twelve hours to wait. Twelve hours! He felt desperate. What had he done? What was she going to say to him? Or he to her? Could he behave himself with decent warmth to her, or did his absurd, irrepressible shock at her story go so deep that he wouldn't be able to, however much he tried?

He got through the twelve hours somehow, stumbling (for he was a little drunk, having had two unaccustomed Scotches and no food) down the familiar stone stairs to the prop room at exactly half-past ten.

She was just putting her coat on, and turned to smile at him as his footsteps sounded behind her.

Nothing had changed. Her face was still ugly—and he still wanted her. He felt a staggering flood of relief because he felt just as before.

"Zalman," she began without preamble. "It's about the money of course. You are quite crazy, and it's taken me three days to calm down sufficiently about it to decide what—what attitude to take." She smiled at him a little shakily. "When I discovered, though, that it was *attitudes* I was trying to decide about, I abandoned all the ones I'd been considering and—" She stopped. "I want to ask one thing. Was the money a gesture, or do you really want me to use it?"

How unerringly she put her finger on his own dilemma! And only the strictest honesty would do—that was the awful thing, or she would see through him at once.

"I'm not sure myself," he said at last. "I only know I had to send it."

She smiled—a sweet, relaxed smile, a reward for truth.

"Then let's wait a while. Say, a month or two. After that, you'll know what you want me to do."

"If I really wanted you to use it—I mean, if you could believe that I did, and it wasn't a gesture—would you?"

"Yes."

Everything cleared in his mind and heart as if a deluge had swept away all the dust and confusion. "I know already. I do want you to use it. I don't want to wait."

He took an exultant step toward her, but her expression of doubt checked him. She looked at him for a long moment.

"Pygmalion?" she asked quietly.

He could only stare at her. She was incredible! It was more than mind reading, for she saw thoughts he hadn't admitted to himself.

Suddenly there was only one thing to do. He put his arms round her and kissed her. He closed his eyes to do it, and the mark of her lips was as indelible as the stain of sweet, dark fruit.

"How can you bear to see people so clearly?" he whispered.

"None too easily," she replied in a voice steadier than his.

He touched the disfigured nose with the back of his fingers.

"Will you have it done?"

She looked into his eyes, first into one, then the other.

"Yes," she said at last. "If it means that you will kiss me with your eyes open."

The operation took some time to arrange, and meanwhile he saw her nearly every day. He felt quite dizzy with excitement as the appointed time drew closer. Soon—soon she would be changed, given the features that would make the whole thing . . . possible. He so successfully projected himself into that future time, that without thinking about it he introduced her to all his friends and went about with her everywhere, quite happily. It was as if the change had already taken place. Ruth smiled and went with him everywhere he wished to take her; the ordeal of meeting people grew gradually less. She, too, was looking forward; the long ugliness was going to end. She could endure it tolerantly in the meantime; suffering for it was senseless now that the cure was at hand.

She chose the nose she wanted from a book of photographs the plastic surgeon showed her. It was a nice, calm, straight one. He said he thought he could lengthen her upper lip at the same time. She did not trouble herself anymore about the money; she could see that Zalman had given it from his heart, which makes no debts. She wanted to repay him by becoming as nearly beautiful as she could.

The operation took place one Wednesday morning. When she awoke, she had a very sore face, and a disproportionate lump of white dressing in the middle of it. She lay squinting at it, dreaming absurd dreams of emerging like a butterfly, totally transformed into loveliness. Everything ugly about the past lay immured in that white bulk; when that was taken away, it would all be sloughed off, forgotten. She thought of her child, and the twin pangs of guilt and relief were both less than they had ever been before.

Zalman came every day to see her. "May I be here when they take all that off?"

"No! And you mustn't come for ten days afterward, either. They say it always looks terrible at first, all swollen and red. Don't even call. Then come on the tenth day. I want you to get the full effect of your—present to me."

He came on the tenth day.

She was back in her apartment now, of course. She did not have a telephone, and she had not yet returned to the theater, so he had written to ask if he might come to see her. She hadn't replied, but he took that for consent, and simply arrived.

He knocked repeatedly on the door, but there was no answer. After a while, he tried it—it was open. With a slight feeling of unease, he went in.

Ruth was standing in the small living-room with her back to him, looking out of the window. The room had a look of automatic neatness, but there was something missing: There should have been an air of renaissance, an aura of celebration, but there was none. Even the flowers he had sent were not to be seen. The room was somehow cold.

"Ruth?"

She didn't move, but clenched her hands briefly. His heart jumped to his throat with terror. What had they done to her? He ran across the room, and turned her around by the shoulders.

He gasped, and then his face relaxed into a smile of joy and relief.

"Darling! It's marvelous! You look beautiful!"

He kissed and kissed her, rapturously, scarcely noticing her unaccountable stiffness in his arms until he tasted tears.

"What's wrong, love?" he asked anxiously. "Is your poor face still sore? Did I hurt it? I forgot how new you are!"

She was gazing at him, and for the first time he saw total bewilderment in her face.

"It's not sore," was all she said.

"Aren't you pleased? Aren't you thrilled?" he kept asking, like a child. He touched the new face with gentle hands, feasting his eyes upon it. "It's almost exactly what I pictured! Oh, darling, it's so gorgeous! We must go somewhere and celebrate!"

"Not tonight, Zalman. Will you forgive me? Not tonight."

He was disappointed, but it was a pinprick to his joy. "Tomorrow night, then—whenever you like." He kissed her again. "See? My eyes are wide open! And when we're married, we'll always make love with the light on, so that I can look at you. . . ."

When he'd gone, she walked slowly to the mirror she had bought as a gesture of faith in the future before the operation—the mirror she had wanted to smash when she had looked at herself with horror in it after the bandages had come off.

She stared at herself. Her nose was different, certainly. But it was a far cry from the trim little one she had naïvely picked out of that fairy-tale book. Neither was it anything like the one she had been born with. It was a strange, unfamiliar protuberance, a sort of elegant beak jutting out of her face—so unlike what she had expected, so at odds with her idea of herself, that she felt a stranger in her own face.

She didn't even have to look in a mirror to be constantly aware of it—it got in the way of her eyes and when she put her hand up to touch it, it felt like a freakish obstacle stuck there irrevocably by mistake.

The surgeon had been delighted with his work, and her protests, made faint by dismay and disappointment, had been met by robust assurances that she had been blessed with one of his finest rhinoplastic triumphs. He admitted that it was not the nose she had ordered. "It doesn't always work out as one expects," he said lightly. "Never mind! It's a very fine nose. Most distinguished!"

To Ruth's anguished eyes, then and now, it looked almost worse than before. Almost, she could long for the poor, familiar, misshapen nose back again—at least she had recognized herself behind it. And Zalman . . . Zalman had fallen in love with her despite it. She had been so deadly certain that the strange new nose would make him recoil from her again that she had not even put powder on it, nor done any of the things to her hair and face that she had planned for the occasion.

And now—this. This incredible, stunning surprise. The new nose mysteriously seemed to please him after all, even fitting into some preconceived pattern in *his* mind.

Or did it?

He was young, too young inside himself to act so well for her sake, however much he might love her. How, then, to explain his reaction? Was it enough to expect the best in order to see what you want to see? Or was he—just possibly—seeing *her* now, so strongly that the face did not matter?

She sat for a long time, letting the slow realization of the security of love spread its healing over her. Then she suddenly stood up and went into the bedroom. In a box at the bottom of a drawer, she unearthed her compact, her lipsticks and the rest of her makeup, all dusty and tarnished from disuse. She carried them back to the mirror, and then, slowly and rather clumsily, she began to experiment.

After ten minutes she stopped, and, abruptly, began to laugh. She was still laughing on a pure, gay note as she went to the bathroom and washed it all off. After that she pocketed some pennies and hurried out to phone Zalman from a local pay phone.

Lynne Reid Banks was born in London, the daughter of a Scots doctor father and an Irish actress mother. Educated at the Royal Academy of Dramatic Arts, she performed in British repertory companies for several years, wrote plays, and finally tried journalism, causing something of a stir when she became the first woman reporter on British television. More recently Ms. Banks has worked as a script writer. Her first novel, THE L-SHAPED ROOM, *was a Book Society choice and a major motion picture. Other works include* HOUSE OF HOPE, CHILDREN AT THE GATE, *and many short stories.*

East of the Sun

by Chloe Gartner

*T*hey first saw the man when they were camped near the border between Norway and Finland on their way down from North Cape. He was the only other human being they had seen for days and he was herding reindeer in a meadow below them. Bob stopped—he and Jan were taking their midday hike—to look at the man through the binoculars.

"What do you know! A nudist and in this climate!"

"Let me look." Jan held out her hand for the glasses.

"As if you never saw a naked man before."

"I haven't in Norway. Or are we in Finland now?" She adjusted the glasses and the figure sprang into view. "He doesn't need clothes. He's as hairy as his flock." She caught her breath as the man stretched, his long back arched, the shaggy head flung back to drink in the sun and wind. "Oh, he's beautiful. He's like Pan. Did the Norse have a god equivalent to Pan?"

"I don't know," Bob said in the voice that meant he also didn't care. "Come on, Jan, we won't get to the top and back before dinnertime."

"Wait. I want to watch him. He's——"

The man was chasing one of the reindeer. It stopped grazing and trotted away from him. He ran after it, outdistanced it and flung himself on it. Man and beast struggled for a moment, then were locked together.

"My God, Bob, look! What is he doing?" Jan handed the binoculars to her husband.

He jerked them from his eyes and thrust them back into her hands. "It's perfectly obvious what he's doing and it is disgusting."

"I've heard about such things. You told me yourself you had seen it in Paris with a woman and a dog."

"That was disgusting, too. Damn it, Jan, don't watch. You're——"

"Disgusting?"

Bob plodded on up the mountain, ankle-deep in new grass. When he was aware she was not following him he turned and said, "Jan!"

The man had released the beast, which shook itself and went back to grazing. The herder threw himself back in a patch of pink wild flowers and lifted his arms to the sun.

Jan followed Bob up the hill. The rocky gray mountains jutted above them. The ground was spongy with newly melted snow. Although it was late June, the birch trees were just coming into bud. The meadows flowered with bell heather, buttercups, violets, and white stars. But Jan noticed none of it.

She was wondering at some aspect of herself she had never known before. It was not something she could tell Bob, and her psychiatrist would give it the worst possible implications, though she was certain there was no element of evil in it. As she had watched the man with the animal, she had felt a communion with it, as if the act had been committed on her. It had not been bestiality but pagan joy, a union of all forms of life.

"Bob." He was fifty feet ahead of her. "Bob, wait. Let's make love."

He stopped, and it amused her that his face was shocked. "Now?"

"Yes. It's a beautiful meadow and I love you." There had been a time before they had left home that she had thought love was dead, but now she was grateful to him for bringing her to this new world.

"I don't think loving me has a damned thing to do with it. And I wish we had never seen that man." Then he added in a kinder tone, "But we could sit on that rock and eat our chocolate."

As he handed her the chocolate bar, Jan wanted to throw it at him. She felt a resurging of the anger and bitterness, the desire to smash things and to scream, which had dominated her for the past year and had finally led to the leave of absence and the journey to Norway.

She had felt better at first. They had driven slowly north leaving spring behind. They had gone to North Cape and sat up all night Midsummer Eve to watch the sun ride over the crest of the sea, the sky bright blue at midnight, and the wind bitter and forceful. They had camped and fished and bathed in white rivers and still, icy lakes, crossed fjords, wound up and down steep-sided mountains in whose folds glaciers glimmered like white gods, and driven through miles of empty tundra. More than once Bob had asked, "Are you really enjoying this?"

She was enjoying it too much. She could not bear to think of returning home to their too perfect apartment, to the pressure and excitement of her job, to their friends and parties, to everything that had been their life. Shouldn't the dread of all that vanish before she could go back?

Bob was not enjoying it. He was tired of the cold, of camp food, of sleeping bags, of no plumbing—he had recited a long list of things he was tired of one night, and then had kissed her and told her he didn't mean any of it when he found she was crying.

He was willing to believe her breakdown existed because the psychiatrist had told him it did. But he didn't understand why. Jan had tried to explain it to him after a month of sleepless nights, when fear lurked in every corner of the apartment and every nerve was raw and quivering.

"I want to go away. I want to go someplace where the world can begin all over again, where there is nothing but essentials, where I can be stripped down to me. I want to see if the little girl who used to be here is still around. The one who didn't have martini lunches, who didn't smoke three packs a day, who didn't have her hair done every week, didn't have to wear clothes that cost a fortune, and spend her life suffering one big hangover. The girl who could bait a fishline, ski, backpack, build a campfire, identify birds, grow a garden, make piccalilli and still have time to read."

"I don't know what the hell piccalilli is and I don't know whether you're talking about Thoreau or the Noble Savage."

"You wouldn't."

"I know what she means," the doctor had said to Bob. "I could give her tranquilizers but she would go right on living the way she is now. It would merely delay the day of reckoning. She is mentally, emotionally, and spiritually exhausted. She needs a complete change, a complete reevaluation."

"Does that mean a reevaluation of me, too?"

"Don't be so insecure, Bob. Just because we haven't been getting along doesn't mean I don't love you."

"Where do you want to go?" Bob asked, beaten. "Wyoming, Montana?"

"No. That would be the same as being here. Lodges and cocktails and tourists thinking they were getting away from it all. I want to go to——to—— Norway."

"Norway!"

"Why not? It's beautiful and empty and rugged and there are plenty of places to fish."

"What's this hangup you have for fishing?"

The doctor had said, "It sounds like a good idea."

Jan, sitting in the sun eating her chocolate, wished Bob thought it was a good idea, wished she did not sense his restiveness. This was a perfect camp. The sun almost warmed the shallows of the stream. There was a meadow where they sunbathed. Their tent was near a boulder which absorbed the sun and shut off the wind; so far the weather had been good, if cold, and at Hammerfest Bob had laid in a supply of English paperbacks. It should have been perfect, and it wasn't.

Jan finished the chocolate bar and leaned back and folded her arms under her head. What time was it? That was the funny thing about the Arctic. She never knew the time of day because it was never dark.

"Come on. I thought you wanted to get to the top."

Stop rushing me. Stop hurrying me. Stop setting schedules for me. "You go. I'll wait here. I want a nap."

"You were the one who wanted to climb to the top."

"And now I am the one who wants a nap." She closed her eyes, but she could not close out Bob's irritation even though he didn't speak.

The grass whispered as he walked away. When she was sure he had gone she opened her eyes and looked into the jungle of pale new grass and wild flowers beside her head, at the blue sky, at the snow shining on the mountaintop. The world must have been as lonely and silent and perfect as this when God first made it.

She let herself sink against the earth as if she were putting down roots, becoming a part of the earth mother. She slept.

Once she half-awakened, thinking Bob had come back. She kept her eyes closed, but she felt him watching her and was almost exasperated into saying, "Damn it, let me sleep." Then he moved away. She slept deeply then, and didn't awaken until Bob was saying,

"Get up, Jan. You'll catch cold sleeping on that damp grass. You should have come. It was great. From up there you really can see forever." He pointed at some droppings in the grass. "An animal has been here."

"Reindeer," Jan said and felt an odd quiver.

The walk had improved Bob's disposition. He made dinner that night and washed up afterward and didn't complain when a sharp, strong wind came up near midnight. All he said was, "You'd better come into my sleeping bag." And as she snuggled against him, "You did take your pill, didn't you?"

"Yes. I took my pill. And when I get home I am going to throw them away. I want a child."

"In this world and with your psychoses? God help the child."

"Only one, Bob. Everyone's entitled to one."

"I'm not sure everyone is. And you'd be a lousy mother."

The next morning he announced he had to write letters. "To let people know we're still alive. The Follett contract will be coming up for renewal and I should tell Fielding what to do about it."

"I'll go for my bath unless you want me to wait for you." Ask me to wait, she pleaded silently.

"Go ahead." He arranged his portable typewriter on the camp table and put rocks on the papers so they wouldn't blow away. "What's the date?"

"I don't know. Does it matter?"

"It'll look damned silly to put 'Somewhere between Norway/Finland, sometime late June.'"

"They'll envy you."

"Mmmm." Already the typewriter was clicking under his fingers.

Jan chose a spot where the reeds grew high. The water, like indigo with white rapids, tumbled over the rocks and against the green bank. It was as cold as the snow from which it had come. She wondered why she martyred herself. Why hadn't she heated a bucket on the fire and sponged in the tent? But as she washed she felt the blood rising and an invigoration of all her senses. Like an awakening. A rebirth.

She scrubbed herself dry and, naked, leaned against the rocks to absorb the pale warmth of the sun. The reeds rustled and Jan thought it was Bob coming, then decided it was the wind. During the sudden cessation of the sound of water she could hear, very faintly in the quietness, Bob's typewriter.

If she could stay here forever she would be cured of whatever the dark bogey was which haunted her.

The reeds bent and parted. The man stood before her. After her first gasp, her fear vanished. The face which she had scarcely seen through the binoculars was kind and childlike, even in its sensuality. The body was magnificent. The hand he rubbed up and down his chest as if in embarrassment was slender and sensitive. And he was going to rape her.

She pulled the towel across her and cried, "No! No!" But it was fright of herself, not of him.

He lunged, throwing her back. They grappled, and Jan found excitement in the fight. Then she remembered the reindeer. She went limp under the man's weight. Her arms pulled him down on her. She covered his chest with kisses and arched up to receive him. He drew back, pinning her shoulders to the ground, and looked into her face. She saw in his own wonder and surprise. Then he laughed and possessed her. Too soon, for Jan, it was over. He rolled off and flung out his arms as if to embrace the sun.

Jan leaned on her elbow and looked at him. His eyes smiled. She stroked his face, touched his hair, his chest, the brown skin of his arms. Passively, he accepted the caresses, but his expression was puzzled. She kissed him as a civilized woman would kiss, forcing his mouth open. She took his hand and held it to her breast. Never before had she so desired a man as she did him. This time the coupling was her doing and left them both exultant.

"Jan!"

The man sprang away so quickly he seemed to vanish.

"Jan, are you all right?"

"I've been sunning." She plunged into the water to wash off the smell of the man. Bob frowned his disapproval.

"You really are a nature girl, aren't you? How can you stand that cold water? I'm going into town to mail these. Don't you want to come?"

She dressed slowly under Bob's gaze and the gaze of the man hidden in the rushes. She wondered Bob did not feel his presence as she did. "Ride forty miles to mail a letter? Not I. I'll stay here if you don't mind going alone."

"Maybe it will be good for us to be away from each other. Do we need anything?"

132

She walked with him back to camp and helped him check the supply chest, conscious that they were being watched. She even walked with him to the car and asked again if he minded going alone.

"I don't mind, but I sure as hell don't understand you. Jan. If anything, I understand you less than I did before we came. You're like a stranger. Sometimes I wonder what our marriage will be when we get back home."

"Probably no different than it was before we left." That was the hell of it.

"I hope you're right. I hope you'll be ready to go back soon." He kissed her more tenderly than he had for days, and waved to her as he drove away, bouncing over the narrow, rutted road. The trees hid the car from sight and the sound of the river drowned the sound of the motor.

She combed her hair, she packed her cosmetics case, she tidied the camp. Then she sat down to wait. She knew he would come. She could feel him there, just a few feet away hidden in the thick forest.

He approached as cautiously as a wild animal, listening, watchful, and watching her. They stared at one another in speechless communication. Jan felt the past dissolving, the shell cracking away from the chrysalis who had been married to Bob. She looked down, expecting a change in her body, but it was her mind that had changed. Bob and the doctor would have said her breakdown was complete. That was civilized talk. She knew she had found herself. She put on her coat, took her cosmetics case, and waited.

The man picked her up and carried her away. After a few steps the camp was hidden from view. They crossed a meadow and the reindeer trailed after them, their bells ringing. They climbed the mountainside where the river became a torrent tumbling down to the valley. They followed a ledge to a hut, part cave, part lean-to, part earthen wall. It smelled of old fires and fish and meat and of the man himself.

He put Jan on the wooden box bed. It was soft with hides and furs. He blew on the fire and put a caldron on. He watched Jan warily, ready to spring, as she walked to the opening at the front. Far below were the patches of meadow, the dark coil of river, the pointed tops of the fir forest, the green mist of budding birch, the black lakes. The wind stung her nostrils and pushed at her as if it were alive. She had come to the edge of the world. She went back to the fire and undressed and held out her arms to the man.

The green Arctic twilight tinted the sky, then turned to brilliant morning. The sun rose just past midnight on the mountaintop. A group of men searched the riverbank. Bob called her name over and over. Once he was very close. She started up but the man held her and made love to her, closing her mouth with his so she could not answer. After a few days there were no more search parties.

The birch forests turned green and feathery. Jan and the man cooked and ate and made love and bathed in the descent of icy water. They fished and hung the fish on racks to dry just as Jan had seen fish drying throughout Norway. She worked with the man, chopping wood, scraping skins, tending the fire which heated the rocks for their sauna. They moved the reindeer to higher meadows as summer advanced. They repaired the corral adjoining the cave. The man spent days making fur boots and a warm coat for Jan, and carving narrow skis from long slats.

The birches turned gold. The twilight came earlier and the sun rose in a blue-black sky. The rains turned to sleet. One day Jan took her last pill and thought, "Now I shall get pregnant." It frightened her but it also heightened her passion.

It was strange that a girl who was a Phi Bete ("an erratically brilliant girl, very close to genius," one of her professors had written about her), who had a career and a salary a man would envy, should be so content. She loved the secret world in which she lived. She never tired of watching the shifting light on the mountains, the storms which roared down. It was joyful to watch the meadows whiten, the forest go bare, to hear the voice of the water stilled by ice, to feel the change in her body.

Her hair was long and she dressed like a Lapp woman now. Through signs and a few words, she and the man had a form of basic communication, but she felt little need for it. She took pride in being able to ski, pregnant or not, on the rough wooden slats as well as she had skied on the Heads, now on their rack in Manhattan. She grew used to the rank smell of the herd brought in for warmth when the snow lay deep. The aurora borealis flickering on the walls through the endless night never ceased to be wonderful to her.

This was what she had wanted: the world as it was when it was new. She turned to the man and he roused in his sleep long enough to draw her closer to him, cupping her swelling breasts in his hands.

The child was born when pink flowers blossomed amongst the patches of melting snow. The same flowers which had been in bloom when she and Bob had come to Norway. It was the first time she had really thought of Bob and the memory depressed her. She grabbed the child and thrust her nipple into its mouth to take her mind off the past. She sang to it and rocked it and the man's face warmed with pride.

The day came when the man indicated she could go to town with him. He had never trusted her before. They walked the entire distance, carrying the baby in a basket like an Indian papoose. When Jan saw the bleak wooden buildings, the Esso station, the coffee *baari*, she felt panic. The people would stare at her because she was unlike them. They would make her go away. Then she saw her reflection in the market window. She would not have recognized it if the woman she saw did not have the child in her arms and had not her man been standing beside her. She felt a moment's horror at what she had become. Then she saw a kind of strong, gaunt beauty and a grace which she had not had before.

While her man bargained over reindeer skins, Jan sat on the bench in front of the store to rest. She dared not show her ignorance of the language by attempting to shop alone. It was then the car came, a new Volkswagen with tourist plates and expensive luggage piled in the rear. Jan knew that luggage just as she knew the driver of the car, though she did not know his companion.

Both men got out of the car and Bob locked it. Bob, a little more dissipated, still young, still handsome in that arrogant, self-confident way which had always irritated her.

"Now you know what you are to ask?" he was saying to his companion. His voice touched nerves and memories she had thought were dead forever. "God knows, if I had had an interpreter last year I might have got some information. She disappeared about this time. She was wearing gray slacks and a loden coat and she had an alligator-skin cosmetics case with her. I thought at first it was deliberate, her going, because she had taken the case. I know differently now. You must ask if they found an American woman or her body or those clothes or that case. Emphasize that she's mad as a coot. You know the word 'mad'?" Bob asked, suddenly uncertain. He tapped his head and said, "Deranged."

"I know," the young Finn said. A college student, Jan guessed. "I know the word 'deranged.'" Then he added softly, "You loved her very much."

Of course he did. He had come back to search for her.

"Of course I loved her," he echoed her thoughts. Jan had forgotten that harsh note in his voice. "It's been hell not knowing what happened to her. Not only that, the laws in my country—you must understand, I cannot marry again or collect her insurance until she is proven dead."

They walked into the store never glancing at the Lapp woman sitting by the steps, though her heart pounded as she caught the familiar odor of Bob. After all this time she recognized the smell of him.

Her man left off his bargaining and rushed out to Jan, his eyes wild with alarm. He plucked at her sleeve, but she smiled at him and shook her head. She pointed to herself and to the baby, and then to him. She held up three fingers, one for each of them, and pressed her hand to her heart.

~~~~~~

Chloe Gartner is an author and world traveler whose main interest is enjoying life and encouraging others to do the same. The idea for "East of the Sun" came to her in a dream after a trip to Europe which included a journey to the Arctic "midnight sun" regions. She lives presently in Menlo Park, California, works part-time in the School of Earth Sciences, and serves as unofficial friend, confidante, and substitute mother to many students. Ms. Gartner is the author of one novel, DRUMS OF KHARTOUM. The story reprinted here brought a storm of mail—some pro, some con—when first published in Cosmopolitan. We agree with one reader who wrote that the story was "pure, poetic, and deeply felt."

Space Ant

by Gilbert Rogin

~~~~~~~~~~

1

When Brownie realizes that his wife is Space Ant, and that she has been sent to Earth from another planet, he is driving through Florida in a rented car. His wife sits beside him, a partly unfolded road map on her lap. She is wearing sunglasses with red rims and slightly convex lenses, which are in between harlequins and wraparounds. Their effect is to make her look like a huge ant. Brownie tells his wife he has discovered she comes from outer space. "This is my otherworldly smile," she says, smiling. "But what is your mission?" Brownie says.

2

Another day Brownie says, "We're going to go out of our way and see what Boca Grande is like."

Brownie's wife says, "You're doing this for me and then you're going to regret it and tell me that you did it for me."

3

Brownie's wife has often mentioned to Brownie that when she was separated from her first husband, Buster Toomey, for the first time, she decided to start her life all over again somewhere else. She was living in Providence, where Toomey was from, and she went to an employment agency that specialized in placing people in resorts. She asked if they had anything waiting on table in Florida, and was told there was a job at the Boca Grande Hotel, which she envisioned as a massive, white, frame building with great porches upon which millionaires rocked after dinner. But she got no closer to Boca Grande than locating it on a map; Toomey, tapering off, came back, with bits of toilet paper clinging to the places where he had cut himself shaving, and said he was beginning to see his way clear.

4

On the way to Boca Grande, Brownie's wife says, "If Toomey had showed up a day later, I would have caught the eye of a millionaire in creamy flannels with dotted lines running up and down them, and he would have carried me off."

Brownie says, "In that event, what would have happened to me?"

5

Brownie drives over the bridge to Gasparilla Island, on which the town of Boca Grande is situated; the island is flat, scrubby, and there are metal signs advertising lots.

"This isn't Boca Grande," Brownie's wife says. "Boca Grande is much greener, there's lots more trees, and the interior is very dense."

As they pass through the town Brownie points out the banyans and the glimpses of the Gulf afforded by driveways that, at intervals, interrupt walls enclosing estates. A block or two beyond town several large brick buildings rise; their windows are blank, they appear empty, in disuse, perhaps soon to become ruins.

"Oh, God!" Brownie's wife says. "A sanitarium."

"The Boca Grande Hotel," Brownie says, showing her the sign.

He pulls off the road opposite the hotel.

"The lady in Providence said the girls who waited on table lived in," Brownie's wife says. "Which would have been the window of my room?"

"There," Brownie says. "On the top floor. You would have been able to see the Gulf."

"I would have never got away," Brownie's wife says, "unless I let down my hair."

"But Space Ant *flies!*" Brownie says.

"It was before I came to Earth and assumed my present form," Brownie's wife says.

6

"There's a blue one in the fastness," Brownie says.

"When you were in nursery school—" his wife says, reaching in among the branches.

"I found a thumbtack on the floor," Brownie says. "The teacher praised me. She said I had very sharp eyes."

It is nearly three weeks after Christmas, and they are finally taking down the trimmings, which date from the marriage to Buster Toomey. Rather, Brownie's wife is; Brownie points out ornaments she's missed. He has never had anything to do with trimming the tree, either, except for fixing the tin star from Mexico to the top, and that he has done because he's taller.

Brownie continues, "Did I ever tell you that although I have been paid any number of compliments since—"

"For what?" his wife says. "Turns of phrase? Your neckties?"

"At various points or moments in the act of love," Brownie says.

7

Brownie and his wife are at a party. Brownie is talking to a girl, whose name he didn't catch, who has paid him a compliment. "When I was in nursery school, I found a thumbtack on the floor," Brownie tells her. "The teacher praised me. She said I had very sharp eyes. Although I have been paid any number of compliments since, this first, being least susceptible to flattery or other impure motives, is the best."

But Brownie can no longer hear the teacher announcing that a thumbtack is lost and that everybody is going to stop everything and look for it. No other children are searching alongside him. He is off by himself, crawling somewhere, and comes unexpectedly upon the tack. "I found a thumbtack," he says, holding it out. The teacher smiles and accepts it. "You have very sharp eyes," she says. She has felt sorry for him.

"I think I'd better find my wife," Brownie says, plunging off.

She is in the dining room, eating shrimp off of colored toothpicks.

"I was looking for you," he says.

"You have very sharp eyes," she says.

I do, Brownie acknowledges. When I drive, I see the deer in their noble attitudes at the edges of woods, in dreams I have beheld all the different fishes streaming in the interiors of lakes, and I can see all of us growing old.

8

Brownie is home alone and penniless; not even carfare to get uptown. He goes to the bedroom closet and gropes for change in the pockets of his jackets, summer and winter, including those he last wore years ago. Putting his hand in the pockets of his old, shiny suits, he realizes he may have been a slightly different person when he wore them, and he tries to remember who that person was.

He doesn't find a cent. He goes to the coat closet in the foyer and feels in the pockets of all his wife's coats. The pockets are surprisingly shallow, worn, even desolate, and warm, as though they still retain the heat of his wife's hands, and they are all empty. No money, no gloves, no matches, no old Kleenex.

Brownie wonders why he had never noticed how small her hands must be to fit in her pockets. He imagines that his hands are his wife's, he her, walking by himself, his hand in his pockets. For a moment, he has a sense of his wife's life. She was someone else, whom he fell in love with.

The foyer darkens, and he is afraid it is the shadow of her wings, and that she is hovering above him.

9

One night, Brownie's wife tries on all her sunglasses. Brownie is lying on his side of the bed, reading. Brownie's wife is on her knees on the floor by her side, hidden, with her pile of sunglasses. She puts a pair on, sticks her head up, drops out of sight, changes glasses, reappears, disappears, and so forth. Brownie's wife must have a dozen pairs of sunglasses, including those which betray that she is Space Ant.

Brownie is reminded of one of those frantic impersonators who turns his back to the audience, does something to his hair, turns around and becomes— Jimmy Cagney! Victor McLaglen! Bette Davis! He is reminded, too, of a swimmer, rather a drowning man, bobbing repeatedly to the surface, his features progressively altered by his experience, appealing for help. Also a child playing peek-a-boo. Is his wife saying recognize me, save me, catch me? Is this the high point of their marriage?

10

While Brownie is doing his push-ups, his wife says to their dachshund, "Josh, if you were Space Ant why would you come to Earth?"

"Why would he?" Brownie grunts.

"To make you talk," she says.

"What would he want to do that for?" Brownie says, getting to his feet.

"So you could tell me what you feel about me," she says.

"But it's implied," Brownie says.

11

One morning Brownie decides it's time to turn the mattress, and discovers that his wife has hidden a notebook between it and the box spring. He reads what she has written:

"Space Ant is in the kitchen cooking bacon and crying. Tears fall into the pan and the hot fat pops. Space Ant sits down on the stool and turns on the radio to hear the news. She cries listening to the traffic. She thinks her mission has failed.

"Brownie says life is largely unrewarding, but one stumbles forward. Brownie says life is hard and he has no time. Brownie says life is exhausting and he goes to sleep.

"Space Ant whispers in Brownie's ear while he is sleeping, 'Wake up loving me and I'll teach you to fly.' "

12

Buster Toomey calls up Brownie and tells him he's working behind the steam table in the Automat on Broadway near Forty-seventh Street. "It's one of the most venerable in the chain," he says. "Do drop in and see me in my little bow tie." The purpose of Toomey's call is to borrow Brownie's portable typewriter. "I want to knock out a few résumés," Toomey explains. "I'm beginning to see my way clear again."

Brownie visits Toomey on the way to work. Toomey is stationed by the toaster. Besides the little bow tie, he is wearing a white cap with a gauze top, which is set at a jaunty angle. When he sees Brownie, he winks and throws him a salute.

Brownie gets a cup of coffee and sits down. In a few minutes, Toomey joins him. "We're permitted five minutes," Toomey says.

"When you were married to her," Brownie says, "did you ever have the impression that she came here from outer space?"

"Not that I can recall," Toomey says.

13

Brownie's goldfish, which he owned before he got married, dies. He had won it at the Feast of Saint Anthony by throwing a Ping-Pong ball into the globe of magenta water in which it frantically swam.

"Are you still upset?" Brownie's wife asks Brownie when he comes back from walking Josh in the rain.

"I had it five years," Brownie says.

"Five years is the normal life-span for goldfish," Brownie's wife says.

"And all the other dogs I see go to the bathroom when it's raining," Brownie says.

"And?" Brownie's wife says.

"The pop-up book," Brownie says.

He goes on to explain that yesterday there had been a pop-up book in the window of the bookstore past which he and Josh invariably walk. The book seemed quite old, perhaps late Victorian, and it was displayed so that it was open to a pop-up that showed children in old-fashioned bathing suits playing in the surf with a large dog or donkey, he has forgotten which. They are all in a bay, the arms of which are high cliffs. The children, the animal, and many of the waves popped up. He had been charmed by the scene and was about to go in and buy the book, when he stopped to classify his emotions. Why was he agitated? Because the illustration so sweetly evoked a lost childhood for which he yearned. But the scene didn't represent his past; it belonged to others, Englishmen now extremely old or, more likely, dead. He was moved by, was pining for, someone else's youth, and he didn't go in. Why did he keep deluding himself? Why did he fail to grasp the reality of his own life? However, today, as he and Josh approached the bookstore in the rain, he became aware that his heart was quickening. The subject didn't matter. What did was a clear sense of momentariness. What happened when the waves broke, everyone came out of the water, the light failed, the day ended, children grew up? However, the book was no longer in the window, and when he inquired he learned it had been sold.

"Would you like to know why I came to Earth?" Brownie's wife asks.

"I would," Brownie says.

"To put my arms around you," she says, doing so, "and to solace your existence."

She doesn't tell him that his goldfish died years ago, and that she had replaced it with one that resembled it, and that that one had died and had been replaced, too.

New Yorker Gilbert Rogin is a senior editor at Sports Illustrated. *Both his short stories and sports articles have been widely anthologized. Although Mr. Rogin was primarily known as a short-fiction writer, it was revealed recently that he'd been writing a "secret" novel for six years—all his short stories published in that period were actually pieces of a novel,* WHAT HAPPENS NEXT, *which appeared late in 1971 and drew a rave review from* The New York Times. *("Space Ant," in slightly different form, is Chapter Seventeen of the novel.) Mr. Rogin lives in Manhattan with his wife and stepson.*

The Wife-Eater

by Myrna Blyth

*H*e came home bearing gifts—a dress for the baby that was two sizes too big, a pair of gaudy earrings that she'd never wear, an orange ashtray for their red and gold living room.

"I love it," she said as each gift was opened, examined, and admired. "I love it," she said as each gift was put away in the bottom of a dresser drawer.

He was feeling good, and his gestures were expansive. He mixed himself a drink, told her the dinner smelled good, played peek-a-boo with Liza. His business trip had been successful. He went to the phone to call his assistant. He wanted to discuss his subtle dealings, to repeat conversations, to gossip and speculate and chew over the past week lovingly, detail after detail. While he talked she whispered to him, "Dinner is ready, darling. Darling, please—" He shook his head impatiently and waved her away. When they finally ate at a quarter after nine he complained that the duck was dry. Marcia slammed down her fork and felt anger burst like a bubble in her throat.

"You should have come when I told you."

"I had to tell Pete a few things."

"They couldn't wait until morning?"

"Can't I make a phone call when I want to?"

They were back to the time before he went away, a time of anger and arguments, silences and pain. She pushed her plate away. "There's dessert—"

"No, thanks." He gave his words an annoyed emphasis and walked off into the living room.

She thought of the apple tart, the cheese and biscuits she had bought because he liked them. Clearing the table, she felt her tears, another enemy, prick at her hot eyes.

Later he slept contentedly, his arm under his head, his mouth open, a great pale fish swept up on the shore of her bed. She stayed awake and watched the pattern of lights on the ceiling, listened to the sound of the city traffic ten floors below. She had been lonely when he was away, but now she was lonely with him next to her. She felt his shoulder; his hip was solid against her hip. But there was no comfort in this closeness. She got up and went into the baby's room.

Liza slept, contented, too, with the sheet in her mouth, her round bottom high. Watching her daughter sleep, Marcia felt love, a physical sensation, course through her and settle like a gentle ache in her back and neck and throat. She knelt down and pressed her face against the crib's bars. She reached in and squeezed the baby's pink clenched hand. But Liza sighed and turned in her sleep. She rolled over and frowned as if to show that love was nice, but sleep was sleep. Marcia rose and went into the bathroom. Sleep was sleep was sleep indeed. She opened the medicine chest. Without a drink of water, she casually gulped a pill.

Larry got a raise. They were going to be rich. She could have . . . a vacation in the Caribbean, a fun fur coat, a secondhand car. Choose one and say thank you. But instead, without telling her, Larry bought stock. He began to read *The Wall Street Journal.* She kept finding little scraps of paper, backs of envelopes covered with numbers. He was figuring out their savings, what their savings would be in five years and in ten. "I think I've made a few rather wise investments," Larry said to the Bannons, a couple they had to dinner. Dave Bannon nodded judiciously, his glasses glinting in the yellow lamplight.

"Oh, we play the market, too," Mrs. Bannon said in a sweet fluting voice. "I got a very good tip recently, from one of the girls in my hors d'œuvres cooking class. An Australian mining company—Double Rock."

Now Larry nodded wisely. "Bought it last week at eighteen."

"We bought it at fifteen—didn't we, darling?"

"Now it's twenty-three," Larry said.

"Twenty-four and a half," she replied. They smiled warmly at each other.

Marcia went into the kitchen to take the tacos out of the oven. She heard Larry say, "If only Marcia would take some interest in the market———"

"Ooohhh, I think it's exciting," the woman trilled gaily. "Money is sexy."

She burned her tongue tasting a taco, she burned her fingers arranging the tacos in a tray. She decided she would go and live in Mexico and doze all afternoon in the warm southern sun. Yes, she would live in a white adobe house with Liza and a maid named Maria. And Maria would have a heavy black shawl, a slight black moustache, and a large comforting bosom. Maria would sit in the doorway and sing sad songs and make tortillas, clap-clap-clap, with her strong but gentle hands.

Larry came into the kitchen to get ice. "Hi," he said and kissed her on the cheek. "Everybody wants another drink." He filled the ice bucket. "Hey, are you O.K.? You look a little pale."

"Everything is grand." She bent to the oven and basted the leg of lamb. "It's too hot in here."

"If you can't stand the heat, get out of the kitchen."

"Fun-ny," he said. "Very fun-ny." He held her around the waist. He tickled her and bit her neck gently. She giggled, not wanting to, then wanting to.

"I don't think money is sexy," she purred and rubbed against him. "I'm old-fashioned. I think sex is sexy."

"Oh, yeah?" His expression was amused but challenging. He picked up the ice bucket and went out of the room, leaving her angry and suddenly ashamed.

"Viva Zapata," she said, trying to be gay as she served the tacos. "Remember? Zapata! Zapata! Zapata!" she cried.

Mrs. Bannon looked at her a shade too blankly.

"Don't you remember the movie? Marlon Brando in a moustache. You must remember. It was great."

Mrs. Bannon shook her neat blonde head. "I'm afraid that was just a teeny-weeny bit before my time."

Marcia sat in the corner of the couch. Shot-down, put-down, put-upon, downtrodden—the words buzzed in her head. The others discussed the advantages of mutual funds while she gorged on tacos. "Do no worry, *señorita*," Emiliano Zapata, nee Marlon Brando, twirled his revolver and whispered in her ear. "*Mañana* we will have our revenge, no? Revenge is sweet, no?" Her stomach began to burn.

In the afternoons she took Liza to the park. The mothers in that park sat half a bench apart to make it very clear they had not come to waste their valuable time and chat. While the children played, they read only the most serious and fashionable books. But the reading was slow. The children fought, cried, fell down. By four the women were in one small tight group, complaining about their cleaning women who didn't clean, about the cost of nursery schools, about the five pounds they couldn't seem to lose. One woman had taken seven months to read *Steppenwolf*. She had finished it in the hospital after her second son was born.

Marcia carried a book of poetry as a shield. Poetry was calming. "I grow old, I grow old, I shall wear the bottoms of my trousers rolled." Finely distilled pain was a comfort. But mostly she watched the children.

Liza had been a placid baby, a good-natured one-year-old, but at twenty-two months she was changing. She threw sand, pulled hair, scratched. All the two-year-olds seemed savage to Marcia. They were like South American Indians, the fiercest Amazon tribesmen who dipped their arrows in snake venom. At two, their world was violent and filled with danger. They lived by cruelty and cunning. Take care! If the piranhas didn't get you, the tarantulas would.

Liza stole Stephanie's horse. Stephanie, shrieking wildly, followed in hot pursuit. She caught and tripped Liza by the playground's gate. Liza wailed while

Stephanie pulled her hair, bit her cheek. Marcia watched, gnawing on a finger-nail, as usual unsure of what to do. Stephanie's mother placidly turned the pages of *The Autobiography of Malcolm X*. Finally Liza struggled free and stag-gered away. But Stephanie was not through yet. She caught Liza again, pushed her down, sat on her chest. She began to kiss her forehead and cheeks while Liza turned her head from side to side with indignation. Marcia ran across the playground. Did she hear a murmur of disapproval from the mother's bench behind her? At the park, "Let-them-fight-their-own-battles" was the current philosophy. She didn't care. She shoved Stephanie away, and bundled Liza into her stroller. It was late and she had to shop for dinner. But Liza, ungrateful and ornery, stretched out her arms beseechingly toward Stephanie. She did not want to be saved. Marcia felt a great wave of exhaustion press down upon her. She stopped at the Italian delicatessen, leaving Liza outside, still crying. She bought a pound of spaghetti and meat balls and would pass them off as her own.

After dinner, Larry stretched, stood up, began to pace the living room. "I feel like *doing* something," he said.

She leaned against her chair and didn't reply.

"Call a sitter, Marcia. We'll go out for a drink. For a late movie. Come on."

"Don't be silly," she said harshly. It was after nine.

He sat on the arm of her chair. "Baby . . . baby . . ." he murmured into her hair.

She shifted slightly. "I don't know why I'm so tired. . . ."

He was up and animated. "Did I tell you what Dave Bannon said about the partnership . . . ?"

She nodded, half-listening. She wanted a cigarette but was trying not to smoke.

"He thinks it looks like a possibility, too. He's sure of it. Well, what do you think?"

"Great. Wonderful. If it happens." They had spent the past week dis-cussing the partnership. There was a rumor spreading around the office. Larry would be offered a junior partnership soon.

"You don't think it will happen? Do you?"

"I don't know."

"You don't seem very confident of my abilities."

"Oh, Larry, it's not that——"

"Most women would show a little more enthusiasm."

"I am enthusiastic. But what more can I say?"

"You could think of something."

"Larry, please." She got up and went to the kitchen, where she had hidden a pack of cigarettes behind the coffee canister.

"Most other women——" He followed her, complaining.

"Look, couldn't we spend one night not talking about your job?"

"What's wrong with talking about my job?" She listened to the sharpness in their voices. The war was escalating again. Fifty thousand Marines had just landed in their living room.

"All right. All right." He had considered. "What do you want to talk about?"

She gave a little laugh. She felt the smoke relax her throat. "I don't know. Anything. Books. Liza. The stock market——"

"Fascinating."

"Let's just not talk then," she said quietly.

"I want to do something. Go somewhere. Marcia, I told you, get a sitter."

"For God's sake, it's nine-fifteen."

"I don't care. I want to go out."

"Then go out. Be selfish!"

"I'm selfish? You're selfish!" And they were shouting at each other, snarling, grimacing, repeating the same words they had said over and over before. She sometimes felt as if they were merely acting out a fight, going through the gestures, growing more and more familiar with the roles they had chosen to play. She got up and rushed around the sofa. She covered her face with her hands, her shoulders shook, but she didn't cry. He approached her, menaced her with his clenched fists. But he backed away shaking his head as she heard herself coolly taunt him. He swore at her softly, groaned, raised his arms high in supplication. They were comic-strip characters, Alice and Ralph on TV, the shrill monsters of *Virginia Woolf*. Deep inside she ached and knew this was vulgar, horrible, and grotesque, but when her cue came she shouted out her lines.

"I'm getting out of this place." Larry struggled into his coat.

"Then go out. Get out. Do what you want. Who cares? Get out——" And he slammed the door behind him. She sunk to her knees and wailed like Liza. Her world also had become violent and full of pain.

She smoked until her throat hurt and she was dizzy, lying across their bed, staring up at the ceiling. How had it happened? Tell me the story. And tell me, too, can this marriage be saved? How could they, once so smug in their passion, have become the people next door who quarreled, the couple at a restaurant table who didn't talk? When she was a young girl, both self-confident and romantic, she had sworn she would never, never be like this. Yet she had become precisely like this—sharp-tongued, shrewish, sullen.

If she wanted to, she thought lighting still another cigarette, she could justify her feelings with complaints. Larry was childish, egocentric, thoughtless. He was too interested in his work, not interested enough in her. But this selfish Larry was part of the Larry she had always wanted and loved. And what did it matter if at times her anger was justified? Or even if Larry was right, and she too often played the shrew. There were no scales upon which to weigh their points of view. Who was there to judge? Heah comes de judge! It was a joke.

For now her discontent was greater than the causes that had first created it. Discontent had become the fabric of their lives together.

He woke her in the middle of the night, standing over her bed, looking down at her. "Baby . . ." he whispered and swayed back and forth above her. He was tired and sorry and a little drunk.

"Hello." She sat up, wide-awake and clear-headed.

"Oh, honey . . ." He knelt at the side of their bed. "I'm sorry, sorry, sorry."

"It was my fault, too." She wanted to be precise.

"We weren't even fighting about anything." He shook his head.

"I know. We were just fighting, keeping in practice."

"Marcia, this can't go on. What's wrong? Will you tell me what's wrong?"

She didn't reply. She felt cold and she rubbed her bare arms. She glanced at the night table. Her pack of cigarettes was empty.

"It's making me sick. I go to the office and I can't work. All I think about is us." In the dim light his eyes were full and wet. She didn't want to see him so vulnerable. "It's just got to stop, that's all. I can't stand it." He pressed his face into her lap. She cradled his heavy head in her arms.

"Please," he murmured sleepily, "oh, please." She stroked his thick dark hair. "Please, let's not fight anymore."

But even this moment was familiar, the making-up scene, part of their usual repertoire. And for a while everything would seem calm between them. But this evening would add to the reservoir of bitterness. Everything they said, did, felt had echoes now. Everything was a reminder of past quarrels, past hurts, even past forgiveness.

"Tell me everything's going to be all right now," Larry said, holding her tightly. "Tell me, baby."

"Yes, yes," she whispered to him softly. She rocked him against her. "Go to sleep, go to sleep," she murmured as if to a child, and she watched his dark, tense face soften as he clung to her and slept.

Larry went to Chicago on another business trip. Her mother came to dinner. "We'll go to the movies," Marcia said, not wanting to talk.

"Spend money on a sitter? Don't be ridiculous," her mother said. "How often do I see you?" She brought a bakery strudel—"Who has time to bake these days?"—and a wine-colored velvet dress for Liza.

"Ma, you shouldn't have," Marcia said, though her mother always brought gifts.

"Please. Besides I got it wholesale. The children's buyer is a friend of mine." Liza twirled happily around the room, declaring, "Pret-ty, pret-ty," each time she passed a mirror.

"Do you remember you had a velvet dress——"

"A blue one with a velvet collar."

"Your father took a picture of you. It's in the book." She shook her head and took her handkerchief out of her purse. "In one lifetime I have so many memories."

Her mother had been a widow for five years. Recently she had taken a part-time job in a department store, joined a diet club and lost twenty pounds. Her salt-and-pepper hair was now carefully tended auburn. And she had acquired a beau, Mr. Applebaum, the neighborhood catch, a widower with real estate. Each evening Mr. Applebaum sat in her living room and together they drank tea sweet with Sucaryl and watched color television.

"How's Mr. Applebaum?" Marcia asked.

Her mother smiled broadly. "We're going to Radio City on Saturday night. Mr. Applebaum is really a very charming man."

Over dinner her mother asked, "Are you tired, Marcia? You look a little tired."

"I'm fine, Ma. Have some strudel."

Her mother counted calories and shook her head. Then she shrugged. "A little, maybe. I had cottage cheese for lunch." She ate her cake slowly, delicately, chewing each bite. She sighed as she put down her fork. "Maybe the house is too much for you. Is the house too much for you?" She wouldn't be deterred.

"Everything is all right, Ma. Really."

"And Larry. How's Larry?"

"Fine, just fine."

"I don't know." The other woman eyed her sharply. "You just don't look right to me."

"Everything is fine. Ma, please——" Her voice was getting sharp.

"O.K., O.K." Her mother shrugged. "I'm glad. Wonderful. That's the way it is. There are good times sometimes, bad times sometimes. Who said life's a bowl of cherries? I'd like to meet that guy."

"I'll get the paper," Marcia said, escaping into the living room. "I'll see what's on television." Together, for an hour, they watched the small flickering screen. Her mother ate grapes, speculated on the ages of the performers, commented on the clothes the women wore. She left early, afraid to travel on the subway after ten. She phoned Mr. Applebaum. He would meet her at the station, walk with her to her apartment building.

"Believe me, Marcia, things change," she said as they kissed good-bye. "That's life. Change. Something different every day." Marcia was relieved when she shut the door. But in a moment she felt lonely, too, alone in the silence with her sleeping baby. There was no one she could talk to. She and her mother couldn't talk. Their relationship was a patchwork of the past, sewn together of bits of pain and affection and distorted memories. The bond between them was also the wedge.

When Larry came home from Chicago they decided to go away for a weekend, assuring each other heartily that was just what they needed, all that they needed. Liza would stay with her grandmother, who had baked brownies, bought a doll who rode a tricycle. Mr. Applebaum would take them to the zoo on Sunday. Everybody was happy.

They drove to an inn in Connecticut where they had gone five years before during the first months of their marriage. "I hope it hasn't changed too much," Marcia said, as the car sped along the quiet highway in the darkening night. In their minds the weekend had become symbolic, a testing ground. What was the point after all if they couldn't even have a good time together? A flat tire or a toothache might be a shadow across their whole future. She thought she should have read her horoscope before she left.

But the inn hadn't changed. It was warm and comfortable. And the room they were given was cheerful with its bright wallpaper and small fireplace and neat Early American reproductions.

"It's very nice," Larry said. Alone in the room, they hugged each other shyly. It had been so long since they were simply affectionate and kind.

They ate an enormous dinner, heavy with hot rolls and relishes and Indian pudding. They sat by the fire in their room, watching the flames, and then slept, holding hands like children under soft clean-smelling quilts. In the morning they took a long walk, collected leaves. They read for an hour in the sunlight filtered through bright autumn trees. After lunch they went again to their room. She took off her dress, brushed her hair. Larry kissed her gently on the shoulder. She turned to him and closed her eyes, willing herself to feel.

Afterward she cried, with relief, with contentment. They kissed, touched, smoked cigarettes. She stood by the window looking out at the pale yellow afternoon. "We should go out. It's nice outside."

"It's nice inside. Come back to bed."

Smiling, she went to him. She liked the way he looked, the hollows in his neck, his eyes closed, and his dark hair against the pillow. She felt gentled by his need for her, her need for him. Her fingers traced a pattern on his warm chest.

"It's all right now, isn't it?" Larry asked almost timidly, awed again by her. She nodded and bent to kiss him.

"Why do we ever fight, Marcie?" he asked. "Oh, baby, baby, why do we fight? Who needs it?" And she shook her head, also amazed. Their quarrels at this moment seemed a child's bad dream. With a change in tempo, in background, their relationship seemed placid and successful. Through the weekend they clung to each other tightly, protectively, as if the threat to their contentment came from somewhere else.

When they stopped at her mother's Liza ran gaily into their arms. Larry whirled her around and around. "We had a good time," Marcia said.

Her mother nodded with approval. "So Liza had a wonderful time, too. Don't forget the doll and the balloon she got at the park. And take some brownies. I baked a few extra and, believe me, I don't need them."

But on Monday morning Larry called, his voice tight and strained.

"I messed up on that last trip. Quoted some figures that were underestimates. Now the other company is balking about signing a contract——"

"Is it so important? Can't you work it out?"

"There's something else, too."

"What?"

"I can't talk now. I'll call you back." He hung up abruptly.

She waited, staying in the house, but he didn't call again. He came home that night an hour later than usual. As she opened the door she knew the weekend had faded already, the feeling of happiness between them was over.

"What's wrong, darling? I've been worrying——"

Slowly he shuffled into the room. He took off his coat, threw it over a chair. "Nothing's wrong," he said thickly. "Everything's wrong."

"You've been drinking."

"Now, that's a good idea. Best idea I've heard today." He went into the kitchen for ice.

Finally he told her, after a drink, after staring out the window, after refusing his dinner, then deciding he had to have it immediately, right then, before the vegetables had time to cook. There would be no partnership offer. One of the top men in the company had told Dave Bannon that no such offer was going to be made. In fact, this man had implied that Larry had become a little pompous lately, a little too-smart-for-his-own-good. There were certain people at the top who were not at all pleased with his work.

"Oh, darling——" He sat, slumped in his chair. He covered his face with his hands. He had worked for the company for seven years, turned down other jobs. All his energy and buoyancy had been fed by the promise of his future. He lowered his hands and looked at her. "Come here. I need you. Make me feel better."

The week went by and then another. Larry came home late, went to bed early. They shouted at each other occasionally—when she forgot to wash his socks, when Liza cried all one night and made them both edgy and concerned. Mostly they were silent and polite, keeping apart. She had the sense of a broken promise between them. One evening Larry was more cheerful. A report he had prepared had been widely praised. Then a man Larry thought was against him was especially enthusiastic. Perhaps Dave Bannon wasn't such a good friend after all. Dave Bannon was ambitious, too, Larry speculated. The partnership offer might be made after the first of the year. He had only to wait.

Feeling good, he poured a brandy, laughed at a television comedian's joke. She felt weary of the Byzantine world of his office politics, weary finally of him. There, she could admit it. Lying across the couch, sucking on the rim of his glass, he seemed to her a great child, absorbing her with his demands, his needs, his kaleidoscopic moods. Larry, Larry, wife-eater, the all-consuming center of her life.

It rained for three days and she and Liza had to stay inside. Her loneliness became a dull ache in the back of her head. They played quietly at first, then Liza grew sulky and impossible. She twisted her dolls' arms and legs, threw them across the room, crying with some inexplicable fury. Feeling neglectful, her head pounding, Marcia called her mother. They had not spoken in over a week. Her mother's voice was full of sighs when she answered.

"What's wrong, Ma?" she asked, already feeling impatient.

"Applebaum is moving to California."

"Oh, no, Mama. Why?"

"His daughter. A great big girl with three children and a husband. She has to have her father there, too."

"What did he say to you?"

"He said come to Los Angeles for a visit. I'd love the climate. He said he'd be happy to show me around."

"Oh, Ma, that's awful."

"Why awful? Did he owe me anything?"

"No, but——"

"So I lost my boyfriend. Big deal."

"Come and stay here for a few days."

"I have things to do."

"What things?"

"You don't think I have a life?" Her mother's voice was fierce. Then she began to cry softly. "That dumbie. That dumbie. He'll hate Los Angeles. He doesn't even know how to drive a car. And his daughter. She'll want him for a month. For a month."

Liza tugged at the phone, calling, "Na-na, Na-na."

"Let me speak to the baby," her mother instructed.

"You're sure you won't come?" Marcia asked, before surrendering the phone to a squealing Liza.

"Please . . ." her mother said as if to sum everything up. "Please . . ."

Weekends were the worst time, because weekends were supposed to be the best time. Weekends were a renewal. Something was supposed to happen. She, too, believed in family fun, picnics in the park, going out with friends on Saturday night. Larry complained, "Why didn't you get a sitter?"

"We weren't going anywhere."

"Well, if we had a sitter, we could go out."

"We didn't have anywhere to go."

"I always like to go out on Saturday——"

"Then go."

"Maybe I will."

Jungle warfare again. They were sharpening their arrows, defoliating the bush.

"I think I'll call the Bannons. See what they're doing."

"Don't. I don't like them."

"You don't like anyone."

"I don't like you," she said lightly.

He snorted and made a face, snug in his ego. "I'm going to call them. She's not bad."

"She's terrible."

"I like her."

"Larry, I don't want you to——"

He grinned and went to the phone.

"Larry," she screamed. "This has got to stop! Right now! Do you understand?"

"O.K.," he said loudly, looking at her uncertainly.

"I mean it!" Another shriek.

"O.K." He studied her for a moment, his head to one side. Their style of argument was changing.

"Go out," she said softly. "Just go out."

He went to get his coat meekly. "I'll get the papers——"

"Take your time. Go to a movie. Have a drink. . . ." But he came right back. They read all evening. He pointed out an article he found interesting. She made a Welsh rabbit as a treat before they went to bed. But she needed two large pills to put herself to sleep.

They took Liza to the park on Sunday. Winter had finally come. The sky was dark and gray and sooty. The low thick clouds promised the season's first snow. The park at four o'clock was almost deserted. A broken plastic horse lay on its side, abandoned. A wheel was missing. There was a jagged puncture in its belly. But Liza went to the horse, her prize, set it right, and began to run with it. She didn't care that the horse moved jerkily, causing her to fall. She ran in wide circles around them, ululating in triumph. She had what she wanted.

Larry sat looking at the river. His face was pale and unshaven, his collar up. He puffed on a cigarette. She thought of her mother fixing an early supper for herself, spending the evening in front of her television set, sucking chocolates for comfort. Oh, perfidious Applebaum.

Larry took her cold hand in his. "I'm sorry," he said.

"I'm sorry, too." He squeezed her hand tightly, hurting her. Was it the beginning of the end? Or the end of the beginning for them? Were they being weathered and was this only the bad, bad time? She didn't know and she didn't want to know yet. She would only keep her head down, turn her face from the coldest winds and try, for a little while longer, to wait the darkness out.

Myrna Blyth, a graduate of Bennington College, has written for radio and TV, and published stories and articles in Cosmopolitan, Redbook, Reader's Digest, Bride's Magazine, *and other periodicals throughout the world. Perhaps Ms. Blyth's expertise as a magazine and fiction editor accounts for the fact that almost all her short stories are bought by one magazine or another. (Few world-famous authors can make this claim.) Although sympathetic to women's liberation, she feels that "emotions are not rational" and that women will continue to find deeper fulfillment in marriage and motherhood than in business or professional successes. Ms. Blyth lives in New York City with her British journalist husband and their two sons.*

Subject to Change

by Sonya Dorman

*T*he grayness of early afternoon came through the vaulted glass roof of the station, was diffused among the great steel beams that crossed and recrossed in a parody of tracks overhead, and was dispersed entirely by the dull yellow lamp and sign lights down below.

She sat on a navy blue suitcase, knitting. Her auburn hair, coarse and vital as a pony's mane, fell long about her fine head, curving forward jaggedly over her forehead and ears, brushing her shoulders. Seen from in front, she had small, delicately chiseled features—dark eyes and an expression of fatigue and endurance—all locked between the long, spiky curves of her hair.

People went by, men passed her; no one turned again to look at the woman busy with her inappropriate task. The gleaming black wool lifted and fell over one forefinger; it grew in a row of ram's curls along the bottom of the white needle in her other hand.

One man looked. He was standing ten feet away and had beside him one suitcase with three cameras lying on top of it. When he looked, she raised her face from the wool in her hands, and met his eyes, which were so deeply set they were difficult to see. He was a short, blocky man with thick, curly black hair and a rather narrow and inexpressive face.

People passed and repassed, following their own timetables, moving between the man and the woman so that their exchange of silence was broken many times. The man at last lifted his cameras about him, hanging them in their leather cases from his shoulder and moved over to her.

"My name's Gilman," he said to her.

"I know. I've seen your photographs at the museum. And in magazines." She began to put the knitting away without watching her hands; something was clasped over the end of the needle to keep the row of curls from falling off; the loose wool was rewound haphazardly on its parent ball; the whole task was stuffed into a cheap cardboard case and the lid snapped over it.

"Hugh Gilman," the man said.

"Yes. I know."

"Are you a photographer? I'm not usually recognized in person."

The woman stood up. She was short and straight, not very graceful, but finely built. "I'm a teacher. A sculptor."

"What train are you catching?" he asked.

"I'm not sure. I have a choice of several."

"Then come and have some coffee with me while we wait. I must wait another half hour for mine; it's been delayed."

"Thank you." She picked up her luggage, and he went back to where he had been standing and assumed his own burden which he had trustfully left there. The cameras dangled at his waist.

"Will you tell me your name?" he asked as they came together after being separated by a wandering cluster of schoolgirls.

"It's Michaeline. I don't like it."

"I'm sure people call you Micky, and you don't like that either."

"No, it's not much better."

"It's awful." He pushed open the glass door with his shoulder, and she passed him and went to the counter, but he came up beside her and motioned toward a booth along the glass wall where they would have more room. They sat down opposite one another, next to the glass wall where people passed and passed.

"Then call me Michaeline, if you prefer that," she said.

They looked over the menu printed on shiny orange cardboard and gave the order to the waitress in her orange organdy dress.

When they stopped watching her, Michaeline and Hugh smiled at each other. "Are you going on vacation?" he asked her.

"Yes, I've got a free week, and I want to go somewhere, away. I haven't decided where yet. I was going to make up my mind after a while."

Hugh reached across the table for her left hand, looked at the back of it, and then with one finger, delicately he touched the pale mark on her bare ring finger.

"He is dead," Michaeline said, and drew her hand away. "Are you going on an assignment?"

"A personal one, a book I want to do with a friend who's a writer."

The waitress set down their plates and cups of coffee, frilled and trembling in her orange organdy, sweetly perfumed with cologne, alive, pretty, but she didn't see them; she was marking down the price of their meal on the check.

Michaeline and Hugh began to eat and drink. He had put his cameras down on the seat beside him, and now and then he put his hand down to feel that three cameras were still there. "I didn't want to bring them all," he explained. "I only wanted to bring one. But Paul asked me to bring them all, in case we wanted to experiment, to try different things. I'm always trying different things in my work. He knows me."

"I would know that, after seeing your pictures. Anyone would."

"No, they wouldn't. People don't look that sharply as a rule. What do you work in? Wood? Stone?"

"Both. And clay, or any other substance. I haven't worked for a long time. I just teach and do some modeling. Someday I'll go back to the other."

"Did he die recently?"

"I don't know what you mean by *recent*. He's been dead eight months."

"I should say that was recent. But perhaps you wouldn't."

"I don't say anything about it."

"I beg your pardon, then," Hugh said. "I wouldn't have spoken of it."

"It doesn't matter. Other people speak of it. My friends do. My relatives. The breath was still in his nostrils when they began talking to me about marrying again."

"And you told them to go to hell?"

"No. I just told them no. I have no more intentions."

"No intentions?" he asked her. "You don't want to be with a man again?"

"I didn't say that. I said I don't want to remarry. I have nothing to offer a man. I'm not pretty. Inside, I'm full of broken glass. What have I to offer?"

"Nothing, to a stranger. One would have to know you better. How could that be done?" He lighted a cigarette. Then he took out the package again and offered her one and lighted it for her.

"I haven't any idea," Michaeline said, perhaps referring to his question. After a moment, she said, "You can't get to know someone in half an hour. Between trains. Sitting behind a table like this."

"Good," Hugh said. "Let's go somewhere else; where we can do better?"

"Your train? Your visit to your friend, the writer?"

Hugh smiled. The smile pulled the skin tight over his hard, wide cheekbones, and the lids nearly closed down over his deeply set gray eyes. "And your train? Your vacation?"

They were silent for a while. Michaeline smoked a cigarette and finished her coffee.

"I have a choice of trains," she said finally. "Perhaps that's the trouble."

"Do you want to make it so that you have no choice?"

She flashed at him, clear and brilliant through the smoke of their cigarettes. "No! I would hate you."

"Then what?"

"Do you live in the city?" she asked.

"Not this one. But you do, don't you?"

Michaeline began putting on her coat. When she had the coat on, she turned up the collar as if her neck felt cold. "It's ten minutes, in a taxi. Do you want to do anything about tickets first?"

"No, I don't want to do anything first," Hugh said, getting up and putting the cameras over his shoulder. "I'd rather think about that later. There's time. I'm afraid you'll become afraid."

"Yes. I am, too."

"Then let's go quickly."

They went out through the door in the glass wall into the mass of moving people and began to flow along with the crowd toward one of the exit doors. They went into the gray, damp afternoon street and Hugh, with a single motion of his hand, brought a taxi toward them.

She unlocked the door of her apartment, and they went in. It was one big room, long and narrow, with three tall casement windows that looked out on the street and the river beyond. Off one end of the room was a small kitchen, and against the wall, a table with four chairs. In a corner the floor was covered with linoleum, and two wooden stands topped with armatures were pushed against the wall. In another corner a couch stood covered with bright cushions. A pair of old slippers lay on the floor by the couch.

Hugh bent and picked the slippers up. They were a small size, even for such a small woman, and once they had been decorated, but now were shabby and bare, and there was hardly any pattern or color left. Hugh put them down on the floor again. Michaeline closed the closet where she had hung their coats and asked him if he wanted a drink.

"No. Nothing now." He paused and smiled the smile that hid his eyes. "You've had too much time. You're afraid."

"Not quite."

They stepped toward each other, the length of the room. She was beginning to run in order to arrive where he was before she became afraid, or remembered, or forgot; she would never be able to tell which it was. She did run to him, moving so fast that she crashed into him with all her weight. He had stood braced, ready for her, so he could stand up to her weight and catch her in his arms.

They kissed. It was on the surface, like two people floating in quiet water; it was strange to them both after her haste across the room and the violence of her body meeting his. Then they kissed deeply. He moved his hands over her back and felt the indentations of her spine. She put her hands in his hair and found it softer than it looked, but dense and springy, like the winter coat of a ram.

"I don't want to explain," Michaeline said when they stopped kissing. "I don't have to, do I? About seeing you in the station and deciding then?"

"Oh good God, no," Hugh said.

She unbuttoned his shirt and put her hands inside, like a child exploring, feeling his ribs, the warm, smooth skin on his chest, the thickness of his back. They kissed and moved to her bed where the slippers lay on the floor.

"You don't want me to talk, do you?" Michaeline said.

"Yes, yes if you want to. I don't mind. But what you mean is you don't want either of us to talk. Isn't that it?"

"I like silence, sometimes. Very often I prefer it."

He put part of his weight on her and rested on his elbows, looking down into her face. With his hands, one at each side of her face, he pushed her hair back so he could see her without that helmet. She did not smile, but her lips moved as if she would have smiled in a moment. Hugh kissed her mouth, and she smiled then; their teeth met and opened. He could feel the strength of her small body, the fineness of her bones and the health of her muscles; the physical desire that she had not withheld from him, not from the first moment, and behind it, or within it, something more, too; something she no longer believed in, but that belonged in her, anyway.

He was heavy and he was not too careful of her, which was better; she would rather take as much of his weight as she could, also. If there had been time to count over each piece of broken glass that she felt in her heart, in her mind where her memory was, she would not be here with him; but at first glance she had decided there was no more time for counting; she must not take that time ever again.

As they lay together in the pale light of late afternoon, she could feel her body becoming fine as lace, transparent and perfectly balanced on an edge of air.

After a while Michaeline turned her head until her lips were against his face. He said, "Now, you see? We can begin to know each other. At our leisure. Are you comfortable?"

"We both are, aren't we?"

After a time he said, "My first camera was about tenth hand, from a hock shop. But I took some good pictures with it. I had a good eye, even then. That was fifteen years ago."

"You must be my age. I'm thirty-four."

"And you're telling the truth, too." He smiled. "You're not a liar," he said.

"I can't be bothered to be one. But I do lie, sometimes, just for convenience, don't you? When you're in the middle of a job, setting up a picture, you don't want to be bothered, do you? You'd like to preserve yourself?"

"Oh, surely," Hugh said. "I'd lie with no conscience at all."

Michaeline looked across the room. "It's after five," she said.

"Is it, really? Will you make some coffee for us?"

"Yes. But I thought you might want to know the time. You still have a train—"

"Stop, now. There are two more trains this evening that I can catch."

"I'll make some coffee," she said. She got up and put her slip on and went into the small kitchen. He lay on the bed, his eyes closed. He waited until he could smell the coffee and hear her put the cups and saucers on the table by the wall. Then he got up and went and sat at the table with her.

"Did you used to wear your hair longer?" he asked.

"Yes, how did you know?"

"It would look better that way." He lighted their cigarettes and drank his cup empty. She refilled it for him. He said, "My wife used to wear her hair short, cut right up the back of her head. It wasn't the style, then. During the war, I mean."

"Does she still wear it that way?"

Hugh leaned over to kiss her neck and said, with his lips near her, "I don't go home more than once or twice a year. I haven't been at home for more than a week in several years."

"I think that's strange," she said moving away from him to look at his face. "Then why do you go home? Or call it home?"

"It's a convenience for us both. My wife doesn't want anything but the house. I mean she wants the name of wife, but nothing else. Not from me or from anyone else, either; her coldness is genuine."

"Just how did you ever marry her?"

Hugh looked down at his hands. "That part is strange, I suppose. We were both twenty, and we've been married ever since. My eye was good then, as I said. She was beautiful. She is now. Only then I thought that was fine enough. It hasn't mattered. You know, I travel so much, I couldn't live with an ordinary woman. I wouldn't be home to dinner for days on end. I couldn't care less about bridge with the neighbors, or any of that. So it's been a convenience for us both for many years."

"Yes, I see." Michaeline filled their cups again, emptying the coffee pot. She suddenly sat up straight in the chair and bent her head back, so the hair fell away from it and hung behind.

"I feel so good," she said.

He said, "Yes?"

"I wanted to some other times I met men. But they weren't right. I can't tell you how, but I knew right away I would have to make explanations; I couldn't be honest and I knew it wouldn't be any good. We'd both be hateful afterward, because of trying to excuse ourselves." She flashed again, "I hate to excuse myself when I'm not sorry! So I'm glad I met you. I knew you were honest."

"I know you did. You didn't pretend not to look at me. It's been a long time since anyone looked at me straight like that, and I was delighted. But I didn't want to frighten you."

Michaeline got up and took their cups into the kitchen where she washed them. When she came into the long room again, Hugh was sitting in a chair, looking at one of the books from the full bookcase near a window. Michaeline sat down on the bed, drawing up her bare feet, and smoked a cigarette.

After half an hour had passed, he put the book down. "Do you want to go out to dinner?" he asked.

"If you like. I'm getting hungry. But your friend? Do you want to at least telephone him?"

"Yes, I'll call him. I'll go up for a few days," Hugh said. He was bending over, putting on his shoes. "What about your plans?"

"I think I'll come back here after we eat. I've got lots of work to do."

While Hugh was phoning his friend, Michaeline put on her makeup and took their coats from the closet. She went over to the metal tub in the corner where the floor was covered with dark linoleum. Slowly she lifted the lid and looked inside. The clay was dried out and had hardened into a crumbling mass. After propping the lid back against the wall, Michaeline got a pitcher of water from the kitchen and poured it carefully into the tub. Then she closed the lid again.

It is conventional for a writer to have had many unconventional jobs before settling into a writing career, and Sonya Dorman is no exception. Among other occupations, she has worked as a riding instructor, cook on a tuna-fishing boat, receptionist, and flamenco dancer. Her stories and poems have been widely published in national magazines, and she is represented in many fiction anthologies. Ms. Dorman has published one book, POEMS. She lives in Westminster, Connecticut, with her husband and daughter.

Lemmings Are Lonely

by Babs H. Deal

Spring arrived in Druid City. Flat out, as the other girls said. The startling red and pink and white of azalea and the delicate yellow of buttercups; blue sky, white clouds, wind in the oaks. Spring. When she went to class in the morning the campus seemed washed and out to dry, new, clean, waiting. It was waiting. For spring holidays. They talked of nothing else on the crowded sleeping porch of the Delta House. Spring holidays—clothes, hairdos, money, the beach.

Lying on her narrow cot Lennie listened to them. It was remote to her, something that passed over her head with the delicate swiftness of wings and went on. She had never been to the beach, never seen the ocean. She had thought about it, there were pictures in her mind. The ocean, stretching forever toward other shores, breaking minutely at her feet on this one. But she had never seen it. In fact she had seen very little except the small town she came from in the north of the state.

She had made shopping trips to Newcastle and to Chattanooga. She had spent an entire week in New Orleans with an aunt, made small family forays into Georgia and Tennessee to visit relatives. But the beach, like New York, like Europe, lay in the future, tinged by dream, remote from reality.

"But you're going, of course," the sorority sisters said. "We take two whole houses. There's room for everyone. Of course you'll go."

"No one's asked me," she said. Aware of the male in the background, the tacit understanding that Mike or Joe or Pete would be going with his fraternity, taking his car.

"But darling," they said, "that's the greatest. No one has to ask you. There are always plenty enough to go around. Just get there, sweetie. There'll be men."

161

There had been men during this freshman year. She dated, because there were Swap Hops and house dances. The dates didn't come back often. She felt shy with them, tongue-tied, unable to talk in the bright fast chatter they used with each other. They didn't come back. But it didn't really matter. There were always new ones. They all looked vaguely alike to her, not-quite handsome, not-quite tall, not-quite spectacular, but almost all of these things. The lovely. The loved.

They were nice to her in a patterned prescribed way because she belonged to one of the best sororities. Her mother had belonged to it and her Aunt Lucy Claire who lived in New Orleans and knew everybody including Chep Morrison and members of the Boston Club. Lennie was a legacy. Not that the girls treated her that way. They liked her; she liked them. For one thing she made very good grades and the sorority could use a few brains this year. For another she looked right, small and brunette with blue eyes and a skin that tanned easily and neat legs and reasonably spectacular breasts. That she didn't feel at all the way she looked they didn't know. She had learned a long time ago to cover up the way she felt. It had occasioned too many amused glances between her mother and her Aunt Lucy Claire. She had learned, very early, not to talk about things like the beauty of nature and the need for love. She hadn't stopped reading because that gave them something to smile about. "Lennie reads" marked her, but not irreparably as "Lennie moons" or "Lennie thinks too much" would.

She took the cool facade to the university with her, and it had served her well through fall and football, Christmas, and midterms. Now she had to decide if it would serve her through spring holidays and the beach.

She knew, hearing the excited chatter, the plans, the breathless preparation, that she was afraid of the beach. Not for any of the obvious reasons. She had learned to handle all the almost-handsome, almost-perfect men early too. But because it was the ocean, and part of the inner life she hid so well. She felt that it might make her vulnerable, and her defenses were very well made, very well polished. She didn't want them breached. Not by all these lovely people. Not now. Not yet.

She had to go, of course. It was inevitable, because to not go would be the very thing to mark her. It wouldn't look right not to go. Not when she had the money and the clothes and the tacit permission of Mamma. Mamma herself would think it strange if she didn't go.

"Of course, dear," her mother wrote on her monogrammed stationery with black ink. "Of course, I read things in magazines about what goes on down there. But I'm sure this isn't among girls of the Delta caliber. There are the wrong kind of people everywhere. You, of course, won't be around *them*."

She had laughed about the letter because it apparently hadn't occurred to her mother that the "wrong" kind of people couldn't afford the annual trip to the beach, and that anything that went on on the Florida shores went on among the right people by simple necessity. It amused her so much she wanted to tell someone about it, but there wasn't anyone. Only the well-groomed, the charming, the beachgoers themselves.

She went to the dress shop with two of the others girls, another pledge, Susie Clanton, and an upperclassman, Helen Jackson. They were like birds in the shop, never still, flitting among the racks, chattering above the cool gray of carpet, joking with the owner of the dress shop, a tall lovely woman with efficient hands and amused eyes.

She bought a new bathing suit and a beach coat, shorts and shirts and a ridiculous beach hat with myriad small objects stuck all over it, a washed denim suit and large pink sleeping cap to cover her outsize rollers. She was a perfect ten, having only to try the clothes on and have them put in a bag. The other girls and the salesgirls oohed and ahhed about it. The other girls bought too-small twelves and had the seams let out, they bought skirts they couldn't sit down in and prayed girdles would take off an inch. They told her how lucky she was.

After finals, and the closed house and reading while the other girls studied —she never crammed for finals—it was over. The street buzzed for two days. Cars were brought around to the front of houses, suitcases and beachbags and duffle bags and straw baskets were packed, crammed, jammed and piled into cars. Everyone had to have an appointment at the beauty parlor on the eve of departure. She went too. She had made her appointment weeks ago for early morning because the girl who fixed her hair said that would be easiest for her.

Lennie packed her bag alone on the sleeping porch because she had waited for the other girls to finish and leave her elbow room. She showered, put on a robe and went for a Coke. She fixed her face slowly, smoking a cigarette, sipping the Coke, relaxing during the last moments while the others buzzed and chattered and ran to the ringing phone and cursed the size of their luggage compartments.

She was driving down with Susie and Helen and three KAs in Helen's car. At the exact time she came down the steps of the house carrying her one neatly packed bag and set it beside the others on the crowded sidewalk. The boys were shoving and pushing and laughing, trying to get the bags into the luggage compartment, complaining because it looked so easy on television. She watched them with a cool detachment, put on her straw hat and sunglasses, and climbed into the backseat of the convertible. She had committed herself to the Florida beach, but she had called upon all the shields and masks of her nature so that it would not, could not touch her. She hadn't wanted her first sight of the ocean to be among the bright ones, but it had to be, so she accepted it.

All the long way down she was charming, socially correct, drinking beer from punched cans, smoking, wearing her sunglasses with the proper amount of dash, thinking of zany things to eat in the small towns along the way where they stopped for meals.

Her date was attentive, but in the cool of coming dark she was able to limit him to hand holding and cool kisses, so that when they stopped for the night he let her go at the door with a minimum of opportunings. As she went peacefully to sleep in the motel bed she could still hear the others arguing on the porch in front of the cabin.

They made good time going down so that the streets were hot and still and waiting in Florida sunlight when they pulled into the filling station at the edge of town. They were all hot and wrinkled and tired and the air seemed full of the smell of asphalt and dust and gasoline. No salt. No sea.

They had the car serviced and drove away through empty streets. Behind them she heard the filling station attendant say to his companion. "It's started." And the answer, "God help us." She smiled.

She soaked in the bathtub while the others struggled into their bathing suits. "Come on," they yelled at her. "We're the first ones here and we can get our tan started hours earlier." Then they were gone, with beach coats and towels and glasses and bags, with cigarettes and suntan oil and portable radios and hi-fis, with money and beer and food and thermos bottles, with records and ukes and inflatable rubber rafts.

She finished bathing and dressed leisurely, looking around the house with pleasure, picking a bed from the cots on the porch she knew to be for the freshmen, unpacking and hanging her clothes neatly behind the striped curtain. She put on her two-piece bathing suit and her beach coat and her sunglasses and went to the path to the beach.

For a long moment she stood at the edge of the path, bracing herself in the dead white sunlight. Then she stepped firmly past the last of the houses and onto the edge of the sand, and looked at the ocean.

It was there. Just as she had dreamed, imagined, thought, through all her life. Immense, improbable, impossible. Stretched grayly away from the earth of home toward infinity, breaking gently toward her at intervals, the tide going out and out, farther out with every coming in, so that the waterline of wet sand seemed to beg for the coming surges, to mourn the retreat, to ask mutely, and to lie deserted and drying as the sea broke farther down, farther down, fickle and uncaring, deserting the shore.

She watched until they called to her. Then she went down to the midpoint of the beach and spread her towel in the gray sand and stretched out on her stomach. The hi-fi was playing and the boys were drinking beer and trying to get a twisting contest going. The sun was merciless and white and hot in the early afternoon. She lay for fifteen minutes, then turned and took off her glasses and shielded her eyes with her hand and baked that side for fifteen minutes. Then she got up and went to the retreating ocean and walked out until the water reached her mouth. She tasted salt water for the first time and marveled at it, felt shocked by it, and happy—immersed in the beginning, bemused until a wave knocked her off her feet and she floated toward shore, feeling the wash against her, letting her face get wet, her new-set hair get wet. Not caring at all, tranquil, swallowed up.

164

The KA named Ted ran out and picked her up and she squealed appropriately and let him lead her back to the others and a damp cigarette and a can of beer.

It accelerated with the falling sun, more people, more cars coming onto the flat packed sand, more music, more laughter, more squeals and splashing. All of them, trying very hard, having a good time.

At nightfall they were building fires at the beach, matching for who was to go in for food and more beer. Bottles were being broken out, ice arrived, and always more people, more barefooted, bare-legged, barebacked people, all laughing, all the right people, all interested only in having more to tell when they got home than the next.

The sun went and the water turned flat and gray before the night. Later there was a moon and they all exclaimed at how wonderful it was that the moon was waxing at just the right time this year. Lennie sat on the sand and talked to her date. She drank beer and ate a hotdog, but refused the whiskey and the ice cream.

Later there was a guitar, a wild flamenco strumming drowning out the surf, and still later there were fewer and fewer standing dancing figures. They lay on beach towels and blankets and in the grainy sand itself, intent, oblivious, merging lips and hands and limbs in the moonlight, inches apart in the sand, uncaring, each in his own darkness.

Ted kissed her a few times, but she didn't respond to him. "Ah, Lennie," he said, the nice handsome right face intent in the washing light. "What's the matter? Come on baby. Give."

She shook her head mutely, not wanting this time to be clever or careful about it. Uncaring, watching her ocean, still out there, untouched, coming up the beach, retreating down the beach, ignoring the half-naked bodies that had gravitated toward it. Perfect. Alone.

He stood up. "Let's go down the beach to the Four Leaf, then," he said. "There's a new combo down there. Come on." He yanked at her hand and she stood up and followed him quietly, stepping over and around the prone bodies, ignoring the sounds, daintily avoiding the feel of flesh on her bare feet.

At the Four Leaf it was frenetic. There were people jammed into every crevice of the room. They sat on tables, they stood jam-packed together on the small dance floor. The combo played and they looked at each other in the half light. It smelled of whiskey and sweat and salt. She felt herself pushed in between two muscular boys in bathing trunks and the wet feel of the trunks and the slickness of their bodies annoyed her. She tried to draw back, but they had crowded in behind her. A girl in a bikini was half-sitting on a boy's leg and she bumped into them while trying to get out. "Watch it, baby," the boy said. "I got all I can handle right here. Just don't crowd me." She looked away from his eyes, bright and a little slimy like his body.

Ted had pushed through the crowd ahead of her. She moved toward him, then stopped, seeing him with a blonde in a pair of tight red hipslingers. He was standing closer to her, swaying to the music. While she watched he leaned over and kissed her. She felt an instant relief. She could leave now. He was happy. She pushed her way through the crowd and out of the sticky room.

She began to walk, up the beach in the moonlight, away from the main body of the crowd, the beach joints, the cars. She struck out toward the tide line, avoiding most of the couples in the darkness farther up the beach. There were solitary fires along the stretch of sand, solitary cars, couples in the sand, but they thinned out as she walked and gradually she reached a place where there was no one. A stretch of beach, narrower than the main one, empty in moonlight. She sat down at the edge of the ocean, letting the waves break across her feet, lying down finally, letting the surf come up and come up until it washed over her body completely. It was a wild sensuous feeling. It even embarrassed her a little. She got up and walked back to the beach house and went to bed, listening to the surf, watching the moon on the floor.

The next day was more of the same, only louder, faster, more frenzied. Ted was gone. She saw him on the edge of the ocean with the blonde girl, holding her hand, running into the water. She was relieved. Others boys came to their group, tried to talk to her. She ignored them. No one noticed her. They were too immersed in what they were doing, trying to drink more, dance more, get tanner, be wilder, love longer.

But today she knew why she had come. She waited until the sun was going down over the ocean, then struck off up the beach. She reached the deserted stretch of the night before and sat down. It was quiet here with only an occasional shrill scream or the sound of pounding feet from down the beach. She watched the sun set, going into the water as though for the last time, leaving the gray flat desert of water, bringing the dark and the moon and light again, the golden wash across immensity, caught glittering in the sudsy surf.

He came on the third night. She might have willed him out of moonlight or ocean. She would not have been surprised to see him rise with trident in hand from the depths, seated on the back of a dolphin, blowing a wreathed horn. Because the solitude and the love of loneliness is a lie at best. Solitude is the beauty we want to share.

He didn't look tall or right or lovely as he came across the sand. He was almost as short as she was, too blonde, too muscular. He looked as though he might be a football player, or a wrestler. Not one of the lovely. Never that. He came across the sand toward the place where the surf washed her and sat down. "I've seen you every night," he said. His voice wasn't right either. It might have belonged to a Yankee or a native. She liked to think so anyway.

"You love the ocean," he said.

She nodded. He sat beside her, silent for a long time. Then he offered her a cigarette from a crumpled pack and lighted it with a Zippo lighter. In the brief flare she saw his face, wide gray eyes, wide mouth, heavy nose. And his hands, with their fingers long but blunt with a dark matting of hair on the back of them.

Everything was strange and moonswept, the sounding surf, the quiet. They did not even talk, holding hands finally, looking at the ocean. She felt at peace for the first time since she had agreed to come here. It was all right. There was someone else here who understood. They didn't even have to talk about it. They had only to look at the ocean and the sky and be still.

Later he kissed her and it was like the moonlight, soft, lingering, not urgent or necessary. Not needed for a good time or to prove anything.

"You taste like beer," she said.

"I'll get some," he said and walked off up the beach, leaving her alone, frightened momentarily until she saw him walk back through the moonlight holding a six-pack.

She sat quietly drinking beer, letting him hold her, beginning to slide a little toward something, thinking No for a moment, then ceasing to care. His lips were less soft now, more insistent and that was right too.

"In the surf," she said suddenly, struggling away from him.

"Yes," he said.

He was standing up, looking down at her. "Get up," he said.

She got to her knees on the sandy bottom and reached a hand out. He put her bathing suit in it. It embarrassed her and she turned her back to him and put it on, hopping awkwardly on one leg, already feeling stiff and sore, conscious of the salt on her limbs and the sand in her bathing suit.

He was lighting a cigarette, then shaking the cans, looking for more beer. She looked at him, watching his face.

"They didn't tell me this would be a first time business," he said. He handed her a can of beer. "Drink up. It'll be better next time."

She shook her head, still standing awkwardly, pulling at the strap of her suit. "They?" she said. "They who?"

"Your friends down the beach," he said carelessly. "Want a fag?" He handed her a lighted cigarette. She took it automatically.

"Who are you?" she said, staring at him, revealed to her suddenly. The almost-handsome, the almost-tall, the lovely. Impossible.

He grinned. "Howard B. Coleman, at your service." He laughed. "Oh definitely at your service. Anytime."

"Where did you come from?" she said. Then, "Put your clothes on."

He laughed again. "O.K. baby. Sorry." He pulled on his trunks, checked in a harlequin pattern. "I'm from Georgia," he said. "Pre-med. SAE. And I know all about you. They told me when they sent me down to keep you company.

"Who?" she said, still trying to get hold of it, place him where he belonged with the others, divorce him from his sudden appearance in moonlight on the edge of the dawn of creation.

"Ted Kendall, for one," he said. He sat down and tilted the beer can. "He said you didn't go for him and needed a man. Baby, I'll say you did. But you've got started now. The rest of the time ought to be great."

He reached out and put his hand on her. "Baby, what you got there don't grow on trees."

"Get away from me," she said slowly and quietly. "Get the hell away from me."

"What's the matter?" he said, the nice voice genuinely puzzled.

"Get out of here," she said, feeling the anger in her, afraid she might hit him and not wanting to feel his flesh in any way, ever. "Get out."

"O.K." He got up easily. "I'll be around tomorrow if you change your mind," he said. "You're O.K."

And when she didn't answer him he began retreating up the beach, still watching her, backing away through the sand. "It'll be better," he called back. "Say. Do you like folk music? There's a new bunch down the beach. We could go tomorrow night."

But she had ceased listening to him.

Later the moon went down. It was cold then, but she sat on, feeling silence grow around her, a little afraid but vastly unafraid too. Because what could possibly happen to her that would make any difference now?

Later she felt morning coming, a freshness in the east, a sighing over the water, a light at last, gray, somber, cold. She got up and began walking back down the beach. There was a small curve around which the main beach lay, and she stopped before turning it, looking back for a moment toward the spot on the beach. The beer cans lay in a forlorn little heap on the edge of the water and around them the sand was smooth, clean, studded with shells. She went on around the curve of beach.

She stopped, staring wide-eyed out across the dawn-lighted beach. For as far as she could see down the expanse of shining gray sand, the beach was littered with beer cans. It was as though a gigantic ship had flown over and dumped the garbage from an alien planet into the beaches of man's morning. She stood still, staring at them. Crumpled, upright, flattened out, on their sides, thousands of empty beer cans, gutted, sucked dry, gleaming in dawn light with the painted legend of promise on their sides. The sea moved toward them, retreated. The cans lay still, mute, finished, sad.

She began to walk through them, not bothering to step around them or over them, feeling the roundness of them under her bare feet, pushing them into the sand with every other step, banging her toes into them. Last night's promise, rejected by sea and man alike.

She did not look toward the sea or the rising sun. She walked to the beach house, sleeping in early morning, and went into the bathroom and took a shower, ignoring the sleepy protests from the porch and the living room. Then she dressed carefully in her denim suit, her white high heels. She packed her bag, and called the bus station to get the time of the first northbound bus.

She had thought she was as drained as the empty cans, as through, as devoid of life, but sitting in the living room, waiting for bus time, she knew suddenly that she was hungry. She wanted her breakfast and coffee. She got up and went into the kitchenette and made breakfast for herself, trying to make as little noise as possible in the sleeping house. She would have liked bacon and eggs but there was only dry cereal and bread and buns. She ate and drank three cups of coffee and smoked a cigarette. Then she went back onto the porch and looked around her at the sleeping houses in morning sunlight. She probed at her mind and her hurt and found nothing much at all. She stood on the porch thinking in jagged little pictures of all the people she had ever known: her mother in her flowered voile, Aunt Lucy Claire proud of meeting Zsa Zsa Gabor, her sorority sisters in their bouffants and cute little pants. And all of it came to the same thing in the end . . . empty rejection by sea and land alike.

She thought of the long bus ride home, hot and stiff in the lurching bus, and it seemed a gesture as empty as any other. There would be only the school at the end of the line. And later the others would all come back. The lovely. Home from the sea. She would have liked to cry, but in the harsh bright sunlight she found that she could not.

She went back into the house and undressed and slept for nine hours. At three o'clock she appeared on the beach, her new tan already showing, her crazy hat on the back of her head.

The ocean was still there, blue now, with sunlight on small whitecaps. But it was only an ocean. Still, she thought, I am only me. But that is something. Ocean and Lennie, part of the universe, finding the shoreline and losing it again. Far out a pelican lighted on the water and rose again, carrying sustenance into the sky. A long way away you could see Spain, if your eyes were good enough. And when night came your eyes *were* good enough to see the stars. She fished a piece of bread out of her beach-coat pocket and walked down the beach to feed it to the gulls.

Babs H. Deal, winner of the Mystery Writers of America Award in 1967 (for her novel FANCY'S KNELL), has written seven other novels including HIGH LONESOME WORLD and THE WALLS CAME TUMBLING DOWN. Ms. Deal, born in Scottsboro, Alabama, and educated at the University of Alabama, now lives with her author-husband, Bordon Deal, and their three children, on Siesta Key, Sarasota, Florida. Her newest novel is SUMMER GAMES.

It Will Pass

by Ella Leffland

She now understood what it was to suffer, though she did not apply the word to herself; it seemed presumptuous in a world where so much real tragedy existed. What had happened to her was ordinary enough: the end of an affair.

She ate, without pleasure; she slept, without resting; she worked, without interest.

"I feel as though I'd died," she confided in her friend Judith.

"You don't believe it now," Judith told her, "but it'll pass. I've been there. I know the course."

She hoped her friend was right.

He had taken the world with him and left the shell. It was as though she crept around inside the shell with her shoulders hunched defensively. But there was no protection. Everything hurt: someone carrying a bouquet of flowers, the smell of frying bacon; cafes, movie houses, restaurants; certain streets, certain songs, certain warm evenings; even the Sunday papers, which they used to read together in bed. Without warning, her throat would constrict and the tears burst from her eyes. And it happened any place, any time: weighing a bag of potatoes at the supermarket, running for the streetcar, sharpening a pencil at the office. It was horribly embarrassing to break down in public, but that was the least of it. The very least of it.

The heavy-lidded gray eyes, the large blunt nose, the slightly pocked skin. Her friends had thought him unattractive, and this had bewildered her. Because the first moment she saw him she had taken a small involuntary step back, as you do when you turn a corner and are confronted by a magnificent view you hadn't expected.

But it was just a matter of taste. She had thought Judith's husband a dreary sort, for instance, but Judith had grown wraithlike after the divorce.

Judith's advice was to keep busy. She said it had eventually worked for her.

So, two weeks after the breakup, she forced herself into a hectic routine of dating. Two of her dates became lovers. Malcolm, who was older, thankful for a girl of twenty-three, indulgent; and Frank, a grad student at Berkeley, thankful for nothing, but zestful and bright.

Every time she looked at Malcolm's kind face on the pillow beside her, or at Frank's clever one, she thought: Oh God, how you bore me! Then she would be filled with shame for her unfairness, and try to be nicer. But she felt Jack's presence in the bed. He was not the intruder. They were.

"They don't help any," she told Judith.

"Don't worry," her friend assured her, "Some morning you'll wake up and find that you've forgotten him."

She shook her head. "Every time I see a maroon car on the street—even if it's a different model than his, even if it's driven by an old lady—I think I'm going to heave, or suffocate."

"You've got it bad. But it won't last forever."

It was a good six weeks after the breakup that she got rid of the things in the apartment that reminded her of him. She took the sand candle that stood next to the bed and deliberately shattered it on the floor; sweeping up the pieces she threw them in the waste basket along with a seashell from the beach, his cigarette lighter, a half-empty bottle of White Shoulders. The two expensive art books he had given her she gave to Judith; the transistor radio she gave to someone else; the white minidress he had liked she gave to the Good Will. Looking around afterwards, she felt she had accomplished something, even though the important items still lay untouched in her bureau drawer. The photographs.

Those she could not bring herself to part with.

At least once a day she would open the drawer, almost surreptitiously, and take them out and brood over them. They had gone together eleven months, and each photograph brought back the whole long span like an avalanche. She would spread them out on the floor and lose herself in the past, studying his face from every angle.

Then one day she resolutely tore them to bits and flung them down the garbage chute. "No!" she cried a moment later, staring hopelessly down the chute. Now his face was lost to her for good.

But of course it wasn't. In her mind's eye he was as close and clear as ever.

She realized she had been wrong to throw out everything that brought him back. She should have learned to live with the mementoes, cherishing the happiness they represented and facing the fact that it was over. But somehow she could not do both.

The second month drew to a close. She took an extension course in the Modern Novel; she cleaned her apartment constantly; she wrote extremely long, dutiful letters home; she broke up with both Malcolm and Frank and became involved with Lou, who was demanding, difficult, and time-consuming. All this, in addition to her job, left her no time in which to brood, yet Jack remained with her in a way she could not fight, as though he flowed through her veins with her blood.

The beginning of the third month Lou took her to a party and the thing she had so long hoped for and dreaded occurred. He was there. She saw him. Her first thought was that he was different: His hair was much longer, he was wearing a suit she had not seen before. She felt a bitter flash of resentment at these things, as though he had purposely set up a barrier between them. Then he caught sight of her, and as their eyes met she felt hers losing control, staring out with a wild regret and at the same time melting with a hope so great that for a moment he was blurred. Then people moved between them and she had time only to glance briefly at the girl he was with before her view was cut off, The girl, she realized with a vicious joy, was nothing special—rather pale, rather plump, with a white shoulder strap accidentally and unbecomingly exposed. But she was a girl. And he was with her. With *someone else*. How could such a thing have come to pass?

But the next morning she woke feeling very good. He had seen her and now he would phone. She waited for his call that day, and the next, and the next. On the fourth day she dialed his number from the office, knowing he would not be in. She was strangely encouraged and comforted by the sound of the ringing at the other end of the line; it was as though she were there, bodily, inside his apartment, listening to the tan phone ringing, sitting on the striped bedspread, under his big map of the world.

Every day for a week she dialed his number and she felt somehow soothed, restored. It would take him a week or two to make up his mind to call, and to get rid of the pale girl, and in the meantime she had this secret daily access to his apartment.

Then she confessed her calls to Judith, and as she spoke, it broke over her like a tidal wave how pointless they were. He and she would never get together again. She looked away from her friend, overcome by a desolation greater than she had yet felt.

"I can't take much more of it," she murmured, ashamed of her weakness and her complaints.

Judith's voice was slow and reflective. "It's hard to believe, but there are things worse than this."

She shook her head.

"Yes. There are," Judith insisted gravely.

The whole month was difficult. It was June. Last June they had gone to the beach every weekend. Now she thought of him swimming with the pale girl. He would not be alone, although she was now alone. In bed she always pretended that Lou was Jack, and she finally decided she could not tolerate this deception any longer. She had broken off with him and since then had kept her dates few and casual. She dreaded the long summer months with their warm nights, the curtain moving softly at the bedroom window. Standing before the mirror she thought she looked flattened and done for.

Judith says there are worse things! she thought savagely. But Judith was crazy. This was the worst. As God was her witness, she had tried everything! Men, lit courses, housecleaning! She had tried and tried and it was hopeless. Twenty years from now her heart would still drop to her feet when a maroon car drove by.

One morning some four months later as she rushed out her door to work she noticed, without any particular surprise or relief, that she was humming. Later that day in the office she found herself doubling up with laughter at someone's joke. And she realized that this was not the first day these things had happened; she had been like this for a while. Degree by degree, the wound had healed and the process had been so gradual that she had been unaware of it until now, when it was completed. Closing her eyes, she brought all her thoughts to bear on Jack. It did not make her feel bad; it did not make her feel good, either. She felt it was finally in the past, that was all.

A few weeks later she was able to substantiate this.

That morning, a Saturday, she took her wash to the neighborhood laundromat and as she came out with it afterwards she saw, only a few yards away, Jack's maroon Olds waiting for the light to change. There in profile was the dark hair—very long now, with sideburns—and the blunt nose and jutting chin. One large familiar hand rested on the steering wheel, the other tapped a cigarette out the open window. As he brought the cigarette back to his lips he glanced in her direction and saw her. A second passed before they nodded, self-consciously.

"How've you been?" he called.

She was neither flooded with memories nor crushed by grief at the sound of his voice.

"Fine. You?" she called back.

It was simply, she saw, that a year of her life had somehow been lost. Scattered by the winds. Nowhere.

"Great," he answered.

And she realized she wanted that year in her possession even if it no longer moved her—she wanted it badly, because it belonged to her, it had *been* her—but because it no longer moved her it could not be found.

The light changed. With a polite wave he drove off and disappeared around a corner. She walked on, stumbling once, vaguely adjusting the bundle of clean clothes in her arms. Though choked with movement, the street seemed strangely still. She felt a deep loneliness on behalf of that old mountain of memories—the warm nights with the sand candle burning by the bed, her shrieks and his shouts breaking up through the roaring surf, the Sunday mornings spent in a welter of funny papers, the heavy-lidded eyes looking into hers with such depths of certitude—that mountain which had somehow crumbled and now lay abandoned, unclaimed by either of them.

Then, that was what Judith had meant when she said there was something worse than trying to forget. You forgot.

Ella Leffland was born in Martinez, California, and studied fine arts at San Jose State College. Unable to decide whether to become a painter or a writer, she chose both. While awaiting success in her double career, Ms. Leffland held several offbeat jobs, including mess girl in a Norwegian tramp steamer, grape harvester, door-to-door salesman of made-by-the-blind handicrafts, and lone white journalist on a black newspaper, the Sun Reporter. *Her short stories have appeared in* Cosmopolitan, The New Yorker, *and many other publications. At present she is completing a screenplay of her first novel,* MRS. MUNCK, *a gothic thriller with women's liberation overtones, which was published last year. Ms. Leffland lives in San Francisco in an apartment decorated mainly with her own paintings.*

Iatro's Djinn

by B. L. Keller

Sherman Iatro's girl stared at the gray stone jar. "Imagine," she marveled, "finding an urn like that in a thrift shop."

So frequently, so fervently, had she marveled since the djinn was uncorked that Sherman called upon that spirit to remove her.

That the demon so elaborated the simple directive "get rid of her" as to deliver the girl—scrubbed, combed, clothed, shod, and bearing a letter of recommendation—to a finishing school near Bar Harbor was only a shiver presaging the convulsion that was to come.

The girl was back on the streets within a week, but that has nothing to do with the djinn, who returned to his jar moments after executing the command.

"Come out and talk to me."

The boy could afford to indulge in whimsical requests. When he had first pried the stone stopper from the jar, the traditional outpouring of smoke had upset him seriously, and the consolidation of that emanation into the striking form of the djinn sent him beyond the conventional terrified prostrations into a catatonic state from which the demon roused him only after hours of incantation.

It was days before Iatro dared inquire, "How many wishes did you say?"

"Infinite."

From the standpoint of a djinn imprisoned in any type of container, it makes little difference how many wishes he is constrained to grant the person who releases and thus possesses him. To serve for all time is the doom. The spirit obliged to grant unnumbered wishes will labor under a torrent of demands in the beginning of any relationship, but in time some possessors become sated, and even the insatiable die—while a djinn's powers are supernatural, they are not divine, and there is only so much he can do.

Contrary to popular misconception, a djinn is seldom passed from hand to hand. The owner of a three-wish demon, after using his wishes, may think of a thing he wants and so barter his bottle, but, more often, in a spirit of pique or spite or pure meanness, he will hide the container or attempt to destroy it. Containers for beings of occult force and temperament were not made frivolously. They are all but indestructible, and the horror implicit in such an assault inevitably shatters the mind of one who seriously contemplates it.

But even the three-wish djinn passes from hand to hand more freely than the djinn of infinite wishes, who is truly beyond all price. The owner of the latter has no need of anything obtainable from mortal agency, so there is no profit in a trade. And the possessor of such an overwhelming power, as moralists and legend makers point out interminably but accurately, becomes possessed. Even dying, he cannot bring himself to entrust it to wife, child, lover, friend, fraternal lodge. He may distribute money, even power, but the possession of a djinn is so awesome that the owner can not bring himself to pass it on.

There are few legal heirs to a djinn.

It is not uncommon, then, for a demon of infinite wishes to languish for centuries until accident brings him again to the hand of one who may free him and bind him.

So had it been with this, a being of such outrageous passion, ferocity, and pride that, after three centuries were expended in his entrapment, he was doomed to grant unlimited wishes to any being who released him, a condition designed to bring him to the deepest possible abasement. To compound the indignity, he was imprisoned in a replica of a simple camphor jar.

Torment is the universe of the bound djinn. To serve the unenlightened whims of a being so fragile that the demon, were he not enslaved, might obliterate him with one careless flicker of will.

To serve, or be enclosed again, inert, swelling consciousness immured in darkness. Blind, deaf, without touch, without voice. Nothing. Nothing. Only rage.

Time passes more slowly for demons than for men, and the intensity of such horror transcends imagination.

In the ages since his ensnarement, Sherman's djinn had been used by only a few.

A vizier who utilized him shrewdly and died, rich and puissant and renowned, at the hand of his only son, in whom the possession of incredible power bred extraordinary vices.

Then darkness, howling soundlessly.

Freed by a merchant with the mind of a maggot.

Again, darkness.

A sailor.

Darkness, centuries of raging.

A courtesan whose vanities became more piteous as she aged, for though the demon kept her young for more than a hundred years, he could not shield her from the inevitable.

Darkness.

Such an alternation of enslavement with nothing would affect anyone. From rage the demon passed to despair, from despair to a cold and terrible acceptance. During his aeons in the jar he was forced back upon his own resources, which were not meager. With ages in which to reason and meditate he became a profoundly interesting being, and while his passions were not diminished, they came under the control of what may only be described as a noble intelligence, encompassing, dignified, and wise.

With a collection of Mason jars, bedpans, nursing bottles, and memorabilia accumulated in the basement of a condemned house in which a senile spinster had died, his jar was picked up by the Saint Vincent de Paul Society's salvage truck and transferred to the thrift shop where Sherman Iatro's girl, who had found her way back to innocence through the casual destruction of her brain cells, stole it in the naïve hope it might contain something worth smoking, injecting, or selling.

Without premeditation, she gave it to Sherman, for she was a girl who found herself constantly and unexpectedly obliged to placate her lovers without understanding why, and when Sherman, after long impatient effort, pried out the stone stopper, the djinn was free again, and thrall.

Having lusted after power without ever taking seriously the possibility or responsibility of possessing it, Sherman was catapulted into profound spiritual crisis, coming close to an inability to act, even to will. When, in a simple reflex of irritability, he ordered the girl removed, the execution of his command failed to excite him.

Committed to the pleasure principle as ethic, Iatro was infected with no sentiments of honor or compassion, and he seldom thought again of the girl who had given him the jar.

His next order, that the demon come out and chat, was a nervous attempt to cope with the anxiety implicit in the possession of such unforeseen potential. Unmanned by the formidable exotic sitting impassive on the mattress beside him, the boy made a few banal thrusts at conversation and then, defeated, asked if it could get him a fix.

It may be of some interest to students of human behavior that, given almost unlimited opportunities and the immediate prospect of myriad gratifications, Iatro lost much of his interest in mind-altering drugs. It is, perhaps, a measure of the resilience of the human spirit that, tentatively at first, then with rapidly increasing confidence, Sherman adjusted to the idea that he could have almost anything he wanted.

As his desires were fulfilled, his imagination soared.

To its limits.

He ordered a Harley-Davidson, a succession of Las Vegas dancers, every garment and accessory from the fashion pages of the dollar magazines for men, a penthouse with sauna, bar, and built-in stereo system.

With increasing exposure to the good life his tastes expanded, and he went on to own a Lincoln Continental, a Maserati, a Bugatti, a number of cinema actresses, a private physician, tailor, hairdresser, manicurist, masseuse, press agent, the biggest cliff-top house in Los Angeles County, and a collection of phonograph records.

Sensing that he was not fulfilled, he observed, he learned, he ordered several old Rolls', a yacht, a jet, and an island with mansion, theatre, pool, and polo field.

"Bring me some old masters for the walls," he instructed the djinn, "and a bunch of old family retainers. And run up a soiree for the international set."

Soon he knew the restricted nicknames of many famous people. He received more Christmas cards than he could display. He was seldom alone. But it seemed to him that a man who had everything should be loved.

His teeth capped, nose narrowed, body sleeked, diction perfected, spectacles replaced by contact lenses in stunning shades, he learned with no effort to swim, speed-read, buy racehorses, and contribute to political campaigns.

He found in power a palliative, in politics a surrogate companionship, and in the combination another form of lust. But after purchasing a number of governments and a large part of the world's economy, he remained hungry.

With enough residences to be at home anywhere in the world, he had had most of the most publicly desirable women alive by now, for besides being a great power, he was twenty-five, good looking, with clean breath, and the confidence, gained from speed-reading, to speak easily about almost anything.

He had long ago gotten around to the most beautiful living woman in the world, and he kept her rather than have people wonder why he did not have the most beautiful woman in the world, but even after she mastered speed-reading she was not enduringly stimulating to a man who had everything else.

With the aid of his public relations staff he constructed some baroque orgies; he had never come to feel at ease with the djinn and was so absurdly sensitive to the indifference with which his thrall regarded him that he sometimes took measures unconsciously designed to win that spirit's approval.

Unfortunately, when stung by what he interpreted as the djinn's contempt, he was apt to behave abominably, wantonly misusing his advantages.

He could not impress the demon.

"Being merely frivolous, irresponsible, callous, and inept, you are something of an improvement over most governments," said the djinn, "and since I am not empowered to enlighten or reform you . . ."

"Back in the jar!" Iatro cried, for he bore still a deep primal fear of that formidable being.

"When you've had one orgy . . ." Sherman conceded finally, gazing without appetite at the beautiful boys and girls, desiccated hags, and remarkable freaks cluttering his conservatory.

It was some time before he ventured to call upon his djinn.

"I suppose there's nothing you can do about souls," he said to the spirit once, in a spasm of desolation brought about, perhaps, by overindulgence in power and other bestial diversions.

"Nothing." And the djinn added, "I am sorry."

Sensing that it meant those words, Iatro was unstrung, confronted, for the first time since knowing the girl who had given him the jar, by a being's concern for him.

"I want . . ." he stammered in alarm. "I want . . . Listen, I'm sick of this most beautiful girl in the world. Bring me . . . the most beautiful girl, but she has to be interesting, all right?"

She turned out to be most interesting. She spoke French, German, Spanish, Mandarin, and Ibanag, wrote essays for *The New Republic*, smiled at the mention of Susan Sontag, and dabbled in Mesopotamian artifacts.

"I don't know if you think you're funny, but you get rid of her and bring me the most beautiful girl I can talk to, for God's sake."

"All right, comedian. Take her back and bring me one that wants to do something besides talk."

"If you ever want to get outside that jar again, you better watch yourself," the debilitated tycoon wheezed at last. "And don't give me the inscrutable gaze. What I want . . . what I want . . ." Overcome by a deliquium of body and soul, the most powerful man in the world found himself inexplicably weeping. "I want a beautiful, gentle, loving . . . I want a woman to love."

Given some room for independent judgment, the djinn was meticulous in carrying out the assignment.

It proved a hideous ordeal.

When Iatro had given simple orders for a woman, confining himself to somewhat mechanical specifics, the djinn had complied effortlessly, as he would in the acquisition of an industry or politician.

Compelled to interpret, he suffered more than servitude or isolation.

The djinn, you must remember, is a corporeal spirit.

Part of the doom laid upon him is that all he may do is serve. Without a specific order from the master, he can do him no disservice.

If the search was painful, the achievement was catastrophic.

Iatro had ordered "a woman to love."

The djinn found her in a Lesbian brothel.

An inexperienced but innovative social worker, she had persuaded a group of San Francisco realtors to sponsor a weekend of seminars and *Gestalt* at Esalen Institute and was trying to convince the girls that it was not charity.

Emerging disheartened, questioning her vocation, she was accosted at the corner of Powell and Eddy by the djinn, who expressed an interest in her work and presented her with a certified check so generous as to provide an excellent education for all the city's tarts, addicts, felons, and derelicts, many of whom went on to pursue distinguished careers in medicine, law, business, politics, and the arts, without, unfortunately, making any lasting improvement in those areas of endeavor; without, alas, making any notable difference.

Naïve in many ways, this girl was exquisitely perceptive and realized at once that the stranger who spoke to her so persuasively was no ordinary man.

Although possessed of the capacity to change size and shape, the djinn in his essential embodiment is not unlike an adult human male. While he comes in a variety of shapes and heights, all impressive, this particular demon stood six feet four inches tall, with a body of such power and symmetry as to challenge the sculptors of Harappa.

Except for the presence of an extra digit on hands and feet, and toenails and fingernails of exceptional thickness and hardness, which, even when clipped short with great effort, tended to curve into talons, he resembled nothing so much as the erotic nightmares of an overwrought maiden gorged on Coleridge, Blake, and the Brontë sisters.

His skin was supple, clear, of a lustrous copper shade similar to that of the North American Iroquois. His hair was thick, black, straight, and possessed of a tensile strength exceeding that of steel wire.

Exquisitely and elaborately wrought, the ears lay flat to the skull with the lobe of the left pierced by a simple gold ring.

While his countenance was alarming, both to men and women, strong-minded women with untrammeled imaginations tended to be entranced by the very strangeness of that face. The skull structure was of an elegance approximated by the Akkadian graver whose head of Sargon stands today in the Iraq museum at Baghdad. His nose was aquiline, but with a slight flattening of the cartilage at the bridge, which gave that otherwise classic promontory a somewhat pugilistic look. His forehead was broad, the brow ridge heavy, black eyebrows peaking over the center of the eyes and winging upward toward the temples.

His eyes were long, deep set, quite inhuman, the pupil, of seemingly infinite depth, shaped like a narrow flame and capable of instant contraction and expansion, the iris shifting in color from the pale of a shroud to a swimming prismal green to unfathomable black. In them were recorded all his antique sins, all his torment, all he had come to be.

His mouth was wide, the teeth large, even, white, the upper canines only moderately elongated, the lips impeccably molded, sensual, betraying at times the lurking satyr smile seen to this day on the lips of the Apollo Veii in the Etruscan museum at Villa Giulia, that archaic smile which bears no relationship to humor.

In truth, an alarming countenance. Only women of great courage and independent judgment could gaze upon it without intolerable uneasiness.

Unfortunately, the girl he had found was a loving, gentle woman of great individuality, strength, and hungers.

The only child of a father whose identity lay in being respectable and a mother engulfed in the pursuit of attention, she had been brought up to give no trouble. As a young woman in the shadow of her mother, the Aphrodite of the Elks Club, Mary Jane suffered from the recurring illusion that she was invisible, and was not unhappy to be sent to a convent school where her ardent nature found some outlet in religious fervor.

She lavished her affections upon the saints, as well as the secular figures she encountered in her studies, suffering impartially for Ahab and the whale. As is common in passionate and severely repressed natures, she became exaggeratedly, even quixotically, romantic. After reading *Alice in Wonderland* as a child, she had spent years trying to talk with caterpillars.

She developed a sympathy for all the doomed exotics in literature and the arts. She was certain that Caligula, Hulagu, and Tamburlaine were scarred by childhood trauma and torn by inner anguish over their abominable acts. She wept for the scaly beasts demolished at the climax of Japanese horror movies, ached for centaurs eternally spurned, believed that Don Giovanni could have been saved by the right woman, never gave up the hope that Herbert Lom would get the girl, and yearned mutely over Leonard Nimoy's Mr. Spock.*

Having little experience outside of home and convent, she tended to stammer in social situations. She earned her doctorate, became a social worker. With an intelligence illumined by humor and grace, she understood that her dedication to ensuring a good life for the underprivileged when her own was so removed from joy was ridiculous—indeed, absurd.

The djinn saw that she was not the most beautiful woman in the world. Her face was not flawless, only lovely, sensitive, and endearing. Her body was not designed for vulgar display, but it stirred in him a disquietude quite inappropriate to his position.

He had never had difficulty in bringing Iatro women. Most were entranced by an invitation to meet the richest young man in the world. Others, women of a certain fierceness, were willing to dare anything in order to remain in dangerous propinquity to the djinn.

But having found what Iatro demanded, a woman to love, the demon dawdled.

His initial appearance before Mary Jane alarmed her. Brought up to avoid making a scene at all cost, she was too inhibited to cry out, and found herself being supported by the firm arm of the accoster, who spoke to her so persuasively she was unable to bring herself to knee him or to send a bone sliver into his brain with the edge of her hand, as prudent young women of this generation are taught.

*A nonhuman character portrayed by actor Nimoy in the U.S. television fantasy series "Star Trek," circa 1967-8, a unique example of a characterization transcending the vehicle in which it appears.

Her mind a turmoil of cautionary tales about soft-spoken strangers who turn out to be lust murderers—"He was always a good boy," the mothers of such rashlings invariably weep—she was constrained by the appearance of this being, fearing that if she were to rebuff him violently, he might be confirmed in his fears that he was somehow "different."

Sensing her disquietude, the djinn transported her to a bar on the alley off of Minna Street, where his appearance and the girl's agitation were noted, but where the insularity of the patrons, mostly newsmen from the San Francisco *Chronicle*, militated against any response so vigorous as alarm.

Assuming she had fainted, reasonably certain she had not been brought to a public place for purposes of criminal assault, the girl was calmed by the dark power of her escort's voice to the point where she was able to accept his check with inarticulate gratitude and only moderate suspicion.

The check cleared the bank. The djinn, driving an unobtrusive Volvo sedan, began intercepting Mary Jane when she left work.

Intuitive by nature, reverent by training, skeptical by virtue of reason, her religious attitudes were liberal, ecumenical, and spiced by a tendency to mysticism. She did not believe in Satan, but she was aware of a universe of infinite possibilities. Her response to the djinn passed from a fearful fascination to a deep admiration, allurement, and awe.

She knew that to ask him anything that might indicate what he was would cause him pain; she understood enough from his eyes to avoid reopening his history.

Conservatively attired, he took her to various cultural events, to the sea, and brought her little things—carpet from Samarkand, parchments from Baalbek, perfumes, oils from Ctesiphon.

Iatro recalled him.

"What the hell! Do you have any idea how long you've been gone? What is this? You do what I told you and get your ass back here pronto."

Crackling between them like flame, an impulse seized the djinn, all but shattering him into a million incorporeal gibbering fragments of will.

Seared by the living, encircling fire of that demonic urge, Iatro managed to gasp only, "Go . . ."

Soaring to penetrate the void—infinite cold—infinite dark—the djinn was hurled back, raging, howling, to pass in torment across the desolate places and return to the place from which Iatro had recalled it, still under the inflexible bond of obedience.

The shock that struck Iatro's island was ascribed to earthquake, but the seizure which left the tycoon curled like a fetus for weeks caused his staff great concern. In the resulting précautionary realignments, scores of lives and fortunes were shattered. Interest rates fluctuated, cutbacks were announced, unemployment soared.

The djinn materialized at last in a Haight-Ashbury flat where the occupants took him to be a heavy apparition. Those who became aware that his presence was constant, regardless of what was smoked or swallowed or shot or not, slipped away silently one by one.

Mary Jane, whose relationship with that spirit had been the only enchantment in a life that stretched back like a landscape of white nylon carpeting, would not forget him. She searched the city, canvassed the acquaintances whom her profession and his generosity had brought her, and inevitably heard rumors of a terrifying trip that seemed to have taken up residence at a flat in the Haight.

"The Haight," a young girl who was turned out and kicked to her death there wrote home a few days before her last, "is a bad scene now." Pasture for all the geeks, freaks, pushers, pimps, dying, cannibals who had driven out the lost and love-struck children.

Mary Jane passed through, and it was bad, but at last she found the djinn.

The unthinkable, unimaginable which consumed him in no way diminished him. Like frost smoke he burned, incandescent in the dun of the room where he stood fixed, insolate, frightful.

He would not recognize her but she would not leave.

At last he told her everything that is set down here.

"Then you're bound to obey," she said. "It's impossible for you to do anything else."

"Impossible. But I will not obey."

"And what will happen?"

"That may not be spoken."

She inquired no deeper into his motivations. Even for her the reality of an infatuated demon, more formidable than her most fevered dreams, was profoundly disconcerting.

She sought out students of the occult.

A djinn, they assured her, is indeed doomed to obey. Rebellion is impossible. The penalty is therefore hypothetical. The hypothetical penalty may be neither communicated nor contemplated.

Banks failed. Mortgages were foreclosed. Crops rotted on the earth. Prices plummeted, wages collapsed, riot and repression spread. The most modern urban household boasted at least a zip gun.

Mary Jane spent night and day with the demon.

"Find him another woman to love."

"There is no other."

"That is absurd."

But part of his bondage was to be literal-minded. "If I were defaced?"

"I could not permit that."

"If only you were capable of fraud," she lamented, desperate and exhausted.

"You'll have to take me to Sherman Iatro," she said. "I'll try to reason with him."

183

"Impossible."

"Djinn, your defiance is causing many people pain. No—listen to me. I understand that your bondage is part of an archaic order, that by disrupting that order you may bring down a chaos beyond my comprehension. But what you're doing to the order I can understand is terrible enough. You're not indifferent, you're not irresponsible, so you must obey or let me try to loosen the command."

"No."

"The last time you confronted him almost destroyed you both. Unless you take me, I will find him myself, and I may . . ."

With a cry of anguish, the demon left the premises.

Recognizing the strength of this woman's will, however, he materialized in her kitchen that night and said, "I see no alternative. But if he refuses to be moved . . ."

"I'm quite conscious of the risk."

The djinn being incapable of error or dissimulation, she was what Sherman had ordered, and a man who has almost everything is apt to forget how to negotiate.

After a long, intense conversation, Iatro refusing to be moved, the demon hovering dire and fulminant, the girl said, "Djinn, I beg you, wait in your bottle. I can't function with your lowering over me."

While Iatro, shaken still by the last terrible encounter, assessed his courage to find if he dared risk another direct order, the girl said to the djinn, "If you trust me, go."

Being incapable of dishonesty, the demon was incapable of conceiving of the possibility of fraud in this woman. He was, however, an experienced observer of human behavior, and so he knew Iatro to be capable of anything. He refused.

The man remained adamant, unmoved by warnings, threats, appeals.

At last Mary Jane said, "Sherman, I will not lie to you. Although you're attractive and well-informed, I don't love you, but I find your ruthlessness exciting. I find the idea of being the richest woman in the world exciting. Under certain conditions, I might be tempted. I would demand specific legal guarantees, to be settled before the marriage ceremony. Certain community property . . ."

The air roiled, reeking of sulphur, but that indomitable female said, "If you would change me, djinn, you must first destroy me."

And Iatro, exultant, dared cry, "Back in your jar!"

Fixing them with a gaze of such contempt it would have congealed the soul of an influence peddler, the demon withdrew deliberately into its container, and Iatro shoved the stone stopper into the neck of the jar.

"That damn thing," he muttered, "is too dangerous to be let out again."

"Then you may give it to me now," said Mary Jane. "A wedding present."

"Power!" Trembling, the tycoon sank into the chair. "Power. That's it.

What a fantastic woman you are! God, what a woman. So long as I remain the most powerful man in the world, then, I can't lose you. How could I give you the means to make me unnecessary to you? I cherish you as deeply as you covet power."

"You may have me or the jar, Sherman."

"Fantastic. No, my dear. I must keep both, for I could never bear to lose you. And we know you could never be bound by agreements, you fabulous, ruthless woman."

All night they negotiated. She was a brilliant adversary, using trickery, guile, threats, fury, ingenuousness, scorn. Blinded by passion, he saw her as even more formidable than she was, and that duel, without the djinn to assist him in any way, was the most exhilarating experience of Sherman's life; he enjoyed it to the hilt because he knew he could not lose.

When she wept, he took it to be another facet of her attack, and he was enchanted by her versatility.

At last, seeing she was becoming genuinely ill, he moved to end the contest, for he did not want this extraordinary being damaged.

"You know you won't leave me so long as I have the djinn and remain the most powerful man in the world," he said tenderly and reasonably. "And so, my dear, you must rest—you've been great. I tell you what I'll do—I'll leave you everything, including the jar, in my will. Providing, of course, that you have been with me all the time until my death, and providing that three physicians of my choice, whose names will remain unknown to you until that time, certify my passing to be beyond your control. If you leave me or seriously displease me at any time from this moment on, I will either destroy the jar or dispose of it where it will never be found. It would be no loss to me, because I never intend to let that damnable monster out again so long as I live."

Drained, fevered, in despair, the girl agreed at last, intending to steal the jar at the first opportunity.

"Let me call my lawyer," she murmured. Iatro had the will and a marriage contract drawn up before noon.

For five years she lived with him, despising her estate, taking to austerity as her indulgence, and becoming a most distinguished woman.

She took care never to displease him seriously. Her surrender seemed to have seared away her loathing for the man, and she treated him with the courtesy she felt due any flawed human being.

He remained entranced, tormented by her meticulous adherence to the agreement, enraged by the decency with which she treated him, afraid to show any serious displeasure for fear she might give up everything and leave him.

Hopelessly in love with her, terrified of losing her, not daring to call upon the djinn, the unfortunate Iatro struggled to remain in power. It was not so formidable a task as one might expect, for power propagates power; wealth,

wealth; terror, terror. But even the greatest empires are not entirely self-perpetuating; vigilance and effort are required to counter the first indications of decay or reform.

To take over what had been wrought by an occult who left no records was not simple. Sherman became an executive, driving himself mercilessly.

Afflicted with bleeding ulcers, migraine, temper tantrums, occasional venereal diseases, he threw himself into more desperate and ornate vices. His resistance thus lowered, he became a prey to frequent head colds, and one evening after ingesting four Allerest, two Sominex, and a notable Châteauneuf-du-Pape, he insisted upon driving himself. His dual suspension Ferlinghetti sideswiped the fuel injection Fescennine of a widely idolized rock group, and the hapless tycoon was riven like Pentheus by a band of prepubescent groupies.

As specified in the marriage contract, Mary Jane inherited everything.

Even disintegrating, the Iatro empire included control of a substantial part of the world's government, industry, armament, agriculture, shipping, communication, air and water pollution, supersonic transport, and sundry corruptions.

In the stampede to bilk, milk, and influence the widow, there was no one mad enough to guess her intentions.

During the funeral festivities, she slipped away long enough to speak briefly with a group she had invited from among the unfortunates she had served once as a social worker.

From these she selected the few who had survived the law, welfare, county hospitals, ghetto schools, and bureaucratic interviewers without becoming dust inside, and they became her staff.

Proceeding swiftly, she sought out the men and women whom she suspected from her investigations of being possessed of grace and infected with her vision.

The surprising thing is that they were so many and that they enlisted millions more. Unfamiliar with the use of power, they were nevertheless determined, as Albert Camus said in a lecture delivered in Algiers in 1956, "to deserve living someday as free men—in other words, as men who refuse either to practice or to suffer terror." Thus, their influence was as nothing to their numbers.

While laboring to convince the world's people to behave decently and reasonably, they began by staffing and supporting enough clinics to provide free dentistry, health education, and medical care, including sterilization and reliable contraceptives, throughout the world, and to underwrite a pension plan for all couples who would bear no more than one child. Asked at what point she would consider the world's birth rate low enough, Mrs. Iatro was said to have replied, "When each child is infinitely precious to us all."

Understandably, a raucous tumult ensued, and she was labeled an atheist, bleeding heart, Communist, capitalist pig, and religious fanatic. It was rumored that her entire body was devoid of so much as a single hair, that she had borne a monstrous child by a prominent spiritual leader, that she had made a pact with the United Nations to undermine the authority of the state.

When her group purchased and distributed all the world's surplus food to the hungry, international consternation mounted. She was called anarchist, do-gooder, anti-Darwinian, free-love advocate, enemy of the proletarian revolution, foe of private enterprise, recluse, and publicity seeker.

In an effort to counter the ecological irresponsibility of the affluent, her group perfected a small, low-powered, emission-free, durable mechanical passenger vehicle in concert with an efficient mass transit system which they offered to subsidize, but polls showed that in all technologically advanced societies users of such Spartan runabouts were looked upon as eunuchoid, intellectual, and cheap, and mass transit patrons regarded as middle-aged, penurious, and careless about feminine hygiene.

Daunted, with the Iatro resources grievously diminished, they nevertheless continued trying to persuade the species to reevaluate their fears and toys, to behave as if they were one household.

There is no point in considering the difference which might have been made at this point by the djinn. Sherman's marriage agreement and will established Mary Jane's ownership of the jar, but there was nothing to compel him to divulge truthfully its location.

A disinclination to leave the enjoyment of such power to the woman he could no longer enjoy, heightened by his inexpressible hatred for the demon who had left him to manage an empire and adore a preoccupied woman, so possessed him that he had a hundred replicas of that jar made and, whether in a spirit of disordered whimsy or of cold malevolence, had them secreted in vile and inaccessible places throughout the planet.

In time the stubborn widow unearthed over ninety, one of them the djinn's.

Five years beloved of Iatro as he descended from passion to lust to mere grossness, five years' intimate connection with power and wealth had been to his wife, with her peculiar temperament, as a mortification in the desert, so that she was left with two obsessions: an assumption of responsibility for all evil, and a determination to find the djinn.

Indifferent to power, recoiling from sensuality, this handsome woman became daily more dedicated, more wretched, and more vilified.

Her refusal to decorate her body with the skins of animals, her interest in feeding the hungry rather than possessing dazzling stones, earned her a reputation for ostentatious austerity.

The world's most elegant women called her dowdy.

Rumor of her appearance in all but the most underdeveloped countries was enough to precipitate a riot. Her heavy investment in the elimination of the pollutants produced by the industries she controlled, her interest in organic farming and in replacing disposable with reusable products had so exacerbated the suspicions of so many that her associates were terrorized, beaten, and imprisoned with some regularity. Their refusal to cooperate in any way in the production or sale of weapons of war was greeted with immeasurable fury by Israel, the Arab world, the Soviet Union, the United States, China, Formosa, North and South Vietnam, North Korea, India, Pakistan, Monaco, the Onassis family, a dissident Wahhabi group, and the Burani oasis. So it went.

Her decline was graphically illustrated by American news magazines. In cover portraits of her at the time of Iatro's death she bore a striking resemblance to Sophia Loren. Three months later she was portrayed as a caricature of Mohandas Gandhi, and in another six months a widely reproduced cover showed her as a multilimbed blue Kali festooned with the severed heads of Walter Keane children of all ethnic configurations, one of her taloned hands disemboweling a farmer stretched across her lap, her upper incisors sunk in the throat of a steel worker, one of her pendulous dugs emblazoned with the hammer and sickle, the other with a reverse swastika, while Mao, Trotsky, George Lincoln Rockwell, Maurice Girodias, an unidentified Tartar, and a slovenly bearded youth wearing only love beads groveled at her gory feet.

About this time *Izvestia* portrayed her as a bloated spider ingesting a young man clad in coveralls while an infant struggled in a web wrought in the form of an American flag and a multitude of poets, composers, and tractor drivers swam desperately in the green venom pouring from her belly.

When unimpeachable sources revealed that she had agents all over the world engaged in purchasing old unwashed and unpolished bottles and jars, the hatred for her exploded in ridicule. It was widely believed that she purchased all those containers because she could not bear to discard her own urine.

Some highly placed informants hinted that she had died with Iatro, and that the sinister forces behind his empire had kidnapped a nun with an uncanny resemblance to the dead woman and forced her to portray Mary Jane Iatro, smoke marijuana, and participate in unspeakable rites.

While her group continued to function, the widespread hilarity brought about by the revelation of her passion for jars was more damaging than any harassment.

It was not long before Harold Robbins began a novel said to be based upon her life. It was rumored that Jacqueline Susann had agreed to try her hand at the screenplay, that Lee Radziwill was bidding for the role of Mary Jane while the producer tried to find out what had happened to Gale Sondergaard. Kenneth Tynan was quoted as seeking a firm commitment from Truman Capote to write a musical to be made from the film as a vehicle for Christine Jorgensen.

Down to one isolated island, Mary Jane sold the last of Iatro's old masters, pursued her work, noted with some surprise that despite all their defeats her group had made some small improvements in several areas.

And she bought old jars.

It was her ritual to spend every night alone in her room opening containers.

The astonishing collection of discarded vessels was utilized by a young technician to make a highly compressed and durable building material suitable for low-cost housing bringing down an unprecedented attack from industry, labor, and scavenger workers the world over.

It was in an unparalleled desolation of spirit that she spent the evening of her thirtieth birthday prying stoppers, seals, lids.

After laboring for hours over a barnacle-encrusted cruet, she worked out the stone stopper, and a luminous violet smoke poured forth.

Enormous, olive green, excessively muscular, betraying, for all his effusiveness, a deep, smoldering arrogance, a most offensive djinn took form and placed himself at her disposal, going so far as to suggest palaces, ambergris, occult knowledge, emeralds like ostrich eggs, in an effort to engage her interest and promote some action.

When she recovered from her first terrible disappointment, she permitted him to wander about her bedroom while she went on opening containers, oblivious to the prowling, muscle-flexing presence.

"Would you like some help?" he inquired at last, bored and restless.

She looked up.

"Could I help you with those lotas?" he repeated.

She was silent for a time while her thoughts took shape.

"Djinn," she said at last, "there is a jar . . ."

More than a little resentful, the djinn went forth and extricated the proper jar from a forty-ton block of concrete cunningly secreted deep off the tip of Tierra del Fuego, where it might never have been located save by occult powers.

Trembling, Mary Jane was seized by a paralyzing shyness at the prospect of opening that container.

"You may go," she whispered to the green djinn.

"Where?" he demanded bitterly.

She was a responsible woman—there was no help for it—and she was obliged to consider him. Solemnly she regarded the looming sullen spirit.

"My dear," she said at last, "first we must do something about your appearance."

With ill grace he transformed himself as directed into a moderately tall, attractive young man with few really alarming physical characteristics. While it was impossible to quench that smoldering menace which would make it impossible for even a stranger to treat him lightly, she gave him a firm command to be good and be reasonable and entrusted him to the care of an ashram conducted by the International Society for Krishna Consciousness where he might become sufficiently imbued with Ahimsa so that she could safely set him free.

Finally she unstoppered Iatro's jar, and the demon to whom she owed so much emerged.

Her composure shattered, she could whisper only, "You are free."

He was not slow to grasp what she had done, and why, and the price, but all he found to say was, "No one frees a djinn."

"I have. Do whatever you wish."

The djinn is a literal-minded being.

Astonished, she cried out, but softly.

A day, a night, and a day passed before she uttered a coherent phrase.

The indescribable carnal ecstasies they shared from that time might well be thought excessive were it not for the unparalleled, if tumultuous, tenderness and regard they bore one another.

Not that their relationship is problem free. Their social life is not the same as yours or mine, lord knows.

Having been brought up with no prejudice against the supernatural, the djinn has no qualms about using his potential for his own delight and to bring about certain improvements which have occurred to him over the centuries. Mary Jane, with generations of Christian tradition and English common law behind her, still thinks in terms of striving, reform, and individual responsibility, and when a social problem is ameliorated as if by magic, she suffers some ethical turmoil. While she has some vehement altercations with the demon, she remains a radiant and truly fulfilled woman.

But the djinn, contemplating the poor cankered planet she so loves, is impaled upon the problem of freedom.

For if her heedless species will not learn to be less than conquerors, to be the loving caretakers of life, what would it mean to preserve them by negating their will?

So the demon is tormented by the dilemma that was a metaphysical conversation piece even before his time.

But who is so simple as to expect perfection in this life?

B. L. Keller, formerly a columnist for the Rome Daily American and mid-eastern correspondent for the San Francisco Chronicle, is an enthusiastic traveler who has lived in Rome, Beirut, and Baghdad and journeyed extensively in the Orient (where she and her two daughters did a great deal of hiking, complete with backpacks). She has written fiction and articles for many magazines, and her first novel, THE MANICHEES, is a suspense story that takes place during the recent Arab-Israeli conflict. Ms. Keller now lives in San Mateo, California.

The Chameleons

by William Harrison

They had already divorced each other twice, but, even so, when Sabra's ingrown toenail began hurting her one weekend she thought of no one else except Barney. Since leaving medical school, after all, Barney had kept a black bag full of ointments, instruments, and bandages. So she dialed his number late Sunday morning, told him her trouble, and within the hour he was ringing the bell at her apartment.

She called for him to come in. He entered her life this time, wearing a checked flannel shirt and blue jeans, looking more like a lumberjack than a doctor. Slowly he strolled across the rug toward the couch where she was propped up among her magazines.

She couldn't believe what she felt. "You've really got a great walk, Barney," she told him just before he sat down on the edge of the couch.

He reached over, moved her hands aside, and pulled the blanket down. Long before he uncovered her sore toe they were reunited again.

It had gone this way for years. Sabra had met Barney when she was a Northwestern co-ed. In those days she had been a sign carrier, involved in causes, rallies, and signings of petitions for peace, the arts, and assorted freedoms. She met him at a demonstration for academic freedom at a meeting hall near the campus. Dressed in his dark business suit, looking like young Gregory Peck slumming from the Chicago investment district, he leaned against a wall and munched a hot dog. She pinned a button on his lapel, smiled at him, and asked who he was.

"Name's Barney," he told her. "I'm just on my lunch hour."

"Are you for freedom of speech?" she asked him coyly.

"Of course," he said. "I love you. I'll carry your placard for you. Give

191

me a date Friday night. Candlelight dinner. Drive around in my cream-colored Chevrolet. Hold hands. My apartment. Kiss on the mouth. You tell me your dream, I'll tell you mine."

"Stop," she said. "I believe you."

They did all that and became engaged. But soon afterward Barney changed his life style. He became a hip medical student down at the University of Chicago, and Sabra, adjusting to his sudden alteration, went into the business world. Because she was abnormally pretty, she became an executive secretary for a firm on Jackson Boulevard. She discarded her sweaters and loafers, bought Saks suits, and learned to sit with her long legs crossed and beautifully exposed under a shorthand pad. She also learned about stock splits, the power of attorney, board-of-trade jargon, and the cosmic importance of producing good onionskin duplicates. In the evenings, giddy with their separate worlds, they would talk, make love, then talk some more. When they became convinced that they would never find each other dull and that sex would always be important but never consuming in their lives, they got married. It was a white wedding replete with parents—and afterward, for nine weeks, they were singularly consumed. Then they began to quarrel. They found their lives bumping along in ruts. Sabra told Barney that she wanted to hear nothing more about cadavers or the boy-doctor crowd that hung around on the South Side; Barney accused her of becoming dull, of trading in her bright, idealistic, and perky personality for the horn-rimmed life of a crusty businesswoman.

"Perky?" she said with disgust. "Drop dead."

They were divorced. But, also, nearly simultaneously, Barney dropped out of med school and Sabra started visiting the offices of the Rush Street entrepreneurs in hopes—of all things—of becoming an actress.

At the same time, Barney, encouraged by the med students of the Washington Park coffeehouse set and by his parents' money, decided to become a tycoon. He opened a rent-a-pet service, his theory being that many wealthy Chicagoans loved small kittens and puppies but were unhappy with adult animals that required more room, more food, and less affection. At the same time Sabra made her appearance on Rush Street in some minor musicals. She always had ten or fifteen lines and at some point in the evening wore a skimpy costume in an off-color skit.

One night Barney showed up backstage. Sabra had grown accustomed to seeing him in a sweat shirt with his hair long and carrying anatomy books, but there he was again in his pinstriped suit. He glowed with success and when he gazed down at her she blushed with a feeling of security and warmth. She also blushed because she wore only sequined briefs and a halter and somehow felt more ill at ease backstage than in front of the footlights. They took a long drive that night, all the way out to a Fox River resort northwest of town where they had supper. They came back the next morning to her apartment near Old Town and four days later they were married by a justice of the peace at city hall.

In the Old Town environment they began to change again. Sabra, though she enjoyed an increasingly higher billing in those flimsy Rush Street shows, grew unhappy with her roles. The pet business thrived for six months more, but the rented puppies and kittens became dogs and cats, and Barney was soon overstocked with animal returnees. He added new features to his business, dressing the growing adult animal population under his care in fancy collars, leather booties, and brightly colored knitted slipovers. But his taste for the rent-a-pet business waned, and he found himself turned on by the young artists and performers who lived above the pottery shops, galleries, and antique stores of Sabra's part of the city. When he got home from his business in the afternoons —he now had nine employees, including an old friend from med school who wanted to buy the business from him—he changed into sandals and jeans and went browsing along the street. Sabra, who left soon afterward for the long night's work at the theater, would have spent the day in apron and anguish trying to learn housewifery: new casseroles, ways to sensible budgets, a few sewing tricks.

When they felt their romance fading, they tried to love all the harder, but Barney's sophomore enthusiasm for the arts bored Sabra and Sabra's glum casseroles disappointed Barney. They tried, though. They bought furniture, took a trip to see all the New York shows, swam together early every morning, but finally even these fierce activities couldn't stave off the inevitable. They were divorced again, happily. They kissed good-bye one noon in front of the Palmer House. Sabra slipped into a cab, and they didn't see each other again for a year.

During that time, Barney was bumming on his family and Sabra was living at home in downstate Illinois, going to the garden club and to bridge with some of her old, dull high-school friends and, occasionally dating boys her own age. She was only twenty-three, yet she had been twice put asunder by her heart. She became cautious and restless. When she couldn't take it any longer, she went back to Chicago and started modeling. She modeled, in fact, for sixty days— until the ingrown toenail and the discovery of Barney's new business telephone number kept her home from work.

She awoke, then, on the sixty-first day of her modeling career, turned over, keeping her sore toe suspended beneath the covers, and caressed Barney's sleeping face. For a few minutes she lay there observing his flannel shirt draped over the foot of the bed, and when he awoke she asked him about his new vocation.

"Are you really a hunting and fishing guide?" she asked.

He edged up on one elbow, looked at her sleepily, and smiled.

"Like it says in the Yellow Pages?" she said.

"I have this office in The Loop," he explained. "I have two employees in the office with me and nineteen contacts up in Wisconsin and Minnesota. All of us wear these same flannel shirts."

He yawned, twisted a stray lock of Sabra's hair, and let his finger trace along her ear.

"Tired businessmen come in during the day and we talk about the great outdoors. I arrange trips for them: bona fide Indian guides and everything from T-bones to beef jerky. We haven't lost a businessman yet. They love to come in and talk, and, occasionally, they even like the trips they take."

"But you just wear a flannel shirt and sit in an office?"

"Mostly," Barney said. "Oh, I've gone up on the lakes some and I've learned a little about angling and like it. But this way I have the best of two worlds: I'm a businessman and I'm an adventurer. I can switch back and forth. It's a way of settling down, you might say, Sabra."

She gave him a big kiss, edged out of bed, and padded off toward the kitchen to fix his breakfast.

They sat across from each other during that breakfast—and for several happy breakfasts afterward—beaming.

"Listen, Barney," Sabra said a few minutes later, "we're interesting people. No one has *ever* interested me more than you. What goes *wrong* with us?"

"I think it's marriage," Barney told her. "I think we have to just stay lovers this time. Some people have nervous systems that, well, just don't do very well in matrimony. Also, we have to think ahead. We have to watch out for the doldrums this time. We're inventive. We'll have to avoid the ruts."

"But why do the doldrums *come?*" she wanted to know.

"I don't have any idea," he said solemnly. With that, he pulled her onto his lap (she smelled of toast) and invented a kiss on her throat. Sabra thought as hard as she could, and Barney's logic seemed perfect.

When her toe healed, she went back for a few modeling sessions. Barney stopped around at her studio occasionally and watched. She was doing maternity clothes for Carson-Pirie-Scott, chic ones with slits, flashy buttons, and short skirts. This is my old Sabra, he told himself one morning. My pretty crusader-actress-model. He took her to lunch afterward and proposed that they go up to the lake country.

"Nature," he whispered over the filet of sole. "Canoes and moonlight. Fresh-air kisses. Call of the wild."

It's my same Barney, she decided, and she said yes.

The Minnesota lake country that autumn was full of the sweet scent of distant fires—chilly and alive with sounds. Barney rented a cabin on one of the far lakes and took Sabra there by canoe and outboard. In the mornings they took long walks; in the afternoons they fished and played rummy; in the nights, blessed with an early frost, they built up the fire in the hearth.

By the fourth day, though, Barney had fallen into some unusual silences, and Sabra asked him what was wrong. "Are you tired of it up here? You want to go back?"

"As a matter of fact, never," he said. "I could stay up here."

"Oh, Barney, you couldn't, either. You're *so* fickle."

"No, I mean it," he insisted. "I'd like to stay up here and write books."

"We don't have to go back soon," Sabra said brightly. "I didn't even tell the agency where I was going. We'll stay on and you'll get your fill of this before long."

After another week Barney still felt the same. They had carried water, chopped wood, bathed in a tub before the fireplace, eaten the same meals—trout and cornbread—many times. But one afternoon when they were out beside the lake, he started talking. He sounded very different to Sabra and she listened intently.

"I have this urge," he tried to explain to her. "And it's all part of what we've been and what we are. I have the notion, I suppose, that we can do anything we want, be anything we want. You're pretty and talented. I'm quick and have ideas. But I have these almost ascetic feelings about what we should do now. We should really change ourselves."

"How do you mean?"

"You asked me the other day why the doldrums come, remember? I said I didn't know and still don't, but it seems to me that we can't go on like chameleons, changing our outside colors to fit new situations. We must need changing inside. Not that I dislike us. I think we're really not ugly people at all, Sabra, but we *must* need changing."

"I suppose we must," she agreed.

"I'm not going back to the city," he said. "I've got to stay here. There's something about nature. I've never tried it before. I see myself now as a person of solitude. I know it sounds silly, but I never want to take off this old flannel shirt as long as I live."

Sabra threw a pebble into the lake. "It does sound a little silly, Barney," she said finally. "For one thing, you're really just changing your appearance and circumstance again. But I'll go back to Chicago and tend to our leases and my job. We can do this, if you're sure."

"I'm absolutely sure," he told her.

In the following weeks Barney sold his part in Field Afar Enterprises for a good profit, Sabra closed down their Chicago apartments, and they rebuilt the cabin as a permanent residence. They put in insulation, bookshelves, and a big slot desk in the loft where Barney sat and wrote short stories. He also took up pipe smoking. Sabra tended to the cruel chores of frontier life with good humor. During the first cold weather, the pipes from the spring froze and broke; the grocery and mail delivery which was supposed to come across the lake every two days grew more and more infrequent and unpredictable; the axhead flew off and was lost in the woods. Even so, they were happy.

"Why shouldn't we be happy? After all, neither of us has ever had an affair," Sabra pointed out when they were discussing themselves one afternoon. "The problem has been staying together—fighting the doldrums. And now I think we've found ourselves. I think you were right about retreating up here. This just might do it."

They became so sure of themselves that when they went down to Duluth to buy winter coats they took out a marriage license. Two weeks later they went back and stood up while a woman justice of the peace named Mary Merrisen pronounced the vows in a strong Swedish accent. Barney smoked his pipe during the whole ceremony.

They returned to the cabin and for a month Barney worked hard. His stories, mailed away to an editor friend in Chicago and to the more hostile publishing forces of New York, all came back with encouraging rejections written in longhand. But in this quiet period, locked away from the frenzy of the city, shut off in silence even from each other while Barney worked, Sabra began to think. She decided that Barney was the unsteady marriage partner, that she'd still be working happily as an executive secretary had he not grown restless in med school, that she had only reacted to him when she took up that silly acting career and, later, that abortive domestic life. She began to place blame. Immediately, almost as if a signal sounded from those deep woods around them, they started snapping at each other. Then they recovered. A week of good times. Friends came up for a weekend visit, everyone sleeping on quilts in front of the fireplace, drinking too many gimlets. Then, left alone again with Barney, it happened: the doldrums. This time, though Sabra grew more restless and melancholy, she didn't blame Barney; she recognized the feeling as the same one she had suffered that time when she went home to her parents.

She felt there was little time. Barney worked on, sitting up there in the loft in his flannel shirts surrounding himself in a haze of pipe smoke, but she felt that something had to be done.

"Barney," she said one morning, "I read your latest two stories last night before going to sleep, you know, and I think I see what's wrong with them."

"Oh?" he said, looking up from his coffee. "What?" A copy of the collected short fiction of Chekhov sat at his elbow and so his tone was superior.

"Well," she said, "I think what you really know and feel is the city—the awful urban life. I think you haven't found your subject yet, not absolutely."

Barney sipped his coffee. Then he gave her the perfect lead: "What do you think I ought to do?"

"Oh, I don't know," she said casually. "Perhaps get back to Chicago. To locales you know." She gave him time to fathom this. The silence gathered between them, then she put in the clincher. "Of course, you'd be a different *sort* of writer, maybe too sophisticated. The penthouse image: You might not like it."

Barney finished off his coffee and gazed out of the window.

"Oh," he said absently, "it might not be so bad."

Back in Chicago, they set up a new apartment on the Outer Drive and Barney started taking walks—to get the feel of the city again, he said. In time, he wrote less and walked more, and one day he came home excited.

"There's all this new construction going on in The Loop," he explained. "I figure the men on the job would go for catered hot meals. I think I can buy a few service trucks and serving wagons and pick up a franchise for this sort of thing. Do pretty well. At least build up a trade so that I could sell at a profit to somebody who wants to carry on. What do you think?"

"Great," Sabra told him. "And, Barney, listen, I've come on a new opportunity, too. Educational television. I talked to an agent today and you'd be surprised how many independent film producers there are in town now. I might even do a few commercials. You like the idea?"

"Sabra," he said, grabbing her up. "You're going to be in movies! That's something! Yeah, I like it!"

He kissed her, she felt, as if she were somebody new. Suddenly there seemed to be a new enthusiasm between them and, at the same time, curiously, a strange distance. She thought hard, trying to analyze it, and she wondered about the days ahead and about herself and Barney, about all the new happy people each of them would become.

William Harrison was born in Dallas, went to college in Texas, studied theology at Vanderbilt University in Tennessee, with further work at the University of Iowa. His short stories have appeared in many magazines and have been anthologized in Southern Writing of the 60's *and* Best Short Stories of 1968. *The author of three novels,* The Theologians, In a Wild Sanctuary, *and* Lessons In Paradise, *Mr. Harrison teaches creative writing and literature at the University of Arkansas, in Fayetteville, where he lives with his wife, three children, and a golden retriever named Beau.*

Names and Faces

by Eleanor Leslie

$\mathcal{W}$ayne opened the taxi door for her and put a tightly folded five-dollar bill in her hand. They kissed gently. Then she was alone inside the taxi with the door closed.

"I want to go to Brooklyn."

Apprehension gave her voice a hard edge. She wished Wayne had told the driver where she wanted to go. He knew how to deal with uncooperative people.

"Sure," the driver answered pleasantly. "What part?"

"Bay Ridge."

"You'll have to direct me."

"Take the Belt Parkway and get off at Eighty-sixth Street."

"O.K., I can get us to Eighty-sixth. Then you direct me."

It was all so easy. He had not argued. She had not been forced to write down his name and number and threaten to report him. She relaxed and opened her purse to get her cigarettes.

"I was afraid you'd argue with me about going to Brooklyn."

"Naw. I take my customers wherever they want to go."

While sorting through the objects in her handbag, she realized that her cigarettes must still be lying on the floor by Wayne's bed. She could manage without one. She was tired and happy. Her watch said two-thirty. She hoped her parents were asleep and would not hear her come in.

"The world is too full of misery without getting into arguments with my customers," the driver said.

"I'm glad you feel that way."

"Right now, I'm not in a position to do anything to straighten the world out; but, when I get myself squared away, I'm going to contribute something. I want to help people."

She made a polite noise of approval and hoped he did not really want a conversation.

"I'm going to become a psychologist. I only drive a cab at night. During the day I go to school under the G.I. Bill."

"Good for you." She tried to force a little sincerity into her polite tone of voice.

"I served in Vietnam."

He paused waiting for her to comment. They were driving rapidly through the empty streets of Lower Manhattan. In the windshield she could see the reflection of a pack of cigarettes that lay on the dashboard.

"I always talk to my customers. I'm very intuitive about people's hang-ups. I don't have big hangups, any more. But now, like yourself, I don't know you. Right? But I'd be willing to bet that religion is one of your hangups."

She did not know how to answer. She was not even sure what a hangup was.

"Don't tell me if you don't want to; but, like look, you're never going to see me again, so why shouldn't we talk?"

"I believe in God and Jesus if that's what you mean," she answered doubtfully. The reflected vision of his pack of cigarettes kept creeping into her consciousness. "I even go to church every so often."

"Are you a Catholic?"

"No." She wondered if she minded discussing her religion. "Give me one of your cigarettes," she said with sudden playfulness, "and I'll tell you all about myself."

"Sure."

He smiled as he handed her the pack and matches. "Are you high?"

"No, I'm just happy."

Her hand trembled with fatigue, and for a moment she could not light the match.

"I'm a Quaker," she said, exhaling her first draft of smoke. "I go to meetings sometimes because God helps me, and I need his help. Sometimes I just sit there and get annoyed because the same dumb people talked the last time I came. Once I got up and went out into the street and had a cigarette. I stood there and prayed to God to forgive me and all the rotten people inside for being rotten." She laughed self-consciously. "You know, I was raised to believe it's bad manners for a woman to smoke on the street."

He chuckled. "No kidding?"

They were in the Brooklyn Battery Tunnel. She had not noticed the taxi enter.

"Quakers don't believe in war, do they?"

"Some fight; some don't. Everyone has to do what's right as he sees it."

"The war in Vietnam really stinks, and I've got the medals to prove it."

"Wars always stink."

They were out of the tunnel now. He paid the toll. She must remember that his tip included the thirty-five-cent toll.

"I was a scout. That's when I discovered that I have—well, that I'm clairvoyant. I always knew where the mine fields were. I knew where the enemy was. I knew where I was even when the maps didn't tell enough. One time the major said to me, 'Sergeant, where's Hill 431?' I said, 'It's right over there, sir.' He said, 'You mean we lost twelve men for that dung heap?' 'Yes, sir,' I said."

The highway was elevated now. She looked at the lights of black Brooklyn.

"I'm tired now, but, God, I really had to stay awake all the time in Vietnam. One time I came back so tired the major told me to go to sleep in the command tent. I woke up because of the gunfire, and I knew I'd been asleep too long. I went outside and found out we were surrounded. They had radioed for reinforcements which weren't coming. I said I thought we ought to try to break out. I had told the major I didn't like the situation."

"What did the major say?"

"The dumb shit was dead somewhere. I knew better to start with, but I'd been too tired. You can't depend on anyone."

"What did you do?"

"We crawled, and we ran. Then we were in this long valley, and the enemy got ahead of us. They were in the rocks on either side where the valley narrowed into a canyon. We were down to sixteen guys. I climbed up in the rocks with a sack half full of grenades—all that we had, all that I could carry and still climb."

She thought for a moment. "I wonder why, out of that group of men, you were the hero."

"Well, first you got to be scared shitless. You don't know what that means, but I do. Then you got to decide you don't give up."

They were driving rapidly along the wide, well-lit highway. She put out the glowing stub of her cigarette in the ashtray.

"Religion does a lot of harm," he said.

"I suppose it does. People hate each other for religious reasons."

"No, I mean people make themselves miserable over something like sex just because of their religion."

"That's ending. Most people do as they please nowadays."

"Do you like sex?"

She hesitated. Probably she should draw the line somewhere in the conversation.

"Yes, I do."

"Good. A lot of women don't. They just pretend they do because they think they're in love."

"How depressing."

"It is."

She wondered if he would make a pass at her. Men usually got around to that. She was not interested, but it would perhaps be a compliment if he tried.

"Was that your boy friend who flagged the cab?"

"Yes."

"Do you love him?"

"Yes."

"I was faithful to a girl once and did without for eleven months. I didn't even understand this girl. When I found out how she thought, I didn't even like her."

She rested her head against the back of the seat and closed her eyes. She was listening, but she also wanted a cigarette.

"When I came back from service, she and her mother and my mother really did a job on me. They wanted me to go into advertising. They thought being a Madison Avenue ad man was a noble profession. Most Jewish mothers, even in the Bronx, have the brains to want their sons to be doctors. What do you do?"

"I'm a caseworker for the Welfare Bureau."

"I thought you'd do something like that. I took a look at you when you got in the cab. Tell me, is everyone on welfare a no-good freeloader like they say?"

"They're people like everyone else, a mixture of good and bad."

"But how many could really hold a job and are lazy?"

"A few."

"O.K. I'm not criticizing, you understand. I think it's great that you're working to help people."

"I try. I don't know how many I help."

"Who knows who really helps who in this world. I say people should try."

"I think it's more interesting that you were a war hero. I never realized that I admired war heroes before."

"If you believe in war heroes, you believe in war."

"That's some indictment of me."

"I once saw three soldiers rape a Vietnamese woman. They were out of their minds. They would have killed me if I had tried to stop them. Right after that we were sent back to Saigon for rest and recuperation. I got all three of them. One guy I couldn't get alone. I followed him all day. Finally, I bought him some drinks and took him to my hotel room."

"I don't understand why you had to do that. It didn't help the woman."

"So tell me I was wrong."

"No. I can't tell you that. I just don't understand."

The Eighty-sixth Street exit sign was ahead now. He drove along the ramp and stopped at the traffic light.

"Which way?"

"Turn right."

As she gave directions, she felt along the seat for her handbag and took out the tightly folded five-dollar bill. When he stopped in front of the brick house that was hers, the meter read $3.60. He switched off the meter and turned in his seat to face her. She held out the money, but he did not take it.

"Keep the change."

"You live here with your parents?"

"Yes."

"I'm on duty until six o'clock. Tonight the loneliness was getting to me. I haven't bothered with a woman in a month. I know a girl I could go see when I get off work. She'll even be glad to see me."

"At six A.M.?"

"Yeah. She says she loves me."

"Probably she does."

"Naw. She thinks it's nice I play the guitar and look a little like Mort Sahl."

"What kind of guitar music do you play?"

"I'm learning classical Spanish."

"I really like that. I have some Segovia records."

"I don't play that well." He paused. "I'm finally getting the right kind of fingertips. Feel the calluses on my fingers."

She touched his fingers gently with her own, then put the five-dollar bill in his hand. He pocketed it without comment. She opened the door slightly, lighting the interior of the cab, and felt glad to see his face before he was gone. It was an ordinary face—narrow and lined and serious. It interested her. As she looked, she realized that he could see her. She must look tired and washed out.

"Well, good-bye."

"Don't go yet. Stay and talk to me."

She hesitated, wanting to put out the light to save her vanity.

"I'll give you a cigarette."

As soon as he spoke the words she wanted the cigarette. She also wondered if his offer showed his negative idea of women. She pulled the door closed, but pride made her refuse the cigarette.

"Sometimes I wish I were a homosexual and didn't need to talk to women."

He laughed to show he was not serious.

"What's your name?"

"Linette."

"Look, Linette. Take the cigarette because I have nothing else to give you."

He held out the pack. She took one and lighted it.

"When I first left my parents' house after coming home from the service,

I had an apartment full of people. There were parties all the time, and someone was always sleeping on the couch. Hell, some girl was usually sleeping in my bed. Then I got to thinking who are all these people? I don't need them. I don't even like them. I cleared everybody out by not answering the door for two weeks. Now I talk to my passengers to pass the time, but I don't really rap with anyone."

"Rap?"

"Communicate. Look, I talk with some girl all evening, and by eleven o'clock I learn only that she is mainly interested in the conversation because her girl friend told her I'm not married."

"It's part of our culture. Every girl feels she has to get married—and the sooner the better."

"Swell. Is that our whole culture—marrying and remarrying? Do you want to get married?"

"Yes."

He laughed.

"Would it help any," she said, "if I told you that I don't want to marry you, at least not at this moment."

"Can I tell you some more war stories?"

"Go ahead."

"Come sit with me here up front."

"No."

"I just noticed. You're nervous, aren't you. I just want to touch you; that's all. Why not come up front?"

"I suppose it's because I don't know you that well."

"You know me better than any other woman."

"Perhaps it's closer to the truth to say that I'm tired and satisfied."

"You're honest. I like that. I suppose you mean your boy friend."

"Yes."

They watched each other.

"What's your name?"

He hesitated: She remembered the driver-identification card and looked for it. The holder was empty.

"Why don't you want to tell me? Is it a name you don't like?"

"Guess."

Her mind went over possible names that Jewish boys were stuck with— Milton, Marvin, Seymour.

"It's a good-enough name. It's Steve."

"I like that."

She felt sudden affection for him now that he had a name and an unhappy face and sat alone in the front seat.

"There are nice ways of killing people."

"There are no nice ways."

"Change the setting on an artillery piece. You don't even see them die. I ate a boy's throat for breakfast once."

"I don't understand," she said, not wanting to hear the explanation.

"We were in this safe village. The place even seemed all right to me. I I was walking along this path not being careful, and this kid hits me over the head with a stick or something. When I come to, I've got nothing but my underwear. I can't even think, my head hurts too bad. I should find a medic, but I follow after the kid and catch him with my stuff. God, the way he looks when he sees me behind him. If he'd been a few years older, he would have known enough to kill me. He was maybe thirteen, fourteen at the most. Even so my hands weren't strong enough. I bit into his throat. He made sounds and bled. I didn't have to do it."

"It was your life or his."

"No, it wasn't. God, you're bloodthirsty."

"It's something of a curse to realize the nature of our acts."

"Talk to me like a human being! Don't give me literary selections! I'm sitting here bleeding all over you!"

"I talk the only way I can! Remember, I'm the girl who smokes on the streets when she's going out of her mind. God understands what you did; I don't."

She put her hand on the edge of the open glass partition, wanting to touch him now because he sounded so hurt. He did not move. His hand was not in sight.

"What do you think of me even if you don't understand?"

"I think it was wrong, but I think you can forgive yourself. My God, what else is there for anyone to do."

She got out of the taxi, looked momentarily up at the dark windows of her home and opened the door to the front seat. He was leaning against the door on his side watching her. She closed the door to make the light go out.

"Thanks for coming in the front. It's like saying I'm not a monster."

"Nobody could possibly think you were a monster."

He reached out a hand to her, and she ran her fingers over his calloused fingertips.

"Feel the calluses on my palm," she said. "I get them gardening. We have a nice little yard behind the house."

"You're great, Linette. Almost mindless and just great."

He moved closer and put his arms around her. She brushed his hair with her fingertips and then she touched his cheek.

"There's a big wisteria vine on the back of the house that's beautiful in the spring."

He kissed her, and they kissed.

"You know, I don't even mind your being with another man tonight."

He kissed her again and touched her face. In the dark his fingers felt the wetness of tears beginning to overflow her eyes.

"I guess I'm crying for you. I don't give a damn about that boy in Vietnam; I really don't."

"So we won't talk about him any more."

"Really I'm not crying. I'm smiling at you."

She put his fingers against her lips to show him.

After a minute he said, "You know you're even fun to kiss."

She held Steve in her arms until she could not hold off thinking about the time any longer. She was parked in front of her parents' home, and it was nearly four in the morning.

"I have to go inside. I don't want to, but I just can't stay here any longer."

"Come with me."

"I can't."

"What's your last name?"

"Hibberly."

"What a WASP name, Linette Hibberly."

His voice seemed to have changed in her ears. He seemed to be closing in upon himself again.

"For God's sake, don't start talking like that."

"I'm sorry, Linette. You know how I am. In fact, I never before believed WASPS could be warmhearted."

She opened the car door.

"Good night, Steve."

"Good night."

She went quickly up the steps and unlocked the door, hearing him start the taxi engine. The car was moving before she had the door closed behind her. She wondered if he would come back. She wanted him back already and tried to think about Wayne instead, but it did not work. She hoped her parents were sound asleep. In five minutes she, too, would escape into sleep.

"I've always written," says Eleanor Leslie, "but I didn't do it full time until I could support myself that way." After graduation from Barnard College, she spent a year in the Women's Air Force as a Second Lieutenant ("I got out just in time . . . they might have made me a First Lieutenant!"), then taught elementary school in New York for several years. Currently a full-time author, Ms. Leslie has had many stories published in Cosmopolitan, Epoch, *and* Redbook, *and has recently finished her first novel. She is divorced and lives in a tiny apartment "just down the street from Norman Mailer's house" in Brooklyn Heights, New York. "To relax," she says, "I date. And write a lot."*

Girl Overboard

by Garson Kanin

$\mathcal{N}$ella? Didi. Listen, you've got to have lunch with me and don't say no for the love o' God because I'm in a no-kiddin' what-a-state here and if I don't get to talk to somebody—no, to you, not to somebody right away—I may go into shock. I mean shocker. I'm in shock now, so don't say no. Beverly Wilshire, Beverly Hills, Bistro, Brown Derby, wherever. He was really the all-the-way worst last night and this morning he—no, I can't on the phone. I won't. You meet me for lunch, y'hear? And don't wear green. I am."

Her throaty speech, normally difficult to follow on the phone, was charged with emotion and required straining concentration this morning.

"I'd love to, Didi, only—"

"Don't say only! Didn't you hear me? I'm in a goddam crisis!"

"How about later? I've got a dentist, one-thirty."

"It can't wait." Her voice broke as she added, "This thing—may be all—over."

"No!" For the first time, Nella's voice sounded interested. "You don't mean it."

"Swear. That's what it looks like to me. Feels like. I couldn't go through another last night no matter what. Humiliated, kicked around. Listen, when I started in modeling—for ten an hour—before I made it right, I was never treated like this. And believe me, I didn't do one thing wrong, Nella. Exactly the opposite. I made every effort. I had everything ready for him when he got home from the studio. I knew he'd had a tough day. They were shooting the tank stuff. You know, where they pull him out of the burning water into the lifeboat?"

"Burning water?"

"Sure. Oil on the water. You read the script. What's the matter with you?"

"Oh, yes."

"All day on that, in the tank, I knew he'd be tired. So I had the Jacuzzi ready, with pine in it. And his terry cloth. And a J&B in a tall glass with nothing but ice. And I rubbed his back and all and scrubbed it in the tub and no foolin' around, I give you my word on my mother's life. Then I put him to bed and all the lights out and that nutty French LP he likes this week on real soft and I left him like that for an hour and a half. Look. I *don't* want to talk about it on the phone, d'y'*mind*?"

"So then what?"

"About eight-thirty, I go out to see if that dopey Helga's done his dinner right the way I told her. By the way, what's with you and your Cecile?"

"She's staying, the bitch. More dough. You know the French. But to break in a new one——So? Go on."

"Well, instead of Tessa taking the tray in, I carry the bloody thing *myself*—did you know females can get hernias the same as men, from lifting?—but I do it because I know he doesn't like servants around any more than he has to, except me, that is, I'*m* a servant. That's what I told him—I mean later when it all got hot. Anyway, I bring him his dinner. Everything. Steak and baked and salad with more damn garlic—he says he *has* to because it helps him remember his lines. I said to him, 'Well, it sure in hell helps me forget *mine*, daddy!'—and a glass of red. A baked Alaska, for energy—and I went and brought him that, too. And the strong Sanka with cream. Then after—would you believe it?—I said, relax for an hour. So he did. And I got ready. God, you should've *seen* me! I must've looked like a high-cost-of-living pro with all that black transparent all over me. But I was doing what *you* said, honey, step by step and all the way. Now I get the bottle of Dom Pérignon in the cooler and the glasses on a tray and I walk in and what I see, so help me, if I don't damn near drop the tray all over myself."

"Why?"

"Why-y? I'm telling you. Are you going to have lunch with me or not?"

"How about earlier? *Before* lunch?"

"I can't. Chet's coming."

"The trainer?"

"Yes."

"I thought you said you gave that up."

"I said I was *thinking* of giving it up. I get so tired."

"So, go on. *Why* did you damn near drop the tray all over yourself?"

"Because. He's sitting there, up in bed, with a cigarette, glasses on, and with his script and doing it, the whole thing, out loud. Can you feature it? I put down the tray and I look at him and I do practically a Salome-where-she-danced up and down in front of him. I'm drenched in Diorissimo—I have to get some, by the way—*drenched!* The fumes are knocking *me* out—but him? I could've had on *buttermilk* for all the effect it had on him. After a while he looks at me—

he doesn't *see* me, mind you, he just looks at me. And he says. 'See if I know this. From the top of thirty-four-G, revised. The pink page.' He throws the script at me. I pick it up. He says, 'Word for word, please. I'm having a full tussle with this maniac. He's a real if-and-or-butter.' So I start in to play the scene with him—and wouldn't you know it? It's that randy beach scene where they're all over each other and he's telling her she's got to come away with him no matter what because hudja budja hudja budja. That's all I needed! There I am—half of the hottest love scene in town only I can't get to first base. So we do it four, five times. The scene. And I come over to him and I sit close and I tell him, 'Word for word for word. Wha'd'y'know? And here's your Oscar!' With that I lean over and let him have a signal right in the ear. Well! You'd've thought I'd hit him or thrown acid or something the way he jumped away. And he says—says! —*screams*, 'Jesus, Didi! You know better than that!' 'Not *much* better,' I say. So he tells me to knock it off and—don't you hate a finger pointing at you?— then he sort of notices me for the first time, what I'm wearing and he says, 'Is that warm enough? I find it chilly in here.' And I say, 'Not as chilly as *I* find it, buddy.' By now we both knew—trouble. Because you know how often he calls me 'Didi'? Once a year, maybe. And me him, 'buddy'? Never. I could feel my boil coming but wouldn't you know it? He beats me to it and he starts in, 'I've got *close-ups* tomorrow morning, you silly bag! Doesn't that mean anything to you?' So I say, extra quiet, extra cool, 'Oh, ever so much. Because I haven't seen a close-up of you around here for a *month!*' 'Use your head, pinhead!' he starts yelling and a lot along those lines till I slam out. What *could* I? What would *you?* The way I felt it in my bones, I knew he'd come in after a while and we'd smooch around and I'd cry and we'd talk about how it was going to be when he finished the picture. Monterey and the cabin and just us. But my bones couldn't've been wronger, baby. He never showed. And I'm sitting there with the little TV on and my earplug in. So, between the Late and the Late, Late—I go to him. He's sleeping. Not only sleeping but snoring. What do *I* do? I take two yellows and one pink together—well, actually, a yellow and a pink and a yellow in that order five minutes apart—you ever done that? In twenty minutes, I'm in the middle of a 3-D color nightmare."

"And what happened this morning?"

"I'll tell you at lunch."

"Tell me now."

"Will you have lunch?"

"If you tell me now."

"All right. This morning, I'm up first. Cold shower—God, how I hate it. You *sure* it does all that for the skin?—and I put on a dandy subtle makeup and my pink Pucci and I'm waiting for him on the lanai when he comes out—good and bleary, too. And I flash him my Shirley Temple, God help me, and I hold out an arm and he keeps coming and as he passes me he bends an inch and kisses some air over my head, big deal. Me? Strictly saint. I pick up the script and I say,

'You want to run through them once, lovey?' 'Would you?' he says, like a kid in a commercial. And we go again. Word for word. Next thing I know, I've lost him to his shirred eggs and the trade papers. And he starts making those awful faces the way you all do when you read them. Frowning, biting your lips, giving terrible grunts. Torture. It figures. What's in there mostly, after all? Who got a job. Who signed for what. Who bought what property. Somewhere along the line one item if not another one is going to bite you, right? Why do you do it? God knows. I said to him, 'Stop screwing your face around like that. Didn't you say you've got close-ups this morning?' It's like he doesn't hear—which is the way it is with him most of the time. He gulps down some more coffee and then he belches. Y'hear? This idol of millions, this Number One pinup—two thousand pieces of fan mail a week, six hundred Gs up front, and ten percent of the gross from the first dollar—belches at his loving wife. Then, he says, 'Do I look as miserable as I feel?' 'Why should you?' I said. 'You had a good night's sleep.' 'How do *you* know,' he says—says!—hollers. '*I had* an *unspeakable* night.' 'I'm sorry,' I said. 'You *should* be!' He's *still* hollering. All of a sudden, soft. 'We've got to have an understanding.' Something like that. I may not have the exact words, what *am* I, a tape recorder, f'God's sake? But he gives it to me like as if he would be my father, and me his daughter. About behavior and respect and sense of values and time and place for everything and responsibility and about my part of the bargain and the function of a partner. I'm telling you—Breakfast with Dr. Rose Franzblau. But I took it—because I kept telling myself, inside to myself—the morning is no time for a screaming contest. Especially what with his close-ups coming up. So I sat and took it like a little major. He ran down, finally, and he got that godawful whiny, self-pity sound in his voice that happens to drive me personally ape—I notice he never uses it any of his pictures—and I tried not to listen for a while because when I hear it, I hate not only it but *him*. The next thing I hear him saying, 'You haven't listened to one single thing I've said, have you? You've just *proved* it! You're like that goddam excuse for a leading lady they've hung on me. She doesn't listen, either!' And on and on. Now he goes and I don't see him till he's about to leave, around twenty to eight. Right before he gets into the car, I say, 'What would you like for dinner?' And he says, 'A wife!' Just like that. In front of Pedro, too."

"Who?"

"Pedro. His new driver."

"Oh. Look, I think you may be making more out of this than——"

"Please! I'd rather not talk about it on the phone, y'mind? I'll tell you all about it at lunch."

"Sounds to me he's in some sort of a work bind, that's all."

"When is he not? So where's the future? He's got only three main worries in life, this Stan of mine: the picture he's on, his last picture, and his next picture."

"You think Julian's not like that sometimes? There was a time—last spring—when he was supposed to do a detached retina on some baseball player. And the whole world started falling apart. You know how many detached retinas he's done? Several thousand, I should think. Then why should this particular one throw him? I'll tell you. It was a complicated one and someone else, in the East, had messed it up. 'It's an insulted eye!' he kept saying. 'A most insulted eye! I may not touch it.' He was like that for a month, maybe six weeks —because he couldn't figure out how to do it. And in all that time, there was nothing I could do to interest him in me. Not one damned anything. And don't think I didn't try. Finally, I gave up. I'll tell you to what point. One night, I went to bed with white cotton gloves on to protect my hand lotion and that yellow Laszlo cream all over my face, and a chin strap, and before I knew it—I was being swarmed. I mean, my dear, it was a regiment of Tartars. The next day, he said to me, 'I know how to do it!' 'You're telling me,' I said. So he said, 'You know what I mean. That sonofabitchin' retina, I've got it licked!' And that was it. You've got to learn to roll with these punches, my dear."

"Keep it. I didn't marry dreamboat to roll with his punches."

"But everyone plays the game. What do you want to be, different, for heaven's sake?"

"Bet your panties."

"Wrong, dear."

"You want to hear my nightmare?"

"Dying to. Wait till I get a cigarette. . . . Go!"

"He's in this tank with the burning water and I'm watching, only it's real not a movie. And he keeps going down and coming up and going down and I'm screaming without a sound and finally I jump in to get him—you know, save him—and as I go through the burning water, I go right through the ceiling of his trailer and he's in there in the sack with his leading lady. You know. Miss Nose Job? And they look at me and they don't even stop! And I'm still screaming with no sound. . . . You think there could be anything in that?"

"Not with her. I know her. She's a patient of Julian's. She hasn't swung for years. Not since she noticed wrinkle number one. She lives in cotton wool."

"Sometimes they start up again."

"That may be, but—look here, I'd rather not hurt your feelings, only it would take more than your boy to bring her back into the fold."

"Don't bet. He's got quite a change-up, this kid, when he wants to use it. She could be it. My whole trouble."

"I think I will have lunch with you. I'd better."

"You think? You already said you would."

"Yes, but this time I mean it. I have to talk to you."

"Don't, thanks. I get the feeling everybody in the world's talking to me. When do I talk?"

"Well, you've been doing not too badly there for a while. Telephone stock went up since you got on."

"Bistro? One?"

"I'll pick you up. Quarter to."

"I'll pick *you*."

"No. Me, you."

"And don't wear green."

The doorbell chimes and the hall clock chimes sounded in unison at eleven A.M. Chet Seaver is never late. Neither is he ever early. He is an efficient, reliable young man. Physiotherapy covers a wide and somewhat vague range. Chet's principal practice in the field of rehabilitation for children occupies the major portion of his days, but is not sufficiently lucrative. That is why he gives his mornings to the business of conditioning, exercising, and firming up a select clientele, most of whom have no idea what it costs.

He has the rugged frame and the stubborn brain of a born athlete. At UCLA, he was a decathlon man. At thirty-four, he has yet to taste his first alcoholic drink, and to experience his first cigarette.

A room off the master bedroom had recently been converted into a miniature gymnasium and sauna room.

It was here that Chet set up the folding massage table and covered it with a pink sheet.

Didi came in, wrapped in a matching pink sheet. She had just showered and wore no makeup whatsoever.

"Good morning," said Chet. "How are you?"

"*You* tell *me*," she replied as she dropped her sheet, mounted the table, and lay face down.

He grasped her ankles and said, "Go. Easy, but steady. Come, pull away. More. You can do better than that. Make out we have to stretch your spine twelve inches or your husband divorces you . . . Go . . . More."

"I can't."

"Very well. Relax."

He moved to her side and touched the outline of her spine expertly with the fingers of both his hands.

"Wow-*ee!*" he said.

"What?"

"Peanut brittle. What's up?"

"Nothing."

"You're uptight as a tick. Here. Roll over." She did so. "Knees up. Way up, on your chest. That's it. Now, clasp them tight. That's it. Now, rock. More. Here, let me help you." After a full minute, he said, "That's it. Now. Tense everything. All over."

"You said I was, already."

"Tenser. Tight, tighter. That's it. Now, let go. Tense. Let go. Good. Now, one by one, take the pressure off every joint. Understand? Wherever your bones join—they're pressing together. Stop it."

"How?"

"Send a message."

"All right."

"Here. This knee. Loose. Looser. Good. Elbow. No press. Other knee. Take your time."

"And would you believe it?" asked Didi. "Within ten, fifteen minutes, I couldn't tell you what tension *was*. He's something else, that boyo."

"It would certainly seem so," said Nella.

Their headwaiter, Pierre, approached and said as he wrote on his pad, "Two vodka martini, imported, rocks, twist."

"You win," said Didi.

Pierre went off.

"You going tonight?" asked Nella, looking around the room.

"To the what—oh, the thing downtown? No. They sent tickets, but no."

"I think *we* may. He says we have to. She's *also* patient. Would you long or short?"

"Well, that's the hell of these things. Long's better for the theatre, naturally, walking in and all—but after, for the party, if you're going to dance these days, you're better off short."

Pierre placed the blackboard-easel menu before them

"Ready to order?"

"Yes," said Didi. "One long and one short."

Pierre frowned in confusion. Nella laughed until she attracted attention. When she had collected herself, she said, "Gazpacho for me."

"Same," said Didi. "It'll go good with this martini."

"*What* martini?" asked Nella, picking up Didi's empty glass.

"Why, the one Pierre's going to get us. Aren't you, Pierre?"

"With pleasure," said Pierre, signaling a waiter to repeat the drink order.

"There's linguine clam sauce today," said Nella.

"Not me. I was one-fourteen this morning. Hamburger rare, sliced tomatoes. No salt no dressing no nothing. A dog's dinner."

"Very good," said Pierre, writing it down.

"The hell you say," said Didi. "But what can I do?"

"Linguine for me."

"You would," said Didi. "No mercy, huh?"

The second martinis were served.

Pierre chirped, "Thank *you*," and went off.

"Skoal," said Nella.

"Boy, am I ever glad you could make lunch. My gorge is right up around *here*. If I don't get to unload, I don't know what. Explode."

"Relax. This taste like imported to you?"

"I think so. Yes."

"Is he doing it a little darker now? Your hair?"

"You noticed!"

"Yes. It's a little darker."

"You like it?"

"I like it both ways," said Nella, judiciously.

"But which better?"

"I don't know. Depends."

"On what?"

"Well, you know. Night or day or whatever. If you wear it up or down or—I think *this* is better. The way it is now."

Didi took a deep breath and exhaled with relief.

The soup course was served and relished as they continued to discuss hairdressing and tinting and styling.

Nella laughed. "Did I tell you what Julian said the other night? He said, 'If women took care of their eyes as much as their hair, I'd be out of business in a year!' "

The subject was abandoned as the main courses were served.

"Coffee now?" asked Pierre.

"Yes," said Nella.

"Later," said Didi.

Pierre left.

"That high protein works for you, does it?" asked Nella.

"If I stick to it, sure."

"I wish *I* could."

"I *have* to. Three, four pounds on and I haven't a thing to wear."

"Speaking of wear, have you seen—you want a taste of this linguine?"

"Cut it out. Seen what?"

"Those new white things at Jax?"

"Which white?"

"The sun stuff."

"No."

"You should. You love white."

"It's the best."

Wardrobe and the imminent necessity for a trip to Paris were the counterpoint subjects for the next twenty minutes.

"Something sweet?" asked Pierre, appearing unsummoned in the manner of a genie.

"Not for me," replied Didi, lighting a cigarette. "Coffee."

"More coffee for me," said Nella. "And——." She turned to Didi. "Listen. Split a Napoleon with me."

"Are you well?" I wouldn't split a Napoleon with *Napoleon,* for God's sake."

"Please. This once. Make an exception. With all your troubles, you owe it to yourself. A little treat."

"Have it if you want it."

"Not unless you do."

"All right," said Didi.

"Two Napoleons," said Pierre. "For two Josephines."

"You're a riot, you know it?" Didi called after him as he moved off.

"You want to hear a great idea?" asked Nella.

"Go."

"Let's have a drink."

"That would make three apiece."

"Who's counting?"

"That is *not* my idea of a great idea. In fact, lousy."

"Small brandy?"

"No."

"Crème de menthe. Healthy."

"How?"

"Settles your stomach."

The Napoleons were served. Didi studied hers.

"I believe," she said, "after this, mine's going to *need* settling."

"Two crèmes de menthe," Nella ordered.

"Frappé?"

"It's the only way."

They began to enjoy their pastry.

"*Oh* boy," exclaimed Nella.

"Glad I talked you into it?" asked Didi, her mouth full.

"You know that new cook of Marcia's? The one she brought up from Acapulco? Austrian?"

"Yes."

"You know what she's paying her?"

"No."

"Hold on to something."

The matter of cooks and maids and gardeners and pool-men occupied them through dessert, coffee, and cordials.

Afterward, a pleasant lassitude overcame them. They sat quietly, smoking and greeting friends in various parts of the room with minuscule waves and meaningful moues.

Didi sighed. "If you'd said no to me today, sweetie, I'd've driven to the beach and walked in and kept walking."

"So. You going to tell me?"

"In a minute."

"You know what it could be with you? Simple depression."

"What's so simple about *that*?"

"A drop in blood sugar or something. From dieting too hard."

"Yuh. I have been going pretty strong on it lately."

"Because, look. Explain this. I get up sometimes—dragging. And every-thing seems im-damn-possible. Can't cope. What's the use? So I take, say a Dexamyl or an Eskatrol? Within half an hour, I'm up there. I feel, hooray—and nothing's changed, mind you. Just me."

"I wouldn't take one of those goofers for anything!"

"But you don't——"

"Never mind. Don't turn me on. They're addictive, those things."

"All right. *Stay* depressed."

"I sure need help, sure. But not out of a pillbox."

Nella slapped the table. "Hey! I've got something. Come on."

"Wait. I've got to sign."

She lifted her hand and snapped her fingers. When they failed to make a sound, she and Nella giggled for five minutes. Meanwhile, the check was brought and signed and the tortuous, stopping-here-and-there exit was made.

On the sidewalk, the sun, in contrast to the dimly lit interior, seemed blinding.

"Mercy!" said Nella, shading her eyes. "What's he got in there today? A thousand-watt?"

The parking boy approached and said, "That's the white Jag today, right?"

"Yes," said Nella, "but hold it."

"O.K."

"Lock it up and let me have the key."

The boy ran off to do her bidding.

"Where we going?" asked Didi.

"Cheer you up. No pills."

When the boy returned with her key, Nella gave him a dollar.

"Thanks," he said. "Have fun."

Nella took Didi's arm.

"Can you walk in those?" she asked.

"How far?"

"Tiffany's."

"What's there?"

"What do you think?"

A new shipment had arrived the day before. Didi and Nella sat in the small back room while Mrs. MacDonal brought them necklaces, rings, and earrings. They tried them on leisurely and knowingly.

The session ended with two grand diamond tiaras—one on each head—and another fit of giggling.

"Thanks, Mrs. Mac," said Nella. "And you'll hold that little turquoise-pearl for me, huh?"

"Certainly."

Out on the street again, Nella asked, "How do you feel?"

"Better," said Didi.

"Wait."

They went to Jax and saw the white things; to I. Magnin's where they each purchased an evening bag; to the Beverly Wilshire drugstore where they browsed and bought each other a present of the largest available bottle of Diorissimo; to Wil Wright's where they had banana ice-cream sodas.

During this time, they talked of sauna baths, oatmeal scalp treatments, the political situation in southern California, and the invaluable ministrations of Dr. Reizner, "the foot-fixer."

They proceeded to Juel Parks and spent half an hour handling lingerie.

They stopped in at The Daisy to see who was there. At this hour, nobody. They sat up at the bar.

"Tee martoonies," said Didi.

When the bartender laughed, Didi and Nella exchanged a puzzled what's-with-him look.

The drinks arrived.

"So, what do you think, Nella?"

Nella took a long drag of her cigarette, let it out slowly, searched the cavern of her thought, and turned to Didi. Her reply had the weight of the burden of authoritative opinion.

"*I—don't—know!*" she said.

It sounded profound, somehow, and Didi nodded, gravely.

"I could never make it modeling any more, face it," she said. "Even part time. I'm too old for the fashion smash, and for commercial you need the energy of a horse which I have not. Got."

"Part-time modeling is a full-time drag," said Nella.

In Saks, they found themselves at Revillon Frères, trying on fur coats, stoles, sables, sheared-otter jackets and, finally, a notable ermine.

"There's nothing like white," said Didi.

She began to twirl, expertly, professionally.

All at once, she found herself at home. In her dressing room, she undressed with abandon, flinging her clothes about.

She took an extended, tepid shower, singing, "Hey, there!"

Wrapped in her husband's favorite terry-cloth bathrobe, she sprawled on the bed and, to amuse herself, imagined it to be a floating carpet.

She fell asleep. Bells were ringing. Chimes. Cowbells. A bicycle bell. Big Ben. A fire alarm. A school bell. Steeple bells. The phone, the phone.

She awoke. The phone beside her was ringing.

She reached out and picked it up.

"Yuh?"

"Where've you *been?*" her husband asked, testily.

"You didn't say hello."

"Neither did you."

"I did."

"You said 'yuh.' "

"I was having lunch with Nella."

"Till four o'clock?"

"We had a few things to do after."

"I'll bet."

"You're not in for dinner tonight, right?" said Didi, gaily. "How come I can always tell?"

"He wants to show us a couple of cut reels. Settle a couple of arguments."

"Show who?"

"The two of us."

"You and Miss Nose Job?"

"Didn't I ask you not to do that?"

"Do what?"

"Call her that."

"*You* do."

"Not when she's costarring with me. And don't you. As of now, she's Miss Paulina Kirk."

"I'll try to remember. About tonight. Can I come?"

"No."

"Oh."

"We're just going to grab a bite somewhere near and right back to the studio."

"How long?"

"I don't know. Depends. He may want to talk a while. He'd better. Can you find something to do? With Nella maybe?"

"I had lunch with her."

"Oh, yes. Anything doing around? Anybody running a picture? Edie? Anne?"

"I don't know. I'll see. Or probably just wait here."

"No, don't do that. It's so dreary for you. And I might be a while."

She had to take a breath, and swallow before she could say, "I don't mind."

"Well," he said, after a pause, "this'll soon be over."

"Yes."

"See you."

"Yuh."

She lay, for a long time, on her back, forcing herself to remember pleasant things: parties, presents, trips, compliments, Monterey, and her healthy portfolio of securities.

She rose, went to her dressing table and began to remove her makeup.

What did he mean, "This'll soon be over?" The picture, of course. You sure? Sure I'm sure. Don't be too sure. He couldn't have meant *me*. Why not?

If he did, would he have come right out and said it? Like *that*, on the *phone?* I mean, after *all!*

She stopped as she realized she had become a misty blur.

"What *is* this with you?" she said aloud. "You look like a special effect in a Disney, for God's sake." She wiped the tears out of her eyes and cleared the image before her. "Cut it out," she murmured. "You're doing fine. Just wait here. Nicely. See what time he makes it in. Get yourself nice and ready. Again? Again. And then see what happens or doesn't. It's Friday night, don't forget. No work tomorrow. No call. If you come up empty tonight, if it turns out no, you'll know."

And then what? she thought. And then what? she echoed. I'll tell you. Next time Mr. Chet Seaver comes to give you a workout, put on makeup before you go in.

"Got it?" she asked.

"Got it," she replied, and began to put on makeup, carefully and deliberately, to see how well she could do it should the occasion arise.

The phone rang.

Garson Kanin, a man of many talents, had a short career as a jazz musician, became a stage actor, then a Hollywood director (his films include such hits as A MAN TO REMEMBER, BACHELOR MOTHER, *and* TOM, DICK AND HARRY), *and screen writer (*ADAM'S RIB, A DOUBLE LIFE, *and* PAT AND MIKE, *all written in collaboration with his wife, the actress Ruth Gordon). Mr. Kanin also authored the play* BORN YESTERDAY, *directed other plays and operas, and has written four novels and many short stories. His latest book is* TRACY AND HEPBURN: AN INTIMATE MEMOIR. *Born in Rochester, New York, he and his wife now stay sometimes at their house in Los Angeles and sometimes at their apartment in New York.*

Marching Through Delaware

by Bruce Jay Friedman

One night, driving from Washington to New York, Valurian, for the first time in his life, passed through the state of Delaware, and felt a sweet and weakening sensation in his stomach when he realized that Carla Wilson lived nearby. All he would have to do is sweep off one of the highway exits; at most she would be half an hour away. Twenty-two years before, at a college in the West, he had loved her for a month; then, in what appeared to be a young and thoughtless way, she had shut the door abruptly in his face. Much later, he became fond of saying it was a valuable thing to have happen and that he was grateful to her for providing him with that lovely ache of rejection. But in truth, and particularly at the time, it was no picnic. He remembered her now as being thin-lipped and modest of bosom, but having long, playful legs and an agonizingly sexual way of getting down on floors in a perfect Indian squat. She had no control over her laugh; it was musical, slightly embarrassed and seemed to operate on machinery entirely separate from her. She had an extraordinary Eastern finishing-school accent, although to his knowledge she had attended no Eastern finishing school. She was an actress; he reviewed her plays for the local newspaper. Members of the drama group, some of whom had been in Pittsburgh repertory, referred to him as the "village idiot." Although she often did starring roles, the most he ever awarded her was a single line of faint praise. On one occasion, he said she handled the role of Desdemona "adequately." He was quietly insane about her; in his mind, the paltry mentions were a way of guarding against any nepotistic inclinations. It was a preposterous length to go to; she never complained or appeared to take notice of it.

Although he remembered quite sharply the night he got his walking papers, he had only disconnected, bedraggled recollections of time actually spent with her. She wore black ordinarily, had a marvelous dampness to her, and trembled without control the first time they danced together. "Are you all right?" he kept asking. "Have you perhaps caught a chill?" There were some walks through town, one during which a truck backfired, causing Valurian to clutch at her arm as though it were a guardrail. "Oh, my God," she said, surprised, delighted, and not at all to demean him, "I thought I was being protected." Her mother swooped down upon them one day, a great ship of a woman, catching Valurian in terrible clothes, needing a shave. In a restaurant, lit by ice-white fixtures, she spoke in an international accent and told them of her cattle investments and of killings at racetracks around the world; Valurian, still embarrassed about his shadowy face, prayed for the dinner to end. Later, he took them back to his rooming house and lit a fire; turning toward them, he saw that Carla had hopped into her mother's lap and gone to sleep in it like a little girl. He had never slept with her, although she gave him massive hints that it would be perfectly all right, indeed, highly preferred. "Oh, I'd love to be in a hotel somewhere," she would say as they danced. Or she would begin her trembling and say, rather hopelessly, "When I feel this way, whatever you do, don't take me out to some dark section of the woods." Ignoring the bait, he gave her aristocratic looks, as though he were an impeccable tennis star and she was insulting him by the inferior quality of her play. In truth, her dampness, the black skirts, the Indian squats, all were furnace-like and frightening to him. A boy named Harbinger had no such problems. She alerted him to Harbinger, saying she had run into the cutest fellow who lived in town and always hung his argyle socks out on the line where the girls could see them. It was as though she were giving him a last chance to get her into hotels or to sweep her out to cordoned-off sections of the woods. But he had always seen his affair with Carla—could he dignify it with that phrase?—as a losing battle, with perhaps a few brief successful forays before the final rout. One night, for example, he surprised her by batting out a few show tunes on the piano, singing along, too, through a megaphone, a talent he had kept up his sleeve. She almost tore his head off with her kisses, although, in retrospect, they were on the sisterly side. Toward the very end, he showed up on her dormitory steps with an alligator handbag, a Christmas gift she didn't quite know what to make of. Inevitably, she summoned him one day to talk over an ominous "little something"; polishing up his white buck shoes, he walked the length of the campus to her dormitory where she told him she had stayed out all night with the argyles boy and that she would not be seeing Valurian anymore. He called her a son of a bitch and for weeks afterward regretted being so clumsy and uncharming. There began for him a period of splendid agony. The first night, he was unable to eat and told a German exchange student —who had suffered many a rejection of his own—that any time he couldn't get fried chicken down he was really in trouble. A week later, he strolled by to see Carla as though nothing had happened; she told him that Harbinger was more in the picture than ever. She started off to rehearsals and he tailed her; she broke into a run, and he jogged right after her, as though it were perfectly normal to have conversations at the trot. On another occasion, he lay in wait for her outside the theatre, grabbed her roughly and said, "Off to the woods we go. I have something to show you, something I'd been unwilling to show you before."

"What's that?" she asked, teasing him.

"You'll see," he said. But she wrenched herself away, an indication that Harbinger had already shown her plenty. He stayed away then for several months, taking up with a green-eyed Irish girl who had great torpedoing breasts, thought all Easterners were authentic gangsters, and with no nonsense about it simply whisked *him* off to the woods. One night, before graduation, he went to a dance, feeling fine about being with the Irish girl, until Carla showed up with the argyles man. He continued to dance, but it was as though his entire back was frozen stiff. He saw her only one more time, paying her a good-bye visit and asking if he might have a picture. "No," she said. "I don't understand it," he said, "a lousy picture." But she held fast—and that was that.

He left school, went through the Army as a second lieutenant in grain supply and then, for ten years or so, led a muted, unspectacular life, gathering in a living wage by doing many scattered fragments of jobs. He was fond of saying he "hit bottom" at age thirty, but, in truth, all that happened was that he developed asthma, got very frightened about it, saw a psychiatrist and, in the swiftest treatment on record, came upon a great springing trampoline of confidence that was to propel him, asthma and all, into seven years crowded with triumphs in the entertainment world—a part in a play that worked out well, a directing job that turned out even more attractively, films, more plays, television work, and ultimately a great blizzard of activity that took a staff to keep track of.

From time to time, he had heard a little about her, not much—that she had gotten married quickly (not to the argyles man), had a child, gotten divorced. That she had settled in Delaware and never left. Although from time to time the thought of her flew into his mind, it was never a question of his wallowing in this particular memory. Valurian had little cause to feel slighted by love. Along with the chain of professional triumphs had come a series of romantic ones, a series of women, each attractive in her own way, ones that Carla no doubt had seen in films and read about in columns. He had as much confidence with women as he did with his work. He *owned* women. When he thought of Carla at all, it was never to wonder what she was up to, but to speculate on whether she read his reviews, the interviews with him, the column mentions. What indeed could she really have been up to all those years? In Delaware. Bridge? Scrabble? The Johnny Carson show? Getting a taste of the sweet life via the *Times* theatre section. The marriage, no doubt, had been to an accountant. Or was it a stock broker? Saturday nights, spell that nites, with three or four other young marrieds, Delaware young marrieds, young married Delaware swingers at Delaware's top nite spot. He could imagine those couples, too. The jokes. The talk about switching. And salves. Bedroom salves. They all used bedroom salves. She had been divorced. After that, she had probably tried to land another second-rater. She loved the theatre; no doubt she'd go after a local theatre notable this time, one who whipped together Chekhov plays and was terribly temperamental. Wore heavy Shetland sweaters. Get rid of the taste of that routine stock brokering first marriage. What *really* could she have been doing with her time? Did she have any idea that Valurian had been to the White House? That, indeed, he was driving back from the White House now. And that it wasn't his first trip. He'd met De Gaulle. Did she know that he had slept with actresses whose names would make her gasp? That he *turned down* dinner invitations from Leonard Bernstein. Lennie Bernstein. How could he explain to her that the only sadness in his life was that the circle of important people he had yet to meet was an ever-shrinking one and soon to be nonexistent. Oh, she had read about him all right. How could she have escaped knowing about him, following his career? Everyone knew about him. And when you consider her special interest in Valurian . . . she probably kept a scrapbook. Far from a preposterous notion. How many lonely, divorced nights had she spent kicking herself for not having spotted the seeds of it in him, his possibilities? How close she had come to an extraordinary life and never, at the time, realized it for a moment. What did that say about her judgment? She probably wondered about that every day of her life. Hadn't she loved the theatre? He owned the theatre. He was the theatre. And who had she passed him up for: an argyles man. Every time she thought of that little stunt, she probably chewed at her wrists in agony. And she had *summoned* him to give him the news. And then refused to give him a picture. *She*, get this, hadn't wanted to give *Andrew Valurian* a picture. It was almost too much for the mind to comprehend. It would take a computer to handle that one. Well, she was probably in a constant sweat about it, night after night in Delaware. In Delaware, mind you. How she must have punished herself all those years. And here he was, Valurian, coming back from the White House on his way to a party at Sardi's that was probably going to bore him to death. How many years of her life would she trade to show up at that party? On his arm. Two, five, a decade? To top it all off, he was only half an hour's drive away from her at most. God, if she knew that. . . . If he ever drove by and called on her, stopped at her dreary, divorced Delaware house, at the very least she'd go right into shock. Faint dead away on the spot. More likely, she'd tear off her clothes and fly at his groin. Would she in a million years be able to find her voice? Never. So she would probably just kneel at his feet and pray and let it go at that. The poor lost miserable wretch.

Oh well, he thought, fuck her, and drove off for the big city.

~~~~~~

While working as an editor of gutsy "men's adventure" magazines in the early 1960's, Bruce Jay Friedman began a second literary career as author of what many critics call "black comedy": savagely funny stories, novels, and plays, which have established him as one of the important (and individualistic) younger writers in America. He is the author of the novels STERN *and* A MOTHER'S KISSES, *and the plays* SCUBA DUBA *and* STEAMBATH. *Mr. Friedman lives in Great Neck, New York, with his wife and three children.*

The text of this book is set in 10 point Palatino with two points leading, using 24 point swash initials at opening paragraphs. Titles are set with 24 point swash initials and 20 point lowercase; author's name is 10 point on 12 point. Palatino is one of many contemporary faces designed by Hermann Zapf of Germany.

Book design by Jacqui Morgan

Jacket, cover and title page by Dorris Crandall

Jacket illustration by Keita Colton